Praise for S. L. Viehl and the *StarDoc* series

"I don't read much science fiction, but I got ahold of a manuscript copy of *StarDoc* and just loved it. . . . I hummed with enjoyment while reading it! Don't miss this one."
—Catherine Coulter

"A fascinating reading experience that will provide much pleasure to science fiction fans. . . . The descriptions of the various sentient beings are so delightfully believable that readers will feel that S. L. Viehl had had firsthand encounters. . . . The lead character is a wonderful heroine."
—*Midwest Book Review*

"A rousing good yarn, with plenty of plot twists . . . a lot of action, a sly sense of humor, and wonders aplenty."
—*SF Site*

"Ms. Viehl writes a riveting tale. . . . With more than a few surprises up her sleeve, this rising star proves herself a master storyteller who can win and hold a bestselling audience."
—*Romantic Times*

"Viehl's characters are the strength of her novel(s), showing depth, history, and identity."
—*Talebones*

Don't miss the other exciting SF medical thrillers
by S. L. Viehl

StarDoc

Beyond Varallan

Endurance

SHOCKBALL

A StarDoc Novel

S. L. Viehl

A ROC BOOK

ROC
Published by New American Library, a division of
Penguin Putnam Inc., 375 Hudson Street,
New York, New York 10014, U.S.A.
Penguin Books Ltd, 80 Strand,
London WC2R ORL, England
Penguin Books Australia Ltd, Ringwood,
Victoria, Australia
Penguin Books Canada Ltd, 10 Alcorn Avenue,
Toronto, Ontario, Canada M4V 3B2
Penguin Books (N.Z.) Ltd, 182–190 Wairau Road,
Auckland 10, New Zealand

Penguin Books Ltd, Registered Offices:
Harmondsworth, Middlesex, England

First published by Roc, an imprint of New American Library,
a division of Penguin Putnam Inc.

First Printing, November 2001
10 9 8 7 6 5 4 3 2 1

Cover art by Alan Pollack
Designed by Ray Lundgren

RoC REGISTERED TRADEMARK—MARCA REGISTRADA

Printed in the United States of America

Some people share the changes in your life;
others change the way you live it.
Best friends are the ones who do both.
For the first novelist I ever met,
the gentlest soul I've ever known,
and the best friend I've ever had,
Marilyn Jordan.

PART ONE

Maternity

CHAPTER ONE

Nascent Inanity

> . . . I will impart a knowledge of the art to my own
> sons and to those of my teachers, and to disci-
> plines bound by a stipulation and oath. . . .
>
> —Hippocrates (460?–377? B.C.)

Hippocrates never had to coach a green cutter, I
thought as I looked at the bloody mess on the table.
Otherwise, he'd have imparted his foot up a certain
eager beaver's southern orifice.

"You used a laser to do this? Not a hacksaw?"

The Saksonan across from me huffed. "You're not
amusing."

"Neither is this." I gloved, masked, then scanned
the entire disaster. "Stomach is history. Ditto on both
kidneys. Large intestine is ruptured in three, make
that four, areas. Spleen is"—I used a pair of forceps
to extract and hold it up for a better look—"totaled.
Nice work, Vlaav."

Thousands of dermal hemangiomas swelled, making
the Saksonan appear like a bristling strawberry. "It's
not my fault!"

"It never is." I dropped the tattered organ back into
the abdominal cavity. "Let's see, cause of death would
be exsanguination, or traumatic shock induced by lack
of anesthetic." I placed my instrument on the discard
tray. "Congratulations, Doctor. You've successfully
murdered your first surgical patient."

"You said I was doing a postmortem this morning.
I didn't realize it was still alive until I started the

abdominal exploratory." With an impatient, three-fingered yank, Vlaav tore off his mask and threw it on the deck. "And this is *not* my first surgical patient."

"If you want to have more, here's a new rule: never cut anyone open until they are under general anesthetic, or you make sure they're not breathing."

"Dr. Torin? Dr. Irde?"

We both turned around. Former League Lieutenant Wonlee stood just outside the exam room with a tray of food. He'd adapted a loosely woven garment as an orderly's tunic to accommodate the thousands of sharp spines covering his body. For some odd reason, they were all standing on end. His hands went lax, and the tray hit the deck.

"You butchered him," Wonlee said in a strangled voice.

The Lieutenant had been a medic, once upon a time, but he'd never done a surgical rotation. Vlaav and I were fairly well splattered with synplasma from the death throes, and I guess the sight of the body was, to an inexperienced layman, rather disturbing.

"It's not a him, Won. It's a training torso." When that didn't sink in, I punched a console button and the botched surgical simulation disappeared. "A dimensional, simulated facsimile. Not a *real person.*"

"Oh." Wonlee took a deep breath, and his spines settled back down. "What happened to it?"

I stripped off my gloves. "Dr. Irde learned how *not* to conduct an appendectomy."

Vlaav peeled his off at the same time. "You said to do an *autopsy.* I swear on my mother's deities."

"Your mom wouldn't appreciate you swearing. And schedule yourself for an auditory scan. Your hearing stinks." A strange odor reached my nose, and I glanced at the deck. I'd smelled nicer things in a biohazard container that hadn't been emptied for a month. "What is that stuff?"

"Your dinner." Won started cleaning up the mess.

"The Captain said you've neglected to take any meal intervals today."

Lately the Captain had been acting like *my* mother. "So he made you come and force-feed me for a change."

That got me a "now, Doctor" look. "Since I was reporting for my shift, I offered to bring it down for him."

I took a step back and gulped. "You programmed it, right?"

"No, as a matter of fact, the Captain prepared it personally."

Personally. "Excuse me." I ran.

After I finished vomiting into the nearest disposal unit, I sat back against the lavatory wall panel and pressed a damp cloth against my hot face. The maniac who constantly tortured my senses with his alien concoctions was going to pay for this. Big time.

The lavatory door panel slid open. "You are ill again."

Speak of the Captain.

"You're cooking again." I took the hand he offered, and let him pull me to my feet. Then I thumped him on the chest, just out of principle. "So this is all your fault."

The Captain was a Terran, like me. He disdained a uniform in favor of his usual black, unornamented tunic and trousers. Some things had changed since we'd met—like his blond hair, which he had let grow and now wore tied back in a queue. There were all kinds of new muscles on his long, swimmer's body, courtesy of training with the Hsktskt and the Jorenians.

Other things hadn't changed. His personality remained as chilly as ever. So did his expression. Carved masks had more life to them. But now it didn't bother me. I knew what was behind Duncan Reever's mask.

"You promised me you'd stay away from the prep unit."

"As you assured me that you would only work standard shifts." He slipped an arm around my waist and guided me to the cleanser unit. "Why are you covered in blood this time?"

"Simulated blood." I bent over the basin and vigorously cleaned my teeth and rinsed my mouth, then I checked my reflection. Still a short, dark-haired, blue-eyed Terran. Maybe a little thinner than usual. I splashed my face with cold water. "Vlaav had another go at a Terran torso on the training simulator."

He folded his arms and leaned against the wall beside me. "And?"

"And the torso lost." I groped for a towel. "Make a note—if I ever need surgery, don't let him near me. *You* do it."

"Hold still." Reever held me by the shoulder and blotted my face like I was a messy little kid. "You are trembling. You must eat, wife."

He liked calling me that. Pleased and annoyed, I blew a piece of damp hair out of my eyes. "You don't run my life, husband."

Two badly scarred hands cradled my face, and before I could say another word I got thoroughly kissed. Reever raised his head after my pulse skyrocketed and I started wrinkling the front of his tunic.

"How do you feel?"

"Pregnant." I grinned as his hand went automatically to my abdomen, and spread over the tiny life growing in there. His fascination with the baby aroused all kinds of feelings in me. Not strictly of the maternal variety, either. "Stop that. You're befuddling me."

"Cherijo." His palm made slow circles on my stomach. "Come back to our quarters with me."

I wanted to. Even after two months of living with Reever, I still hadn't quite made up for lost time. But then there was Vlaav. "Not now. I need to talk to my resident about taking a refresher course in Why We Employ Anesthesia Before We Cut."

"Do it tomorrow. Come back with me now." His mouth landed on mine again, long enough to make me *really* wrinkle the front of his tunic. Against my lips, he said, "I want to sleep with you, beloved."

"Oh really?" Vlaav could practice sterilizing instruments. "Then you shouldn't have kissed me like that."

I dragged him off to our quarters.

Several hours later, I left our sleeping platform and went to check on the ship's status. I didn't want to wake Reever, so I left off the lights and audio. I pretended I wasn't sick to my stomach, and covered in a glassy sweat. But I was.

The nightmares did that to me.

This time I hadn't relived the horrors of the past. No, this bad dream had sprung from a signal I'd received from the *Sunlace* earlier that day. The latest batch of test results weren't too promising. Squilyp, the Omorr Senior Healer on the Jorenian ship, wanted to perform another series. No drastic decisions about what to do could be made yet.

Mostly because I hadn't told Reever about the problem.

Guilt had made me dream about what his reaction would be when he finally heard the news. Reever shoving me away. Reever flying off in a shuttle. Reever leaving me for good.

Reever won't leave. It was only a dream, let it go.

According to the vidisplay, the L.T.F. *Perpetua* was close to Te Abanor, our next scheduled stop. We were halfway through our mission to return all the Catopsan slaves to their homeworlds.

Where's the Sunlace? I checked the external viewer and located the other ship off our port side. *Hi, guys.*

My adopted family, HouseClan Torin, manned the

Jorenian star vessel *Sunlace*. My adopted big brother, Xonea Torin, had been adamant about escorting us during the mission. Once that was over, they'd probably go exploring the galaxy again.

I wasn't sure if we'd tag along. League mercenaries were still hunting me, and rumor had it the Hsktskt Faction had recently put out their own bounty on me.

That thought made me look at the third ship in our little fleet—the *Truman*. My creator, Joseph Grey Veil, had sent the unarmed, drone-piloted League vessel from Terra as a gift for me—some sort of gesture of truce or something. Reever and the Jorenians had thoroughly checked it out before towing it along with us. Personally I'd never liked Joe's present, and regularly expressed my desire to see someone blow it to smithereens.

Reever was more practical. *We may need to make use of it, Cherijo.*

I cleared the screen and accessed a new file I'd been working on since we'd escaped the Hsktskt. Being pregnant made me realize how important it was for me to record the facts behind the strange twists my life had taken over the last three years.

I want you to know the truth, lump. I spread my hand over my still-flat abdomen. *You wouldn't be able to hear the whole story from anyone else but me.*

I scanned through the entries I'd already made about what had happened from the day I'd left Terra. The file headers read like ads for one of the space operas so popular on my homeworld.

Promising thoracic surgeon discovers she's a genetically enhanced human clone.

Clone escapes brilliant but insane scientist creator.

Insane creator pursues runaway clone across the galaxy.

I'd spent my first year of independence as a trauma physician on Kevarzangia Two, treating nonhumans. My love affair with an alien pilot named Kao Torin had collided with a race to cure a mysterious plague. The fight for my own freedom came soon after, when my creator Joseph Grey Veil had tried to reclaim me as property. HouseClan Torin had come to the rescue, just in time for me to watch Kao die in my arms. Worse, I'd killed him with a transfusion of my own poisonous blood.

I closed my eyes for a moment. *Kao, I hope you forgive me for what I did. Maybe someday I can do the same.*

The next entries covered the year I'd served as Senior Healer on the *Sunlace.* Where I still might be, if not for a demented killer and the Allied League of Worlds. We'd caught the killer, but the League had cornered us on Joren. The Hsktskt had arrived on the scene to make things even more interesting.

I'd been oblivious to everything but saving Joren, which meant betraying the League to the Hsktskt. Finding out my own husband was a Hsktskt collaborator had shattered our marriage.

Being a slave doctor had been about as much fun. So had enduring torture, and discovering some of the guards were actually eating the prisoners alive. Healing and befriending a disfigured female Hsktskt guard had nearly salvaged my sanity. Until she'd sacrificed her life to protect me.

We're almost done with this mission, I wrote in my new file. *Still I think I'll spend the rest of my life trying to atone for my mistakes.*

"As will I."

I jumped and swore. Reever had gotten out of bed and presently stood directly behind me. His warm palms slid over my shoulders as I frowned up at him.

"You scared me. Cough or something next time."

"I apologize. What are you working on?"

"A journal file." I felt my cheeks burn. "It's for the baby. What's this 'as will I' business?"

"You are not the only one with regrets, Cherijo."

"You have nothing to be ashamed of. You were great—putting your life on the line, pretending to work for the Hsktskt while you were smuggling slaves off Catopsa," I said. "What have you got to feel bad about? Even the Jorenians forgave you, and you know how they feel about revenge."

He reached over, saved the entry, and deactivated the console before swinging my chair around. "Why don't you write about your own victories?"

"I am."

"Did you enter the data about the thousands of lives on K-2 and millions on Joren that you saved?"

I shook my head. "That was pure luck."

He took my hairbrush from the vanity unit and started untangling my hair. He liked doing that. "Luck had nothing to do with the destruction of the slave depot on Catopsa."

"That was luck and a working relationship with a sentient crystal," I pointed out, enjoying the soothing sensations the long, slow strokes through my hair sent over my scalp and down my spine.

"You have nothing to be ashamed of."

"Sure. I can just skip the part about how I killed Kao, and all the Torins who died in mercenary attacks on the *Sunlace*, and the League prisoners who fought the Hsktskt after I turned their ships over to the Faction." And then there was the baby. "Piece of cake."

"The streak in your hair looks a little wider." He traced the silver slash that started just above my right temple with his finger. "You have been devoting too many hours in Medical."

"You won't let me learn how to calibrate the engines." If I sat there much longer, I was going to melt all over the chair. I got up. "We've arrived at Te Abanor."

"I know."

He always knew. Reever took the job of running the *Perpetua* very seriously. I was lucky if I remembered what shift it was. "Where are we heading once we've finished this mission?"

"We will find a new world to settle on. A place where we can raise our children and live without fear."

Considering how widespread the League and Hsktskt Faction territories were, that wasn't going to be soon. Or easy. I'd avoid thinking about the other problems for now. One migraine at a time. "This Eden is located where? On the other side of the universe?"

"We will not have to travel that far." Duncan picked me up and carried me back to the platform. Like Kao, he enjoyed carrying me around. It must be a guy thing. "You need to get some rest."

"We were going to fight over names tonight, remember?"

He stretched out beside me and held me against him. "You did not like the last suggestions I made."

I could feel his heartbeat against my cheek. "You suggested Ggddkktt or J-byn." I shuddered. "Why can't you pick out something with vowels in it?"

"Very well, what do you think of"—he made a low, whistling sound—"for a female, or"—he made something that sounded suspiciously like a suppressed belch—"for a male?"

"I liked Ggddkktt and J-byn better. And I hate them." I thought about the list of baby names I'd pulled from the computer earlier. "How about Dian-the? Or Daniel?"

"Dian-tha means filthy water in Habarroo. Daniel is a command to jump high in the air while screaming on Andorrii."

I propped myself up with one arm. "Do they really mean that, or are you just making that up?"

"I will access the linguistic database, if you like."

"Hmmm." I eyed him. "What does 'Cherijo' mean?"

"It means nothing in any of the languages I know. I think that is why I was initially drawn to you."

My name came from an acronym for Comprehensive Human Enhancement Research I.D. "J" Organism—the title of the experiment that had resulted in my creation. However, Reever knew a lot of languages. I wondered if he was telling me the truth, or Cherijo meant something like "pond scum" in Trytinorn.

"How about Duncan? What does that mean?"

"In Terran Gaelic, it means dark warrior. In Svgan, burning spear. In Loracian, ice crystal. In—"

"Okay, okay." I ran my fingers through his shaggy blond hair. "*Dark* warrior, huh?"

"My coloring was not a consideration at the time my parents named me." He stroked the small of my back. "Have you confirmed the gender of our child yet?"

He knew I'd been having tests, but I'd passed them off as the usual prenatal exams. "No. I don't want to know. That's like opening Christmas presents in July." I squeezed my eyes shut. Maybe now was a good time. "Duncan?"

He was rubbing my stomach again. "Hmmmm?"

"I need you to know, I . . ."

"Look." He pressed my hand under his. "Can you feel the curve there? The child is growing."

There would never be a good time.

I lifted my head as something crawled over my foot. Saved by Reever's ambulatory pet mold. "I really wish you'd keep your Lok-Teel out of the bedroom."

He reached down and gently removed the undulating blob from my leg, then set it on the deck. He'd brought a couple of them from the slave depot on Catopsa, where he'd used their ability to take on any form to conceal his features. The moving mold had since happily adapted to life on board the ship, reproduced and were now all over the place. The Lok-Teel oozed off to clean something else, while Reever brushed my hair back from my face.

"Better?"

"Yes." He was always fooling with my hair. "I have an idea. I'll name the baby if it's a boy, and you name it if it's a girl. You have to use vowels and consonants."

"I agree. What is your choice?"

"Michael. Yours?" He told me, and I smiled. "Hey, that's not bad. I sort of like it."

"Go to sleep now, Cherijo."

I slept, but the nightmares returned. This time I didn't dream of losing Reever, but of a disaster so ominous that it destroyed everything I loved.

"I want you to report over here before you go on this sojourn," Squilyp said.

My former surgical resident, now a full-fledged doctor and currently the Senior Healer in charge of Medical on board the *Sunlace,* looked very annoyed. Squilyp was an Omorr, so he did that very well.

"I'm busy."

The white, meter-long gildrells around his oral membrane went into icicle-mode. They made him look like he was wearing a starched beard. "You're being irresponsible."

"Oh, like you'd know."

"Doctor."

Okay, so he was mad. He'd get over it. "This trip will only take a few hours. We can run the final series when I get back."

He thumped down the chart he'd been holding in the spade-shaped membranes that served as his hands. "Shall I consult with Captain Reever for his opinion on this matter?"

Now *I* got mad. "You say one word about this to him, and I'll tie a big knot in your face."

He sighed. "Cherijo, I know you are avoiding a decision, but you cannot continue to conceal this from your mate. He has the right to know what is happening, and what you propose to do about it."

"Yeah, I know. I know." I felt the beginnings of a tension headache start tapping inside my temples. "Just, give me a couple more days, okay? When I'm done with this sojourn, I'll have Reever bring me directly up to the *Sunlace*. Then you can run as many tests as you like." And I could finally figure out what to do, and how to tell Duncan.

"I don't know why I argue with you," he said. "I always lose."

"You're nothing but a big softie." He was anything *but.* I smiled. "Thanks, Squid Lips."

With an impatient gesture, he ended the signal.

I sat back in my chair, and read over the chart in my hands again. Trace bilirubin levels—leftovers from blood cell destruction—appeared in the latest sample. The antibodies had crossed the breach and were attacking.

"Cherijo?"

Alunthri appeared in the doorway. Like me, the feline Chakacat had been condemned as a nonsentient life form—in its case, from birth. We'd met on K-2, where its owner had subsequently died from the Core plague. I'd freed Alunthri from domestic slavery, and Reever had done the same when the Chakacat had tried to immigrate to another world run by slavers. It was the gentlest creature I'd ever known.

"Hey, pal." I cleared the console screen. "Haven't seen you around lately."

"My studies keep me preoccupied." It smiled, baring glittering small fangs. Alunthri was obsessed with all forms of art, and recently had been working on some kind of multispecies thesis. "You are going on the sojourn to Te Abanor?"

"Can't get out of it." Couldn't wait to go was more like it, but I wasn't going to dump my problems on the Chakacat.

"I wish I could join you, but I am still working on data I collected from the last world we visited." It cocked its bullet-shaped head to one side, making light shimmer across its silvery pelt. "Would you mind recording any examples of cultural self-expression for me?"

"No problem." It took a minute before I realized it was waiting and added, "Vid and audio okay?"

"Yes, thank you." Its colorless eyes met mine, and its pointed ears flickered. "Cherijo, is everything well? You seem rather preoccupied yourself."

"Just thinking about the sojourn," I lied.

Alunthri seemed to accept that answer, for it thanked me again, and then departed.

I hadn't been thinking about the sojourn. I was thinking about my husband. I had two, maybe three days at the most before we had to act. That meant I had to tell Duncan today. Not exactly something we could chat about on the way down to the planet.

Later. I loved that word. *I'll do it later.* I grabbed my pack and headed for the launch bay.

The sojourn to Te Abanor required us to take one of the *Perpetua*'s shuttles down. Reever, who unlike me was perfectly at ease with any sort of tech, manned the helm himself.

I strapped myself in behind him and looked over his shoulder. "Are we there yet?"

"No." He gave me a bland look. "Would you prefer to pilot the mission?"

"Please. I'd like to get there in one piece." Back during my time as Senior Healer on board the *Sunlace*, I'd barely passed the mandatory pilot training all crew members were required to take. I was good with living things, medical tech, prep units, and that was about it. "How's the atmosphere look?"

"We shouldn't encounter much turbulence. How is your stomach?"

"Okay, for now." I had a container stowed under my seat, in case that changed.

The flight took much less time than I'd thought, and as Reever predicted, there were only a few bumps along the way. Te Abanor's stratus shroud parted to reveal a gray-and-black world that looked inhospitable from above. Not a green speck of vegetation or geometric outline of civilization was visible.

"There, you see?" One of the former Catopsan slaves pointed out the darker mottled areas along the equatorial regions where the bulk of the Meridae civilization dwelled. "That is the epicenter of my home throng."

I grinned. It might have been ugly, but home was home. "I bet your family will be happy to see you."

"They will fill the skies," the Meridae male said. He had a homely face that was rather endearing. "I should warn you, Doctor, our atmosphere has a lower oxygen content than you humanoids are accustomed to."

I imagined everyone stepping off the shuttle and instantly turning as blue as a Jorenian. "Exactly how low?"

"It will be breathable, of course, but you may wish to curtail your movements."

My Saksonan resident's nubbly derma started swelling. "Do we have breathers on board the shuttle?"

"Calm down, Vlaav," I said. "If the air's too thin, we can always hop back on the shuttle."

"You are always so confident of success," he said, sounding peeved.

I repeated what had been hammered into my head through four years of medtech. "We're surgeons. Success is the only acceptable alternative." I caught his pout and sighed. "Will you stop worrying about everything? We escaped the League. We beat the Hsktskt. We can handle a little oxygen-poor air."

Vlaav mumbled something about spare ventilators and started rummaging through his medevac case.

Reever signaled Planetary Transport as we landed a few minutes later. I couldn't help but notice how even more depressing Te Abanor was when we set down. Gray. Black. Lots of uninterrupted rock. That was it.

Reever, Vlaav, and I gathered our equipment, then waited until Te Abanor's automated transport monitor gave us final clearance to disembark. When the hull doors parted, I noticed the change in the air at once.

What air? my lungs argued. I fought to keep from hyperventilating. Had to be a good example for my nervous student cutter.

Te Abanor's Transport Center seemed empty, except for some gliding forms circling overhead. I guessed they were the natives when they spiraled down and began landing in front of our group.

This particular brand of Meridae were naked, drab colored, with rounded heads covered by long, wrinkled skin lappets. Out of hidden snouts, long extensible tongues covered with spiny papillae flicked out.

"Why do they look different?" I asked Reever.

"That is a female."

I knew at once I would *not* be sharing the traditional Jorenian kiss of welcome with any Meridae. There are reasons I am a terrible diplomat. Papillaed tongues is one of them.

More Meridae arrived and landed. A distinct ammoniac odor emanated from their bodies, which were studded with oval bristle clusters. I saw why when one began grooming its fur.

Built-in hairbrushes. I could use something like that.

What impressed me the most was the natives' dorsal wing. While they stood on the ground, they held the jointed flap folded against their spines. Fully extended in the air, the wing stretched over ten feet long, and worked like a sail. Evidently the low gravity and air currents gave them lift, for once they were up, all the Meridae did was tack to or against the wind. It was obvious they loved it, too. Our passengers were already tearing off their borrowed tunics and taking off.

Reever offered greetings in a high-pitched shrieking language that made me cringe until my vocollar adjusted to the portable database, dampened the sound, and began to translate.

"We greet you, honored Meridae," my husband said. "Duncan Reever, Captain of the *Perpetua*."

One batlike creature screeched back at Reever. "Welcome. The Meridae offer thanks for the safe return of our kinsmen."

After an exchange of a few more pleasantries, the Meridae asked if we would care to visit the community's epicenter. Reever accepted the offer, which oddly surprised the envoy.

"Do you think this is a good idea?" I asked him.

"They are not members of the League," Reever said. "Their leaders will need information about the war."

We were escorted by the Meridae to the epicenter, if you could call it that. Several more landed and at some unseen signal approached each of us. Approached as in hopped over and extended these claw-things toward us.

"Uh, honey?" I said to Reever with a cheerful smile as one of the Meridae headed for me. "What are they doing? Exactly?"

"They're going to fly us to the epicenter," he replied. "Don't resist, you'll insult them. He won't hurt you."

I looked at my escort. *Fly* me to the epicenter. *Not* eat me.

The Meridae's hind appendages had small curved talons—the claw-things—which he gently slid under my arms. I experienced a slight jolt as he jumped up, and spread his wing.

Suddenly I was *flying*. It wasn't so bad after all.

My escort seemed unaffected by my weight. I saw the other natives had no problem carrying Reever and Vlaav, who were much larger and heavier than me. The Meridae were exceptionally strong, graceful, and hopefully, not prone to clumsiness.

We soon arrived at a group of bizarre, treelike structures that grew from wide, thick bases to soar hundreds of feet upward. Te Abanor's warm orange sun gleamed dully over the grayish-brown, lengthy branches. They weren't trees, judging by the lack of vegetation, and the sculpted appearance of the bark indicated they were Meridae-made. But from what? Soil?

The natives gently set down our team around the base of one of the biggest structures, where the ammoniac smell was much stronger. I performed a discreet enviroscan.

"Let me know if anyone feels dizzy," I told the others in a low voice. The fumes were chemically similar to ammonia, but not as dangerous. I pressed a hand against my abdomen and swallowed hard. Throwing up would make a lousy first impression.

The ground beneath us was flat and consisted of dense, nonporous rock. The aviaries couldn't be made of soil; there *was* no soil.

Reever touched my shoulder, startling me. "Look."

I followed his gaze up. Above us, a huge group of the Meridae were descending gracefully from the upper portion of the tree-structures. They flew unlike anything I'd ever seen on Terra—darting, floating, playfully weaving patterns with their bodies. In a moment we were surrounded by the winged creatures.

One wrinkle-faced female landed close to me, and I saw she supported a cluster of smaller, immature Meridae. It didn't look like being a mom was an easy job, either. Each infant hung from her face, a skin lappet tightly gripped between their small blunt teeth. Ouch. No wonder their faces were stretched out.

"That's got to hurt," I murmured to Reever.

"Not at all," the female replied.

She was wearing a standard League wristcom and understood every word I'd said. They were *all* wearing wristcoms here. Good thing I hadn't said something like, "What an ugly baby."

After hearing some of what the former slaves had endured, two of the Meridae led Reever off to discuss the Hsktskt/League war with their leaders.

Vlaav and I obtained permission to conduct a standard sojourn survey. As I had been during my time on the *Sunlace*, I was responsible for the medical and anthropological data. Reever thought it was a good idea to collect as much information as we could on non-League civilizations.

I suspected it was a ploy to keep me out of trouble.

"What a wonderful family you have," I said to the female with the kids hanging from her cheeks. Apparently that was the right thing to say, for she detached one of the infants and offered it to me. I cuddled the baby, and only had to gently discourage it from trying to latch on to the only significant protrusion on my face. "No, baby, you don't want to bite nice Doctor Torin's nose."

After that, the Meridae practically adopted us, and were happy to describe their culture. They performed nearly every function of life on wing, alighting on their tree structures only for rest, prolonged nourishment, or nursing the young.

I learned the Meridae had no formally trained med pros or treatment facilities. Each family unit (called "throngs") had a "fosterer"—usually an unmated female—who provided all health care. They even performed complex surgical procedures with a high success rate.

When they learned we were physicians, they brought

up a mysterious problem with persistent ulcerations among some of the younger males.

"Could it be some type of plague?" Vlaav asked me, afraid to touch the adolescent Meridae.

"Not according to my scans." His agitated shuffling was wearing on my nerves. "Get a grip, will you?"

The smell of their bodies took some getting used to, but I found after several hours I no longer noticed it. To deal with the ulcerations, Vlaav and I set up an impromptu aid station and began performing routine examination scans.

I examined the painful raw spots on several young male Meridae, and concluded it was likely due to excessive grooming. They were in their first season, and acting like love-struck teenagers do all across the galaxy. Doing dumb things, trying to impress some desirable but unusually fickle young *female*. I pointed out the betraying marks left by the comblike bristles, and prescribed an emollient to facilitate healing.

"I'll leave a supply of it with you," I said, after I'd treated the last of the males. "It might help if the young lady decides who she wants to mate with. Soon."

One of the older females chirped, "Preening until they bleed, the young paramours! I'd give my wing to be in first season again."

"Hush, you will embarrass our visitors," another female said, and eyed me and Vlaav with obvious pity.

Another one peered behind me, as if to make sure I wasn't hiding a wing somewhere. "How do you bear being planet-bound?"

They thought we were *handicapped*. "We're grounddwellers," I told her. "Most of us aren't born with wings—um, a wing."

Vlaav finished recording his scan data. "Haven't you seen other offworlders without wings?"

"No other visitor has ever come to our epicenter," the older female replied. "The escort teams say it is because they fear they will be dropped. Such ill-bred behavior!"

Glad I hadn't spoken up back at Transport. The females weren't done asking questions. On the contrary.

"How do you secure a mate without wing?"

"How can you hunt? Do you remain on the ground always?"

"Does it not hurt the bottoms of your feet?"

In the end I had to promise to leave an in-depth report on ground-dwelling humanoid cultures and physiologies for them to study at their leisure.

While discussing dietary particulars, we discovered the only source of vegetation on Te Abanor grew in the caverns beneath the surface. Apparently all surface flora and topsoil had been eradicated during the volcanic prehistory of the planet.

The caves, however, hosted thousands of plant species and a horde of mammals which fed on them. The Meridae preyed on the smaller mammals, which they caught while combing the network of caverns in organized hunting packs. Their quarry was either consumed on wing, or brought back to the aviaries to be divided.

Vlaav and I politely refused their offer of a meal. It was easy. Vlaav was a vegetarian, and I personally had treated too many types of patients to eat the flesh of anything. Plus my stomach was definitely upset, to the point of knotting with cramps.

What appetite I had disappeared when I learned exactly *how* and *from what* the Meridae built the aviary structures.

"Throngs are made up of nonrelated broods, to ensure proper breeding," I was told. Sensible enough. Over time, inbreeding had destroyed countless species in isolated areas on other worlds. "When a throng reaches capacity, a new throng is initiated, and we collect for a new aviary."

"Collect what?" I asked.

"The throng members defecate in a clearing until the proper amount of material is accumulated, shaped, and dried."

Yuck. The structures were nothing more than hardened, sculpted *waste.* I remembered not to make a face, and surreptitiously scanned for contaminants. I found none; the fecal material was extremely sanitary.

"Would you care to ascend?" one politely offered.

"No, thank you." Sanitary or not, no way was I going to stand on a pile of dried-up, decades-old Meridae droppings.

Remembering Alunthri's request that I check into any obscure, artistic expressions I came across, I asked about the Meridae forms of entertainment.

"Let us perform for you," one throng leader offered. And up they went.

The Meridae *danced* in the air. Their movements were unbelievably fast, intricately weaving patterns as groups flew up. Soon the sky above us was filled with throngs, floating, diving, winding around each other. Others flocked to join them, until it seemed the sunlight itself would be blocked out by their mass. My neck muscles strained. I couldn't have cared less.

The crowd above parted, and each Meridae made a brief, personal promenade. Some fluttered slowly, drifting like a feather without aim or purpose. Others tightly spiraled down to the surface, only to swoop up at the last moment and soar into the heights.

The young Meridae were particular geniuses when it came to comical acting. A group of them began making the oddest movements, lurching and jerking, turning their heads, and flapping their chin lappets. I laughed until my sides ached.

Reever stood next to me. He wasn't laughing, but I could see a flicker of warmth in his eyes.

"That's the funniest thing I've ever seen a non-

Terran do," I gasped, holding my ribs. "I wonder what they call it?"

A throng member murmured to Reever, who told me, "An Imitation of Our Visitors."

Vlaav looked indignant. I tried to. It was even funnier, now that I knew where they had gotten their material from. We must have looked pretty strange to the Meridae, with our walking, gesturing, and talking. I burst into laughter again, and the throng member chirped along with me.

The sky had gradually turned from tangerine to crimson as the performers finished their acts and spiraled down to perch on the aviary. Finally there was only one group left in the air, and a noticeable hush fell over the throng.

"Is this the grand finale?" I asked the Meridae next to me.

She stroked one of her face flaps. "You could say that, Healer."

The group above us arranged themselves in an almost-stationary circle, while two other Meridae occupied the center. One was obviously a female, the other a fledgling with a still-discernible wing wobble.

The little one began circling the female with odd, clumsy movements, which gradually slowed as if the fledgling was exhausted. A male broke out of the circle just as the small Meridae stopped flying. I started to yell just as he caught the child in his forelimbs. The female cradled the fledgling from the other side, and they revolved together. The others moved in, and the entire group huddled together around the trio.

Then it became clear, even to my offworld eyes. The throng comforted the male and female. The fledgling didn't move.

It was a dance of death.

I touched my stomach. *Oh, lump, how am I going to tell him?*

"Cherijo." Reever was there beside me, and slipped his arm around my waist. "You are upset."

"I'm okay." I let him lead me a short distance from the others. "Did you tell them what they needed to know about the war? Are they going to get involved?"

"That is not important. What is wrong?"

"I'm just tired. Tell me about your meeting." Do anything, I thought. Keep me from crying my eyes out in front of these people. Another stitch bit into my side and I gasped, alarmed at how severe it felt.

"What is it? Cherijo!" He caught me before I doubled over, then turned his head to the side. "Dr. Irde!"

Vlaav hurried over, agitation making his nubbly hide pockets swell. "Dr. Torin? What happened? Are you ill?"

Wrenching pressure began to build in my lower abdomen. I knew what it was, but I didn't want to say it. "Pain. Here." I grabbed onto Reever. "Duncan, get me—"

That was when one of the Meridae fosterers swooped down, and plucked me up in her talons. I screamed. Felt the desperate hands clutch at me as Reever and Vlaav tried to grab me back. A moment later I was soaring straight up, far from the ground and any hope of help.

"Please," I said, trying not to scream. "Please, take me back down . . . I need . . ."

"I know what you need," the female said. "This will help."

Gravity clawed at me, making the cramps worse. I felt a hot trickle between my thighs that quickly soaked the crotch of my trousers. Lack of oxygen made my eardrums press in and black spots appear before my eyes. My hands and feet went numb.

The baby—

CHAPTER TWO

Separations

I came to on the floor of the launch, with Vlaav hovering over me. I already knew from the rhythmic pains and the blood seeping from between my legs that I was having a miscarriage.

"Duncan?"

"He is taking us back to the *Sunlace*." Vlaav eased a folded tunic under my head and adjusted the thermal wrap over me.

I took a couple of deep breaths as the cramping got worse. "What happened?"

"You're hemorrhaging. We'll get you to Medical as soon as we arrive."

I closed my eyes. *My baby.* "Why did that bat thing grab me?"

"I'm not sure. Apparently it was an attempt at some kind of native medical treatment." Vlaav ran a scan over my lower abdomen. "Your uterus is contracting and there is placental matter and amniotic fluid in the blood sample I took." He met my gaze. "I—I'm so sorry, Doctor."

"Save it." No tears. Odd, I should have been crying my eyes out. "Give me that scanner."

I fumbled with the instrument until I could run another series on myself, and confirmed everything Vlaav had said. The pain became a deep, tearing agony that seemed to gouge at my spine from the inside.

"You're right," I gasped the words out, and dropped the scanner.

Vlaav gave me a reproachful look. "Of course I was right."

I controlled my breathing and panted through the next contraction. Coming down off it made me snap at him. "Resident, if you mope every time someone follows up on your work, you're never going to be happy in this job. Right now I'm having a miscarriage—concentrate on that. You can sulk another time."

Duncan left the helm as soon as we landed inside the *Sunlace*'s launch bay, and lifted me up in his arms.

"Put me down. You're getting blood all over your tunic," I said as he carried me out. His arms tightened and he walked faster. "I'm all right, get a gurney."

"Signal Medical," he said to Vlaav. "Have them prepare for her."

His voice had turned positively glacial. Belatedly I realized the Meridae's "help" must have scared him, too. I reached up and awkwardly touched my husband's face.

"I'll be okay, Duncan. But the baby"—my throat tightened—"we're going to lose the baby."

"We can have other children." Now he looked at me, and his eyes were anything but cold. "I will not lose you."

A team of nurses helped Reever get me on a trauma berth when we reached Medical, and Vlaav and Squilyp took over. I tried to relax as the Omorr performed the necessary pelvic scan, but discomfort and fear made me bite the inside of my cheek. Duncan never let go of my hand, even when Vlaav asked him to.

"Residual fetal tissue?" I asked.

"Placental matter, yes." The Omorr looked at me over his mask. "No residual fetal tissue detected, Healer."

We'd talked about what we'd do, Squilyp and I, in a worst-case scenario. This was as bad as it got, and I had no options.

I tried to let go of Reever's hand. "All right, Squilyp. Get me prepped."

The Omorr glanced at Reever. "Did you tell him?"

Reever's hand tightened on mine. "Tell me what?"

In that moment, I could have cheerfully cut Squilyp's heart out with a blunt probe. "No time like the present, I guess." I took a deep breath and addressed my husband. "Duncan, things started to go wrong with the baby a few days ago. We tried a couple of drugs to stop it. But . . . nothing worked."

His eyes never left mine. "What happens now?"

"Squilyp is going to have to perform a dilatation and curettage on me." I ignored the small sound the Omorr made. "It has to be done, to prevent infection. I'll be fine."

Reever touched my face. "I'll go in with you."

"No." I put my hand over his. "No, you can't. It won't be pretty and you know how squeamish you are about surgery." Before he could say anything else, I closed my eyes. "Please. Please do this for me. Please wait for me in recovery."

A few minutes later, Squilyp leaned over me as I was being wheeled into the surgical suite. "I hope you know what you're doing."

"Don't worry about me." The effects of the sedation made me miss him when I swatted at him. "Worry about being perfect, because that's what I need you to be. Right now."

The operation went off without a hitch. An hour after it was over, I woke up in recovery, with Duncan at the side of my berth. His coloring looked grayish, and dark half-circles bruised the skin beneath his eyes.

I wasn't feeling too great myself. "Hey. Haven't they chased you out of here yet?"

"You're awake." He stood up, and signaled for a nurse. "How do you feel?"

"About as good as you look." I tried to sit up, but some Doctor who was going to get my fist in his gildrells had put me in full limb restraints. "Where's my chart?"

Squilyp came in, released me, and picked up a syrinpress. "Shall I sedate you now, or will you behave yourself?"

Without a word I held out an arm.

He put the instrument down on a tray table with a thump—Omorr are lousy bluffers—and turned to Reever. "Captain, would you give me a few moments alone with your wife so I can examine her?"

Reever hesitated, then nodded and left the room.

As soon as the door was closed, I tried to sit up again. "Let me up. I'll do the scans myself."

"You will stay in that berth and let me scan you, or I will go out there and tell that man exactly what happened in surgery."

I scowled. "You try, and I'll spray your face with skin seal."

"Cherijo." He heaved a sigh. "At least allow me to perform the postop examination. There is much we have to discuss. Particularly the reasons why you are lying to your husband."

"I'm not lying. I'm just not volunteering information," I said through gritted teeth, then relaxed and let him scan me. As the minutes ticked by and he remained silent, I lost my patience. "Well? Did it work? Were there any complications? What happened?"

"It went much the way we anticipated. There are no apparent complications. Your immune system has already begun to heal the damage." He noted something on my chart, then caught me inching up. "Don't even contemplate getting out of this berth."

"Okay." I dropped back against the pillows. "For now."

The Omorr sat down beside my berth and took my hand with one of his membranes. Since Squilyp's people practiced touch-healing, I didn't object. But he wasn't interested in healing my physical injuries. "Cherijo, you must tell him."

"What? What precisely do I tell him? That I'll never be able to carry a child full-term? That my own body will kill any baby I try to have? That I'm a monster?" Tears streamed down my face. "No, Squilyp. I'm not going to tell him what we've done. Not now. Maybe not ever."

"Very well. I will respect your wishes. My advice remains the same—tell him the truth. He will need time to adjust to the idea."

I wasn't going to think about it. I couldn't. I wiped the back of my hand over my eyes. "Did you determine the gender?"

"Yes. Female."

I touched my flat belly. "A girl. We had a little girl." Reever would have loved that.

"Do you want to see—"

"No." I looked over at the room console. "Signal Xonea. I need to talk to him right away."

"Why?"

"Just ask him to come down here for a minute. Tell him it's HouseClan business."

Xonea arrived a few minutes after Squilyp sent the signal. Like all Jorenians, my ClanBrother was nearly seven feet tall. His sapphire skin contrasted sharply with his all-white eyes. He wore his Captain's tunic, and had his long black hair in its customary warrior's knot.

He made a handsome, if somewhat intimidating, big brother.

After touching my brow with his in an affectionate manner, he sat down beside my berth and took my hands in his. "I cannot rejoice in what has happened, ClanSister."

Jorenians normally celebrated death, so it was a gesture of sensitivity and understanding I'd never expected from him.

"Xonea, lock the door." I considered how I was going to phrase my request as he did that. When he sat back down, looking even more worried, I gave him a wan smile. "It's not that bad."

"Nothing good ever comes of your securing access panels."

"I only have one request, and you probably won't even have to do it. You're my ClanBrother, the one I trust most to carry out my wishes."

He knew what I was going to ask then, and got to his feet. "I will speak to the Omorr. There must be more that can be done—"

"Relax, I'm not dying. I'm fine. Sit down." I waved him back down to his seat. "Xonea, I know HouseClan protocol. I can do this any time. I can invoke it any time."

"You said you remain on the path." His troubled white-within-white eyes met mine. "Why do you insist on this now?"

I thought of my premonition of disaster, and shuddered. "Because there are all kinds of separations on the path, ClanBrother."

"I know I am in trouble when you quote journey philosophy."

"You're not in trouble. You're simply going to be my Speaker." I sat up a little straighter. "Now, this is what I want you to do."

Reever and Alunthri came to visit me later that day, but I slept through most of it. When I woke up twelve hours later, I felt as if nothing had happened.

That was exactly how I intended to handle it, too.

While I looked for my clothes, Squilyp hopped in. Omorr have four limbs, but use three like arms. That left one to get around with. My former nemesis did it with a peculiar, dignified sort of bounce I admired.

I certainly would have looked ridiculous if I'd been obliged to hop instead of walk.

"Would it kill you to rest for another forty-eight hours?" he asked, watching me dress.

"No, but your life expectancy would be seriously abbreviated." I checked my reflection in the mirror of the wall vanity unit. I should have looked like death warmed over, but I practically glowed with health. Courtesy of my loathsome immune system. I went back to packing my sojourn case. "Besides, you know you'll be happier to have me out of your gildrells. I'll round up Viaav and we'll head back to the *Perpetua*."

"That is the other problem I wish to discuss with you before you leave." Squilyp went over to close the door to my room, and leaned back against the panel. He was tall and rangy, and his pink derma looked great in the white-and-blue physician's tunic. He'd earned that, working for me. "The Saksonan has expressed a wish to remain on board the *Sunlace* and serve as a surgical resident in Medical."

I whirled around. "He *what*?"

"Dr. Irde wants me to take over his training."

"You're pulling my leg, right?" The Omorr shook his head. "I don't believe it. That ungrateful little snot." I slammed the lid down on my case. "After all I've done for him."

"Judging by the fervency of his request, I suspect you have completely terrorized him." Squilyp made an impatient gesture. "Don't glower like that. You have never been successful at terrorizing *me*."

"That's only because you're as conceited and arrogant as I am." I didn't want to admit it, but I was hurt. What had I ever done to Vlaav, other than give him the finest training a surgeon could ask for? "Is it because of the simulator runs?"

"He did not cite objections to a specific task."

"I only made him do two per shift, you know." I started to pace the deck. "My resident trainer used to make me do four. And I didn't yell at Vlaav when *he* messed up." Squilyp's expression of disbelief put me on the defensive. "Okay, so I yelled at him, but not very often."

Squilyp folded his membranes. "Cherijo, I've served beside you for more than a year. You are, without a doubt, the most gifted and competent surgeon I've ever worked with."

I arched a brow. "High praise."

"You are also short-tempered, demanding, and extremely hard to measure up to. That I can also attest to from personal exposure."

I scowled. "It isn't a competition. As for you, you know *exactly* how good you are, so don't hand me that 'I-don't-measure-up' waste."

"I measure up. Vlaav doesn't think he will," Squilyp said. "As far as skill goes, it's always a competition. You've simply never been in a position to worry about your own competency. You were the best surgeon in your training facility on Terra, correct?"

"Yes."

"And you became the best surgeon on K-2 as well?"

I glared. "Yes."

"I can tell you, you were the best surgeon on the *Sunlace*. You've always known you'd be the best, wherever you go. You're the epitome of confidence."

I threw up my hands. "But that's part of the job! How else are we going to have the nerve to cut people open and rearrange their insides on a daily basis?"

"Perhaps you're right. I don't know how else one can be a surgeon. I'll tell you what I do know: That young Saksonan will never be half the surgeon you are."

"Of course he won't!" I yelled. "He won't train with me!"

"If there's ever a chance of him coming close, he *can't* train with you. Did you know he's gone without adequate sleep intervals for weeks, studying your methods, trying to emulate your techniques?"

I *had* noticed how tired Vlaav had been acting lately. Residency demanded a lot. Still, I would never have guessed he was losing sleep, trying to please me. Trying to imitate me. "Okay, maybe I've been a little too hard on him."

"A little?"

"I've praised him, too. A few times." I rubbed the back of my neck, feeling sheepish. "Not enough, apparently."

"He is losing confidence in himself, Cherijo. I think he's afraid of going back on the simulator. He puts it off, says he can't clear his thoughts. He must be constantly second-guessing himself."

A luxury a surgeon never had time to indulge. "Squilyp, I honestly didn't know it was that bad." And all my fault. Like everything else.

Squilyp accurately read my expression. "It's not your fault. He didn't air his concerns, and I know how busy you are. Vlaav admitted he couldn't bring himself to ask you about the transfer. The boy idolizes you."

Or was scared to death of me. That didn't make me feel better. It made me feel like Joseph Grey Veil. "Not much of a role model for him, am I?"

"Let me work with him for now. When he's got his focus and confidence back—"

"No. You take over his residency from here on out. It's for the best." I felt like banging my head against the nearest hull panel. "You can use the extra hands, anyway."

"Have you talked to Reever yet?"

"No." I picked up my sojourn pack. "Don't go behind my back and tell him, either."

"I may not have to. The man is a telepath, Cherijo."

"I'm not telling him now." I held up a hand when he would have argued the point. "Stay out of this, Squilyp. It's personal."

The ship suddenly lurched, and shuddered. We grabbed each other to keep from falling on our faces. The ship slowly restabilized, and the Omorr hopped over to the room console and signaled the helm.

"Are we under attack?"

"No, Senior Healer. We passed through a small meteor swarm, but sustained no significant damage. Jorenian alloys are impervious to such bombardment." The ship's Operational Officer glanced at me. "We were able to shield the *Truman,* but I regret to report the *Perpetua* was not as fortunate."

I shuttled over to the now-crippled *Perpetua,* which looked like it had been put through a molecular sieve. I went directly to Medical, and walked into total chaos. Patients were yelling, nurses were shouting, and orderlies were running back and forth fetching supplies.

I put two fingers in my mouth and whistled to get everyone's attention. The room fell silent. "Triage nurses, report."

Three of my nurses came over and delivered the stats on the injured. Most of the crew members had reported in with only minor assorted lacerations and fractures, but at least a dozen were going to require surgery.

I got on the console and signaled the *Sunlace.* "Squilyp, I'm going to need a full med-support team over here. You and Vlaav, too, if you can be spared."

"We will shuttle over and be there in a few minutes."

A nurse appeared at my side. "Doctor, we've got a

complicated spinal injury over here you'd better look at."

"On my way." I pulled on some gloves. "Surgical team, prep and ready! Two minutes!"

My spinal injury case turned out to be three broken vertebra compressing the patient's convoluted spinal cord, according to my first scan.

"Fifty cc's of prednisyone," I said, and performed a second pass. "Looks like we've got three fractures between C-eighteen to T-fourteen in the cervical."

The patient was unconscious, so I had to rouse her. She was one of the Tingaleans we'd rescued from Catopsa, and strongly resembled a large snake with six pairs of stunted limblets.

"Can you hear me?" I glanced at the nurse. "What's her name?"

"GySikk."

"GySikk," I said, and patted her leathery cheek. Slowly her triple-lidded eyes opened. "You've had an injury to your spine. I'm going to probe your abdomen and lower body now. I want you to tell me if you can feel it touching you."

"Yes." She was slurring her words, but that was normal for a Tingalean.

By probing, I determined that GySikk's legs and a third of her trunk were paralyzed. She had trouble keeping her second eyelids from drooping, too.

"Upper ten limblets reactive, lower two nonreactive. All webbing nonreactive to probe." Another scan showed the tissue around the fractured vertebra was swelling, despite the corticosteroid drugs we'd administered. "Set her up and wheel her into room one. She'll be my first." I leaned over and put a hand on the Tingalean's triangular brow ridge. "GySikk, I'm going to operate on your spine, to relieve the pressure and repair the broken vertebra."

GySikk tried to look down at her body, but the restraints strapping her to the spinal support board didn't allow her to lift her head. "Will I . . . be paralyzed?"

"No. Your spinal cord is intact." I smiled down at her. "Just relax and let us take care of you now." I waited and watched her vitals until the sedation kicked in, then went to the cleanser to scrub.

The assisting nurse popped up beside me. "Doctor, what about her blood?"

I thrust my hands into fresh gloves. "What about it?"

"It's extremely poisonous. Lethal upon skin contact."

I nodded and put on another pair of gloves over the first. "Analyze a sample and set up the whole blood synthesizer to duplicate it. And don't spill any on yourself."

Squilyp came in with Vlaav and a team of Jorenians just as I headed for surgical suite one.

"I've got a spinal cord compression I've got to work first," I called over to him. "I'll be an hour, maybe two."

He nodded. "I'll take the next one. Vlaav and Adaola will cover triage. Go."

I kept my hands up and backed into the surgical suite. The team had the Tingalean rolled over and her back prepped and sterilized.

"Everyone in double gloves and full face visors? Good, let's get moving." I powered up the laser rig and positioned it over the upper half of the snakewoman's body. "Okay, GySikk. Let's see if we can't get you back up on your belly."

The spinal procedure went smoothly, and I was able to repair the fractures and relieve the pressure on the patient's cord. If all went well with her post-op recovery, GySikk would be slithering around the ship again in no time.

When I finally got a chance to access a console, I tracked my husband down in Engineering. He was too busy to talk, though. Once we finished treating the injured and performed post-op rounds, I went down there to find out how bad the situation was.

Reever was working three consoles, accessing ship schematics on one, consulting with the Senior Engineer on the second, and receiving updates from work crews on the third.

When there was a brief lull in the madness, I leaned over and kissed his cheek. "Captain. You're earning your paycheck today."

"I do not receive compensation for my position." He glanced at me. "You should be in Medical on the *Sunlace.*"

"What can I say? I got bored." I sat down beside him and studied the latest transmission of repair estimates. "Whoa. Looks like the ship got slammed pretty good."

"The hull could be restored, if we had engines to get to a more advanced system. We don't. Damage from the residual debris is our primary concern at the moment." He accessed one console, and brought up an interior view of the stardrive section, which was deserted. "The drive initiators are offline, main fuel cells have ruptured, and radiation levels are climbing."

Radiation was never a good thing. "Can you get anyone in there to purge the cells?"

"No, the exposure would kill them in a few minutes. It's not coming from the cells, but from radioactive fragments lodged in that section of the ship. Even if we had propulsion and could land safely on Te Abanor, it would take weeks, possibly months to remove all the debris."

I doubted the Meridae would want us to expose them to that much radiation. "Can the Lok-Teel help us out?"

"They would try. Unfortunately, the radiation would prove fatal to them as well."

I gnawed at my lower lip. "So basically the ship is unfixable."

"For want of a better word, yes." Reever sat back in his chair and rubbed his eyes.

"We can transport everyone over to the *Sunlace* temporarily." I looked at the upper deck, mentally tallying the number of former slaves and crew members left on board. "It would be cramped for a while, but the Torins will be glad to help us out."

"There is another possibility." He steepled his fingers. "We can inspect the *Truman,* and see if it will serve our needs."

"Bad idea. Knowing Joe, he's got it rigged to send a signal beacon to the nearest mercenary base the minute we step on board."

"You know we have already performed several scans, and found no weapons, beacons, or explosive devices on the ship. The computers remain offline and can be fully reinitialized. It appears harmless."

"Yeah, that bowl of porridge is just right." His expression didn't change, and I rolled my eyes. "Another joke I'll have to explain to you someday, Goldilocks."

"Since the Meridae's native resources were incompatible with the *Sunlace*'s power core and dietary needs, the Jorenians are presently running low on both fuel and supplies now. They can't sustain the additional demand of extra passengers on their equipment for longer than a few days. The only other alternative would be to strand us on Te Abanor while the *Sunlace* replenishes their supplies at the nearest non-League planet. That would be BiTned, which is more than three weeks away."

Three weeks marooned on a planet with little oxygen, animal flesh for food, and dwellings sculpted from fecal matter. "Okay, we take a look at Joe's gift horse."

"I think that would be best."

"Just you and me, though," I said. "There's no reason to risk anyone else until we know it's safe."

"It will take several days to inspect the vessel."

"So we'll evacuate everyone to the *Sunlace*, then pack some clothes and take Jenner with us."

While I assembled what we'd need for the trip in our quarters, Reever sent a signal to the *Sunlace* and made arrangements with Xonea for the evacuation, then notified the crew. Squilyp agreed to supervise the medevac and cover the patients while Reever and I took care of checking out the *Truman*.

I checked on Alunthri, who thankfully had been working on the *Sunlace* when the meteor swarm hit, and made sure it hadn't been injured. "I am well, Cherijo." After I told it what we were going to do, it added, "I hope you and Duncan will be careful. Your creator is a devious individual."

"Don't worry. If I see so much as a recording drone hovering around us, I'm setting the ship on self-destruct."

I ended the signal and started to pack. Fifteen pounds of silver-furred Tibetan temple cat jumped up, then sprawled out beside my case on the sleeping platform. Indignant blue eyes inspected me with mild hostility. I could guess what he was thinking.

You left me again. Alone with that blond guy who never pets me and those disgusting blobs.

"Hey, pal." I gave him a thorough scratching around both ears and under his chin. "Miss me?"

Please. He yawned and closed his eyes. *I have a full schedule of naps to take.*

"I'll bet." I finished folding my garments, then went to Reever's side of the storage container. It still felt odd, handling his clothes, picking up his grooming items. The intimacies of married life. "How would you like to take a little trip?"

Jenner's head lifted, and his whiskers twitched.

About as much as I like getting wet. One of the Lok-Teel flowed past him, and he gave it a single, disdainful sniff. *And these things.*

I saved bringing out the animal carrier for last. By now Jenner knew exactly what it meant when that appeared. Fortunately for me, he'd gotten too fat and lazy to run very far or fast.

I caught him and carried his struggling body over to the platform. "Come on, come on, you know the drill."

I put a handful of dry mackerel treats in the carrier to placate him. He immediately kicked them out through the vent slots and yowled.

Do you really think you can bribe me?

"I tried."

I met Reever in the nearly empty launch bay, and handed him the garment case as I climbed in the shuttle with Jenner. Strapping the carrier in only made my poor pet's yowls get louder.

"You are injured." Reever took my hands and extended them.

"Just a couple of scratches. Jenner doesn't like taking trips."

He eyed my darling feline. "I will never understand your attachment to that irate creature."

"You love me," I pointed out.

"You do not scratch me when I transport you."

"I don't? You sure have a short memory." I patted his back in a particular place. "Everyone get off the ship all right?"

"Yes." He went to the helm, and initiated the flight shield. "Come and sit with me."

Normally I would have sat beside Jenner and tried without success to soothe his shattered nerves, but I had the feeling Reever wanted to talk about the baby. I'd been successfully avoiding the subject since the miscarriage. But it wasn't just my baby, and I was sure he needed to vent.

Don't think. Don't talk. Just listen.

Slowly I went up and strapped myself in beside him. I also put up the mental walls that would keep my husband from accessing all my thoughts. I'd been doing that since the miscarriage, too.

We flew out of the launch bay and into space before he said anything. "I regret the loss of our child, Cherijo."

I stared through the view screen at the looming outlines of the *Truman.* Squilyp was right, I did have an obligation to tell him. "Duncan, how would you feel if we could never have any more kids?"

"I have you," he said, as if that was all that mattered. "We made this child. We will make other children together."

For once I hated the fact I was female, and I had the uterus. "What if I can't? What if I can't and you find out I'm not enough?"

I knew how difficult it was for Reever to express himself emotionally. So it didn't surprise me that the words that came from him were slow, and drawn from a place he was still getting acquainted with.

"Cherijo, I have never loved anyone in my life before you. It was not my choice to experience these emotions, but I have them. I have come to know them very well."

"If it's any comfort," I said, feeling slightly miffed, "I didn't want to fall in love with you, either."

"So you understand how I feel. I had greatly anticipated the birth of our daughter, and I deeply regret her loss. But your concerns are unnecessary. We are both young and healthy. There will be other children. I look forward to them."

We were approaching the docking entrance for the *Truman*'s launch bay, which was a good thing—I was about ready to burst into tears and ruin everything.

Not now.

"Okay." I wiped my eyes quickly and straightened

my tunic. "We'd better get up to Command and take a look at Operations first." Something strange shimmered in front of the launch bay. "What's that weird glow out there?"

"It is produced by the vessel's flightshield. The League apparently recently developed technology that would maintain it continuously."

I didn't know much about flightshields, only that they encased a ship in a bubble of power that allowed them to jump to light-speed and slip in between space. Then something he'd said registered. "Apparently? You mean you're not sure?"

"The ship is unlike any the League has produced thus far, and represents a considerable advance in star vessel construction. Xonea's engineers inform me they will have to disassemble the ship itself in order to ascertain the exact design specifications."

I was all for chopping it into pieces. Maybe they'd let me watch. "Is it going to let us dock?"

"Yes. We sent a probe and an unmanned launch through first." Without hesitation, Reever flew right through the yellow glow and into the bay. He scanned the exterior compartment and performed the routine decon procedures before opening the hull doors. Before I could disembark, he took me in his arms.

"Tell me you love me."

That surprised me. He never asked. "I love you, Duncan."

"I will not let you go, beloved."

I felt terrible. Guilty as sin. Because I was going to hold him to that promise.

The *Truman* was evidently the latest and finest development in star vessels that Terra had to offer—only the best for my creator, of course—and its dimensions made it roughly about half the size of the *Perpetua*.

"I don't think I've ever seen a cleaner ship," I said as we walked down one sterile, empty corridor. The

Lok-Teel Reever had sitting on his shoulder was going to have a rough time finding something to eat. "Or a more boring-looking one."

"You are spoiled by the Jorenians' penchant for vivid decor," my husband said as he swept the level ahead of us with a proximity scanner. "Gray is perfectly acceptable as an interior color scheme."

"They could have used more than one shade of it." I sniffed the air. All star vessels had a particular odor. The *Sunlace* smelled vaguely floral. The *Perpetua* still reeked faintly of pulse weapon discharge.

But this hulk didn't smell like anything. Pure oxygen had more of an aroma to it. It was making me really nervous. Could it be that new?

What's wrong with this thing?

Jenner's yowl from inside the carrier got my attention. "Do you think it's okay if I turn him loose now?"

He'd already put down the Lok-Teel, which started climbing up the nearest wall panel, searching in vain for some dirt to eat. "Yes, let him out. He may detect something I cannot."

"Hey." I glared at my husband before I bent down to release the carrier door. "He's not a bloodhound, okay?"

On one of the other ships, Jenner normally would have taken off like a shot. Instead, he sniffed once, then arched his back. Fur bristled. He hissed and tried to climb up the side of my leg.

I'd seen him do it before. "Joe must have been on board sometime before he sent it from Terra. Jenner only acts like this around him." I picked up my pet and winced as he dug his claws into my shoulder and chest and slammed his head against my chin, over and over. "It's okay, pal. If nasty old Dr. Grey Veil shows up, Duncan will shoot him in the head."

Reever reached for a hatch panel. "And if I don't?"

I took out the syrinpress I'd taken to carrying in

my pocket since leaving Catopsa. It pays to be overly prudent where Joe's concerned. "Then I poison him."

The panel opened to a cross section, and Reever made a slow sweep with the scanner, from right to left. He stopped about halfway into the left region and held the scanner steady. Before I stepped over the threshold, the sound of footsteps made both of us freeze.

"Who's that?" I whispered, pressing myself up against a corridor wall.

"It does not show as a life-form on the scanner." Reever activated his weapon. "Don't move."

"I don't plan to."

The heavy thuds got closer. Reever hid just around the edge of the hatch opening, waiting, ready to shoot whatever stepped through. I held my breath. Jenner hid his face against my neck.

"Life-forms detected."

A small, bipedal drone stepped through the hatch and halted between me and Reever. It was about half my size, encased in bright alloy, and had innumerable sensors paving its upper chassis. Vid receptors scanned me, then Jenner, then Reever.

"Welcome to the *Truman*," it said politely. "Maintenance Unit Nine-Six-One, programmed to assist. How may I serve you?"

"God." I slumped against the wall and put Jenner down. Now he took off like a shot—away from Nine-Six-One.

Reever scanned the little drone, then powered down his weapon. "Nine-Six-One, are you programmed to commit harm to any life-forms?"

"Negative."

"That's not good enough," I said. There were all kinds of things this drone could do to us that would not be considered harmful to any life-form, and would still incapacitate us.

Reever nodded. "Nine-Six-One, state your program parameters."

"Caution. Fulfilling this directive will take approximately one hundred, twenty-seven minutes. Digest response is recommended."

"Please, pick the digest response," I told Reever. I didn't want to stand there listening to the damn thing for two hours.

My husband addressed the drone again. "Delay digest response for one quarter stanhour. Escort us to the helm."

The drone made an abrupt about-face. "Please follow me."

The helm was in the very center of the vessel, behind a series of protective grids and multiple reinforced corridors.

"Why all the security?" I asked Reever as the drone deactivated yet another bioelectrical grid.

"Control of this vessel was very important to whoever designed it."

Control. As in who was in. "That doesn't sound very reassuring."

"Considering Hsktskt ship-to-ship technology, and the prospect of impending war with the Faction, it is likely a mandatory and standard design application for all new League vessels."

I wasn't quite so analytical. "Joe probably has it set up so it can be controlled from a remote ship. That's the only reason he'd allow that kind of safeguard—if he had a back door in."

"You are too suspicious."

I scoffed. "Spend a few years being chased by Joseph Grey Veil, then come talk to me about my paranoia."

The Command Center was compact and efficient, and acted as the brain for the entire vessel. Controls over all levels and systems were at our fingertips. Only

the main computer was offline, waiting to be reinitialized.

Reever sat down at the console, but before he
touched the keypad, I grabbed his hand.

I had the strongest urge to pull him away from the
controls and run all the way back to the launch. "What
if you reboot this thing and it decides to fly straight
back to Terra?"

"The Jorenians have already downloaded the entire
mainframe computer core via the probe we sent in,
and have extensively examined the data. There is
nothing in it that presents a danger to us."

"What if they missed something?"

He squeezed my hand. "Then I will be able to see
where you grew up."

"Very funny."

Reever tapped out the required codes, and an image
popped up on the vid screen. It was my creator, Joseph Grey Veil.

"Hello, Cherijo."

"Damn, I knew it!" I slapped the console with my
hand. "He can't even give me a present without spoil-
ing it."

Joe smiled. "As you know by now, my daughter,
there is nothing that will harm you on this ship."

"You lie like a floor covering," I told the image.
"And don't call me your daughter."

"It is prerecorded, Cherijo," Reever said.

"I don't care. He still doesn't get to call me his
daughter."

Joseph continued. "The *Truman* is the latest and
fastest of the new scout ships being designed and built
on Terra. There are sufficient supplies and living areas
to accommodate you and a maximum of two hundred
additional crew members. I hope you and your friends
will use it to attain the freedom you seek."

"He's being too nice," I said, stepping away from

the console. "There's definitely a bomb on this ship, or something."

He wasn't done, either. "I have taken the liberty of entering a special signal relay program into the mainframe system." The code appeared briefly below his image. "If you are ever in need of assistance, access the communications array, input this code and a direct relay will be sent to me here on Terra."

He still expected me to come running to him for help. After everything he'd done to me. The man's ego knew no bounds. "When pigs fly."

"Good luck, my dear." The image vanished.

I wasn't his dear anything. I turned away from the console, feeling the familiar outrage building inside my chest. "Erase whatever code he put in the computer, Reever."

"Cherijo—"

"Do it. *Now.*"

CHAPTER THREE

Endamaged

Reever had to reinitialize the computers before he could locate and erase the code. I stood there watching until he did. Then he listened to the drone spout a lot of programming directives, while I paced along the length of the helm and brooded.

"I'm hungry, Reever," I lied. "Let's go see what kind of food this heap has to offer." A couple of weeks on Te Abanor with the bat people were starting to look pretty good to me.

The little drone thumped over and put itself in my path. "May I escort you to the galley?"

"Go jump out an air lock," I said.

Nine-Six-One started to head for the entrance panel, when Reever stopped it and canceled my directive. When I glared at him, he merely raised one blond eyebrow at me.

"We can use the drones," he said, taking my arm. "And a meal interval would be welcome."

"When did you get to be so nice?" I said as he guided me out into the corridor. "I don't remember you being this nice on Catopsa. Or the *Sunlace*. Or K-2."

He paused to remove the Lok-Teel from the wall

panel and put it back on his shoulder. "Would you prefer I return to my previous persona?"

"Which one?"

"You accused me of having many. Corrupt, evil, traitorous, oblivious, inhuman—"

Anyone else would have thought he was serious. But I'd been with him long enough to recognize Duncan's personal version of humor. "Cute. Very cute. No, you can stick with being nice. I suppose I'll get used to it eventually."

"It may even influence your own personality."

"Ouch. That was a low blow, darling." I pretended to clutch my abdomen. Then I went still, thinking of the miscarriage. "Sorry, I didn't mean to— Sorry."

The little drone led us to the galley level, and went into some rambling dissertation about the functions of the prep units. I nudged it aside and started dialing.

"What are you hungry for?" I asked Reever over my shoulder, deliberately forcing a cheerful note into my voice. "And don't pick anything from that third planet in the Tupko system. I can't handle food that talks back to me."

"A simple vegetarian dish will suffice."

The program produced two reasonably attractive Tuscan salads, along with Jorenian morningbread and two servers of mint tea. I checked everything first with a scanner before I let Reever touch a single crumb, but found no trace toxins.

"He had to rig something on this ship. He's not capable of simple decent human behavior." I cautiously tasted my tea. It was on the weak side; I'd have to fiddle with the unit's preparation submenu algorithms later. "If not the drones, the computer, or the food supplies, then what else could he have sabotaged?"

"Perhaps he truly meant what he said. He wanted you to attain freedom from the Hsktskt and the League."

I gave him an "oh, please" look as I fed the Lok-Teel a crust. The blob enveloped the scrap of bread and ingested it immediately.

"People are capable of changing, Cherijo." He gave me a slight smile—something he'd been working on, practicing in the mirror for months. "You changed me."

"You never told me what you were like before I met you, so I can't exactly judge." I sampled the salad. Not bad. "Joe hasn't changed. He's just trying a new angle, like the good little mad scientist he is."

"Do you want to know what my life was like before I met you?"

It would keep me from having to come up with dinner conversation. After that thoughtless remark I'd made before, I was all for that. "Sure."

"When I was a child, traveling with my parents, I often considered suicide."

I spilled my tea, and the Lok-Teel oozed over to mop it up. "What?"

Duncan calmly picked up his server and took a sip. "It seemed a logical solution. My experiences were for the most part unpleasant, mentally and physically."

"Okay." He was serious. "What changed your mind?"

"Establishing telepathic links with other species. Sometimes their emotions filtered through. They were all different, and often confusing. Only one thing did they all seem to have in common. A desire to love, and to be loved. I didn't understand it, until I met you."

"This is the part I don't get. What's so special about me? Other than the fact I'm a genetic construct being hunted by everyone on this side of the galaxy."

"I wasn't sure myself at first. You are physically attractive for a Terran, I suppose—"

I sat back in my chair. "You *suppose*?"

"And you are a skilled physician and surgeon. But it was more than that. I have spent most of my adult life living among and communicating with thousands of other species. Yet all I had to do was see you, hear your voice, and I knew I had encountered someone more unique than any life-form I've ever known."

I was still burning over that he-supposed part. "And you got this from just seeing me at the Trading Center on K-2?"

"It was not limited to that. I watched you. I could feel the emotions emanating from you, more clearly than anyone I'd ever met before. You immerse yourself in what you do for others. Yet you rarely if ever give a thought to what will benefit you personally."

I shifted, uncomfortable with the picture he was painting of me. "Don't make me out to be a saint, Duncan. I'm not."

"No. You are completely dedicated to your work. You devote yourself to healing the sick and the injured, no matter who they are or what they have done to you, when others would simply let them die."

I thought of SrrokVar, the Hsktskt physician who had tortured me and dozens of other slaves on Catopsa as part of his research into xenobiology. I'd mutilated and nearly killed him with a pair of bonesetters. "Not always."

"You fight for freedom, for yourself and others like you. Alunthri, the slaves on Catopsa. Even a Hsktskt OverSeer."

I didn't want to think about FurreVa. After fighting so hard to give her a normal face and learning to become friends in spite of our differences, losing her had been agonizing.

"That's just doing the right thing," I said. "Any decent person tries to live their life like that."

"Then decent persons are rarities indeed, for you are the only one I know."

"I keep telling you, you need to get out more."

He reached for my hand, and the light fell on the terrible scars crisscrossing the back of his. "All of this drew me to you, but when we linked for the first time, I felt your emotions through you, as if they were my own. I began to understand how empty my life was. How meaningless it had always been, until I met you. I had finally found the reason to live."

"So, that's when you fell in love with me?"

He shook his head. "No. That was when I decided I was going to have you as my mate."

I made a face at him. "And love just happened to get in the way later?"

"I knew I loved you the day you limped into the medical bay on the *Sunlace*, your hands broken and torn, your leg bleeding from an open artery. And still you went over to the cleansing unit to scrub for surgery."

That seemed a pretty gruesome moment to pick. "What, the sight of all those compound fractures and third-degree burns dragged you completely under my spell?"

"No." He looked away for a moment. "Before I came to Medical, I had been told a Healer had been blown out into space when the buffer on level seven reformed. I thought it was you." He paused. "A few minutes later I came to Medical and saw you there. Alive."

He'd never told me that. "God, Duncan." I started to shake as I remembered that day. That moment. The same moment I'd finished reading the list of the injured and dead, and hadn't found his name on it. The exact moment I'd realized I'd fallen in love with him. "You know, on the cosmic scale of coincidences, this one blows everything away."

His eyes narrowed as he looked at me. "You felt the same? At the same time?" I nodded. "Then it is simple, isn't it? We were meant to be together."

"I suppose." When he frowned, I winked at him. "Gotcha back."

*   *   *

I found the quarters Joe had prepared for me about an hour after we finished our meal. Reever gave me a proximity scanner and a pistol, the latter of which I promptly returned to him.

"If there are hostile life-forms on board—"

"Then you get to shoot them," I finished for him. "And if you do shoot them, make sure you don't hit anything important. Otherwise, you get to assist me in surgery again."

He pocketed the weapon. "I will go with you."

"You will go work on the computers while I take a look around," I said in a firm, don't-argue-with-me tone. "I'll take the drone with me. Nine-Six-whatever your name is, you'll protect me, right?"

The little drone immediately stepped between me and Reever. "Affirmative. Safeguard function activated. Step away from the doctor, Captain."

I grinned. "You know, this little guy is starting to grow on me."

Nine-Six-One dutifully protected my body and led the way as we walked through the *Truman*'s sixteen levels.

"Where's Medical located?"

"Medical is located on level sixteen."

Bottom of the ship. We were only on level eight. It figured.

When we passed through the two levels of crew quarters, the little drone stopped in front of one chamber located at the end of the last corridor.

"Notification. Dr. Joseph Grey Veil assigned this compartment to you, Dr. Torin. Would you care to inspect the rooms?"

"Not really. What's in there?"

The drone had to process that for a minute. "Contents of compartment C-1, food preparation unit, entertainment unit, communications console, personal computer terminal console, utility storage unit, garment storage unit, sleeping platform, lavatory—"

"Discontinue inventory. I get the idea." I looked at the closed panel again. "Is there anything in there that will harm or incapacitate me?"

"No such item is listed on the compartment inventory file, Dr. Torin."

Okay, so maybe I was a little curious. "You go in first."

Nine-Six-One directed a sensor stalk at the access panel, and the door panel slid silently open. He walked in, and after a moment, so did I.

I don't know what I expected to see—maybe something sterile and utilitarian—but certainly not my old room back at The Grey Veils, the family mansion on Terra.

"God, this is . . . creepy." I walked around, still in a state of total disbelief. Everything was there—my Parrish prints, my personal entertainment unit, my collection of archaic jazz discs, even the clothes I'd left behind, hanging in the garment unit.

I went over to a shelf where I had photoscans of Maggie and me when I was little. I picked one particular frame up and turned it over. I'd dropped the original a few years ago, and nicked the back of the case. There was no scratch on this one.

So he'd hung on to the originals and duplicated everything. But *why*? Joe didn't make sentimental gestures. He didn't do anything without a specific reason. Especially where I was concerned.

Why had the drone told me about this room? "Nine-Six-One, were you programmed by Joseph Grey Veil?"

"Negative."

"Well, then who programmed you?"

"Full programming was scripted by Willa Cline Industries, auto-format download unit—"

"Never mind." I went over to the utility unit and opened a door. My old medical case sat inside. Along with a pair of boots I'd forgotten to sterilize. There was still Terran soil caked in the treads.

It's not the same. It's simulated. The real boots are back on Terra. So is Joseph.

"Cherijo."

I jumped, swiveled around, and yelled. "Will you stop doing that!"

My husband stood in the open doorway, and didn't look a bit sorry for scaring ten years off my life. "These quarters are already occupied?"

"Yeah. By me. Back on Terra." I swung my hand around. "Joe replicated everything that was in my old room."

He studied the stark, colorless decor that had been the latest trend three years ago. "It is not very appealing."

Three years ago.

"He hasn't changed a thing since I left. I just realized that. Joe has the entire mansion redecorated every six months, and yet this room hasn't been altered in the slightest degree. There's even a copy of a pair of old muddy boots I left behind." I didn't know whether to be amused, or sick. "It doesn't matter. I'm not sleeping here tonight." Or ever. "How are things going with the computers?"

"It will take several hours for the core to ascertain there are no errors from initialization." Reever held out his hand. "Come with me. I want to show you something."

He took me down another eight levels, to sixteen, where Medical was supposed to be located.

Level sixteen *was* Medical. The entire deck was one huge medical treatment facility.

"Only the best for Cherijo," I muttered under my breath as I walked around. "Look at all this stuff, Reever. Diagnostic simulators, full medsysbank array, multispecies drug and plasma synthesizers, and if I'm not mistaken"—I opened a panel and looked into what had to be the most advanced surgical suite I'd ever seen—"yeah, there it is. My own personal paradise."

Jenner padded in, and planted himself next to my ankle. Absently I picked him up and started stroking him.

Reever was busy fiddling with the database. "Your creator knows you very well."

I closed the panel without going in. "My creator doesn't know that I'd trade all this fancy tech in a heartbeat for a chance to be a FreeClinic trauma physician again."

That seemed to surprise him. "You would return to Kevarzangia Two?"

"If it wouldn't put the colony in danger, yeah, I would." I picked up a new style of syrinpress I'd never seen before. "No chance of that, I'm afraid."

A signal came in over the main console, and Reever acknowledged it.

It was Xonea. "ClanBrother, ClanSister, we are reading some minor fluctuations in the flightshield surrounding the *Truman*. Are you experiencing any power loss within the vessel?"

"No, Xonea." Reever frowned. "Have you located the source of the fluctuations?"

"It appears to be coming from the stardrive. It would be best to run a simulation on it before we transfer your passengers." The screen went blank for a moment, then Xonea's face reappeared. Suddenly he wasn't smiling anymore. "Our signal is being jammed. We are reading multiple vessels closing—"

The console went dead. Something smashed into the side of the *Truman,* sending me, Jenner, and Reever sprawling on the deck.

We ran back to the helm, and found our three ships were surrounded by a horde of star vessels in attack formation. No one was firing on anyone, from what we saw on the viewer, but the *Perpetua* was spinning out of control, showing huge, new gaps in its hull.

They wanted to be sure we couldn't use it.

"Thank God we got everyone off," I said as I went to the communications station and secured Jenner in a storage compartment next to the unit. He didn't like that, naturally, but he'd have to yowl for now. "*Truman* to the *Sunlace*. Xonea, what's your status?"

His signal came in, audio only. "We have sustained damage to the Command control and ship's Operational, along with minor casualties on four levels. Are you and Reever unharmed?"

"Yes." I looked at the viewer. "Where did all those ships come from?"

"We do not know. Even now they do not appear on our scanners. Salo speculates they are using some form of energy shunt to conceal their ships and stardrive functions."

That was when our attackers overrode both our signals, and took control of communications.

"League Scout Ship *Truman*. Is Dr. Cherijo Grey Veil on board?"

I wasn't going to let them fire on my family again. "I'm here, you bastards."

"You are ordered to stand down and prepare to be boarded."

"By whose authority?" Reever asked.

"By the authority of—"

Suddenly the *Sunlace* was firing on the biggest ship, and I was pounding on the console. "Xonea! No!"

The mercenaries returned fire, and we had to sit there helplessly and watch as two more levels sustained heavy damage.

"*Truman*. We will suspend the communications block for sixty seconds. You will advise your allies to stand down at once, or we will destroy all your vessels and the colony on the planet you orbit."

My hands started to shake. There was no way the

Meridae could defend themselves against that many ships. When I looked at Reever, he nodded. I pressed the console keypad again. "Xonea. Listen to me. We can't fight them." I relayed the mercenary's threats, then added, "I invoke my Speaking."

There was a brief silence, then Xonea acknowledged in a voice as cold as death, "As you wish, ClanSister."

I shut down the signal, then opened one to the mercenaries. "This is Dr. Cherijo Torin. I surrender. Come and get me." I shut down communications and turned to Reever. "Don't look at me like that. Go down to the launch bay and take the shuttle back to the *Sunlace*." I opened the storage compartment and took my disgruntled pet out. "Take Jenner with you."

He only shook his head and did something that made the engines rumble.

I wasn't going to lose him or Jenner. Not to mercenaries, not like this. "Duncan, don't you dare."

"They will pursue us. It will give Xonea time to transition." He set coordinates, and powered up the engines.

"You really think they're going to chase us if we run?"

"You are why they are here. Where you go, they will follow. Put your harness on."

I put Jenner back in the compartment, which got me a couple of good scratches in the process, then pulled the rigging over my shoulders. "Don't warn them. Just do it."

"I will, as soon as we're clear of the planet."

For a few minutes Reever successfully dodged a continuous volley of pulse fire as he maneuvered the *Truman* out of orbit and away from the *Sunlace* and the *Perpetua*. As he predicted, the mercenaries followed us. I started digging my nails into my chair's arm rests.

"When did you learn to fly like this?" I asked him as the ship went into yet another rolling maneuver.

"When I was on Terra." He frowned as his fingers moved rapidly over the flight control panel. "I once entertained the idea of becoming a transport pilot."

The mercenary ships were fanning out, trying to flank us on both sides. We were still too close to the planet to initiate the stardrive. "You never told me that."

"You never asked."

We both were jerked against our rigs as the flanking ships began firing at us from both sides. There was no way Reever could dodge the cross fire, so he did something completely unexpected. He cut the engines entirely, which made us drop back and under the pursuing ships.

"Good move," I said, peering at the viewer. "Can you initiate the stardrive from here?" No answer. "Duncan?"

"I just tried to." Reever sat back. "Cherijo, there is no stardrive on this vessel."

"What the hell are you talking about? Of course there's a stardrive. It's a star vessel."

"No, it's not." He calmly unfastened his rigging and stood up. "I believe the reason for that is about to present itself."

The little drone I'd left down in Medical came through the helm door panel. "Simulation sequence complete. Dimensional grid shutdown in progress."

I watched with wide eyes as the helm began to slowly dissolve. Equipment, consoles, even the view screen vanished. In a panic I grabbed Jenner and hauled him out of what I thought had been a storage compartment. It disappeared, too. Soon everything was gone, and we were left standing in a large, empty compartment lined with some kind of glowing, yellow mesh.

I thought of the thoracic training unit, the lack of odors, and groaned. "I don't believe it. How could I be so stupid? It was all a simulation."

"Yes." Reever kicked aside Nine-Six-One, who had turned into a simple recording device on rollers, also covered with the glowing mesh. "We should exit this area now."

We went out into the empty corridor. It, too, was lined with mesh. "The shuttle. We brought the shuttle over from the *Sunlace*. That's real."

"I doubt we can reach it. They're probably on board by now."

He was two for two, I thought, as I heard the thundering sound of many footsteps running toward us. "I knew Joe's present would turn out to be a lemon."

Reever turned and caught me in his arms. "Cherijo, whatever they say or do, don't fight them."

As it turned out, neither of us had a chance to fight anything. A small panel opened on the corridor wall beside me, and I turned a few seconds too late.

"Reever, look out—"

A bright, hot beam of energy burst over us. I fell to the floor, my vision already going dark. Just before I lost consciousness, I felt Reever's arms close around me.

"Dr. Grey Veil."

The voice was feminine. High-pitched. Cheerful. I wanted to slug whoever owned it.

"Can you hear me, Dr. Grey Veil?"

Certainly I could hear her. There was no way to avoid that kind of voice, other than puncturing my own eardrums. It acted like a parietal drill on my skull, drilling in to meet my huge, throbbing headache.

"It's time for you to wake up now."

Was she nuts? Some lunatic had beaten me, glued my eyelashes together, and lined my mouth with hundred-year-old waste. Every muscle I had felt torn and abused. Unless I got to return the favor, I wasn't ever going to wake up again.

The Truman. *Why aren't I on the* Truman?

Recalling that made me force my sticky eyelids

open. A smiling Terran female face floated above me, her features partially obscured by light gleaming off a surgical visor shield. Or her toothy smile. Either one could have produced all that mega-shine.

I could knock a few of those pretty white teeth out, I thought. See if that helped cut the glare.

Before I could take a swing, she slid the shield up and out of the way. "Good, you're awake. I'm so glad. How are you feeling?"

She said that like she meant every word. I spotted the glittering, brand-new gold insignia on the collar of her trendy physician's tunic, and went stiff.

Oh, God. They'd stuck me with Doctor Sunshine and Happiness.

"Don't be afraid." She patted me the way she would a shivering dog. "You're safe now and doing just fine."

Afraid? I was terrified. She was such a rookie, she still believed it actually mattered what she looked like. I started yelling—or tried to. "Where am I?"

My croak made her chipper smile become more sympathetic. "Poor thing," she crooned, stroking my forehead. "Don't remember a thing, do you?"

I remembered how to inflict severe head trauma. I took a deep breath to tell her that, and immediately started coughing. What was in my lungs? It felt and tasted like someone had poured laser rig coolant into them.

"Slow, shallow breaths now. We just took you off the machine, and you're still transitioning."

I didn't transition—Jorenian ships did. Was I on one?

I looked around. Monitors, berth optics, a vitals array. Medical. I was in some kind of medical facility. Then I remembered I'd been captured by the League. Apparently now they were going to start experimenting on me.

Time to exit the premises.

She touched my face again with her soft hand. "Please, don't try to move or speak, Doctor. You've been in sleep suspension for an entire cycle."

"A *cycle*?" Where was Duncan? And Jenner? I yanked against my restraints and ignored the scraping sound of my voice. "Where's my husband? Where's my cat?" They had me strapped down tight. "Let me out of these things, you stupid twit!"

That dimmed the smile a few watts. "In due course, I will." She picked up a chart and made some notations on it. Her short, honey-colored hair gleamed as she glanced over at me. I'm Dr. Lily Risen. Call me Lily. Please, don't struggle. I'd hate to have to sedate you again."

"Again?" Call-me-Lily hadn't even run a scan on me yet. If she really was in charge of me, I was lucky to be alive. "Where am I?"

"You're on board the L.T.F. *Stephenson.* We've just gone into orbit above Terra. Now, relax and try to stay calm while I take your vitals."

"My vitals are fine. Where is my husband and my cat?"

She hesitated, then went over to a console and accessed it. "Linguis Reever and the animal were brought out of suspension yesterday and have been transferred to the detainment area."

"You put my *cat* in *jail*?"

Doctor Sunshine walked back over to my berth. "Of course not. Once it was revived, the animal refused to be separated from Linguist Reever." She rubbed her forearm, which I saw was bandaged.

Jenner *really* didn't like strangers handling him. "He's got some claws, doesn't he?"

She gave me a prim frown. "Yes."

That was my boy. "Are they all right?"

"Yes. We also discovered the most extraordinary form of mold on the ship—it appears to be ambulatory."

Lord, they'd even found the Lok-Teel. "That also belongs to me. Where is it?"

"Right over there, in a specimen container. Now, here." She leaned over me, holding a syrinpress. "No, don't be afraid. I'm going to administer the last corrective to bring you all the way out of the suspension. It won't hurt you."

"What corrective?"

"They told me you'd be demanding," Lily said as she infused me at the jugular. The sting of the drug spread through my neck, and made me arch against my bonds again. "I know it's a little uncomfortable. But we'll have you out of this chamber in a few minutes, and then you can see your father." She smiled again, as if expecting me to sob or cheer or something.

No one had bothered to brief Dr. Risen about my relationship with my creator. Which, when I thought about it, was terrific.

"My father's here? On this ship?" When she nodded, I let my lips curl up on both sides. "That's great news. I can't wait to see him. How about letting me up now?"

"Sure. Just remember, take it slow and easy."

Oh, goody. Nobody had bothered to brief her about *anything*.

She released the straps holding me down. "You're on your honor now. Please don't try to escape. I'd hate to have to call security."

Was there anything she didn't hate to have to do?

"I won't try to escape." Try, hell, I was *going* to escape. I sat up, then pushed myself off the suspension unit. It took a minute to get my legs steady, so I took the time to study my surroundings.

They'd put me in a typical League medical bay. All the berths were empty, though, and Dr. Risen was the only med pro in sight. Excellent. One on one was a lot easier than one on twenty.

Even better, she'd also neglected to deactivate the

console. She'd have used her password, and she just might be a Primary. Primary physicians had access to the entire database. Every bit of information I'd need was right there, waiting for me.

Now I just had to get rid of Sunshine.

I eyed the chart in her hands, then a dermal probe and syrinpress. All three were easily within my reach. Decisions, decisions.

"Are you the Primary here?"

"Yes. Look at me, please." She held an optic scanner up and checked my eyes.

They were making airheads like her Primaries. Mother of All Houses. "First assignment, right?"

"Is it that obvious?" She even laughed pretty. "Yes, this is my first offworld assignment. Takes some getting used to, you know, working on a troop freighter, being around all these nonhumans."

"Uh-huh." There were barely discernible bags under the makeup she'd blotted around her sparkling brown eyes. Establish rapport, Cherijo. Lull her into thinking you're the Sunshine and Happiness Patient. "Must have been pretty rough. You look a little tired."

"You were a very naughty patient, Doctor." She wagged a manicured fingernail at me. "I had to remain awake for the entire jaunt because of you."

The chart. It was closest; the obvious choice. I moved my hands into position under it and locked my fingers together. "Why's that?"

"Trying to keep you in suspension was really a challenge. You kept waking up, no matter how much sedation I—"

I hit the bottom of the chart as hard as I could with my joined hands. The edge flew up, smashed into her chin, and sent her staggering backward. Lily shrieked and grabbed her face, but by then I had retrieved the syrinpress, tackled her, and sat on top of her.

"No!" She sounded funny, and struggled as I calibrated the instrument for a hefty dose of Valumine, then pressed it against her jugular. "What are you . . . ?"

"Don't you hate it, Lily, when someone infuses you with something and they won't tell you what it is?" I smiled. "Have a nice nap."

I got to my feet as soon as her eyes fluttered shut, and started stripping her down. Sunshine was a foot taller than me, so I had to roll under the hems of her sleeves and cuffs. I put the syrinpress and the dermal probe in the pockets of her lab coat. On the plus side, she had small feet, so her footgear almost fit me.

Once I was dressed, I dragged her over to the berth, heaved her up on it, and clapped her into the restraints. A strip torn from the berth linens made an adequate, if not quite fashionable, gag.

"Don't go anywhere now." I checked her vitals. Yeah, she'd be out for a couple of hours. Then I draped her to make it look like I was still in the berth, huddled under the linens.

At the console, I pulled up a schematic of the ship. According to the screen, Reever and Jenner were being held in a compartment two levels below me. I knew just where it was, since the *Stephenson* was the same class of League ship as the *Perpetua,* and the layouts were almost identical.

I figured there would be security outside the door, so I needed to disguise my face. I spied the Lok-Teel undulating listlessly in its specimen container, and rubbed my chin.

"If you can do it for Reever, I bet you can do it for me." I took it out and felt it caress my fingers with warmth and what had to be a form of mold-affection. "He did this telepathically, right?"

I wasn't much of a telepath, but I had been able to successfully communicate with the Pel on Catopsa. And the Pel had used the Lok-Teel as housekeepers. Should work.

I cradled the Lok-Teel between my hands and concentrated, forming a mental image of my own face, masked and transformed into Dr. Risen's features. The Lok-Teel stopped moving for a moment, then crawled up my arm toward my neck.

It was unnerving at first, to sit quietly as the mold flattened and oozed up and over my face. It worked its way over my lips and my nostrils. I guessed my job was to trust it, hold my breath and keep the image of the Lily's face—and air holes—in my mind. That, plus no screaming.

Slowly the Lok-Teel covered my entire head, and enveloped all of my hair, pulling it up and flattening it against my skull. Then I felt silky, shorter strands of hair brushing against the thin surface of the mold coating my cheek, and carefully got to my feet.

A glance in a wall unit mirror made me grin. I was the spitting image of Dr. Lily Risen—even down to the smooth, blond hair style.

All I had to do now was walk out of Medical at a brisk pace, carry a stack of charts, look harried, and hope whoever had a weapon fell for my act.

It worked. The guard at the panel never twitched a muscle. Once I got to the lift, I punched it and secured the doors until I reached Reever's level.

More crew members passed me as I walked down the corridor. I pretended to read a chart, and no one said a word about how odd it was, that Lilly had suddenly shrunk a foot. Maybe height wasn't something everyone noticed. A few nodded and smiled at me. Using Dr. Risen's face, I smiled and nodded back.

The guards at the detainment area were big, armed, and looked bored. They gave me the once-over.

"What do you need?" one asked.

"Not much." I pitched my voice to an equally bored, colorless pitch, hoping Dr. Risen wasn't always as chipper as she'd been with me. "I'm here to do the last prisoner check before they go onplanet. Open it up for me."

"He's not in a good mood," one of the guards said, and jerked a thumb toward the access panel. "Broke both arms of the last guy on shift when he took in his meal. They just sent him over to Medical."

Not good. What had the other guy done to Reever?

"Poor thing." I made a face with Lily's face. "I'd better hurry up and get this over with so I can get back and take care of him."

"Want me to go in with you?"

"No, thanks. If he gets antsy with me"—I lifted the syrinpress and waggled it—"I'll just stick him."

I held my breath as the guard slowly unlocked the panel and opened the door. Then I walked into the dark compartment, and waited until the door closed before I said, "Hello?"

He was on me in two seconds. Strong arms pinned me to the wall. Something hard with a ragged edge pressed against my neck. "Don't move. Don't breathe."

"Gee, honey, I missed you, too."

"Cherijo." Whatever he had against my neck fell to the deck. Lights came on. Hands that had been creating bruises now ran over me, and peeled the Lok-Teel mask from my face. The helpful mold reformed its mass into its neutral old self and slid down in front of my tunic. "What did they do to you? How did you get away? I thought they were going to transport you in a suspension unit."

Jenner started butting my ankles, and I bent down to stroke him. "I don't know, I knocked out the dim-wit they left me with, and we're going to steal a shuttle. Let's go."

"I think not."

Jenner hissed. If I'd been a cat, I would have joined him. Slowly I turned my head to see my worst nightmare standing in the open door panel, flanked by a quartet of guards. Then I hissed anyway.

He wasn't very tall. Like me, he had black hair that reflected a gray sheen in the light. No silver streak in his, though. He had the same exotic-looking dark blue eyes. The same slightly beaky nose.

Understandable. I'd been created from his own DNA, so that made us twins. If you could be twins with a man you'd called "Dad" all your life.

"Hello, my child," Joseph Grey Veil said. "Welcome home."

CHAPTER FOUR

The Inevitable

"You should have let me stab him," I said to Reever as they marched us to the launch bay a short time later. I felt a small sense of relief when I heard Jenner yowling, and spotted his carrier stowed inside the shuttle, under the seats. "A dermal probe to the aorta, and all our problems would be over."

"There were too many guards around him."

"I could have gotten him in one shot." And I would have, except Reever had grabbed me, then the guards had grabbed and searched both of us. So much for my syrinpress and dermal probe. "After everything he's done to us, don't I deserve the chance to hack his heart out?"

"Killing your creator now will not improve our current situation." Reever looked over the interior of the shuttle, the rigging they were putting us in, and the distance to the helm. His mouth still bled from the tussle he'd had, trying to get me away from Joseph's guards. "Another, better opportunity will present itself."

I thought of the Lok-Teel, which was still hidden under my tunic. Maybe Reever was right. Not that I was going to stop nagging at him. "Okay, but I get dibs on his heart. Assuming he has one. Hey, cut it out," I said to the guard manhandling me. "I'm not talking about stabbing *you*."

"Shut up," the Terran said. He had a blunt, ugly face that hadn't been improved by Reever's fists.

"If I throw a stick, will you go away?"

He grabbed the front of my tunic. "You shut up or I'll knock you out."

Reever jerked against his bonds. "Let her go."

"Guard. Release her."

Joseph came in the shuttle and took a seat across from me and Reever. At the same time, Jenner let out a low, scary sound that make me smile. Joe had better have secured the latch on that carrier tightly.

The guard let go of me as if my tunic had scalded him, turned, and bowed toward my creator. "The prisoner was making threats against your life, sir."

"She generally does." Joseph gestured for the guard to leave, then watched me and Reever for a few minutes.

Outwardly, my creator hadn't changed that much in three years. He had always looked remote, attractive, and powerful. And short.

Evidently he'd gotten some cosmetic work done since I'd left him—the faint silver strands in his hair were gone, and some minor wrinkles around his dark blue eyes had been lasered away. His body appeared even more muscular than it had been when I'd lived with him, but he'd always been obsessed with developing his body. That was his compensation for being so short.

"How did you get the streak in your hair?" he asked me.

I turned to Reever. "Did you hear something? I could have sworn I just heard something. Sounded like a . . . a rodent, squeaking, didn't it? A small, diseased rodent, maybe?"

Joe smiled faintly. Or sneered. It was always a toss-up. "You cannot provoke me into anger with your childish insults."

No, but I was going to try. "On second thought, it's not a rodent," I said to Reever. "Could belong to a lower order. Like slime. Slime sounds like that when it oozes out from under a rock."

Joe fastened his harness as the shuttle's engines came online. "Evidently your natural capacity for violence has tripled. I had to treat Dr. Risen for severe contusions. You nearly fractured her mandible. Extensive psychological evaluation will have to be performed on you."

My *natural* capacity? I felt a twinge of guilt at learning I'd almost broken Lily's jaw, but ignored it. "Then again, slime sounds much more pleasant than that. Waste. That's it. Has to be unprocessed waste."

Stop taunting him, Cherijo. Reever slipped into my mind without effort. *He is unpredictable and we are vulnerable like this.*

I tried to casually throw up my mental blocks, hoping he would think I was sulking. Even now, I couldn't risk Reever knowing what was on my mind. *You never let me have any fun anymore.*

Reever leaned forward.

"What are you doing?" Joe asked Reever, his gaze bouncing between our faces.

Reever bent down and pressed his mouth against mine, then gave Joseph one of his blank looks. "Kissing my wife." He sounded almost amused.

"She is not your wife. Marriages with nonsentients are not recognized under Terran law." Still, Joseph seemed fascinated by what Reever was doing. Namely, rubbing his cheek against my hair. "She routinely responds to your tactile stimulation?"

"Yes, she does." Reever made it sound like I tore off my garments and danced nude for him whenever he touched me.

Which wasn't an unappealing idea, actually.

"I find that quite intriguing. She demonstrated no interest in exploring her own sensuality before she left Terra."

He had no idea what I'd explored since I left Terra.

Cherijo. Despite the blocks, Reever could tell how angry I was getting. I looked at him. *Don't respond to it. Ignore him.*

Oh, I'm going to respond to it, Duncan. With a blunt, cold instrument.

"What are your intentions, once we reach the surface?" Reever asked my creator.

"Due to the League's involvement in reclaiming my property, there will be an official hearing before representatives of the World government." Joe shrugged, like that wasn't consequential. "Cherijo will be legally remanded to my custody, and then I will continue my work with her."

He's lying. I nuzzled my husband's neck.

Reever rubbed his cheek against my hair. *How do you know?*

You can hear it in his voice. He never tries that hard to sound confident. Something's wrong.

Joe wasn't finished, either. "If you will convince my daughter to cooperate, Linguist Reever, I will recommend the committee show lenience toward you. It is likely you will have to serve some time on a penal colony for your role in the Varallan disaster, but with my recommendation, the length of your sentence could be drastically reduced."

Don't, Cherijo—

I shoved Reever out of my mind. "You think dangling that carrot is going to work, don't you? You son of a bitch. He's not like you. He won't use me."

Reever stopped the rest of the stuff I planned to yell with another kiss. *You're only giving him more ammunition to use against you.*

I thought about biting my husband on the lip, then sighed into his mouth. *All right.*

By that time the shuttle was landing at a Terran Transport Center. New Angeles, from the look of it. The guards double-checked our bonds before we were permitted to disembark.

This was the world I'd been born on. I'd never thought I'd see it again. Now that I was here, I couldn't wait to get off it.

Soon. We'll escape, and find a way back to the Sunlace. *We have to.*

"How long has it been for you?" I asked Reever as we stepped onto Terran soil. "Since you've been back, I mean?"

"Twenty-two years, six months, three days, nine hours, and two minutes."

"Not long enough."

We went from the shuttle directly into a secured glidebus, where they chained us to the seats on separate sides. Joseph sat behind me. Because my hands were tied, I ignored him.

"When you were here, did you ever spend any time in New Angeles?" I asked Reever as the glidebus pulled away from the cargo-loading zone.

"No. My school was in Paris."

I watched the impeccably manicured landscape whiz by my window. "You didn't miss much."

I'd never liked the tasteful, precisely sculpted scenery surrounding the sterile structures that made up downtown New Angeles. Not one tree had been planted too close to another, not one stray blade of grass grew untrimmed. Three years away from the homeworld had only increased my aversion. What I wouldn't have given for a walk through a nice, uncivilized jungle, like the one surrounding the colony on K-2.

"The region resembles Paris a great deal." Reever wasn't looking at the scenery. He was watching the guards. "Terrans appear to embrace consistency almost as fervently as their xenophobia."

"They're picky about things like shrubbery and the threat of genetic pollution."

"You are both Terran," Joseph said suddenly.

We turned to glance at him. I laughed. Reever only went back to watching the guards.

My creator leaned forward and without preliminaries started interrogating me. "Your vitals indicate a recent trauma involving blood loss. However, I found no evidence of internal injuries. What caused it?"

I wasn't going to tell him about the baby. "I ran into a vampire. He reminded me of you."

"Have your menstrual cycles been regular?"

No topic was sacred. That was my dad. "Make someone happy, Joe. Mind your own damn business."

He didn't like me calling him "Joe." I could tell from the way he tightened his jaw. "You are currently ten pounds lighter in weight than when I last had you scanned on K-2. Explain the difference."

I pretended to think for a minute. "I've always wondered—how many angels, do you think, could dance on your head?"

"Your flippancy serves no purpose. Answer the questions."

"I'm kind of busy now." I gave him a lovely smile. "Can I ignore you some other time?"

The glidebus came to a stop at the back of a large federal building. More guards came on to remove me and Reever. We were marched into a private lift and whisked up to the top floor, where we were shoved through more biodecon and weapon detectors.

"They're clean," a guard said to the two standing in front of a large set of double doors.

"And healthy. And vocal," I added.

"Shut up," our guard said with a growl.

"You may proceed," one of the door guards said, and both stepped out of the way.

Inside was a huge, empty assembly room occupied by a sea of vacant chairs. In the center was a round presentation platform, with a single table. Six Terrans of different races sat at the table, each sporting a personal terminal.

Given my personal notoriety, the room should have been packed. So it was clear—this was all going to be under the table.

"You didn't extend an invitation to the general public?" I asked my creator. "I'm so disappointed. I expected a big, crazed homecoming mob lobbing rotten vegetables and screaming for my blood."

A pulse rifle jabbed me in the back. "You will remain silent until you are called upon by the committee."

"Oh, I'm getting called upon? Wonderful. I have so much to tell them. Where do I start?"

That got me another, harder jab. "Move."

All the continents had been represented, I saw as they escorted me and Reever down to the platform. North and South America, Africa, Asia, Euro-Common, and the Polar Nations.

Just one representative from each, however. It was much easier to bribe a single rep, versus a whole delegation.

The North American rep, a bilious-looking male with thinning hair, heavy body frame, and slightly protuberant eyes, spoke first. "The committee recognizes Dr. Joseph Grey Veil."

Everybody recognized Joe. He was the official Poster Boy for Terran medicine.

"Thank you, representative." My creator took a file from the briefcase he carried and stepped up to the podium in front of the committee. "My petition has already been presented to the committee. I have apprehended the experimental construct, Cherijo Grey Veil, and her accomplice, Duncan Reever. All that remains is a petition review, and the rendering of your final decision."

"Why have they been placed in restraints?" The

Euro-Common rep, an elegant Parisian female in an immaculate tunic, looked faintly alarmed. Obviously she was used to a much better class of experimental construct.

"Dr. Torin and Linguist Reever are dangerous fugitives, representative, both of whom have long eluded the League's efforts to recapture them. The restraints are for your safety, as well as theirs."

The Frenchwoman sniffed, as though Reever and I were giving off a bad odor. "If that is so, sir, please move your prisoners *away* from the committee platform."

That was okay with me. The smell of her expensive perfume was starting to get to *me*.

Joe directed the guards to sit us down on opposite sides of the assembly area. I would have started yelling about that, but Reever caught my eye and shook his head.

Maybe he'd found a way out. I went to my seat quietly.

"If you are ready to proceed, representatives, I am prepared to answer any questions you may have regarding the petition."

"I see no legal grounds to even support such a petition. The construct represents gross negligence of World Law," the Asian rep pointed out at once. He was a small man with beady eyes and a shrill voice. "According to current legislation, she must be destroyed at once, and you, Dr. Grey Veil, imprisoned for violating the statute against genetic experimentation on humans."

I liked him. Especially if he could get Joe thrown in jail.

"You will find a full waiver exonerating me of any wrongdoing in your copy of the petition, representative." Joseph held up the page for the committee to see. "Attached to the main file, subsection four, granted by the World Assembly three decades ago."

He'd gotten his waiver thirty years ago—just before I'd been born.

"Thirty years ago!" The rep from the Polar Nations echoed my thoughts with about as much shock. "That was when the original legislation was introduced and passed into law. Created and proposed by you yourself, Dr. Grey Veil."

Which made absolutely no sense to me, either. Why pass a law and then allow the man who'd basically written it to immediately break it?

"Yes." My creator folded his hands. "It was determined at that time to release only a portion of the experimental data involved in composing the prohibition against human genetic experimentation."

Six very powerful people nearly dropped their jaws in their laps. I could almost hear what they were thinking: Just *who* determined *that*?

Joe ignored the gapes. "Ladies and gentlemen, as you are well aware, Terrans have rightfully formulated a deep and abiding distrust of alien life-forms. In order to safeguard our DNA, certain measures had to be taken. The first was enacting the GEA and preventing any random or thoughtless experimentation here on Terra.

"The second was to empower me to map out future evolutionary prospects and therefore strengthen the species against involuntary genetic pollution. The first was made public. The second was not."

The South American rep's dark face flushed. "And this construct you've brought here today—you created her to represent what lies ahead for the human race? She is Caucasian!"

The other members of the committee looked uncomfortable. It had been a long time since Terrans had openly bickered over their *own* skin color. Now all they cared about was preserving the pristine condition of their race's DNA. They probably thought of themselves as supremely enlightened that way.

"She contains the genetic secrets that will permanently safeguard our genetic heritage, representative. This includes the heritage of *all* native Terran races."

"She is a criminal guilty of treason and murder," a familiar voice yelled from the back of the assembly room. "I request permission to file a counter-petition with the World Law committee. At once."

I didn't have to turn around to see who it was, but then, I'd spent a year dodging the man.

"Who is this being?" the North American rep demanded. "He is not human." No one answered. "Why are you here, alien?"

"He's depriving some poor village of their idiot," I said in a helpful way. That got me another rifle jab from the guard standing behind me.

"I represent the Allied League of Worlds," Colonel Patril Shropana said as he approached the committee, followed by a long line of armed guards. His canine face was thinner, but just as nasty as ever. "I am granted permission to apply to this committee, through the most recent version of the Accord Treaty. This construct must be turned over to me immediately and executed."

Well, Colonel Shropana's appearance certainly threw a wrench in Joseph's plans. The entire committee all tried to speak at once, while my creator's guards went toe-to-toe with the Colonel's troops. Everyone was well armed—apparently the military guys got to bypass the weapons scanner—and I was deciding if I should drop to floor and hide, or stand up and add my dulcet tones to the yelling, when I finally realized someone significant had left the party.

Reever. He was gone, and no one, not even me, had noticed.

I sat back down and forgot about protesting or getting shot. *He left me.* How had he gotten out of his restraints? Why hadn't the guards seen him go? Where had he gone?—all the doors were secured.

Duncan's smart. Maybe he's on the floor, crawling under something.

I got down and ducked my head under the row of seats. All I could see were the combat boots the guards wore and Joseph's handmade Italian footgear. No sign of Reever anywhere.

The guard yanked me back up. "Stay where I can see you."

I glared at him. "You're not as stupid as you look, are you? You couldn't be."

He looked under the seats, then over at where Reever was supposed to be sitting. "Where is he?"

"Search me." I got snatched out of my seat. "Not literally, stupid."

The guard dragged me over toward the platform. "Dr. Grey Veil? Doctor!"

Joseph made a waving gesture toward the guard and kept arguing with Shropana.

Reever's just gone to get help. I wasn't going to think about how he'd left me on Joren, and how he'd left me a couple of times on Catopsa. *No, he's definitely gone to drum up some allies.*

Only we were on Terra, and no one was going to help a man branded throughout the League as a Hsktskt collaborator.

"Gentlemen!" The North American rep banged his datapad on the table a few times to get everyone's attention. Joseph and Shropana, who were now in each other's face, turned and looked furiously at the committee. "We will debate the merits of both your petitions. Please, put your men at ease and sit down so we may conduct this hearing in a reasonable and orderly fashion. Guard." He pointed at me. "Move that prisoner away from this platform."

"Sir, the other—"

"Now!" the representatives shouted.

The guard took me back to my seat, then motioned over four of his pals and told them about Reever. The other guards began discreetly searching the assembly room. There should have been more, but some of Joseph's men were missing.

Out looking for Reever already? I hoped my husband knew how to hot-wire a glidecar.

Meanwhile, the committee debated the petitions. God, how they debated. They talked about genetic responsibility and the influx of undesirables to Terra and the League's droit du seigneur attitude toward prisoners.

Joseph made a good argument—but that was his specialty. "I created this construct to serve a greater purpose than to be a sacrifice for a League Commander's pride. Cherijo is the schematic for all future Terran generations."

"Why don't you simply create another clone?" the Asian rep wanted to know.

"Before my property escaped, she destroyed thirty years of data. She is the only source of the genetically enhanced material left available to me for study and replication."

"Don't you lie to them!" I shot to my feet. "I didn't destroy anything!"

"Dr. Grey Veil," the Euro-Common rep waved her thin hand toward me. "Instruct your property to remain silent, or I will have her removed from these proceedings."

"You can't seriously believe what this man says. He's deranged, xenophobic, and a murderer"—they stared at me, unimpressed—"oh, I forgot, that makes him a model citizen here, doesn't it?"

"Cherijo, if you value this animal"—Joseph lifted a familiar carrier up for me to see—"then create no further outbursts. If you do not comply, I will have the guards shoot it."

I sat down and shut up.

Shropana continued where my creator had left off. "Dr. Grey Veil would have you believe this female is a mindless automaton, under his control. She is not. She has collaborated with the Hsktskt Faction and betrayed hundreds of League members to them. She was solely responsible for the debacle in Varallan. Countless sentient beings are dead because of her. I assure you, I will see that she is exterminated before she can harm anyone else."

I guess he'd forgotten all about that time I saved his worthless hide.

The committee asked Shropana and Joseph to wait as they discussed the petitions. I could tell the Asian and North American reps were leaning toward granting the League's request—they had the most to lose in tech contracts with other worlds. But Terran concerns, I would bet, came first.

The decision was announced without any discussion or emotion by the African rep.

"The petition presented by the League is denied. The petition presented by Dr. Grey Veil is granted. The construct, Cherijo Grey Veil, will be remanded to the custody of Dr. Joseph Grey Veil, to serve whatever purposes he determines are appropriate, for the remainder of her existence."

Did I know my own species, or what?

I didn't raise too much of a fuss when the guards marched me back out of the building and into a private glidecar. Hoping Reever would magically appear to snatch me away from all this kept me quiet and alert.

But Reever didn't show. Worse, nobody seemed worried about that—not even Joe.

"Hey." I was shoved in the back of the vehicle and squashed between two guards. "Where are you taking me?"

Joe got in behind the wheel. "Home."

"That would take a few hundred light-years," I said.

I couldn't stand not knowing anymore. "Where is my husband?"

"I'm not sure at the moment, but I will find him."

So Reever had taken off. I grinned. "I doubt it."

"He is in no position to help you, Cherijo."

"Keep telling yourself that, if it makes you happy." I pretended to stare at the scenery as it whizzed by, while trying to plot my next move. Reever would come after me. I wasn't going to let the mistakes of the past let me doubt that. And when he did, I needed to be ready.

And if he doesn't?

I hated that sour little voice inside my head. *Then I get out of Joseph's cage and I go find out why he didn't.*

The massive estate I'd grown up on was located just outside New Angeles, right over one of the prime epicenters of the San Andreas fault. My creator had bought the land dirt cheap, shortly before the New Angeles Corps of Engineers had permanently stabilized the fault. Land value had skyrocketed since then, which left Joe sitting on a gold mine.

Maggie had told me I'd been born on the grounds, so it figured that Joseph had his laboratory stashed somewhere on the estate's nine hundred acres. Maybe somewhere up in the mountain range just behind the house. The only other thing up there were some Future Agers and a couple of Indians living off the land.

Joseph's mansion had undergone yet another overhaul, I saw as the glidecar pulled to a stop outside the front entrance. Another three stories had been added, making a towering total of seven. Instead of the stately marble-and-glass facade that I'd hated so much when I'd lived there, someone had completely redesigned the entire exterior in a trendy polished alloy with sculpted faux-stone accents.

The sight of it made my stomach clench.

"Let's go."

The guards forced me out of the glidecar and up the long cobblestone walk to the front entrance. We followed Joseph inside, where the icy temperature of the air conditioning made me realize how much I was sweating. An automated housekeeper greeted us in a metallic voice.

"Welcome to The Grey Veils." It turned to me. "Identify the female Terran, please."

"This is my property, Dr. Cherijo Grey Veil."

"Welcome, Dr. Cherijo. It has been over three revolutions since your last occupation. Please respond for an updated entry into the household database voice-recognition program."

"This place still resembles a mausoleum."

"Thank you, Dr. Cherijo."

Joseph instructed the drone to prepare an evening meal for two, then dismissed the guards. Once we were alone, he lifted Jenner's carrier and gestured for me to proceed him to the wing I had once occupied.

He still had my cat, so there wasn't much I could do. Yet.

"I'm not staying," I said as I trudged down the endless hall. "So don't get too comfortable with the living arrangements."

"I have no doubt you will try to escape." Joe ushered me into my old room, which, like its duplicate on the *Truman,* was exactly as I had left it. "You have one hour to cleanse and rest before dinner. Then we will discuss why escape would be unadvisable, and what the future holds for both of us."

Our future was a snap to predict. I would be leaving. He would be in traction.

As soon as the door panel closed, I tried to reopen it, but he'd locked me in. Then I started searching for anything I could use as a weapon. All my medical and sports gear had been removed. Anything made of alloy or plas had also been confiscated. I sat down on my old sleeping platform, and thought for a minute.

The treasure trove.

Joseph didn't know what a sneaky kid I'd been. There were always little things I'd picked up that he'd demanded I dispose of—pretty rocks, feathers—the usual kid junk. I'd pretended to throw them away, then had secretly squirreled away my treasures. Even Maggie hadn't known about my stashed collection.

Before I went after it, I'd have to find all the recording drones he had planted in here and disable them. That would take some time—probably more than an hour.

So I'd cleanse, dress for dinner, and wait until later.

Unlike the replicated room on the *Truman,* Joe had provided me with a brand-new selection of garments. Very attractive, feminine outfits with plenty of sparkle and matching accessories. He must have forgotten how uncomfortable I was in that kind of thing. Luckily I found one of my old physician's tunics in the back of the storage unit, and put that on, making sure the Lok-Teel was still secure in its hiding place.

The door panel opened precisely an hour after Joe locked me in, and one of the drone staff hovered outside in the hall, evidently waiting to escort me.

"Any chance I can reprogram you to get me out of here?" I asked it as I walked out.

"All input by Dr. Cherijo must have Dr. Joseph's approval before the unit may comply with any directives."

"That's a shame."

Joseph stood waiting for me in the main dining room. Dining hall, I reminded myself. My creator liked formality almost as much as he liked experimenting on helpless children.

He frowned at me as I entered the cavernous room. "Good evening."

"You're still breathing. What's good about it?" I was starving, but wary of the food the drones had laid out for us. "Where's Jenner?"

"Safe, for now. Please"—he swept a hand toward my old place at the table, just to the right of his chair—"sit down. You must be hungry."

I sat. "I'd like to have a scanner, please."

He took his place beside me. "You're not feeling well?"

"No. I want to check this food for drugs before I put it in my mouth."

Amicably he reached over, took my plate, and ate some of the fancy seafood from it. Then he handed it back to me. "You may observe me as long as you wish, but I assure you, the food has not been drugged."

Instead of eating, I handed him my crystal flute. "Try the champagne while you're at it."

He didn't take a sip of that, but called for a drone and had it removed. I sat and smirked until he gave me an irritable glance.

"You are only delaying the inevitable."

"The inevitable what? Lab rat tests?" I picked up my fork and toyed with my shrimp. It wasn't spiked, but he'd touched it. "Why the drugs?"

"You indicated you'd try to escape. A mild tranquilizer would inhibit such impulsive behavior, and make what lies ahead less stressful for you."

He really wouldn't try to sedate me without a good reason, and his idea of stress would make someone else have a nervous breakdown. "What lies ahead?"

"Revelations." He ordered a carafe of plain water from the attending drone and gestured toward my plate. "Please eat your meal now. We will discuss my plans for your future after dinner."

I accepted the water after I saw him drink some from the same container, but I didn't eat. How could I? I was sitting next to a monster, the man directly responsible for nearly every miserable moment of my life. Besides, I couldn't eat and listen to him at the same time—I'd throw up. And Joe never kept quiet when he had an audience.

He didn't disappoint me. "The reports I've received since the Hsktskt captured you at Joren have been few, and very sporadic. A number of colonial aliens have sent signals to Terra regarding your heroic actions on the slave world. I will need more details about your activities since you left me."

Left him. Like we were married or something.

"Let's see." I made a show of thinking it over. "Not much happened. I treated alien patients. I avoided the League. I got married. I was away from you. I was happy." I tapped my finger against my cheek. "I heard you started a war between the League and the Hsktskt. You get *that* bored while I was gone?"

"I did not initiate the hostilities between the Faction and the League. They have been ongoing for decades." He put down his fork and instructed the drone to clear both our places and bring dessert. "I merely offered my opinion before the Fendegal XI delegation as to a possible solution to the perpetual border disputes and colonial attacks."

"Such as wiping out the entire Hsktskt civilization. Good solution." When the attending drone would have set a plate of fruit in front of me, I pushed its arm away. "When millions die as a result of your opinion, Doctor, tell me—how are you going to feel about that?"

"The Terran involvement in the conflict will be marginal. The balance of the League's forces are not human."

"Don't feel bad. A lot of people have no hearts. Of course, everyone else besides you is a cadaver."

His brows rose. "It is obvious you wish to provoke an altercation with me."

"Gee, you're quick. Want to show me how fast you can run out in front of a glide-bus?"

"We will continue this discussion later." He folded his napkin, placed it on the table, and rose. "You will accompany me now."

I got up, too. "Where?"

"To my laboratory. Where you were born, Cherijo."

I'll confess, I wanted to see it. The facility I'd been created in wasn't located on the estate, but rather *under* it. Joseph took me to a lift I'd never seen before, hidden in the back of his study, and guided me in.

"How far down?" I asked as he closed the panel and rapidly input a code into the panel. I watched so I could memorize the numbers.

"I had the lab constructed five hundred feet below the fault line," he said. The lift began to silently descend. "Also, for your information, I change the access codes daily."

I was glad I hadn't eaten anything at dinner. My stomach was starting to roll again. "A bit paranoid, don't you think?"

"Where you are concerned, my child, I find unnecessary precautions are absolutely imperative."

"Don't call me your child. I'm not your child. If anything, I'm your sister."

He didn't comment on that as the lift continued to drop. It came to a smooth stop and the panel slid open to reveal a huge, empty white room.

White walls. I'd had nightmares about them, I remembered. So they were real. *How many times did he drug me and drag me down here?* He went to take my arm, and I jerked away.

"Don't touch me."

"I intend to do a great deal more than simply touch you. But for now, I will allow you your distance. Come. I will give you a complete tour of where you were created."

I stepped out of the lift. "Does it come with an Igor?"

"I beg your pardon?"

"The lab, Dr. Frankenstein."

He shook his head. "I never understood your fascination with those ancient fictional texts. They were poorly conceived, absolutely without the slightest scientific foundation, and luridly composed. Although they were not quite as bad as those disgusting romance novels."

Those disgusting romance novels had kept me from turning into *him*. "You never liked my taste in anything."

The interior temperature equaled the warmth of Joe's personality, a few degrees above frost formation. I shivered. Beyond the open, empty area we were standing in were five separate corridors lined with other door panels.

"Where's the dissection room? Got your lascalpel rig powered up?"

His upper lip curled. "We'll start with Central Analysis. Follow me."

Central Analysis was a research scientist's fantasyland, fully stocked with all the latest in medical examination tech. Some of the scanners were so new I didn't recognize the models. Several worktables stood ready for human subjects, but there was a sterile, unused feel to the room.

I wiped up a little dust from a console with my fingertip and examined it. "Been suffering mad scientist block lately?"

"I generally work in Development and Engineering." He pointed to another panel. "Through there."

I walked through the door and entered an equally sterile, cold environment. However, here there were signs of ongoing experiments, centrifuges spinning, culture dishes cooking, and an entire wall of containers stuffed with organs and other, less recognizable objects preserved in duralyde solution.

I nodded toward the wall. "Spare parts in case you mess up?"

"Some are continuing experiments in cloned organ scaffolding. Others are failures. As were these."

He pressed a button on a console, and an entire section of the opposite wall slid away. Behind it were endless rows of glittering plas bubbles, filled with black liquid and hooked to dozens of data cables. Each had a drone clamped to its base, and from the flickering lights many were still active.

That didn't get my attention as much as the contents of the bubbles. Inside the murky fluid were small, pale objects enmeshed in a web of monitor leads. They were human. Human fetuses in various stages of development.

Hundreds of them.

I could feel the color draining from my face. "Embryonic chambers, I presume?"

"That is correct. This one"—he went over and placed a hand on the only empty chamber—"was where I developed you."

I walked toward it, morbidly fascinated. Memories stirred with every step.

The sea of warm, black fluid . . . the intricate web held my body suspended . . . warm and safe. . . .

"How long did it take to develop me?" I asked as I got close to the technological horror that had been, in essence, my mother.

"Synthetic growth hormones cut the gestational period by a third. You were full term at twenty-seven weeks."

"Prematurely mature." I touched the outer curve of the chamber. The flexible chamber housing felt warm against my palm. Old sensations washed over me.

Unexpected light . . . ferocious pain . . . pulsating strands stabbing into my tiny body . . . tearing at my bones and flesh . . . changing me . . . a younger Joseph staring at me through the plas . . . the fluid draining away . . . clawing at myself . . . unable to breathe . . . cold . . . empty . . . blind . . .

"You probably have some residual recollections of the chamber. Tests indicated you were fully cognizant and aware of your environment by your third month of development."

"Second," I told him, not caring if he believed me. "Yes, I was. I remember when you took me out of here."

A note of eagerness entered his voice. "Tell me what you recall."

"Fear. Disgust. Horror. Outrage." I slowly took my hand away and faced him. "I won't let you do this again. It's wrong. You can't create human beings like this."

"I was telling the truth, Cherijo, when I said I would not repeat my past mistakes. Even if I wanted to, I now know the success I achieved with you is singular. There will be no more clones raised in embryonic chambers in this facility."

I let out a breath I hadn't known I was holding. "Good." Then I got skeptical. "What *are* you planning to do to produce the next perfect human?"

He sat down and regarded me steadily. "I'm going to impregnate you with my own DNA."

"Oh, please." I couldn't help it. I started laughing. "You can't be serious."

"I am."

"You're a geneticist, Joe. You know the damage that can be created by analogous gene pools mixing."

"That can be prevented."

"By two nearly identical twins producing an offspring? Get a grip. Artificially inseminating me with your own sperm will only produce babies who have the I.Q.s of broccoli." I wiped my eyes with one hand. "God, I haven't laughed that hard in ages."

"In-utero adjustments will have to be made, of course."

He was absolutely serious. He had the talent and knowledge to repair whatever damage came of blending our mirrored DNA. He could get me pregnant, but could he control my immune system response?

Of course he could. He was an expert at organ transplant techniques. If anyone knew how to keep a body from rejecting foreign tissue, it was Joseph Grey Veil.

He could have prevented my miscarriage. And there was the ultimate irony—Joseph Grey Veil likely represented my only hope of ever having another child.

For a moment, I entertained a revolting idea. Just for a moment. Then it hit me: He had engineered my body to reject my unborn children. He was directly responsible for my miscarriage.

"If you will look over the project specs with me, I can show where I—"

He never completed that sentence. I lunged at him, and knocked him flat on his back. My first punch broke his nose. My second drove the air from his lungs.

"You are *never* going to use me again!"

Just as I was preparing to follow through with a knee to his groin, something grabbed me and pulled me off him. It was one of the maintenance drones. I struggled wildly, but couldn't free myself of the unyielding mechanical grip units.

"I'm going to kill you!" I shrieked at my creator. "Your days are numbered, I swear to God!"

"There is no God," Joseph said in a distinctly raw, nasal tone. He grabbed a cloth and held it tightly against his nose as he turned away from me and addressed another waiting drone. "Bring in the prisoner now."

The drone went to the lift panel, and opened it. Two more drones wheeled out, dragging a semiconscious man clamped between them. He was battered and bleeding from several small wounds.

I took a step forward, but Joseph grabbed me by the hair and spoke softly against my ear.

"You can save him, you know. Cooperate, and I will let him live."

I made a low, helpless sound, then called to him. "Duncan."

My husband slowly lifted his head. The pain in his eyes tore an invisible hole in my chest.

"Continue to resist," my creator said, "and you can watch him bleed to death right here."

I didn't bother to look at Joseph when I said, "Fine. You win."

CHAPTER FIVE

Dancing with Christopher

Joseph wouldn't let me touch Reever. He treated my husband's injuries, while I got to cool my heels in one of the clear-walled treatment rooms in his Research and Development lab. Trying to see what he did as he sterilized and sutured Reever's wounds made me clench my fists. By the time he was done, blood stained the edges of my fingernails.

Joseph had one of the drones wheel Reever's gurney into the adjoining treatment room, and lock him in. Then he came over to look in on me.

"You made the correct choice. We will begin the new trials tomorrow. Good night, Cherijo."

"Is he all right? Was anything fractured? Let me take a look at him."

"I will return in six hours. Sleep well."

"Why don't you answer me? What did you do to him?" I called after him as he left the lab. "Oh, you're dead the minute you let me out of here."

One of the drones trundled over to the clear wall. "No talking. Take your sleep interval now or you will be sedated."

I had no doubt the drone would drug me if I kept shouting, so I stalked over to the medical berth that served as my bed, and flung myself on it. The interior lights dimmed as the drone made another pass in front of my cage. I wondered if it was going to sing me a lullaby.

Cherijo?

My mental walls snapped up as I saw Duncan lying on the other side of the plas wall, watching me. I pushed my berth over until it lay against the wall, like his.

"Are you okay?"

He shook his head and tapped his ear. The treatment rooms were soundproof—he couldn't hear me.

I eased myself into the link, trying to clamp down on my hostility. *Hey. How are you feeling?*

I have had better days.

He was blocking most of his thoughts from me, too. From the sweat on his brow and the way he was breathing, I could tell he was in pain. Then I dug my hands into the berth mattress until linen tore. *He didn't give you any analgesics.*

It doesn't matter. I prefer to be clearheaded. He pressed his hand against the wall. *Has he harmed you?*

No. I'm okay. I matched the outline of his fingers with mine. *We've got some problems. The committee turned me over to him. Unconditionally. You should have stuck around. The only good part about it was seeing the look on Shropana's face when they announced it.*

I would have liked that.

Where did you go when you snuck out of there? How did Joe catch you?

Reever shook his head. *I didn't escape. One of the guards infused me with a narcotic and removed me from the hearing. I woke up here.*

You mean he had you kidnapped?

Did you think I would leave without you?

No, I thought— He knew exactly what I thought. *Yeah, I did.*

You have a very poor opinion of me.

I'm working on it. Duncan, he's really crazy. Seriously deranged. He told me tonight that he wants to impregnate me with his own DNA.

My husband's mental blocks fell away as his thoughts became elemental. Images of Joseph dying in various gruesome ways filled his mind.

Honey, have I ever told you I like the way you think?

He curled his hand against the plas, until his knuckles turned white. *We have to get you out of here.*

Us. Us out of here. Tomorrow he'll start testing me again. It'll give me a chance to get the layout of this place, maybe find a weapon or a way out. You'd better rest now. Those drones really did a number on you.

The drones did not inflict my injuries.

No, I could see that now, from the images of the beating he was remembering. The man who'd done it had taken prolonged, vicious pleasure in doing so.

Joseph did this to you? It must have happened while I was dressing for dinner.

Yes.

One more reason for me to dismember him in his sleep. God, I'm sorry, Duncan. I got up and started pacing.

You should sleep while you can.

I can't. Not here.

He intensified the link, until he gained control of my body, and brought me back to the berth. He hadn't taken me over like this since we'd left Catopsa, but I let it happen, and everything but the two of us dissolved away. Then we were transported to a very familiar place.

Now you can.

Show-off. He'd created an illusion around us, to fool my mind into believing we were back on the *Perpetua*, in our bed. I couldn't feel homicidal here. *You sure like watching me sleep.*

His mouth touched mine. *Just for tonight, beloved.*

*   *   *

Exactly six hours after Joseph left (five hours after I fell asleep with a luxurious sigh), a lab drone woke me up. Not the way Joe had sent Maggie in to shake me awake, when I was a kid. Instead the drone hit me with a shot of static discharge. Right in the upper arm.

"Ah!"

I jumped off the berth and collided with a wall, then saw the little hunk of junk at the panel.

"What the *hell* did you do that for?"

"It is 0500 hours, Dr. Cherijo, the scheduled time for your initial examination. You will remove your garments."

"Go fuse yourself." I turned and headed back to bed.

The lab drone trundled over to Reever's treatment room. My husband was still asleep. "You will remove your garments or this specimen will be disciplined."

Specimen. Disciplined. Two of my creator's favorite words.

"I'll do it. Get away from him." I forgot about going back to sleep and slipped the Lok-Teel out from under my tunic. I formed an image of it hiding under my pillow, and it obediently oozed out of sight. Then I went through the motions of stripping off my clothes as I edged toward the door.

The drone opened the panel. I kicked it over and bolted.

A second, more vicious discharge knocked me off my feet. I hit the floor, then lay there for a moment, gasping. The drone rolled over to stop beside me.

"Advisory: applied static discharges will increase in severity and duration with each unauthorized action."

My hair was practically standing on end. "Now you tell me."

"Stand and follow me, Doctor."

The drone led me out to Central Analysis, and indicated a recently sterilized table. "Recline here, Doctor."

"I'd prefer to stand."

"Recline or receive further discipline."

I wouldn't be much good to Reever unconscious, so I reclined. As soon as my back hit the table, automatic restraints shot out of slots in the table and snapped around my wrists and ankles.

"Hey!" I jerked at the alloy cuffs. "I'll cooperate, take these things off!"

"All input by Dr. Cherijo must have Dr. Joseph's approval before the unit may comply with any directives." The drone went to one of the consoles and activated something. "Please remain still as the scanner passes over you."

I stopped fighting the restraints as a hot, white beam charted its way down the length of my body. Someone had been experimenting with thermal residual imaging—this felt much more intense than any scanner I'd ever used.

"No parasites or other corporeal infestations located."

"Record and file," Joseph said as he walked into the room.

I lifted my head. "You think I'm carrying around body lice?"

"How many times were you required to administer discipline to Dr. Cherijo?" he asked the drone.

"Twice, Dr. Joseph."

He kept ignoring me as he went to the console. "Initiate fluids sampling sequence."

Thin, hollow probes emerged from the table, and attacked me. One stabbed into my neck. Another in my arm. A third in between my legs.

I felt like shrieking, but clenched my teeth. "I would have been happy to voluntarily donate some blood and urine to the cause. All you had to do was give me a syrinpress and a cup."

"You have clearly demonstrated your unwillingness to cooperate with me." Joseph turned around. "My tests require sterile samples. The probes will not harm you."

There were all kinds of harm. "If this is how you're going to run things, I'll fight you every step of the way." That would almost certainly mess up his tests.

"What will happen if I agree to remove your restraints, and invite your cooperation?"

I felt like snarling. "I'll be a good girl, *Daddy*."

He pressed the keypad on the console, and the restraints slid away. I was tempted to run—who wouldn't be?—but I had to do what Reever said. *The opportunity will come and we will escape.*

I just wished the opportunity would hurry up.

Joseph spent the next several hours performing various tests on me. Scans of every intensity and variety. More fluid samples, scrapings from my gums, snips of my hair. Two more probes tapped my bone marrow and spinal fluid.

I didn't cooperate with him as much as I endured his proximity, and bit my tongue. By the time he handed me a plain patient gown to put on, I felt like I'd chewed off half of it.

"Is that it? Or do I have to run through a maze and find some cheese now?"

"Follow me." He led me out of the Central Analysis and down a corridor to a small room containing a large console and one chair. "Sit down."

When I did, the console screen blinked on. A series of questions appeared.

"Answer each of the queries."

I read the first couple. "I did this before. For three days on K-2, for your League buddies."

"These queries cover events which occurred *after* you left the colony on Kevarzangia Two."

"What, didn't Dhreen fill you in on all the details?" Dhreen, the Oenrallian who'd helped me leave Terra and escape Joseph, had been my friend—or so I'd thought. I'd depended on him, confided in him, even gone crazy and pulled him out of the wreckage of his crashed star vessel. All that time, he'd been reporting back to Joseph with details of everything I'd done.

Finding out Dhreen was my creator's spy had broken my heart. If I ever saw him again, I planned to do the same to his face.

My creator ignored the question and walked to the door panel. "I will return for you in one hour."

I turned back to the console. "Good thing I can type fast."

The questions covered a hundred different topics; everything from what I preferred to program for my meals and how often I ate to how many times I'd had intercourse and with what type of life-form. There was no particular order to them, either. I amused myself by providing some creative answers.

Query: What three evening meal interval programs did you select most frequently while serving in space? My answer— 1. Vegetarian lasagna. 2. Coq au vin. 3. Serada baked with shredded nyilophstian root.

Query: What form of contraceptive did you employ while entertaining a nonhuman partner? My answer— I never entertained a nonhuman partner. I'd been too busy having orgies with dozens of them.

I chuckled and worked my way down the list, until I got toward the end. Then I stopped, and sat back.

Query: Have you become pregnant in the last two revolutions? If the response is affirmative, please list the date of delivery, gender of progeny, and inseminator's name, age, and species of origin.

It stopped being funny. I tried to skip the query, but the screen wouldn't let me bypass it.

Query: Have you become pregnant in the last two revolutions? If the response is affirmative . . .

I didn't answer any more of the questions. The console beeped at me. I stared at it.

Query: Have you become pregnant . . .

My fist smashed into the screen, shattering it. Sparks

flew. The console erupted into frantic beeping and flashing. The door panel behind me slid open.

"Why did you do that?" Joseph asked me.

"I got tired of typing."

"You will repeat the exercise later." He looked at my bleeding hand. "Come back to the lab with me so I can treat your wound."

I cradled my throbbing knuckles as I got to my feet. "The day I need your help, the brain damage will be too extensive to merit saving me. I'll do it myself."

Reever watched me walk in, his eyes moving from my face to my hand, then to Joseph. If looks could kill, Joe would have been in a lot of itty-bitty pieces sprayed against one of the interior wall panels.

Expecting a fight over the hand, I was pleasantly surprised when Joseph backed off and let me fix it myself. Surprised until I noticed him making clinical observations of my one-handed dexterity with the scanner.

"Want to see me jump through hoops after this?"

Joseph had no sense of humor. "Your ability to leap is insignificant. I am conducting a scientific analysis of a transcendent achievement in genetics."

"What did Thomas Love Peacock say? 'I almost think it is the ultimate destiny of science to exterminate the human race.'" I used a dermal probe to extract a couple of tiny plas shards from my knuckles.

"Peacock was a foolish man."

"Oh, I don't know about that." I dropped the shards into a specimen container, so he could analyze them. He analyzed everything. "By the way, when did he meet you?"

My creator put down his datapad. "What is your prognosis?"

"I'll never be able to play the violin again." I flushed the lacerations, then activated the suture laser. As I sealed the deepest gash, Joseph placed a folded stack of garments on the table beside me.

"Change into these."

I didn't see Joseph standing there waiting until I finished dressing my hand. He had that weird look in his eyes again. Reever was pacing back and forth, the way he did only when he was extremely upset.

What was going on now?

"You want me to change." I didn't touch the clothes. "Leave and I will."

"Your modesty is superfluous."

"So is your face."

He handed me a bunch of monitor leads. "Attach these as is appropriate for cardiovascular monitoring."

"So now I run the maze and find the cheese." I put them down beside the clothes. "I'll put them on. As soon as you go."

Joseph's eyebrows rose. "Will sedation be required?"

"To put up with you? Plenty. Make it continuous."

He went over to Reever's treatment room, and addressed him for the first time. "How do you tolerate her flippancy?"

Reever said something in Hsktskt that I was fairly sure didn't mean "let's talk about it sometime," then he hit the plas wall. Blood splattered in a wide arc as his knuckles split, and the panel cracked. My creator swiftly backed away.

Oh, Duncan. My heart ached for him.

"Joe, you'd better leave and let me calm him down. I don't think your drones could hold him right now, not even with all the static in their discharge units."

"You have ten minutes." Joseph gave my husband a filthy look, then retreated. I heard the sound of the access panel being secured as I went over to let Reever out. The minute I did, he was all over me.

"Did he hurt you?" He touched my face, my hair, then ran his hands over me. "What did he do to your hand?" He clasped it between his, getting his blood on my nice clean bandage. "I am going to take him apart one limb at a time."

I stood on tiptoe to press my cheek against his. "He didn't, I hit a console, and you'll have to wait your turn." His arms came around me, and we stood like that for a minute.

The drones refuse to give me any information. I can't tolerate not knowing what is happening to you. Have you found a way out?

I shook my head. *The whole place is crawling with drone security. He never leaves us alone, did you notice?* I looked over at the maintenance unit sitting a few feet away. Its sensors were active. "Let me take a look at that hand now." *You shouldn't pick fights with plas walls, you know.*

He fingered the bandage wrapped around my knuckles. *Physician, heal thyself.*

Very funny.

After I took care of his hand, which was in worse shape than mine and required bonesetters, the maintenance unit made Reever stay in my cell. Three other units repaired the damage he'd done to his. I hooked up the monitor leads and changed my tunic for the lightweight shirt and trousers Joseph had given me.

As soon as I was finished dressing, my creator came back in, followed by four drones toting a funny-looking treadmill. It reminded me of the kind of equipment SrrokVar had used on me on Catopsa.

"What's that for?"

"Test trials." Joseph had the drones set it up and indicated I should climb on.

"What sort of test trials?"

"Cardiovascular status."

I checked it over and noticed the vid screen positioned at the front, and two-way feeds. "What are you going to do? Make me watch vids of your lectures to see if I can run and nap at the same time?"

"It is time to begin now. Assume your position on the treadmill."

I climbed on, and hooked myself up to the monitors. The lead cables were long enough that I wouldn't get brought up short unless I fell off.

Joseph started the treadmill's track at a slow pace. I walked. Nothing happened for a few minutes as he made some adjustments on his consoles. Then the track started to pick up speed, which forced me to trot.

The screen at the front of the unit flickered on, and I saw a vid of myself, stepping out of a junky-looking star vessel. It was the *Bestshot*, Dhreen's old ship, which had been destroyed when he crashed on K-2. I smiled, remembering how shocked I'd been by the first alien world I'd ever seen. My smile faded as Dhreen joined me on the Transport platform.

"Wow, look, home movies. Did you pay that two-faced, orange-haired liar to make recordings of everything I did on his ship, too? Watching me cook must be enthralling."

Joseph didn't say anything. He was already engrossed in the readings from his console.

The track speed increased by increments, until I was running. The screen began showing a series of vids of my life on K-2.

There were the sparse, utilitarian rooms I had occupied in Colonial Housing. Scenes from that first night, when I'd come home to find Jenner gone, later returned by a giant, alien kitty cat who not only walked upright, but talked—my pal Alunthri.

My first couple of weeks had been rough, until I'd made some friends and had some good times. That was before the Core infiltrated the bodies of the colonists.

I ran in place, mesmerized by the recordings of patients I'd treated, meals I'd eaten, friends I'd made. Ana. Dr. mu Cheft. Lisette. Ecla, my flowery charge nurse. It made my heart twist. I hadn't seen them in two years now.

But Joe had. He'd made sure I'd go to K-2—all part of his experiment on me—while I'd thought I'd made a clean getaway. I'd never noticed the tiny recording drones he'd sent to monitor me and document my activities.

"How did you camouflage the drones, Joe? Make them look like insects? Weave them in my clothes? What?"

"They were attached to some of your personal belongings. Whenever you moved, motion and heat detectors activated the track/record function."

On the vid, a handsome, alien pilot appeared beside me outside the Trading Center, and I tripped and nearly fell.

It was *Kao*.

How dare he do this to me? It wasn't an experiment anymore, it was some kind of sick, twisted game he wanted to play with my head. I looked away from the smiling image of my dead lover.

"Shut it down."

He touched his console, and a mild discharge pulse hit me, making me stumble again. "Watch the screen and continue running."

I jumped off the treadmill, and got a second, far nastier zap that made me drop to my knees. When I could unclench my jaw, I yelled, *"Shut it down!"*

Joe came to stand over me. "Get up and continue the test, or I will have the drones fracture the linguist's other hand."

I glanced over at the treatment room. Reever looked ready to do it himself on another wall. I couldn't let this get to me. I was a big girl. I could handle it.

"Enjoy yourself, Doctor, because the payback for this is going to be colossal."

I dragged myself up, waved and smiled at my husband, then climbed back on the treadmill. The track and the screen started up again, and I got to watch Kao and me eating at the Trade Center as I went from a walk to a steady run.

Thank you for saving me from hearing all of Paul's EngTech tales for the fifteenth time. I would like to see you again, Healer Grey Veil. Perhaps we might share another meal—alone?

I remembered how stunned I'd been, to be asked out on a date by an alien. Especially one as good-looking as the Jorenian pilot. What had I said? *If you can find me off duty. Until then, Kao Torin.*

Now the screen showed us saying good-bye to each other. His white eyes crinkled as he smiled down at me. *Walk within beauty.*

He'd given me that—a walk within beauty—and much more. As the scenes of our rather unorthodox courtship flashed on the screen, I ran faster, harder, as if doing that would help me escape the overwhelming regret and heart-shattering sense of failure.

I'd killed Kao, trying to save his life. He'd contracted the Core pathogen early on during the epidemic on K-2, and when he'd stopped breathing, I'd desperately infused him with my own blood. Without testing what would happen. My immunities had brought him back, but only for a little while. After wiping out the Core, my blood had poisoned Kao.

Which, combined with what I'd done on the *Sunlace* before we were captured, made me just as much of a monster as Joe.

Cherijo.

I slammed up every wall I had. *I'm okay, Reever.* No I wasn't. I was running and weeping silently and almost hyperventilating. *He's throwing more ammunition at me.*

Reever projected something into the link that made the pain go dim and quieted my thoughts. *Do you remember the Marine Province simulation you programmed in the environome on the* Sunlace?

The beach?

Yes. He entered my mind, and for once didn't complain about the walls. *Close your mind to what is happening. Summon the image of that shoreline.*

I did, and suddenly I was running down a long stretch of amber sand, right beside Reever. Bunches of scarlet flowers rustled with a melodic hum in the soft, salty breeze. I looked over at him. *How do you do this?*

Does it matter?

No, I guess not. Anything was better than being on that treadmill. *How long can you sustain this . . . whatever it is?*

I don't know. He reached out, and took my hand. *I've never tried it for longer than an hour with you before.*

Can you do it again when he— I cut that thought short. *Do we have to run?*

No. He stopped, and so did I. On another level I was aware I was still running, back in the lab, but it didn't seem to have any effect on me.

Good. I pivoted toward the dark purple ocean, hopping over a cluster of feather-leafed grasses as I whooped and tore off my shirt and trousers. *Come on, Duncan! Last one in is a rotten egg!*

Reever was able to maintain the link between us for an undetermined amount of time, until something malfunctioned in the treadmill unit, and I was pulled off. I left my husband in the Marine Province illusion and returned to reality.

A reality filled with aching leg muscles, burning lungs, and a lab filled with smoke.

"Hey!" I coughed, stepped away from the motionless track, and waved my hands in front of my face. "What happened?"

Joseph was at the console, hammering on the envirocontrols. The air replacement units kicked on, and a few seconds later, the air cleared. He straightened and turned to me. "You burned out the motor on the treadmill."

"Really?" I walked in a circle, trying to stretch out my cramped muscles. "Guess instruments of torture don't hold up like they used to. Maybe if you return it, they'll give you your credits back."

He came over and ran a scanner over me. "Remarkable." He paused to note the results on a chart, then repeated the scan. "Did you take up long-distance running after leaving Terra?"

"No. Why?"

"Because you just beat the world's record for the forty kilometer by ten minutes." He shut off the scanner and stared at me. "There is minimal muscle strain and elevated respiratory activity, but no significant increase in your blood pressure or heart rate."

I shook some sweaty hair out of my eyes. "Your equipment must be malfunctioning. Look what happened to the treadmill."

He came closer. "Apparently it is. We will repeat this test tomorrow."

Reever was standing at the wall again, fists clenched. Joe was close enough for me to smell him. He still wore the same cologne, and too much of it, as always.

"I'd like to take a break and have a meal with my husband."

"You will not be given the opportunity to have intercourse with him."

As if I'd do that, where he could monitor everything. "I'll try to restrain myself."

I walked over to the only prep unit in sight, hoping Joe would take the hint and leave. He did. The maintenance unit trundled over to Reever's treatment room and opened the door panel. When Reever would have walked out, it blocked his path.

"Wait here. Dr. Cherijo will bring your food to you."

No utensils, which meant no chance of getting my hands on a knife to pass to Reever. There were only three things listed on the main menu: vegetarian lasagna, coq au vin, and serada baked with shredded nyilophstian root.

That'll teach me to be a smart ass. I prepared two trays, and carried them over to the room before I addressed the drone. "Get lost."

"All input by Dr. Cherijo must have Dr. Joseph's approval before the unit may comply with any directives."

"At least get out of my way."

I went in, and placed the trays on the table before turning to Reever. He was watching me closely, so I blocked most of my thoughts off behind a smooth, impenetrable mental barrier.

"I regret your creator reminded you of times best forgotten."

I smiled sadly. "He's just yanking my chain. Besides, I don't want to forget Kao. He was very important to me." Before he could react, I reached over and kissed him. "Don't. You're not competing with his memory. I loved him, and I love you."

He nodded, and sat down with me. His expression changed slightly when he saw what I'd programmed for him. "Serada? But how—"

I gave him a steely-eyed look. "Don't ask. Just eat."

We ate together companionably, and eventually the drone seemed to lose interest, because it went to perform maintenance on the ruined treadmill. Reever lingered over his herbal tea as I cleaned up our servers.

Why are you blocking your thoughts from me?

I nearly dropped the dirty plates. *Because I don't want you to know the kind of homicidal fantasies I have.*

My own are probably worse.

They were—he'd seen more horrible things than I had—but I wasn't abandoning my only good excuse.

Reever, I've never been completely comfortable with the way you can access my thoughts. Right now they're kind of ugly. That was the truth. *Do you mind so much if I keep that away from you?*

Reever looked at the drone. *He intends to kill me, you know.*

I knew. How, I couldn't say, but Joe would kill him, and soon. If only I could somehow fake his death, the way I had with the Aksellans on Catopsa. . . .

I looked at a drone passing by the panel. It was the same model used in hospitals, and that gave me an idea.

Reever, if I get one of the lab drones in here tonight, and disable it, can you reprogram it to help us escape?

Your creator monitors us through them.

No, actually, I don't think he does. He downloaded their data banks this morning; if they were on output monitor, he wouldn't have bothered.

What about the recording drones inside the lab?

I'm going to have a sudden attack of modesty and get Joe to agree to put up privacy screens in our rooms. The dark will do the rest. Well?

If you can disable it without damaging the power supply system, I can reprogram it.

I grinned, leaned over, and kissed him. *Then we're in business.*

An hour later I wasn't thinking about escaping or disabling drones or even Reever. Joe had me hooked up to a nervous-system analysis unit, usually reserved for diagnosing and treating paralysis victims. I was being bombarded with stimulation pulses sent through a tight alloy webbing he'd wrapped me in.

The effect was like getting stabbed by thick needles—thousands of them—over and over.

I hadn't resisted until after the first preliminary test was done, and I thought I was getting off the table.

Joe had used restraints when I tried to roll off the table, and told me to get comfortable.

That had been about thirty minutes ago.

Oh, God. I twisted in vain, trying to avoid the continuous, red-hot pinpoints of pain. *How much longer do I have to take this?*

"Probably an hour or two," a familiar voice said. "Considering what he did to you when you were a toddler, this is a walk in the park."

Maggie.

Unlike the other times I'd gotten a cerebral visit from my maternal influencer, I wasn't overjoyed to hear her inside my head. She'd been a part of this, and had some other bizarre plans for me. I'd discovered during our last little reunion that she hadn't even been Terran, but an alien.

I didn't feel like talking to a dead alien's ghost, especially one who had subliminally programmed herself to pop into my synaptic recesses whenever I was under tremendous stress.

Get lost, Maggie.

"Is that any way to talk to your mother?" She didn't sound upset, just amused.

I gritted my teeth as the stimulation pulses increased in strength and duration. *You're not my mother.*

"I'm the only one you ever knew."

You're an alien who helped him, lied to me, got paid for it, and died before I could find out what you'd done. As a mother, Maggie, you stink.

The dark well that would lead me to Maggie opened up behind my eyes. "Come on, kiddo. Do you really want to throw a tantrum when you could be finding out more answers?"

Answers? All you do is drop lousy hints and make worse jokes.

"This time I have the real deal for you, baby."

One last time. I'd let her draw me in, one last time,

and if she didn't deliver, I'd find a way to purge her damn subliminals out of my head.

All right.

I dropped into the warm, safe darkness that smelled faintly of Maggie's illegal tobacco and the distinctly bawdy perfume she'd worn for special occasions.

I landed right in the middle of my sixteenth birthday party.

"Cherijo, I'm so happy for you!" Muriel Foster, the wife of one of my father's Medtech instructors, was holding my cheeks between her frail, arthritic hands. She smelled of talcum and Earl Grey tea. "You're going to be the youngest graduate we've ever had—and off to your internship tomorrow, too!" She let go and turned to her silver-haired husband. "James, aren't you proud of our little doctor?"

James Foster beamed at me, too. "I certainly am; she shows great promise. Now all you have to do, young woman, is follow in your father's footsteps. You won't have trouble finding them, big as they are."

Before I could tell the Fosters what I thought of my "father," Maggie came up alongside me. The sight of her low-cut, too-tight burgundy party dress made Muriel gasp, and James's grin widen. "Mind if I steal the birthday girl away from you two for a minute?"

My paid companion hustled me away to the banquet area, and thrust a plate in my hands. "Here. You need to eat something."

"Let's skip the usual song and dance, shall we?" I threw the plate to the floor, and suddenly the partygoers vanished, leaving me alone with Maggie. "Get on with it."

"Hanging around those big blueberry guys has made you real feisty, Joey girl." She picked up an open bottle of my father's most expensive spicewine, and took a swig. "Daddy's princess mad at me because she was stupid enough to get caught and have her butt hauled back to Frankenstein's lab?"

"I don't need this." I knocked the bottle from her hands and pushed her back. "You can go back to whatever hellhole you crawled out of."

"Well, well." Something like admiration gleamed in her eyes. "Feisty and then some. My little girl, all grown up and ready to kick ass. About time, I say. As for hell, sweetie, I've been there, and to tell you the truth, it doesn't suck as much as you'd think."

She thought everything was funny. That only made me angrier. "*What* do you *want*?"

"I want you to serve your purpose." She used a reasonable tone. The same one she'd used to get me to go along with whatever my father had wanted me to do. "The purpose you were created specifically to undertake and fulfill."

Whenever her vocabulary improved, it made me nervous. "And that would be . . . ?"

"Soooorrrry." She patted her mouth, faking a yawn. "Couldn't risk corrupting the data with the subliminals I downloaded into your head. They're a bit too unstable to trust. You'll find everything you need in Joe's house."

"What is it? *Where* is it?"

"Discs. I put them in your little treasure box."

"How did you know about that?"

"Oh, honey, you thought you were being so clever." She grabbed a chilled shrimp from the banquet table and popped it in her mouth. "I had to edit the room vids every time you pulled that little box out so Joe wouldn't confiscate it."

"When did you put them in there?"

"The day before I was hospitalized for the last time."

Then she'd gone and died on me a week later. It had broken my heart—but I was getting over it. Fast. "All right. I'll get them, if I can." I tapped my foot on the polished oak floor. "Are we done?"

"No. We need to talk about a few more things.

Like, why you lied to Reever, and why you ever thought, even for a moment, of letting Joseph fix your baby problem."

"Let's see: Reever is none of your business. My fertility is none of your business. End of talk. Can I go?"

She got a wistful expression. "You really thought it's the only way you'd have a child? Or is it that you love him that much?"

"Your species must be incredibly stupid. Yes to both. I want a child, and I really love Reever. Can I go *now*?"

"What's your hurry? The party's just started." She waved a hand, and music started playing in the background. "Do you remember Christopher Hamilton? The son of that podiatrist who worked in the office next to Joe's old downtown practice? You had a crush on him when you were . . . eleven, right?"

"Twelve. So what?"

"Poor boy came here one afternoon asking to see you. Apparently it was a two-way crush. Joe took him into his study, and told him you not only didn't like him, but you thought his overbite was repulsive."

"What? How come no one ever told me Chris was here?" I was stunned. "And I *loved* his overbite. That was what made him so cute."

"Exactly." Maggie trailed her finger down my nose and tapped the end once. "The kid went home, totally crushed, so I gave Joe a piece of my mind. That's when your dad told me what he had planned for you. I talked him into waiting until you'd had a chance to mature and experience life."

She'd known he wanted to use me as some kind of incubator. "Thanks. Thanks for nothing." Nauseated, I looked around. "How the hell do I get out of here?"

"Joe had planned to breed you for the first time when you turned sixteen." Maggie patted my cheek as I gaped. "That night, I stepped up my plan to get you off Terra. I'm sorry that I died before I could finish making all the arrangements. But you got away, that was the important thing."

More cryptic hints. "Why are you telling me this? So I'll be grateful to you, and do whatever it is that's involved in this 'purpose' you keep babbling about?"

"Didn't you wonder why he didn't try this before? I kept him distracted, away from you. Believe me, baby girl, it was *not* the happiest ten years of my life."

Maybe I didn't want to think of her as my mother, but it was obvious she did. She'd somehow gotten the maternal instinct to protect, anyway.

That didn't make up for the rest of what she'd done. "Okay. So I owe you one. I'll find your discs and I'll listen to them and I'll try to do whatever it is you want. Satisfied?"

"I'll have to be, won't I?" She snapped her fingers, and a tall, black-haired boy appeared next to her. He had dark, intense eyes, a great smile, and a very slight overbite. A throbbing, sensual tango began to play.

"Why is he here?"

"So you can have a dance before you go. For old times' sake."

"To a *tango*?"

"Oh, pardon me, Dr. Uptight." The music changed to a slow, elegant waltz.

"Better."

Maggie grinned, blew me a kiss, and sauntered away.

I turned to Christopher, who was staring all around him with complete fascination. I refrained from sighing and held out my hands. "Hi, Chris. Want to dance?"

"Yeah, sure." He gingerly took me into his arms. "This is some dream." He rubbed the top of his head and chuckled. "Haven't had hair up there since I graduated medtech. Wow, I'm a kid again."

"It's just a dream," I told him. Not that I was entirely sure it was. "So what have you been up to for the last, what, fifteen years, Chris?"

He slowly moved me around the floor. "I took over my dad's practice. Married my high school sweetheart, Jenny. We've got two girls, and one on the way."

More babies that might have been mine. "Congratulations. You're happy, aren't you?"

"Sure. I'm really lucky to have Jenny and the girls." He hugged me closer. "I never forgot you, though."

"Oh?" At twelve I thought I had been pretty forgettable.

"You broke my heart. At least, I thought you had. I didn't figure out what your dad had done until my oldest girl got her first crush. The boy came to ask me if he could take her on a date."

"Uh-oh. I bet that brought out your paternal side."

"And then some. Surprised me when I thought about doing the same thing to him, just to keep her safe." He twirled me around, and grinned. "That was when all the pieces fell together."

"Did you? Chase off your daughter's boyfriend, I mean?"

"No. I remembered how awful I felt, gritted my teeth, and let them go to a movie."

I laughed and kissed his cheek. "You really are a great guy, Chris."

"Thanks, and just for the record, Cherijo—your father was a genuine asshole."

"News flash: He still is."

"Are you okay now?" At my blank look, he added, "I saw the report on the vid, when they brought you and that linguist guy back to Terra. All I could think was, that's the girl I could have married instead of Jenny."

"Lucky escape, huh?"

"No. I love my wife and my kids, but I'll wonder what it would have been like for you and me. We could have had something terrific together."

Just before he faded away, he bent down, and kissed me on the cheek. Suddenly I understood why the people we love but can't have are almost as wonderful as the ones we get.

"Yeah, I think you were right."

The darkness came up so suddenly that one moment I was doing a graceful pivot, and the next I was standing alone, completely blind.

"What the— Maggie?" I tried to turn around, but I was paralyzed. "Maggie, stop it!"

"One more thing, Cherijo. You must never let him know what you did on the *Sunlace*."

She knew. "I'm not going to tell Duncan anything."

"You should tell Duncan *everything*. He loves you." She appeared in front of me, in her elegant, alien body. "But if Joseph finds out, Duncan will die, and you will never leave Terra again."

PART TWO

Paternity

CHAPTER SIX

Leyaneyaniteh

Joseph had to inject me with stimulants to rouse me from my semi-comatose state, or so he informed me as the lab drone peeled the stimulation webbing off me. There were no wounds from the prolonged session, but the memory of pain made my muscles slow to respond. That, combined with the abuse from the forty-kilometer run from the day before, made me promptly keel over.

He helped me up. "You withstood the trial well, Cherijo. I was correct in my predictions of your nerve tolerances. I think it is safe to assume my other estimations will be as accurate."

"Don't be so humble. You're not that great." I swayed on my feet. "Could I get some sleep now? I'm really tired. And a privacy screen would be nice, too. I'm sick of all the drones watching me undress."

The whine in my voice was artificial, but very convincing. Joseph instructed the lab drone to give me what I needed, and said his usual good night to me. He felt brave enough to touch me, and caressed my cheek with his cold hand.

"Sleep well, daughter."

The man still thought of me as his child. He really was pond scum, minus the pond.

The drone obligingly draped the walls of my treatment room with privacy screens, then turned out the lights. Reever had been moved back to his own room, now that the plas wall had been replaced, and lay apparently asleep. A few moments after the lights went out, he groaned softly.

"Reever?" I sat up and looked through the dividing panel. "Are you okay?" All I got was another groan. "Maintenance unit?"

"No talking. Take your sleep interval now or you will be sedated."

"Linguist Reever is ill. Service emergency medical override protocol, priority one, directive file S.O.P. four-two-seven." I crossed my fingers, hoping Joseph hadn't removed that directive from the unit's database. It was part of the original factory programming package, and consequently no one ever thought about erasing it when creating new command sub-menus.

It clicked and hummed for a moment, then said, "Service emergency medical override protocol initiated. What are your instructions, Doctor?"

I went right to the door panel. "Provide me access to the patient, and assistance." The drone let me out, then escorted me into Reever's room. My husband had curled over in a fetal position, and was shaking violently. "Reever, what is it? What's wrong?"

All he did was groan again.

The lab drone went to the edge of the berth. "Inquiry: Should Dr. Joseph be signaled to attend to this patient?"

"No, that's not necessary," I said, and pulled the power supply board out of the back of the unit. It went completely dead. "Please help me get him on his back," I continued, for the benefit of the recording drones.

Reever allowed me to roll him over, and while I

blocked the view of the maintenance drone, pulled the unit's panel and began reprogramming it.

Everything was looking great, until all the lights went out.

"Is it the power grid?"

"We're not going to wait to find out." Reever grabbed my hand, pushed the unit out of the way, and hauled me to the door.

Someone bumped into us. Someone short and wearing strange garments. Too short to be Joseph. Another drone?

"You the patcher and the code talker?" a high-pitched voice whispered.

"Who wants to know?" I whispered back.

"Come to spring you two out of here." The intruder turned on an optic emitter and swung it toward one of the corridor access panels. "This way."

I started out the door panel, but Reever held me back. "Who are you?"

"Milass." His voice bordered on shrill. "I hov' with the alien underground. Caught word of your troubles, craved to help."

The alien underground? "I've never heard of that," I said.

Reever stepped in front of me. "Nor have I."

"Not like we advertise, get it?" He spoke an odd variety of inner-city slang, one I hadn't heard in three years.

"Can you speak stanTerran?"

Milass made an impatient sound. "You two crave strolling out of here, or not? The junkers will be on us in a blip."

I wasn't taking another step without my cat or the Lok-Teel. "Reever, get Jenner."

While I retrieved the Lok-Teel from my cell, Reever managed to smash open the plas unit Joe had imprisoned Jenner in. He leaped up in my arms and stared at our rescuer. He didn't hiss, but the fur on the back of his neck stood on end.

"He's okay, pal." I stroked him, not sure if I was comforting the cat or lying to myself.

A small, square hand gestured for us to follow him. "We got to stroll, *now*."

I looked at my husband, who hesitated another moment, then nodded.

We followed our diminutive rescuer into one of the corridors and down past a number of equipment storage areas. Emergency lights illuminated everything with a blood-red glow. At the very end of the corridor was a wall panel with a small, square hole.

Milass pointed to it. "That way."

Reever crawled in first. I put Jenner in, then followed. Behind me, Milass got in, then sealed it. That plunged the narrow crawl space into total darkness.

We crawled forward, but not for long. Reever pulled himself out into a larger area, and turned to grab Jenner and help me. When the smell hit my sensitive nose, I stopped at the very edge.

"What is that stench?"

Beyond me appeared to be some kind of tunnel with smooth, perfectly rounded walls. Someone had strung a couple of optic emitters along the very top of the tunnel. A stream of sluggish mud covered the bottom of it.

"Take my hands, Cherijo."

I held on to my husband's hands and pushed myself out of the crawl space. And stepped into something that was definitely *not* mud. "Where are we?"

"Old sewer pipes," Milass said as he emerged. "We got to hike through it to get to *Leyaneyaniteh*."

That wasn't anywhere I'd been in New Angeles. "Le-what?"

"It means, 'The Place of the Reared Under the Ground,' " Reever said.

Our rescuer climbed down and walked toward us. "You got word on my tribe, code talker?"

I saw his garments had been fashioned from some sort of animal hide, and covered with primitive symmetrical symbols. He looked as though he'd stepped out of a history text.

"I understand your root language."

Code talker. A name for linguists who'd used obscure languages as encryption devices during the old wars. How did I know? Joseph had dragged me over to the Four Mountains reservation to watch him make his annual address as the official shaman for the Native Nations of North America. Sometimes I'd slipped out of the tribal assembly hall and wandered around the adjacent museum building.

"You're an Indian," I said. I concentrated for a moment, rolling the word around in my head. The only Indians for miles around were the ones up in the canyons, beyond the mountain range. "Navajo?"

"No."

When he stepped into the circle of light, I saw he wasn't a young boy, but a very short, thin man. Milass had the typical bowed calves and dark coloring of the Navajo, so I didn't think he was telling the truth. He wore his long brown hair loose, with some white feathers hanging from a single thin braid by his right temple. The feathers contrasted sharply with the livid burn scars marring his face and neck. He might be childsize, but he looked like a guy nobody messed with.

"You're tasty looking," he said, giving me a leer.

"You're not," I said.

"We'll spout later." He started down through the conduit. "Move your gear."

I looked at Reever, saw how my cat was struggling to get out of his arms. "Give me him, he's scared."

Reever handed me Jenner, and I propped my frightened cat against my shoulder. He sank his claws into me, and shivered.

"It's okay, pal."

I continued to murmur wordless sounds of comfort as we worked our way farther into the archaic sewer system. When I saw the rats lining either side of the conduit, I realized Jenner wasn't frightened as much as he was *hungry*.

"You can't eat those things," I told him. "Look where they live."

Reever put his arm around me when we turned into a cross section and had to climb up into another, smaller pipe. This one had several inches of waste at the bottom, and I made a face.

"That has to be at least two hundred years old. So why is it still wet?"

My husband took my arm. "It's below the water table."

I cringed as my footgear became saturated. "Lovely."

We slogged through a series of waste-lined conduits for some time, until we reached a man-made breach in the pipes. Milass led us through that into a much larger tunnel, filled with what appeared to be an ancient transport system.

I studied the alloy rails, huge, decaying transport vehicles that resembled glidebuses, and heard the faint hum of electricity. The little Indian went up to the first of them and wrenched open a door. A shower of rust flakes rained down around him. Hinges squealed and groaned.

"I never saw anything like this when I lived on Terra," Reever said in a low voice.

Me neither. "Have any idea what it could be? Besides junk, I mean?"

"Apparently some type of primitive electrical conveyance system. It might be what was once called a 'subway,' a system of underground transport."

I could think of half a dozen archaeologists who would have fainted at the sight of an intact subway system. "Can't be. Subways haven't been used in about five hundred years."

Milass came over to us, clearly impatient to go. "It's solid. Let's jam."

We entered the long, box-shaped transport and sat down on two of the cracked, stained seats. Reever was utterly fascinated and started touching everything.

"This pole is aluminum," he said, then felt the seat. "And this feels a little like unrefined plas."

"Plastic," I said as I watched our rescuer. He'd gone to the front compartment and was sitting at some kind of console.

"If this is a subway transport, it is too old to be functional."

"I wouldn't put credits on that." I watched as Milass activated the power system, and the entire car shook. "Grab something, Reever."

Metal whined, electricity crackled, and the transport shuddered and groaned as it began to slowly move on the rails.

Reever got that rapt look on his face, the one he had whenever he was updating a linguistic database or crossbreeding some kind of rare flower. "Incredible."

"Uh-huh." It might be incredible, but it was also five hundred years old, or worse. I held on and prayed the thing wouldn't collapse on us.

It didn't. It gathered velocity until we were doing about half the normal speed of a glidecar, and rattled along the tunnel railway. Someone must have spent considerable time and effort maintaining this ancient system. Still, every couple of seconds there was a new whine, hiss, or bump. I started to sweat when I saw the rivets in one of the old aluminum panels beginning to give way.

After an hour of this joyride, I called to Milass, "How much farther?"

"Almost there," he yelled back.

I closed my eyes as we finally decelerated. "There is a God and He listens to me."

When the transport came to a full stop, I got to the door and out of there. In the pitch-black tunnel outside, I opened my mouth to give the little man a piece of my mind, when he took out a small black device and pointed it at the wall.

The wall slid to one side, revealing yet another tunnel—this one much smaller and hacked out of solid stone. Tiny optic emitters sparkled, casting a faint glow.

Milass glanced back at us, then waved his arm and stepped down into the tunnel.

Things weren't adding up. Indians involved with an alien underground. Transport systems that shouldn't exist but still worked. Stone walls moving like door panels by remote control.

"Reever, I've got a bad feeling about this."

"We have no choice but to go on. Unless you prefer to return to the estate and try to find an alternative escape route."

"So what's a bad feeling or two?" I stepped down into the tunnel. The air at once became cleaner and cooler, and I took a deep breath. Jenner perked up and struggled to get down again. "Not yet, pal. Pardon me, but how much farther is it?"

"We're near getting. Wait." He held up a hand as he pointed his device at a red optic light set in one side of the tunnel. Something beeped, and the light turned from red to green.

"What's that?" I asked, looking back as we passed it.

"Watch." He used his remote again, switching the light back to red, then picked up a pebble and tossed it. A bioelectrical field snapped and crackled, bouncing the pebble back at us. At the same time, half a dozen thin, sharp-tipped silver rods shot out of the top of the tunnel and buried themselves in the floor.

"A containment field. And . . . spears. Very nice."

"The buzz keeps meddlers out. The chuks clinch they don't get another go." He was already walking away. "Grip your animal and stay near."

"Absolutely." Seeing as I didn't have a handy-dandy remote device myself.

We passed at least a dozen more traps that Milass had to disarm, emphasizing that wherever we were going needed lots of security. From the slope of the tunnel and the temperature drop I judged we were descending even farther beneath the ground. The deeper we went, the more optic emitters I saw. Then other tunnel openings began to appear.

"This place reminds me of Catopsa," I said to Reever. "All it needs is some hostile lizards and killer *tul* crystals."

Strange pictographs also started appearing on the walls of the tunnels. They ranged from abstract circular designs to more elaborate primitive symbols. Some strongly resembled the patterns in the Navajo wool rugs my creator collected. We also heard sounds of other footsteps, faint, clanging noises, and from one tunnel opening, drumming and low-pitched chanting.

The little man took a final turn and lead us out into a huge, natural cavern. It was so enormous and unexpected that I yelped. Dozens of dark eyes turned to look at us for a moment, then paid no more attention.

It was exactly as if a small Indian village had been dropped into the center of the earth. There was a big fire burning in the center of the cave. Men crouched near it in small groups, talking and drinking from small pottery servers. Women sat near them, some of them weaving on huge looms. Children ran around, some of them naked, and played games with sticks and balls. Some thirty small, rounded huts built of mud and wood lined the walls of the cavern.

I'd been to reservations and museums. I'd seen the

way even the most conservative Native Americans lived. None of them had ever tried recreating a historic habitat like this. "This is impossible."

"No." Milass's scarred face lit up with a satisfied smile. "This is *Leyaneyaniteh*."

While I stood there gaping along with Reever, our rescuer strode away and walked around the cavern. He didn't do anything for about ten minutes.

"I don't care what he says. They're Navajo," I said to Reever.

"How do you know?"

"The Navajo consider it rude to barge in and say hi the minute they arrive somewhere. They like to wait and give people time to finish whatever it is they're doing before they interrupt them."

Once Milass judged the time to be right, he strode casually to the center of the cavern and climbed up on a big, flat boulder there. By then everyone had finished or set aside whatever they were working on and gave him their full attention.

"Got in, got out, got 'em here." The Indian pointed to us, then smacked his little hand against his chest and made a pushing-away gesture. "Junkers never stuck a sensor on me."

Everyone in the cavern made a high, trilling sound, something like a cross between laughter and cheering.

He strutted around the top of the rock, detailing our escape. Then he said, "The chief gifts you two more to connect—she's a patcher, and he's a code talker."

From my rusty grasp of the man's patois, and my even scantier knowledge of Indian customs, I thought he was saying we were going to join the tribe. "Reever, did you get that?"

"Yes. He thinks we're going to join them."

"I didn't say anything about joining them." I scanned the faces around us. Most of them weren't completely human. "Did you?"

"No."

I started edging back toward the tunnel we had come from. "I mentioned my bad feeling, too, right?"

"Yes." Reever stopped me. "Wait, we should hear what he has to say."

I waited. That was my first mistake.

Milass climbed down from the rock, and headed straight toward us, flanked by two bigger men.

"Nice cave." I looked around again for the exit. "So, can you take us up to the surface now?"

"Spill and spout on that later."

Later. In Indian terms, that could mean anytime, from this evening to next year. "May we speak with your chief?"

Milass tapped his chest. "I'm the chief's *secondario*." He gestured toward the biggest man. "Kegide, the chief's other arm."

More like his other *army*. Trytinorn females would have fallen in love with Kegide, who stood nearly seven feet tall and had to weigh close to four hundred pounds. Lighter skin and short-cropped black hair should have made him seem less menacing than Milass, but it didn't. His expression seemed a little vacant, and his mild brown eyes wandered. He didn't say anything at all.

"Hok, the chief's shoulder-talker."

Hok's title must have meant advisor, but he really did only reach Reever's shoulder. Not because he was short, but due to the contorted condition of his body. The hump on Hok's back must have been due to a severe spinal injury, or an untreated case of scoliosis. To add to his problems, he also had scars all over the lower half of his face. It looked like he'd been born with a cleft palate, and someone had done a terrible job on the oral reconstruction.

Hok wore his dark hair in a long braid that hung over one hunched shoulder, and he had shrewd, black eyes. Not that it was easy to catch his gaze. He seemed mesmerized by the ground.

"Cherijo Torin," I said. "My husband, Duncan Reever. May we speak with your chief now?"

"Come." Milass pointed to the fire burning in the center of the cave. "The chief craves you break and chew with us. Spout our tales together."

Considering how much he'd helped us, I couldn't see refusing his hospitality. "All right."

That was my second, and worst mistake.

When we were seated on woven mats near the fire, Milass directed some of the women tending it to bring us food and drink. Reever and I were handed servers of strong, dark tea and handmade bread stuffed with some kind of cheese.

I cautiously tasted the tea and bread, and smiled. "This is delicious, thank you," I said to the woman who'd given it to me. She merely gave me a strange look and wandered away.

The little Indian man sat down beside me and nudged me with his arm. The contact made me jump. "You're a body patcher, like the Shaman, solid?"

"I'm a thoracic surgeon." I nibbled on the bread, trying to figure out how these people had established an underground village. "Why are you people living like this?"

Milass explained a little about it. From what I grasped of his speech patterns, the Night Horse Clan was formed from Navajo refugees and half-Navajo, half-alien fugitives, some ten years ago. They'd bought land here after leaving the reservation, and had discovered the tunnels by accident. The hybrid fugitives decided to move underground to prevent being deported. Their human family members divided their time, living above ground part of the year, and moving into the cavern in the winter months.

"We got back the *Diné* ways," the little man said. "Here we do like the old ones."

Diné was what the Navajo called themselves. "I thought you said you aren't Navajo."

"We are not. We are Night Horse."

Jenner, whom I'd been holding with one arm, sniffed at the bread in my other hand. Absently I broke off a piece for him and put him down between me and Reever.

"What made you decide to leave the Navajo reservation and form your own tribe?" Reever asked.

Milass scowled. "Whiteskin laws. The people hang on them now. Whiteskin law say all brids taboo, have to go from *Dinéteh,* go from Terra. Rico fetched the brids and their kin away, fetched them here."

"The way you 'fetched' us here?" I asked.

The little man shrugged. "Some. They crave it now."

"You solid, patcher? Decent?"

The beautiful voice asking me that came from Hok, and for a moment, all I could do was stare. Finally I realized how rude I was being, and nodded. "Yeah, I'm a pretty decent patcher."

"Crave a new mug, Hok?" Milass said. His squeal of laughter was as mean as his eyes. "No patcher decent enough do that." He laughed, and Kegide grinned.

"You'd be amazed what I can do," I told Milass, angry that they'd ridiculed him. An image of Furre-Va's beautifully reconstructed face, and me pulling a berth linen over it, made me bite my tongue.

But the little twerp wasn't done.

"Bet this hairball do the job," he said, and held Jenner up by the scruff of the neck. "What you spout, Hok? Crave a good scratchin', better up your mug some?"

I got to my feet. "Put him down."

"Snap your lip, patcher." The little man shook my poor cat. "I ain't marring him."

I wasn't going to wait and see if he meant *at all* or *yet.* I grabbed Jenner from Milass, pressed him against my chest, and ran. For about ten feet, until someone literally picked me up off mine.

Kegide grinned down at me as he carried me suspended between his huge hands back to the fire.

"Milass making fun," Hok said to me as Kegide gently put me back down between him and Reever. "No grief, patcher."

I looked at my husband, who was staring at the hunchback, evidently fascinated by his melodic voice. So I elbowed him.

"Thanks for helping me rescue Jenner," I said, heavy on the sarcasm.

"You get wrathful easy, little patcher," Milass said. "Your animal ain't marred."

"We'd like to make arrangements to leave Terra," Reever said. "Do you have any contacts with interplanetary transportation?"

"We'll spout on that tomorrow. Come." Milass rose to his feet. So did the other men. "I'll guide you to your night hogan."

We were both so tired we fell asleep as soon as we were shown our "night hogan," one of the little mud-and-stick huts at the back of the cavern. It felt good to curl up with Reever and Jenner. All we had to do was get back to the *Sunlace,* and I'd be a happy girl.

One of the Night Horse women came in to wake us the next morning, and brought some water to wash with and two servers of their eye-opening tea. I assumed it was morning, anyway. The cavern remained lit only by dozens of optic emitters.

We must be a good mile underground.

Reever waited until the silent woman departed before he spoke to me. "I am getting the impression the chief does not wish us to leave."

"From what?"

"If they meant only to help us escape your creator, why are they keeping us here?"

"Indian hospitality, I guess. Don't be a pessimist." I splashed my face and dried it off with the edge of my tunic. Almost as an afterthought, I replaced the Lok-Teel in its accustomed spot under the tunic. "They'll probably make us honorary Horses or whatever, then take us to the surface."

Jenner refused to budge from the blankets we'd slept on, so Reever and I went out by ourselves to the center cooking fire. This morning it looked like the entire tribe was gathered around it, sitting cross-legged, heads bowed. Hok stood off to one side, chanting something that sounded religious.

I stopped. I didn't know much about Indians, but I knew they took their rituals and religious practices very, very seriously. "Maybe we should wait until they're done."

"Cherijo, Duncan." Hok gestured for us to join them, then continued his low, haunting chant.

We sat down on the outer fringes of the group. Someone passed us a cup made out of hard clay, and made hand motions for us to drink from it. I pretended to take a sip, and wrinkled my nose. *Ugh.* Whatever it was, it smelled like wet, burnt wood.

Reever made a similar pantomime before passing it along. "Ashes," he murmured against my ear. "Mixed with water."

"Maybe they ran out of tea," I whispered back.

Hok finished his chant, and I nearly jumped out of my skin when the entire tribe yelled *"Ayi!"*, then got to their feet and walked away from the fire. Reever and I got up, too, but Hok waved us to come closer and sit with him. Milass and Kegide took positions behind us.

I could feel Milass staring at the back of my head as I spoke to Hok. "Thank you very much for letting us stay overnight, and your generous hospitality. But we really need to get out of here before someone comes looking for us."

"No heat, patcher. Gunboys never find *Leyaneyani-teh*." He handed me something, and I saw it was two wristcoms. Milass and Kegide wore them, too. "Clap it on. Make it simple for us to spout."

Reever only shook his head when I handed one to him. "I don't need it."

Of course he didn't. The man only spoke about a million languages. I put mine on and adjusted it. "So, what do we need to talk about?"

Hok's voice came through the wristcom very clearly, unfortunately. "Our chief wishes you to stay here."

If Reever said, "I told you so," I was going to smack him. "Why? You don't even know who we are. We could be mass murderers."

"I know what you are," he said. "Not all of my tribe hides underground. We have many hogans up in the canyons. We have vid equipment."

So Hok knew we were fugitives. "Are you going to turn us in?"

"No. Some of our tribe play for the New Angeles Gliders. We need you to help them."

"The Gliders?" I was totally confused for a minute, until I placed the name. "You mean they play shock-ball?" He nodded. "You want to help them, make them quit."

"That would be unacceptable to our chief."

"Okay. What's the problem with your players?"

"Their appearance." Hok traced a circle in the air around his own face. "As long as a player can run and kick, the junta doesn't ask a lot of questions. The problem is with the random commission inspections. They require physical alterations to better pass as full Terrans."

Physical alterations as in surgery, I assumed. "Why me?"

"Our team physician says you're the best cutter he knows. You're blood, too. You owe it to your people to help them."

"You are not my wife's people," Reever said, very calm and cold. "The fact that Cherijo has Navajo ancestry doesn't obligate her to provide her services to your tribe."

"You're not blood, whiteskin," Milass said, dismissing him with a flick of his hand.

They meant to keep us here. But that couldn't happen. We had to get back on the surface and get off Terra as quickly as possible, before Joseph found us again. I didn't need the additional headache of escaping our rescuers. But there were only two of us, and a whole tribe of them.

Panic made me surge to my feet. "I'm flattered by your invitation, but I have to refuse. You'll find someone else to help you out. We really need to leave now."

"You'll do what you're told," Milass said. "All the blood follow the chief's orders." He clamped a hand on my wrist.

"Let her go," Reever said.

Milass pushed me aside, and pulled out a knife. "You don't challenge me. I'm *secondario* here. My words come from the chief's mouth."

"Then you should both shut up." My husband produced a blade similar to Milass's. He must have stolen it—Reever always liked to be armed, for some reason.

"Wait." I stepped between them. "We can talk about this, work something out."

"Cherijo, get out of the way," my husband said.

Milass shifted the knife back and forth between his hands. "Hide behind your woman while you can, whiteskin."

I looked at Hok. "Don't let him do this."

Hok only motioned to Kegide, who strode over, picked me up like a doll, and hauled me to the sidelines.

Milass jumped forward and slashed at Reever, who circled back and around the fire. The Night Horse silently gathered to watch. Kegide held on to me, and didn't make a sound, not even when I kicked him repeatedly in the shins.

I shrieked when Milass's blade caught Reever's shoulder, and left a gash that saturated the front of his tunic with blood.

"Reever!" I twisted around and yelled at Hok. "Stop this!"

My husband instantly went on the attack, using his blade with precise, calculated sweeps. He cut Milass on the forearm, chest, and forehead before the Indian could even react.

"Yield," Reever said, but Milass only wiped the blood out of his eye and slashed back.

It took a few more of those soundless, rolling moves Reever knew how to make, but in the end Milass ended up flat on his back on the cave floor, bleeding from a dozen shallow wounds.

"I prevail." Reever wrenched the Indian's knife from his limp hand. Hok came over and dragged Milass to his feet. A tribesman I hadn't seen before joined them, steadying Milass and speaking to him in a low voice.

Kegide put me down as Reever started to walk toward me. Milass came up behind him, and thumped my husband on the back. "Good fight. Too bad you lost."

Reever went still. Kegide finally turned me loose, and I ran over to him. His face had gone pale and glassy with sweat.

"What's wrong? Did he . . ." My voice trailed off as I glanced down. There was a knife sticking out of Reever's side. Milass was still holding the hilt and turning it, slowly.

I didn't think, I punched. Milass staggered backward and crumpled. Then I had to grab Reever as he dropped to his knees. He pressed his knife into my numb hand.

"Use . . . this . . ."

"Oh God." I was sobbing, clutching at him. "Hold on." Gently I lowered him to the ground. The tall one came to stand over us, and I brandished Reever's blade. "Back off."

"I am Rico, chief of the Night Horse."

A cold, invisible finger ran down my spine. I shot up and held the knife to his throat. "You're going to transport my husband to a hospital. Now."

"You may make use of our medical alcove." Apparently unconcerned that I was ready to slit his throat, Rico snapped his fingers. Two men appeared, carrying a litter. Before I could blink, he added, "When you agree to join us."

So the fight had been a setup. I pressed the edge of the knife in, until a trickle of red ran along the blade. "You should be more concerned with your jugular."

"You have much to worry about, too."

I felt twin sharp pricks on either side of me. Kegide loomed on my right, Hok on my left. Another tribesman crouched next to Reever, and held a blade to his throat.

Rico simply looked amused. "The whiteskin will assuredly bleed to death before I do. Decide."

"Okay." I let go of the knife and let it fall to the cave floor. "I'll do whatever you want."

I'd never operated on someone I loved before. The closest I'd come was taking care of Kao, before he'd died, and the surgery I'd performed on Dhreen, when his ship had crashed on K-2. Now, running beside the makeshift gurney Kegide and Hok were carrying Reever on, I faced a surgeon's worst nightmare.

What if I botch the job?

What if I can't stop the bleeding?

What if he dies on my table?

I wasn't perfect. Every doctor made mistakes. Now

Reever's life was in my hands, and one error on my part could snuff it out. Just like that.

I could hardly think about it. Him, dying. Life without Reever was . . . unimaginable.

Squilyp's voice rang out in my had. *You've simply never been in a position to worry about your own competency.*

Well, I was now. I wondered what the Omorr would say about that. What Vlaav Irde would say, if he knew how frightened I was?

You are always so confident of success.

I recalled my reply to what he'd said, and cringed at my own arrogance. *We're surgeons. Success is the only acceptable alternative.*

I had to shut down the voices, and the doubts, or I'd freeze up. I knew that; I'd seen it happen to other surgeons. Reever wasn't going to die. I didn't fumble instruments, I didn't make mistakes. I was the best. I'd find the damage and fix everything, and the man I loved would live.

And if he didn't, then I'd deal with that, too.

Reever regained consciousness for a moment and squeezed my hand. *I know . . . you will . . . my beloved. . . .*

Reading my thoughts again. "Stop that." I couldn't let him know how frightened I was. "I bet you're just congratulating yourself for marrying a surgeon."

Hok gave me an odd look, and I realized I'd spoken aloud.

I laced my fingers through Reever's. *It'll be okay. I've done plenty of kidney work in the past. Relax and let me take care of you, okay?*

It is . . . difficult. . . .

I knew Reever didn't even like watching surgery—it made him physically ill. *Trust me, please.*

He slid back into unconsciousness, just as we crossed over the threshold of a man-made alcove in the rock wall and into a makeshift treatment room. There were no air replacement units; it was cluttered with junk, and everything was filthy.

As soon as I met their "cutter," I was going to kill him.

I directed the men to carefully set Reever down on the floor, and grabbed the first scanner I saw.

"You." I pointed to Kegide. "You're officially my assistant for the next hour. Clean that refuse off the exam table."

Kegide looked at me, then at Hok, puzzled.

"He doesn't understand," Hok said, and tapped the side of his head. "He's not right here."

"Great. Then you're elected."

Hok shrugged and began to move the dusty boxes from the ancient exam table. I leaned over Reever and scanned the wound site. The blade had penetrated his kidney, which lay skewered on the end like a choice tidbit.

"Looks like you'll be running on one from now on." Automatically I scanned the opposite side of his abdomen, saw the readings, and swore. Reever didn't *have* a second kidney to spare. I felt like slapping him. "Damn it, what did you do with the other one?"

There were no scars to indicate he'd had prior surgery—I knew that, just from living with him. His vitals were weakening, though he hadn't lost much blood. If I'd pulled the knife out back in the cave, he might have bled out before I could have gotten him prepped. I looked over at Hok, who had stripped off the stained linens and was wiping down the table with a strong-smelling liquid antiseptic.

"I need to operate on him. Get me whoever can handle assisting me, an air replacement unit, sterile field generators, full-spread thoracic setup, a lascalpel rig, and a whole blood synthesizer." Hok merely stared at me. "Do you have a brain problem, too?"

"Our cutter can assist you. We don't have many instruments and no laser array. Our synthesizer isn't very reliable, but you're welcome to use it. What is a sterile field?"

I could have screamed. "You people actually expected me to work on your athletes? Under these conditions?"

Hok shrugged. "Our cutter never complains."

"Your cutter never graduated medtech. He should be locked up."

A tall, thin Caucasian male walked in. His physician's tunic was covered with stains and had a shabby, frayed look to it. His close-set eyes widened when he saw me.

I imagined mine were doing the same thing. He had the same long, oily hair and cheesy smile that he'd sported when we were in school.

"Heard Milass cut him a whiteskin." He grinned. "Cherijo Grey Veil. So the psycho little dwarf pulled it off after all."

"Wendell." I could have wept, but I was too angry. "*You're* their cutter."

Wendell Florine was quite possibly the most inept medical student I'd ever had the misfortune to brush shoulders with at medtech. He was a drunk and a gambler, and had cruised through classes relying on his dubious personal charms and his father's money to obtain passing grades. He'd nearly killed a patient in our last year of internship.

I turned to Hok. "You assist me."

"Don't be a bitch, Cherijo." Still grinning, Wendell shuffled over to the exam table. "Quasimodo here doesn't know a clamp from a rib spreader. "I'll give you a hand. It's what the chief wants me to do, anyway." He cocked his head to one side as he looked at Reever's wound. "What did he hit? The liver?"

I turned to Hok again. "You're assisting me."

Chapter Seven

Choices

Wendell objected again, long enough to give Hok a chance to escape, so I ended up stuck with him. It took a few minutes to stabilize Reever enough to put him under. Instead of intravenous sedatives, I had to resort to inhalant chemicals to knock him out.

"Liquid antiseptic. Liquid anesthetics. What kind of a slaughterhouse do you run here?" I slammed down the container of inhalant. "This stuff is completely unreliable."

"It's all we could get." Wendell looked around. "What did you do with all my books?"

"For God's sake, he could wake up in the middle of the procedure—what are you talking about, books?"

"They were in boxes on the table." Wendell yawned. "Stop complaining about the inhalant, will you? If he regains consciousness, I'll just pour more over his mask."

"Go scrub," I told him. "Before I douse you with some myself."

I catheterized Reever, infused him with an auto-transfuser, which would pump the blood he was losing back into his body, then laid out the instruments to soak in a pan of antiseptic. I eyed the stacked boxes lining the walls of the alcove.

"You've really got books in here?"

"Couldn't get my hands on a medsysbank. A couple of the Indians found some kind of old storage vault when they built this place. I got all the medical volumes out of there."

"You've been treating patients using books." It was unheard of. "Real books, made of paper?"

"Yeah. Down here, you work with what you can get."

"Uh-huh. And these books are *how* old?"

"Couple of centuries. They survived in pretty good condition, actually. And some of the procedures and illustrations in them are just hilarious."

I closed my eyes for a moment. A practicing physician who had never made it to residency, treating patients using ancient texts he thought were funny. It was a wonder he hadn't wiped out the entire tribe.

The old-fashioned titanium scalpels Wendell had unearthed for me gleamed, cold and menacing. I'd been trained to cut with a blade as well as a laser, and once I'd even been forced to resort to using a chunk of razor-sharp tooth to perform surgery.

But this was Reever. I wanted only the best for him. And I'd ended up stuck with the worst.

Quickly, I scrubbed up beside Wendell, who was whistling as he leisurely used an old brush on his grubby nails.

"Tell me, Florine, how did you end up down here with these Indians?" I asked him. It was better than beating him over the head with a torso brace.

"I met Rico through the shockball junta. I, uh, owed them a bit of creds for some games I bet on."

"Why didn't your father bail you out?"

Wendell assumed a pained expression. "Dad sort of got tired of my hobbies. We parted ways a few years ago. When Rico came to me, we got to talking, and he said he needed a cutter. Said he'd pay off all my debt chips if I worked for him. So here I am."

"Rico got a raw deal," I muttered, but Wendell heard me.

"Well, not all of us can be top of the class, slave-until-you-drop Cherijo the Goddess Grey Veil, you know."

I ruined my sterile scrub by grabbing the front of Wendell's none-too-clean tunic and pulling him close. "Listen. That's my husband on the table over there. You're going to be top of the class today, or I'll excise your lungs with a rusty spoon, minus inhalant. Got it?"

"Sure. Sorry." He glanced over at Reever as I let go of him. "You positive you want to do this yourself?"

"You're not touching him." I scrubbed again, furious at myself for wasting precious moments on someone as slimy and self-interested as Wendell. "Hurry up. I want to get started."

We went to the table and I cut Reever's tunic off, then sterilized his abdomen.

Wendell noticed the knife, still buried in Reever's side, and scanned the wound. "We're doing a, uh, nephrectomy, are we?"

"No, you idiot." I checked the infuser lines, then Reever's pupils. "He only has one kidney, we can't cut it out."

"The renal trauma looks bad—his ureter has been severed, and there's extensive damage to the cal—cal—"

"Calyces."

"Right. And the glomer— glomer—"

"Glomeruli."

"That's it. Are you sure you can repair it?"

I glared at him over my mask.

"Stupid question, right." He took position by the instrument tray.

I held out my gloved hand. "Scalpel."

My hand shook a little as I placed the sharp edge of the instrument against Reever's skin. Blood welled up as the tip sank in.

Oh, God. I was cutting open my husband's body. Not a patient, not an anonymous collection of organs to be repaired. Reever. I was cutting into Reever with a knife.

I can do this.

The trembling disappeared, and I made the long, straight incision.

"Uh, Cherijo, shouldn't you remove the weapon from the wound before you do that?"

"Shut up, Wendell. This isn't a teaching class."

If I'd had a scope, I could have repaired most of the damage without cutting Reever open. As it was, I laid open the tough inner muscles of his abdominal cavity and spread his ribs out of the way.

The kidney itself lay tucked under his liver, a tiny organ only five inches long. It appeared in worse shape than I thought; it should have been enlarged to make up for the missing kidney. Instead, it appeared to be slightly withered.

"The renal artery's been nicked. Suture laser—" I closed my eyes. There were no lasers. "Suture silk."

"We've got Vicrol synthetic or PDS. Take your pick."

"What? That stuff hasn't been used since the turn of the century."

Wendell smirked. "PDS lasts longer, but has double the absorption rate and doesn't handle as well. I recommend the Vicrol."

"Good idea." I took the needle from him and started sewing. "Save the PDS for your mouth."

"Don't be mean." Wendell leaned over, blocking the overhead emitter. "Wow. I've never seen such small stitches."

"Get out of my light, you moron."

"Sorry."

"Suction." I repaired the artery, which was fed directly from the aorta, and then gingerly extracted the knife. I threw it across the room, heard it slam into the wall. Too bad Milass hadn't been standing there. "Pack the entry wound with sponges. Have you at least got a cauterizer?"

Wendell held up the small instrument. "Voilá."

"Take care of those small bleeders." I started inspecting the glomerular filtering units and the medulla. The organ was literally ruined. With any other patient, I would have performed a nephrectomy and yanked the kidney out. As it was, I had to patch what was left together and hope it would hold out until I got Reever to a hospital and on hemodialysis.

That meant I had to go back to Joe. Maybe he'd find us first. Which was fine. I'd do whatever I had to, to keep Reever alive.

Wendell swore, and dropped the cauterizing tool. "Sorry."

I looked over, saw the mess Wendell was making of the simple job. The thin thread of my patience finally snapped, and I tossed the bloody probe in my hand into the tray. "Get out."

"Excuse me?"

"You heard me. You're done. Get out of here."

"But, Cherijo—"

"Get out!" I shrieked, and Wendell ran.

I took several deep breaths, then looked down at Reever's face. He was still out, thank God. I added a little more fluid to his mask, then went back to work.

Two hours later, I finished closing, and put the Lok-Teel on the table to clean up the blood. Wearily, I stripped out of my gear and sat down beside my husband. The monitor showed his vitals were low, but steady.

"Well, honey, we made it." I rested my forehead against his motionless arm, and wept for a long, long time.

Even after the tears finally stopped, I couldn't get rid of the ache in my heart. The only kidney Reever had left wouldn't last very long, even with the repairs. I might have bought him a few weeks, but in the end it was inevitable: He was headed for complete renal failure.

I had two choices: put him on dialysis, or come up with a transplant organ. If I didn't do one or the other, Reever would die.

After the surgery, I spent the rest of the day monitoring him. Kegide brought me food I didn't eat, and lingered.

The way he stared at me got on my nerves, fast. "What?"

He didn't answer, but pressed his hand against his throat.

Maybe he had laryngitis, and wanted something for it. I scanned him, and was surprised to find he had no vocal cords. They hadn't been surgically removed, so Kegide must have been mute from birth. What had Hok said? *Not right up here.*

A second scan showed distinct developmental malformations in several sections of the brain. Mute and cerebrally handicapped. He probably had the mentality of a small child.

"I'm sorry, I didn't know."

Kegide picked up the clay pot of the stew he'd brought me, and placed it in my hands.

"Thanks, but I'm not hungry." I gave it back to him. "You can eat it, if you want."

He sat down and polished off the stew. As he did, Milass walked in.

"The chief wishes to see you. Come with me."

"Your chief can drop dead. And you can go sit on a knife."

"You might be tasty looking, but you have a foul mouth." Milass went toe to toe with me, his eyes level with mine. "If you were my woman, I'd poison your food."

"If I were your woman, I'd eat it." I stepped in front of Reever. "I can't leave him alone right now. He's still in danger."

"Kegide. Go fetch Burrow Owl to sit with him." Kegide lumbered out, while Milass looked at Reever over my shoulder. "You did a good job on him. He should be dead."

I could have happily buried a scalpel in *his* kidney at that moment. "So should you."

"You have a discourteous mouth, patcher." He put a heavy hand on my shoulder, and squeezed. Bones shifted under his grip, but I didn't twitch an eyelash. I wouldn't give him the satisfaction. "Take care what comes out of it, or I will see you squirming on the end of my blade."

"Do you know how many people I've cut open since I picked up *my* first blade?" I leaned in and lowered my voice to a whisper. "Thousands."

Kegide came in then with one of the women, and Milass shoved me away. "You come to the chief's fire. He waits for you." Then he stalked out.

I spoke with Burrow Owl, who had only a rudimentary knowledge of first aid, but seemed agreeable and understood what to watch on the monitors. "If anything fluctuates, send Kegide to get me at once."

I went out into the tunnel and back to the central cave. Rico was standing with Hok and a group of other men by the fire. A beautiful young girl was clinging to the chief's side.

It was easy to see why. Rico had the commanding presence of a chief, and wore his primitive garments with ease and style. A thong pulled his long black hair back from strong, defined features. He didn't smile much, but when he did, it was as potent as a slap.

He looked over, saw me, and said something to the

girl before gesturing for me to approach. She sauntered off, but not before giving me a dirty look.

"You sent your psycho dwarf for me?" I asked, planting my hands on my hips.

"These are the players you must fix," Rico said, waving a hand toward the dozen or so men. All of them showed obvious external indicators of their hybrid blood—some more blatantly than others.

It was unusual to see so many half-Terrans, given the GEA, but not a surprise. Most of the galactic humanoid races had proved to be cross-fertile. It had stunned twenty-second-century Terran scientists, who had always snottily insisted it to be impossible. Until they'd gotten hold of some alien DNA and found out just how wrong they were.

Now they debated whether Terrans had, like other humanoid species, descended from an original founding race. Popular opinion was an unwavering *no,* but what could you expect from a species that had once thought their world was as flat as a pancake *and* the center of the universe?

I looked over the group. There were facial corrections to be made, pigment and other dermal mutations to be altered, and in a few cases, some major reconstructive work. All of which I couldn't do with the limited quantity of medical supplies and instruments the tribe had.

"I'll need better equipment, numerous pharmaceuticals, and someone with medical training to assist me in surgery."

"Wendell—"

I lowered my eyebrows. "Not Wendell."

"Very well. Talk to my advisor." Rico thumped Hok on the back. I saw the wince before the hunchback could conceal it. "He will get you whatever you need." With that, he went after his girlfriend, who giggled and threw her arms around his neck. He disappeared with her into the largest of the lodges.

Must be pretty nice to be the chief around here.

I turned to Hok. "Have you got something to make a list with?"

"Just tell me. I'll remember." At my skeptical glance, he gave me a twisted smile. "I am a *hataali,* patcher. I can remember songs that take three days to sing. I assure you I will do the same with whatever you tell me."

I gave him the list. He made no comments about my demands, but shook his head when I got to the dialysis rig. "That will not be needed."

"How the hell do you know what I need?"

"I worked as an orderly in a hospital on the reservation. You don't need to perform any kidney operations on our tribe."

"If my husband dies, I'm not going to operate on anyone. Get the damn rig."

"There aren't many to be had anymore. Organ cloning is the treatment of choice." He gave me a thoughtful look. "I can get you the components to make one."

"Fine. What about nurses?"

"A few of the women have practical knowledge."

Practical knowledge. They probably smeared patients with colored clay and rattled things over them. 'Not good enough. What about you? You said you worked in a hospital."

"I sterilized equipment." He actually blushed. "I have had no training."

Again with the training. Was I ever going to be in a situation where I had competent help? "You're the brightest one I've met down here so far. I'll train you myself."

"If the chief permits it."

I glowered. "The chief will permit it, or he and I are going to have another little chat."

I went back to Medical, dismissed Kegide and the Indian woman, and performed another series of scans on Reever. He was running a low-grade fever, but roused as soon as I tried to wake him.

"Hello, wife."

"Hi, yourself, husband." I adjusted his infuser and injected a standard antibiotic, to deal with the budding infection. "How do you feel?"

"Sleepy." He looked around. "Where am I?"

"In my new medical facility. One room, no equipment, and the supplies are at least a century old. Sort of reminds me of the FreeClinic on K-2." He tried to touch his side, but I caught his hand. "No messing with my suture site."

"Were you able to repair the damage?"

"Mostly," I lied. "Want to tell me what happened to your other kidney?"

"According to my parents, I was born with only one."

"That explains why you don't have any surgical scars." I paused, wondering exactly how much I should tell him. I'd been in a similar situation before, with Kao. But with his sensitive Jorenian physiology, he'd already known he was dying.

I couldn't keep Reever in the dark. He had a right to know.

"Duncan, I was able to temporarily fix the damage, but your kidney will eventually stop functioning. Hok is getting me what I need to set up a dialysis rig for you, and once I find a replacement organ, I'll perform a transplant procedure."

"If you don't?"

"Then you'll die."

He curled his hand around mine. "I have much to live for. Do what you can." Then he drifted off to sleep.

I shut off the light emitters, sat beside him, and felt something brush against my legs.

Jenner. I picked him up and held him on my lap. He sniffed at Reever's hand, then nudged mine.

"He's okay," I told my cat as I scratched gently around his ears. It didn't sound like I was deluding myself. "He's going to be fine."

I set up an adjoining alcove in the tunnel as an outpatient treatment room, and started working on the first hybrid.

Small Fox didn't quite live up to his name. He was a walking hulk who played as a frontline blocker, and used his massive torso to keep other linemen from attacking the center kicker. None of that made any sense to me, but I wasn't much of a shockball fan.

Small Fox's problem was the genetic heritage his alien father had passed along to him. Namely, an extreme case of hypertrichosis, resulting from an abnormal androgen production level, stimulated by his alien DNA. Small Fox's body was, quite literally, covered with hair. If that wasn't bad enough, the hair was bright green in color.

"No one ever called you the Jolly Green Giant?"

"Not after I passed three hundred pounds."

"Hmmm." I ran a bioanalysis on a hair sample. It was copious, it was green, but it was plain human hair. "How have you managed to conceal your condition so far?"

"I shave before every game," Small Fox told me, and winced as he rubbed the grassy stubble on his face. "Twice a day, every day."

I used a small vat of depilatory cream to de-hair him this time, then prescribed a daily dose of an androgen-suppressant compound.

"If that doesn't work, we'll have to use electri-stim on the follicles directly." Which would take about forever. "Report back to me in a week and let me know how you're doing."

A second player presented a more complex problem for treatment: leg bones that curved inward, which often made him trip when running upright, like a human, instead of on all fours, like his alien equine parent. Protruding bony knobs at his knees and ankles didn't help.

I trimmed away the protrusions, which served no purpose, and dressed the sites. If he'd been a child, I could have operated on his legs to correct the abnormality of the tibia and fibula. Since the bones were ossified, I'd have to approach it from a physical therapy angle.

I prepared a couple of weight packs, and showed him how to stretch the tight muscles with some simple exercises. "Once those patches heal, work on your legs with these, every day. Get them loosened up, and you'll be able to keep your balance with your legs spread farther apart."

He hobbled out, and I went to check on Reever. The fever had improved, but he wasn't ready to go waltzing yet. I'd get him up and walk him tomorrow, I decided.

My next patient was waiting for me when I went back to the treatment room. Thousands of small, dark purple discolorations covered his face, hands, forearms, neck, ankles, and feet.

"Hi, there. Who are you?"

He folded his arms and glared at me. "Spotted Dog."

"Great name."

The rest of his body appeared unaffected, and although he had an unusual arrangement of genitalia, without the discolorations, he'd easily pass for Terran.

"If you were a lot older, I'd say these were age spots." I circled around him, trying to figure out why his torso only had a couple of spots here and there. "Do they pop up anywhere else?"

"Sometimes on my legs, and chest. They go away in winter months."

I stepped back and studied him. Of course. Everywhere his garments covered him, his skin was relatively normal. The discolorations occurred only on the parts of his body that were constantly exposed to the elements. I took a blood sample to be sure.

"Okay, Spotted Dog. You've got a serious case of anaphylactoid purpura, also known as Schönlein-Henoch purpura. The spots are caused by inflammation of the blood vessels beneath the skin."

"What does that to me?"

"I don't know yet, but whatever it is, it's environmental and you're highly allergic to it. Did your alien parent have any kind of a severe physical reaction while on Terra?"

"My father had to take Mother back to her home-world. She had trouble breathing. They left me behind with my Terran grandparents."

Since he didn't sound too happy talking about it, I let it go. "I'm going to start you on a series of shots. We'll determine what exactly is irritating your derma, then come up with a counteragent. That should get rid of the spots."

That was all the patients I was sent for the day. I went back to sit with Reever, and Hok limped in, carrying a heavy box of pharmaceuticals.

"Your drugs, Doctor."

I checked through the collection, which according to the labels had been taken from a dozen different area hospitals. "Where did you get these?"

"Does it matter?"

"No. Why didn't you report here today? I could have used some help moving some of this junk out of here."

"The chief needed me elsewhere." He shuffled toward the door.

"Tell the chief I need you tomorrow." His limp seemed more pronounced today, and I frowned. "Are you in pain? Do you want me to check you out?"

"No. I am only tired." He paused at the alcove's

entrance. "I'll bring you the components for the dialysis rig tomorrow."

"Good. Be ready to start your training, too."

Hok delivered boxes of supplies and equipment to Medical every day after that, and generally stayed a few hours to assist me. Remembering how I'd screwed up with Vlaav, I took great pains to be a kinder teacher.

I started to move Wendell's books out into the tunnel, then one of the boxes fell over and I picked up a perfectly preserved volume on surgical theory. I knew I shouldn't have wasted time with it, but my curiosity got the better of me. Then I started sorting through the books and pulling out a few reference volumes. Nothing I could really use, but as reading material, they were utterly fascinating.

Hok and I built the dialysis rig together, and set it up beside Reever's makeshift berth. Signs of kidney failure were already beginning to show in his daily scans, and I knew it was only a matter of time before I had to put him on the rig.

Milass and Kegide also made regular visits. I had the feeling the *secondario* only came to make sure I was working and to report back to Rico on my progress with the hybrids.

Kegide brought me things—food most of the time, but sometimes pretty crystals, pebbles, and one time a small brown feather he tried to stick in my hair.

At first I thought he meant to pet me, the way he did the cat, and grabbed his big paw. "Uh-uh. No scratching behind my ears."

"He wants you to wear the feather," Hok told me, then took it from Kegide's hand and tucked it in his tunic. "No, brother. She does not want it."

"I can wear a feather in my hair, if it makes him happy." I'd have to sterilize it first, though.

Hok snorted. "You have shown no desire to be a

part of the blood. Why would you lower yourself to emulate our ways?"

He'd made other, similarly snide comments over the past week, and I was getting sick of it.

"Look, pal. Unlike you and Man Mountain here, I was never allowed more than a brief and largely superficial exposure to my ancestral cultures. But just because I was raised like a 'whiteskin' doesn't mean I hold them, or your culture, in contempt."

"Is this the truth?" Hok swept a hand out toward the tunnel. "I see you among the blood, but you do not speak to them outside of this room. You eat our food and sleep under our protection and hear our songs, but you never offer thanks for any of them. You watch us with your whiteskin eyes, but you do not see who we are."

"Huh?" The laugh I couldn't help. "Wait a minute. I don't recall being invited to any of your conversations, ceremonies, or whatever you call these little nighttime *soirees*." I planted my hands on my hips. "And, in case it's slipped your mind, my husband and I were brought here, and are being held here, against our will. I don't think we're going to be grateful to you for kidnapping and imprisoning us. *Ever.*"

"If you condescended to learn more about the blood, perhaps you would agree to stay voluntarily."

Kegide gave me one of his beseeching looks. The same way he did whenever I was bordering on a knife fight with Milass.

Some of what Hok said made sense. It's hard to be righteous when you haven't considered the other guy's point of view. Not that I'd ever consider staying here, when all I wanted was to get back to the *Sunlace*. "Okay. When's the next dancing or singing thing?"

"Tonight we will celebrate a new marriage among us. You and *Nilch'i'* are welcome to join us."

A wedding. And I had nothing to wear. *"Nilch'i'"*?

"That is what they are calling your husband. It

means 'the wind,' for the way he moves when he fights with a blade."

"How is Chief Rico going to feel about me and The Wind showing up at this wedding?"

Hok gave me a twisted smile. "Who do you think wants you there the most?"

I wasn't going to touch that remark with a ten-foot dermal probe. "What time, and which hogan?"

"We are going above, to the canyons. I will come for you when it's time."

CHAPTER EIGHT

Topside

"I don't want to try to escape tonight," I told Reever as I helped him dress. Since I'd destroyed his tunic prepping him for surgery, I'd borrowed some clothing for him from Kegide. "You're too weak to go running around the mountains in the dark."

"I can make the journey."

I told him what Hok had mentioned—that teams of men—whiteskins—had sporadically been spotted in the general area above the tunnels. Then I added, "They have to be working for Joe."

"Joseph will not capture us. I will be fine."

"You will be dead if you don't listen to me. We'll just see how you get from this cavern up to the surface, and plan to make our own trip when you're feeling better."

"Cherijo." He put his hands on mine and stopped me from lacing up the front of the decorated, animal-hide shirt I'd put on him. "You could go without me."

I could have—that was the terrible thing about it. I wanted to get off Terra and back to the *Sunlace* so badly it actually tempted me.

I tugged on the laces. "Sorry, that would violate my

marriage contract. Times like these, that little 'until death do us part' clause kicks in."

"We have no such marriage contract."

"Well, whatever the Jorenian or Hsktskt equivalent is, then." I used a piece of suture silk to tie back his hair. "You need a haircut."

He fingered my braid, which was so long now the end reached past my hips. "So do you."

Once I finished his outfit, I started putting on mine. One of the women had brought me a two-piece dress called a *biil* to wear, and it took a minute to calculate exactly what draped and knotted over that. I liked the bold stripes and diamond patterns woven into the garments, which were both lightweight and warm.

"There." I turned around slowly. "How do I look?"

"Like an Indian."

"Then I must have it on right."

Hok met us in the tunnel. He seemed to approve of my costume, then asked me the strangest question. "Doctor, are you having your menstrual cycle now?"

"No, I'm not." Not exactly something I'd ever expected to be asked, outside of an examination room. But then, Joe had wanted to know the same thing. Was I that cranky? "Why?"

"Women who are actively menstruating are considered unclean and are not permitted to attend a wedding ceremony."

Religious taboos. I will never understand them. "That's really silly, you know."

He gave me his equivalent of a shrug. "That is our way."

I thought Hok would take us out to the central cavern, but instead he led us through the labyrinth of tunnels out to the old subway station.

"Why is everyone waiting?" I asked as we joined the others leaving the tunnels and walking toward the old transport system. "Don't tell me you've got this thing running up to the surface."

"We use the lift," Hok said, and guided us around the rusting transports to a raised platform.

"The lift?" Then I saw something sliding back down the strange arrangement of mechanisms and machinery at the other end of the platform, and blinked. "That's the lift?"

Hok nodded.

Somehow the tribe had cannibalized one of the subway transports, and rigged it on pulleys to slide up what had been some kind of mechanical stairway. When the empty transport came to the bottom of the stairway, it filled with people, who grabbed the main cables, which had been run straight through the transport, and pulled. By pulling the cables, they hauled the huge rusting box up the stairway.

"Just out of curiosity, how many people have to be in the lift to be able to pull it to the top?"

"At least ten."

Which is why they went up in groups, and had no problem with me and Reever seeing how they traveled to the surface. There was no way we could do it by ourselves.

Two more groups went up before we had our turn pulling the lift to the surface. Even with twenty-five of us, it wasn't easy. Reever kept giving me very intense looks. I knew what he was thinking—this probably would be our only chance to escape, unless we figured out how to get back to Joe's lab.

While I knew if we tried, given his condition, the attempt might kill Reever.

The lift connected at the top of the stairway to a huge mechanical clamp, which allowed us to release the cables and get out before the transport was lowered back down. The last group to come up, Hok told me, would keep the transport locked in place until we returned from the wedding.

We got out onto another platform which led up a

short flight of regular stairs. Sunlight filled my eyes as I emerged from there to the surface.

I was momentarily distracted by how wonderful it felt, simply to be outside again. The sun was just about to set behind the mountains, and although the temperature was on the cool side, just being able to stand without millions of tons of rock over my head was sheer pleasure. I lifted my face and closed my eyes, relishing the last touch of sunlight against my skin.

"I miss the warmth on my face, too," Hok said, startling me.

Anyone who would rather live in a cave than on the surface, in my opinion, was crazy. "You don't have to."

He just gave another of his shrugs and started hobbling over the path that cut through the narrow canyon in front of us, toward a cluster of boulders. Reever took my hand and we followed him at a discreet distance. I checked behind us to see Kegide and some of the other Night Horse men bringing up the rear.

"We have to go now," Reever said in a barely audible tone.

"They're watching us."

"Later, then. At the first opportunity."

I scanned the surrounding area. Rocks, brush, scrub pine, and dirt. I hadn't done much exploring of the region around my birthplace, but I knew there were thousands of canyons and trails in these mountains.

We had no food, no water, and no survival equipment. It was late autumn and that meant heavy frost. Even if we could steal what we needed from the surface community, we had no idea of where we were. We could be a mile away from The Grey Veils, or a hundred miles.

It didn't present much danger to me. Besides being hardened after a year of slavery, I knew it would take a lot more than temperature and starvation to kill me.

I could get off this miserable world and get back to the Sunlace. *But I can't leave Reever behind.*

There were also Joseph's search teams to reckon with.

"We can't. I don't know where we are. You're too weak, and I don't have so much as a single lousy bandage on me. We'll die of exposure if we try."

His eyes, which had become a colorless, chilly gray, met mine. "We have to try."

"No, we have to live. We can do this when we're better prepared."

The path abruptly shrank and Reever and I were forced to squeeze single file between the boulders. Beyond them a wide, flat expanse of land stretched out, hemmed in on all four sides by sheer vertical rock cliffs.

A cluster of larger hogans identical to the ones underground had been built in the center of the canyon. I could see the immediate appeal of the location—evidently the only way to get to it was through the concealed trail between the boulders, or from the air.

These people were Navajo, or at least descended from Navajos, but again they'd broken with tradition. From what I remembered seeing on the Four Mountains reservation, the traditionalists preferred to live far apart from each other over wide tracts of land. Here the hogans had been erected close together, and the sense of a tightly bound community was very strong.

Like a cult, I thought uneasily.

Corrals occupied by horses, sheep, and other animals lay behind each hogan, and there were signs of crops growing in small cleared areas beyond the village. Hok and the others headed for a specific hogan, at the far end of the community. Then, just before we arrived at our destination, everyone stopped and pretended to study the ground for several minutes.

"Definitely Navajo," I said to Reever.

The bride's family eventually came out of the hogan and greeted us. No hybrids here. Dressed in brilliantly colored, handwoven garments, our smiling hosts greeted and spoke with every guest individually, leisurely working their way through the crowd. Hok introduced me and Reever as whiteskin friends of the tribe.

The bride's mother, who had the rather menacing name Veda Wolfkiller, gave me the once-over. "You don't look much whiteskin to me."

"I'm only half-white," I said, repeating the lie Joe had told me since childhood. In reality, I had no idea if I had any Caucasian blood at all.

"What is the other half of you?"

I tried to keep a straight face. "Some Navajo. Mostly Apache."

"Apache?" Veda's eyebrows rose. "We know some Apache families. Perhaps they share blood with you. What is the name of your mother's clan?"

Before I could try to explain my way out of that one, the bridegroom's party arrived. Veda promptly excused herself and returned to the hogan. Hok stayed with me and Reever to explain what was happening.

First the bridegroom's family presented the dowry gift to the bride's family. This consisted of traditional gifts—rugs, blankets, silver jewelry, baskets, pottery, and a saddle—all beautifully worked and obviously precious. The groom and his family immediately went into another, larger hogan, to sit down by the fire, while the bride and her family sorted through the gifts.

I nudged Reever. "How come I never got any wedding presents like that when I married you?"

"Conventional Hsktskt union celebrations include sacrificing a warm-blooded animal. The newly united pair must drink the blood for luck."

I cringed. "That's a good reason."

Veda Wolfkiller emerged from the hogan, carrying a beautifully woven basket, inside which was an equally elaborate clay pot. It held special ceremonial corn mush, Hok told me. She was followed by other female family members, bearing platters of food. They walked through the village to a large, obviously recently constructed hogan. Hok told us to follow them inside.

Bundles of dried corn cobs and beautifully patterned wool rugs lined the walls of the hogan. It was crowded, and a little stuffy, but Reever and I found a place out of the way by the door. As we watched, Veda handed her basket to her daughter, and embraced her. The bride then joined her groom on the opposite side of the fire, and with great formality presented him with the mush. Once that was done, she sat down on his right.

"Now the ceremony begins," Hok said in a low voice.

My scalp prickled, and I felt a low, distinct sense of awareness hum over my nerves. Although I hadn't seen him yet, Rico had to be somewhere close by, and he was . . . preoccupied?

My new empathic warning system proved to be right as Rico, dressed in an elaborate Navajo costume, abruptly walked through the entrance to the Hogan. He carried a wicker jug and a strange-shaped vegetable over to the wedding couple. As he approached them, everyone fell silent.

"Is that a squash?" I asked Hok in a whisper. Seemed like an odd wedding gift.

"No, a gourd ladle for the water in the jug."

Rico handed the gourd ladle to the bride, then poured water from the wicker jug into it. The bride turned and poured the water from the ladle over her groom's hands. She then handed him the ladle, and he repeated the same process with Rico for her.

"Now he will take out his bag of corn pollen," Hok told me.

"You people sure have a thing for corn," I said.

Rico removed a small bag, from which he pinched

some pollen and squatted down to sprinkle it over the basket of mush. He did this from right to left, then up and down. After that, he made a circle of pollen around the basket, then tucked the bag away.

I made a mental note to test Spotted Dog for pollen allergies.

The chief stood and addressed the tribe. "If any here have protest to the turning of the basket, speak it now."

Hok anticipated my question and said, "It's symbolic of turning the minds of the bride and groom toward each other."

No one had any protests to make, so Rico turned the basket of mush. "Take a pinch of the corn mush at the edge, where the pollen ends at the east," he told the groom.

The groom took it, and put it in his mouth. The bride did the same. They continued by taking pinches of pollen from the pattern sprinkled around the basket, and eating that. When they were finished, there were sudden, startling shouts of approval from the tribe.

I couldn't help smiling. "That means they're married now?"

"Yes."

I looked at Reever and remembered the daylong ritual he'd made me go through on Catopsa. "The Hsktskt could learn a thing or two from these people."

Rico called for everyone to begin the feast, and Hok went with us to the tables set up along the back wall of the hogan. We were handed enormous plates of food and servers of hot tea, and smiled at by everyone.

"They seem pretty happy, don't they?" I said in a low tone to Reever when we sat back down. "I guess no one cries at Navajo weddings."

"Not every culture considers marriage a tragedy," Reever said.

Hok left us there, and we listened to some of the

bride's family talking about another wedding being planned. Veda, I noticed, was missing. When I asked where she was, so I could thank her for allowing us to attend, one of the bride's brothers explained the custom of the mother-in-law leaving after the presentation of the bridal corn mush.

"It is so she can avoid looking upon her daughter's husband," he told me. "It is bad manners for her to stay, just as it would be impolite of my sister's husband to enter our mother's hogan."

"Why?"

The man shrugged. "It prevents trouble in the family."

The feast was delicious, and I was happy to see Reever eating well. Once everyone was done, one of the groom's relatives stood up and made a speech. He thanked the bride's family for the food and their reception, and the gift of their daughter.

When he was done, Rico stood over the bride and groom, and started instructing them on how they should conduct themselves as man and wife, including what they needed to do on their sleeping mat. The latter was put in such frank terms that I was appalled.

"Whiteskins never talk about proper conduct in the making of children," the bride's brother said, when he saw my wide eyes. "That is why we think so many never stay together."

The Night Horse had no problem with Rico's candid instructions, and joyously accompanied the bridal couple to their new lodge.

That left me and Reever and Hok standing in the ceremonial hogan. "They will stay in there together for four days and nights," Hok said. "We will go back to *Leyaneyaniteh* now."

"May we have a moment alone?" Reever asked him.

Hok nodded and limped out.

"Don't," I said, as soon as we were alone. "You're

already exhausted, and we still have a long walk ahead of us. We'll find another way out of this, when you've recovered."

He brushed his lips over my hair, then my nose. Then he hugged me, hard enough to displace a few vertebra. "I could distract them while you go."

"I'm not leaving. I'm *never* leaving you." I was instantly, irrationally furious. Bad enough I had to deal with my own desperation, but did he have to keep pushing me away? "Don't ever ask me to do that again."

He sighed. "We'll go back."

Once we returned with the Night Horse to the underground tunnels, I took Reever to Medical and performed a thorough scan.

"I'm fine."

"You're not." I went to get a syrinpress, and found my wrist clamped by his hand.

"Come with me."

I went, mostly because I didn't want to fight with him anymore. Then I saw his eyes as he hauled me into the hogan we'd been given in the central cavern. They weren't cold and gray any longer.

"You're in no shape to do this," I said as soon as he let go of me. "You've already pushed yourself too hard tonight. I should have you on continuous monitor in Medical. Your incision hasn't healed yet, and your kidney—"

"My kidney will be fine." He closed the door flap and reached for me. "I have other concerns."

"Oh? Like what?"

"I'm not sure what the source of this perpetual ache is. Perhaps you should examine me."

He wasn't angry—he was *teasing* me.

By the light of the small fire in the center of the hogan, I could just make out the muscles flexing as he pulled off his borrowed shirt. For the first time since his surgery, I didn't use my physician's eye to inspect him. Tonight I could relax for a few hours and be a woman.

His woman.

I moved closer and placed a hand in the center of his bare chest. "Something wrong with your heart?"

"Here." He pressed my fingers against his skin, rubbing them over the strong, steady pulse beating there. "It sometimes aches."

"Angina attacks. Hmmm, not a good sign in a man your age." I leaned forward and kissed the smooth skin. "What else hurts?"

"My hands." He moved them up my arms, over my shoulders. "They feel heavy. Empty."

"Could be osteoarthritis setting in." I took his wrists and moved his hands down, until I could slide them under the hem of my tunic. "Try to keep them warm. Anything else?"

His eyes became glittering slits as he pulled my tunic over my head and dropped it behind me, then stared down at my breasts. "My . . . mouth. It aches, too."

"You've been depriving yourself again." I lifted a hand and traced the firm line that never seemed to bend. "Maybe you're just a little hungry."

"Hungry." He bent down, pulling me up off my feet at the same time. "Yes. That's it. I'm hungry." His warm breath touched my lips. "For you."

More like starving, I thought, my neck arching back under the force of his kiss. But he shouldn't have been lifting me. I wiggled out of his grasp, backed up to our sleeping mat, and held out my hand.

"Come to me, Duncan."

The firelight made small, jumping shadows that passed over his face, briefly illuminating, then hiding the beads of sweat on his brow. He came toward me, then paused and pressed a hand to his side.

The physician in my head mentally kicked me in

the libido. "Maybe continuing your, um, deprivation is the best."

"Give me a moment. It will pass."

No, it wouldn't. He didn't want to admit it, but he was in pain. With a silent, admittedly selfish groan, I resigned myself to another couple of nights of chaste cuddling.

I lifted my outstretched hand and faked smothering a yawn. "You know, I'm really tired. How about a rain check on this?"

"You are a terrible liar." Reever eased down beside me and took my hand. His breathing sounded rapid and shallow, and his skin temperature felt icy. "Im sorry, Cherijo."

"You can make it up to me when you feel better." I pulled a blanket over us and warmed him with my body. "Go to sleep, Duncan."

He fell asleep in my arms.

I wasn't so fortunate. Reever had a way of arousing all the basic feelings in me, and they weren't going to let me get off that easy. Eventually I extricated myself from his embrace, rose from the mat, and wandered out in the cave. Everyone was still asleep, but someone had left a pot of tea warming beside the banked fire. I poured myself a cup, and sat down.

Hok had been very canny, to invite me to the wedding. No doubt all part of his campaign to have me voluntarily join the Night Horse. It was even logical, in a sense. I needed sanctuary. The tribe needed a doctor.

What would it be like, if I had no other choice but to stay with them? Would they allow me and Reever to live on the surface? Could we make a place for ourselves with these people? My ancestors had once lived like this, and for the first time in my life I understood the allure of a simple, uncomplicated existence.

Like the wedding ceremony. A "whiteskin" couple in my former social sphere would have spent thousands of credits on a huge, elaborate service held in some pristine religious shrine. Compared to the Navajos' simple bonding act of sharing food and gifts, a traditional Caucasian wedding seemed almost sterile.

Then I thought of what I had left behind, and all the attraction abruptly faded. These weren't my people, this wasn't my world. I needed to get off it, to get back to my real family.

Something made the back of my neck tingle, then a long shadow fell over me.

"You do not sleep tonight, little patcher?"

I put aside the cup. "No, chief, I was only thirsty."

"Stay. I wish to speak with you."

That was the very last thing I wanted to do, but I couldn't think of a plausible reason to go—not counting this bizarre, unwelcome awareness I had of him.

He sat beside me. "What did you think of our ceremony?"

Might as well be honest. "It was lovely."

"You have done well with my players. Small Fox no longer must shave before and after the games. Blood Warrior's legs grow straighter. And Spotted Dog now seeks a new name."

"My success rate isn't one hundred percent." I thought of the one player I had sent back to Rico untreated. Removing the hard layer of keratin plaque covering Black Otter's entire body would have killed him.

"You do what can be done. That pleases me very much. I am glad you have joined us."

"I haven't joined anything. I can't live in a cave forever."

"Why not?"

"I don't know, I guess I've been spoiled by the little comforts, like running water and automated waste disposal."

"You will grow accustomed to our ways." He chuckled and put his arm around me. I felt him tug at my braid. "You should wear your hair like our women do."

He was suggesting hairstyles, while putting his hands on me and radiating what felt like intense, focused desire. I didn't think it was due to the fact he wanted to see me look like an Indian maiden. Reever lay sleeping just a couple of yards away. If he woke up—

"I'm not a member of the tribe."

"You have been made welcome, haven't you?"

"I have my own people, my own clan."

"Tell me about them."

I told Rico how the Jorenians had saved me from being abducted by the League from K-2. He asked about the year I'd spent serving on the *Sunlace,* and what my visit to Joren had been like.

When I was done, he said, "They are not your blood."

"No." I thought of Joe, and Maggie. "But they are my family."

"We are your family now."

I stared at him. I'd never really looked at his face before, never noticed that his eyes weren't brown or black, but dark blue. He had the Navajo bone structure, and the dark skin and hair, but I'd bet there was some Caucasian blood in his veins. The narrowness of his face, the long chin, and his height indicated that.

He was without a doubt the handsomest man in the tribe. I could acknowledge that much without violating my commitment to Reever.

He yanked on my braid again. "Loosen it for me."

"Why?"

Rico's gaze wandered over my face, then went south. "I have never seen you with your hair down."

He had never seen a lot of other things, either. The trouble I was in abruptly quadrupled. I felt like slugging him, but I suspected one shout from Rico and I'd find myself nailed to the nearest hogan door.

I'd try to be diplomatic. "That's getting a little too personal."

He moved closer, until his mouth hovered just above my ear. "When I get personal with you, patcher, you will know it." Then he grabbed my braid and started unraveling it himself.

The hell with diplomacy. "Please don't."

He ignored that, and put his other hand on my arm to keep me from moving away. I thought frantically, and recalled what Hok had said about attending the wedding ceremony.

"Wait. I just started my menstrual cycle; it's what woke me up."

He took his arm away as if I'd scalded him. "You're unclean."

"Yes." Thank you, Hok, for your ridiculous taboos.

Rico got up and turned his back on me. "Return to your hogan."

I did, and nearly broke the speed of light.

After I fastened the door covering and curled back up beside Reever, I listened. If the chief left the fire, I didn't hear him go.

Finally I fell asleep, and dreamed of the Night Horse ceremony. This time I was the bride bearing the basket of corn mush. I set it down in front of my dark groom, and took my place at his side. When he turned to me, he was smiling.

He was also Rico.

A lifetime of using synthesizer units had spoiled me, and as a result I'd never given much thought to the alternative methods of food preparation. Not until I woke up the next morning, went out to the central fire, and got to see some of the Night Horse women preparing one of their communal stews.

A long tray of vegetables sat on a flat boulder that doubled as a kind of worktable. One woman deftly plucked potatoes, onions, and carrots from the tray and sliced them up for the pot.

Her companion was chopping something else—something that lay in a small, bloody pile next to her. It took a moment for me to realize she'd skinned and was dicing up a dozen or so small animals. Rabbits. Birds. Squirrels. And last but not least, what appeared to be several large, plump rats.

"Good morning," I said, when they looked at me. I pointed to one small corpse. "Are those rats?"

They looked at each other, then giggled. Of course, they were rats. Was I blind?

I thought of the few times I'd sampled one of their stews, and shuddered. Better to find out late than never. "Did I mention I'm a vegetarian?"

That just made them giggle harder.

A small, furtive shadow crept up to the pile of bodies, and the woman preparing them went still. A moment later, she seized and held up a small, clawing animal. "Look, sister. This will add spice to the broth."

"Wait!" I grabbed her hand before she could slice its throat open. "You can't eat that. That's a cat."

"Yes, patcher, we know what it is."

"It was just hungry. You can't kill it for being hungry."

"I will kill it so our *tribe* does not go hungry," she told me, the way she would a not-too-bright child.

"It's awfully scrawny. Would you mind giving it to me instead?"

The two women eyed each other. The younger said, "Whiteskins keep useless animals as pets and waste food on them. That is not the way of the People."

I thought desperately of how I could convince them. "A cat is not a useless animal. They hunt rats, and will bring them as offerings to the humans who care for them. Think of all the stew you'll be able to make."

"*Ayi*, is this true?" Both women seemed intrigued by the idea, and I realized that rat must figure prominently on their menu.

I didn't think throwing up was going to support my case, so I nodded and held out my hands. "Please."

"Very well, you may have it."

I took the cat from the woman's impersonal grip, and hugged it against my chest. The small feline curled up against me, yowling and shivering. "Thank you."

It was filthy and full of fleas and in need of some immediate medical attention, so I took it to my medical alcove. Jenner followed me, griping for me to notice him, until he saw what I put down on the exam table. He jumped up to have a sniff, and nearly got his face clawed.

I'd never had Jenner neutered, so his interest was only natural. "Back off, Romeo. She doesn't want to make friends right now."

I scanned her thoroughly. She was female, domestic shorthair, and fully developed. She was also full of parasites inside and out, malnourished, and had a dozen infected bites in her scraggly black fur. Apparently the rats fought back.

"Well, Miss Juliet, you look like you've been through a couple of catastrophes."

Juliet bit my thumb to let me know what she thought of my opinion. Jenner cried plaintively at my feet.

I hated sedating her, but it would make the worming and wound treatment easier on both of us. Once I rid her small body of all the pests, I carefully cleaned out and sutured the gashes. She'd lost part of an ear some time ago, and it had healed raggedly, so I fixed that, too.

Then I sat and held her until she came out of the sedation. She was already used to my stroking hands when she opened her wary green eyes, and sniffed at me.

"Hi, there." Jenner was pacing around my ankles.

"Want to say hello to your new boyfriend now?" Juliet peered over my lap at her anxious suitor, sneezed once, and curled up against my chest. "Well, pal, it looks like this one is going to take some convincing."

"I know how he feels." Reever stood in the entrance, arms folded, watching me.

"Nothing worth having comes along easily," I pointed out, miffed. Then I noticed how pale he was. "You okay?"

"I feel somewhat tired."

"Don't eat the stew they make here anymore, okay?"

"Why?"

Reever probably wouldn't object to rabbit, bird, and rat with vegetables, given his weird food preferences. However, I had to kiss him, and I did. "Trust me. Just don't."

Juliet had fallen asleep again, so I carried her over to the makeshift cat bed I'd improvised out of the supply container, and carefully set her down in it. Then I grabbed my scanner and waved Reever over to the table. "You're next."

I told him about how I'd saved Juliet as I went through the renal series, and saw my repair work was still holding up. We might even have as long as a month before things got critical. I thought of what would happen if his kidney failed, and what had nearly happened with Rico the night before.

"Reever, we have to get out of here."

"I've done some discreet exploring."

"What? As weak as you are?"

"I did not go far. The outlet tunnels are rigged with proximity beacons and trip sensors. It's possible I can disable them, but without a map, I doubt we can negotiate our way out once we're past them."

"I don't think they use maps." I saw a hulking form hovering outside the entrance, and lifted a finger to my lips. "Come in, Kegide."

Kegide went immediately over to Juliet's container, and peered down at her. Jenner joined him, and he cautiously stroked my pet. For once, His Majesty let him without making a fuss, and Kegide grinned at me like a kid who'd been given a treat.

"How many pets do you plan to acquire while we're here?" Reever asked me.

"Don't look so peeved." I patted his cheek. "Just be glad I'm not a rodent lover."

"Why did you leave me last night?"

I went over to the table and started cleaning up the mess I'd made from treating Juliet. It was the only way to keep Reever from seeing the guilt on my face. "No reason. I couldn't sleep."

"What did he do to you?"

My hands stilled. "He talked to me. I told him about the Jorenians. That's all."

"Is it?"

I tried to think of a way to reassure him. Then I turned, and saw Reever was gone.

Juliet gradually healed, but she never completely lost her scraggly appearance. Jenner didn't care. He fell, and fell hard. Wherever she went, he followed. And wherever they went, Kegide wasn't far behind. I often found the three of them playing a game of chase-the-suture-silk in the tunnel outside Medical. Once Juliet was back to her old self, she and her two boyfriends began going out regularly and hunting rats in the tunnels.

How did I know that? From the pile of fresh kills laid at the door of our hogan every morning.

The Night Horse women were impressed by the contributions Juliet and Jenner brought for the cooking pot, and praised both animals frequently. They graciously ignored the fact that Kegide constantly stole from their stores to feed his small companions.

Reever and I never discussed what had happened

that night after the wedding ceremony. I tried a few times to talk to him about it, but he always changed the subject. By unspoken agreement we never brought it up again. He became distant, and it started eating at me, like a wound that wouldn't heal.

I kept hearing rumors of men searching the surface regions above the tunnels. Hok informed me they'd even inspected the Night Horse village, looking for us.

Joseph wasn't giving up. I suspected he never would.

Kegide showed up one morning after I'd treated Spotted Dog (now called Handsome Runner) with his weekly allergen suppressant, and gestured for me to come with him and the cats. Puzzled, I grabbed the impromptu medical case I'd thrown together, and followed him into one of the outlet tunnels.

I stopped just short of the proximity beacon. I liked Kegide, but there was no way I was getting a bunch of spikes punched through me for him. "Kegide, we can't go any farther here."

Kegide did something on the wall, and the lights winked out. Then he showed me it was safe by walking through the trip sensor. With a sigh, I trailed after him.

The tunnel he took me into from there was part of the old sewer system Rico had originally brought us through. I recognized it from the smell.

I suppressed my excitement and trudged along, pretending to be miffed, and memorized our path. Was he taking me to the subway? Another access hatch to the surface? Why?

We didn't go to the subway or the surface. Instead, we entered a cross-section that had once held some kind of equipment, long ago rusted away. Salvaged panels and other junk had been used to make a small, dilapidated shack. I smelled a fire, and heard someone coughing inside it.

"Hello?"

Kegide stuck his head inside the shack, then stepped

back as an emaciated figure trudged out. The man was one of the Night Horse hybrids, judging by his coloring and dress, but he looked awful.

"What do you want, whiteskin?" he asked me.

"I'm a patcher. Are you ill? Do you need help?"

He just shook his head and went back in the shack. The salvaged panel that served as a door slammed shut.

"Okay." I turned to Kegide. "Now what do I do?"

Kegide gave me a beseeching look and gestured for me to go inside.

"He didn't exactly put out a welcome mat," I said, then sighed as Kegide kept waving his big hands at the shack. "Yes, I'll go in. But you're coming with me." I tightened my grip on my bag and went in.

CHAPTER NINE

Many Mistakes

It was hard to see at first, what with the smoke and the gloom. When my eyes adjusted, I saw the sick man and a dozen more hybrids lying on the floor of the shack, curled up on filthy sleeping mats. They were all asleep or unconscious, and from the condition of their bodies, they hadn't been interested in or capable of keeping up with their personal hygiene. A shallow hole dug in one corner of the shack had been used as a cesspit. The stench from that alone made my eyes water.

"How long have they been like this?" I asked Kegide, before I remembered he couldn't answer me. I walked around and performed a brief visual exam of each of the shack's occupants.

Some of the hybrids were coughing, others were in a sludgy, semicomatose state. Once I'd made sure they were all still alive, I knelt beside the man who had come out of the shack.

His hair had fallen out in patches and his skin looked almost gray in tone. Both eyelids and the lymph nodes under his jaw were swollen. Thick, gray patches of tissue surrounded his mouth. Two open chancre sores glistened, raw and red, on his lips. The other exposed areas of his body were covered with a crop of pale red rash spots.

Whatever he had, it was potentially contagious. "Kegide, go outside."

I scanned my patient, and found an odd, spiral-shaped bacterium rampant in his bloodstream. I didn't recognize it, but a weird sense of déjà vu came over me.

Where have I seen this bug before?

The scanner was unable to identify the spirochete as well, which was really bad.

I went to the door of the shack and stuck my head out. The Man Mountain was sitting a few feet away playing with some stones. "Kegide. Don't go anywhere."

He nodded.

I went back to my patient, who opened his eyes and said something nasty.

"I'm here to help," I said, hoping I could. "Tell me what's happened to you and the others here. How long have you been like this?"

"Weeks. Maybe months."

"And the others?"

"The same. It is why we're here."

Not good. "How is the sickness affecting you?"

"I have aches in my head and my bones all the time. I'm tired, but I can't sleep or eat much. Fever gets bad at night."

I looked at the other hybrids, spotted more hair loss and open sores. "Do they have the same symptoms?"

"Yeah." The man rolled over and covered his face with one arm. "Now go away."

I took the opportunity to extract a blood sample instead, and left the shack to analyze it with my scanner. Being away from the smell cleared my head, and I took several slow, deep breaths as I watched the results of the analysis scroll onto the scanner's display.

"Barbiturates?" That made absolutely no sense.

The amount of barbiturate in his bloodstream was almost as potentially fatal as the infection he was suffering from. "How did he get hold of drugs like that?"

Kegide stopped rolling the pebbles he was playing with and looked at me, bewildered.

"Did Wendell see these people?" I asked him.

Kegide nodded.

"That stupid, negligent, homicidal maniac—I'm going to strangle him." I marched back inside and crouched down beside my patient. "Who gave you the drugs? Was it Wendell Florine? Was it the whiteskin patcher?"

The man rolled back over, and looked at me for a moment. Then the swollen lids closed over the filmy black eyes. "Go away."

I didn't go away. I scanned and examined every occupant of the shack. The strange spirochete was present in all their bloodstreams. Most were in various stages of barbiturate poisoning as well.

A search of the shack turned up an ample supply of the drug they had been taking, hidden in a pouch tucked under one of the sleeping mats. I took the old-fashioned oral concentrates with me when I finished my rounds. A few of the hybrids noticed and protested, but no one was strong enough to stop me.

Outside, Kegide slowly rose to his feet and gave me a hopeful look.

"I'm going to need to go back to Medical, then return here. Right now."

The big man silently guided me back through the tunnel system to the alcove. I walked in to find Reever sitting on the exam table, one of my scanners in his hand.

"What do you think you're doing?" I took the scanner away from him and checked the display. He'd keyed it for a kidney sweep. "Checking up on my work?"

"No." He watched as I went over to the scope and put one of the blood samples I'd taken into the analyzer. "Where have you been?"

"Looking at some new patients." I peered in the scope at the spirochete. If it had progressed to the bloodstream and lymphatic system, there was little hope of localized treatment. "Very sick patients. Kegide took me to them. They're suffering from some kind of bacterial infection, complicated by barbiturate addiction."

Again I had the feeling I'd viewed the nasty little spirochete before, but when? Where?

Judging from the location of the chancres, the bacterium had likely entered the body through the mucous membranes, or through the skin. That meant close body contact or body fluid exchanges.

Yet without a diagnostic array, there was literally no way for me to identify the anonymous spirochete. And until I knew what was causing the disease, I couldn't prescribe treatment.

"All I need is a medical database. One lousy diagnostic unit. This is so *frustrating*."

"My sentiments exactly."

I turned around to see Wendell lounging beside Reever on the exam table. "Kegide took me out into the sewer pipes to see some very sick people. Have you seen them?"

"In the sewer?" Wendell pursed his lips and looked thoughtful, then shook his head. "Can't say that I have."

He was lying. I could feel it. "Well, you can come with me when I go back. There are about a dozen of them, and they've been infected by a bacterial pathogen. I'll need help nailing down what they've got."

"The great Dr. Grey Veil needs *my* help? Never thought I'd see the day." Wendell gave me an insulting grin. "Well, Doctor, if they're infected, that means they're contagious. I'm not going near that shack."

I put aside the second slide I was preparing and walked over to him. "I didn't say anything about a shack."

Wendell blinked, then recovered quickly. "I'm sure that's all they could scrape together out there—"

Reever put a hand on Wendell's arm. "A small piece of advice. Don't lie to her. She dislikes it intensely."

I folded my arms. "Well?"

Wendell shoved his hands in his tunic pockets and shuffled his feet. "Okay, so I've seen them. I don't know what it is. There's nothing you can do for them but leave them alone."

"Ah, but I have to, Wendell," I said, very softly. "I took an oath."

"I didn't." He pushed off the table and tried to walk out.

A cold knot formed in my stomach as I blocked his path. "You've done more than see them, haven't you? You tried to treat them."

He flung out his arms. "So what if I did? I'm the only person down here who can do anything. You know what they do when someone gets sick? They *sing.* That's their idea of treatment."

"While yours was, what? Giving them a little something for the pain?" I didn't wait for him to answer me. I already knew. "What were you thinking, you moron?"

"I did what I could."

"You gave them these." I threw the pouch of barbiturates at him. Pills pelted his face, chest, and scattered all over the stone floor. "Sedatives. For a bacterial infection!"

"I didn't know what it was!" he shouted back. "I've never seen anything like it!"

"Yeah? Guess what? You not only didn't help them, you turned them into drug addicts!"

"Cherijo. Dr. Florine."

I whirled on Reever. "Don't you dare call this quack a doctor!" Then I started back in on Wendell. "I can't believe you didn't run a blood analysis. A simple blood analysis, Wendell. Go look in the scope— there are so many spirochetes on that slide they're practically crawling up the magnifier!"

"I thought it was cholera."

I had a handful of his tunic in my fist before he could blink. "And you'd treat cholera with barbiturates? They shouldn't have kicked you out of medtech, they should have thrown you in prison!"

"Calm down, Cherijo." Playing the peacemaker, Reever stepped between us and made me let go of Wendell. "This is not going to solve the problem. Both of you must set aside your differences if you're going to save these people."

"Here's an idea—keep him away from anything that breathes," I suggested. "That should up the survival rate considerably."

"Okay, so I didn't know what to do. You think you're so perfect." Wendell sneered at me. "If you're such a magnificent cutter, then why is everyone topside hunting for you? How many patients have *you* killed?"

"Cherijo." My husband started looking a little worried. "Don't."

"Reever, get out of my face." When he did, I got in Wendell's. "You pathetic excuse for a floor sweeper. Don't you try to shrug this one off the way you did back in school. Those people are barbiturate dependent now. *You* did that to them. On top of the goddamned pathogen!"

"I'm not going to take any more of this waste from you, you sanctimonious little bitch."

Wendell walked out, and when I would have gone after him, Reever stopped me.

"Let me go."

"Hitting him will solve nothing."

I scowled. "It would make me feel better."

"If you're feeling that aggressive, why don't you take it out on me?"

"You haven't committed malpractice." I glared at him. "Oh, come on, Duncan. You can't possibly be on his side."

"You might have found out more information about the infected hybrids if you hadn't attacked his competency."

"He has zero competency." I went back to the analyzer. "And the day I need help from that jerk, I'm calling it quits."

Hok showed up a short time later, and I vented my spleen on him. Or tried to. He stood silent and impassive as I ranted about the contagion and Wendell's gross negligence. Then he refused to get me my diagnostic equipment.

"What?" I stopped packing my case and turned on him. "Are you out of your mind? Those people are suffering. They need treatment, *now*."

"It is not a decision I can make. You must get permission from the chief first."

"Stuff the chief. I want that equipment."

"I will take you to him and see if he will grant your request. That is all I can do."

I made Reever, who was not my favorite person at the moment, stay in the alcove while I went to deal with Rico. Along the way, my temper subsided, and I noticed once more how badly Hok hobbled.

"What caused your physical problems? Are they congenital birth defects?"

He gave me a twisted smile. "I don't know."

I speculated. It could have been Treacher-Collins or

Pierre Robin syndrome; he had some of the clinical signs. In addition to the clumsy repair of the cleft palate, he had the abnormal jaw and facial distortions.

"It looks like someone tried to do soft-tissue and osteomic transfers to build up your nose." Whoever had done it had given him separate but uneven nostrils, and they didn't work. "You have to breathe through your mouth, right?"

"Yes."

"Choanal atresia, then. You don't have eyelashes or eyebrows, and your ears have some of the macrostomia associated with the defect." I was starting to get angry again. "Whoever worked on you should be shot, Hok."

"Hawk."

"Excuse me?"

"My name is Hawk, not Hok." He clearly enunciated the difference for me.

"Oh. Sorry." I studied his face again. "Who did the work?"

"A doctor on the reservation did the first operation, when I was a baby. Wendell gave me my nose."

Dr. Disaster strikes again. He was lucky it wasn't on the side of his head. "Do yourself a favor, Hawk. Stay *away* from Wendell."

"I have no complaints about what he did. Children no longer run away screaming when they see my face now." He gave me a twisted smile. "Most of the time."

"I could help, if you'll let me."

He shook his head. "Thank you, but I'm content with how I look."

"That's fine for your face, but what about your back? The scoliosis distorting your spine is only going to get worse. You could suffer partial paralysis as a result."

"I will manage."

We entered the central cavern. Rico was nowhere

in sight, but Hawk sent one of the women to summon him. We sat down by the speaking rock, and I absently made us both a server of tea.

"Ahe'ee zer ch'il gohwéhé," he said.

"Which means?"

"Thank you for the tea."

"You're welcome. Tell me something. How did Rico convince all these people to live underground? I thought Indians liked the wide, open spaces."

"We do." His stark, beautiful voice was amused. "But those who came here were not permitted to enjoy them. The clans living among the Four Mountains rejected or exiled all of us. Rico came to our hogans and spoke to us about forming a new tribe."

"And that's it? You guys just went with him?"

"You do not know the chief well. The Navajo call him *Nohoilpi*—He Who Wins Men, the Divine Gambler. He offered protection to the hybrids who were facing deportation, and their human families. He challenged us to build a place for ourselves, hidden in the earth, as told in the old legends of the Leyaneyani, brother of Whirlwind and Knife Boy. We came here, made this place, became the Night Horse."

The Divine Gambler? Knife Boy? Was he kidding?

"So basically you all moved into a cave because of some old story Rico told you?" He nodded. "Didn't any of the hybrids ever consider immigrating to their alien parents' homeworlds instead? And why are you here? You're not one of them."

"You whiteskins ask so many questions."

"You Indians do some really weird stuff."

"We remind you of who you are, beneath the skin."

"I'm not one of you." I took a sip of my tea, which was getting cold. "I don't belong here. You know that."

"I know you are here now."

"Not by choice. You know that's wrong. You could help me and Reever a great deal just by getting us out of here." I thought of Joseph, and tried a not-so-subtle threat. "Those men who searched the village—they'll be back. Eventually they'll find a way down here. They'll notify the authorities about you. Help us, and you'll be protecting your tribe."

"No." He got awkwardly to his feet. "I do not betray my chief."

"Glad I am to hear it, my friend," Rico said from behind us, making me spill lukewarm tea down the front of my tunic. "Doctor. You wished to speak to me?"

Hawk limped away. Everyone else in the cavern found something else to do or look at. That left me to handle the chief.

"Yes, I do. You have a real problem that needs taking care of, right away."

Rico crouched beside me and offered me a colorful square of linen. "Tell me about this . . . problem I have."

After I mopped up the tea with that, I related how I'd found the hybrids in the outer sewer system, and what I'd discovered from examining them. I explained what a spirochete was, how it was responsible for the symptoms, and presented my request for a diagnostic unit in order to find a cure. I used simple, nonclinical terms as much as possible.

He listened at first, but by the time I got to the part about the equipment I needed, I had the feeling he'd lost interest.

I speeded up my delivery. "The bottom line here is, I have to identify this bacteria first, then I can treat the infected patients. I'll have to check the other members of your tribe, and temporarily isolate anyone who tests positive for the spirochete. We can have it under control immediately, and hopefully once we find out what it is, and how to treat it, have it completely cleared up in a few weeks."

Rico, who had been watching Hawk hobbling on

the other side of the cave, picked up a small stone and tossed it into the fire. "No."

I wasn't sure what part of that he was objecting to. "I beg your pardon?"

"No, you will not get the equipment, treat the infected, test the tribe, or isolate anyone."

"Maybe I didn't explain this right. The hybrids living in the sewer system are very sick. The sickness they have is highly contagious. I'm positive there are others here who—"

"You do not have to repeat your words, patcher. I heard and understood every one of them."

"Then what's your objection?"

"It is simple." Rico stood up. I did, too. "The outcasts you examined are unclean and worthless to me. They are cursed."

"But—but—" I shook my head, trying to process this bizarre reaction. "Chief, you don't understand. They're not unclean or cursed, they're sick. They need medicine. They may have infected other members of the tribe, who aren't showing signs of sickness yet."

"They will perish. If any more of the Night Horse become cursed, they will be cast out and perish, too."

"You can't do that," I said, getting angry. "It's not their fault. You can't simply ignore them."

"That is our way," he said.

"Your way? Your *way*?" My voice climbed several octaves. "Is it your way to allow innocent people to die from a preventable illness? Or is that why you had Wendell keep them drugged? So they wouldn't bother you? So you don't have to look at them?"

Rico's attention wandered away from me, and fixed on someone entering the cavern. "Wendell. Join us."

Wendell came over, looking a little nervous. "Chief. Doctor."

"Dr. Torin tells me she's been taken among the unclean. She tells me you gave them drugs."

Wendell blanched. "It was only to keep them quiet, Chief."

"You're a real humanitarian, Wendell." I was mad, but something was starting to worry me. Something was wrong. Wendell had gone completely white. And Rico, Rico was radiating something very peculiar. He should have been angry, but he wasn't. He was happy. At least, something like happiness.

"Wendell makes many mistakes, Doctor." Rico stepped forward, and tapped his hand against Wendell's cheek. "Many, many mistakes. Like bartering with the unclean."

I felt sick. "You *sold* them the drugs?"

"Chief." Now Wendell sounded desperate. He even got on his knees. "I only took a few things. They didn't need all that silver anymore."

"What are you planning to do with it, Wendell?" Rico asked.

"Let me go topside. I can get a good price for the stuff, start over somewhere else." He held up his hands in entreaty. "I won't tell anyone about this place. I swear."

I got disgusted at once. "You deliberately addicted those people to barbiturates, just so you could get out of here?"

"They needed it for the pain. There was nothing else I could do for them anyway." He gave me a filthy look. "You'd do the same thing, if you had the chance. You want out of here as much as I do." He turned back to the chief. "I have to get out of here. I can't stand it anymore."

"I will let you go, Wendell," Rico said in a gentle, reassuring way. Then he grabbed Wendell by the hair, and before I could stop him, whipped out a knife and cut his throat.

The blood hit me first.

"No!" I caught Wendell as he fell, and jammed my hands around the throat wound, applying direct pressure. More blood from the jugular and the carotid arteries sprayed directly in my face. I looked desperately at Rico. "Help me!"

The chief reached down, wiped the blood from his knife onto the sleeve of Wendell's tunic, then straightened.

I kept yelling. No one came to help me. I tried to lift Wendell myself, but slipped in the blood. By then it was everywhere. I tried to drag him, until I saw Rico still standing there, watching my futile efforts.

"Help me get him to Medical. There's time. I can save him."

"No."

Rico leaned over then and did something that I would have nightmares about for weeks after. He licked some of the blood from my cheek.

As Wendell's life drained out between my fingers, the chief of the Night Horse smiled at me, and then simply walked away.

I managed to drag Wendell toward the nearest hogan, but whoever was inside quickly shut the door covering. I yelled for help, for anyone to help me. Every door I could see was closed. Everyone had disappeared inside the hogans, and they weren't coming out.

Why wouldn't anyone help me?

I changed direction and dragged Wendell toward the tunnels. I kept shouting until I was hoarse. No one came out. He was too heavy for me to pick up, but I tried that a couple of times, too.

Wendell went into full cardiac arrest near the entrance to the tunnels, staring up at me, his face filled with horror and disbelief. When I heard that last, choked breath leave his lungs, I dropped his arms, knelt beside him, and performed CPR. When that failed to bring him back, I just sat there with him.

I don't know how much time passed. All I could

seem to do was sit there on the cold stone floor and look at him. Bleeding to death made him look whiter than ever.

"Cherijo."

Reever was there, lifting me up, wiping my face with something. I looked at him, but I didn't really focus on his face. All I could see was Wendell, lying there, dead.

Hands were running over me. "Did he hurt you? Are you cut anywhere?"

I focused on my husband's face. I guess all the blood made it hard to tell. "No. It's his. I'm . . . I'm fine."

Reever knelt and checked Wendell's pulse. I'd taught him that. With a little work, my husband might make a decent medic one day. If he ever got over being so squeamish.

"He's dead."

I looked down. "Yeah. He's dead."

"Did you do this to him?"

That got to me, when nothing else would have. Still, I felt frozen and disconnected as I returned the favor. "Do you think I could have slit his throat?"

"No. Who did it?"

I saw Rico's smile, heard the soft pleasure in his voice, and then the terrible slash of the knife.

"Rico." I started to shake, and wrapped my arms around myself. "Right here. Right in front of me. One stroke, severed both arteries. Then he"—I swallowed bile—"then he licked some of Wendell's blood off my face."

Reever pulled me up against him and started rubbing his hands up and down my back. "It's all right, beloved."

"I couldn't carry him. I tried to. The blood made my hands slippery and he was too heavy. I yelled for help, but no one came. No one would help me. I had to drag him. He was too heavy. He stopped breathing." I lifted my eyes to look into his. "I tried, Reever, but I couldn't save him. Why did he do it? Why wouldn't anyone help me save him? Why did they leave us alone like that?"

"You did what you could." He guided me away from the body. "Come with me now."

A woman stepped out of the tunnels—the young, beautiful woman who had been hanging all over Rico before. She didn't look very pretty now, not with that smirk on her face.

The girlfriend came toward me. "You need to wash, patcher. You stink of whiteskin."

"Move out of the way," Reever said.

"You know who I am, whiteskin?" She turned her smirk on Reever. "I'm Ilona Red Faun. I belong to Rico."

The girlfriend was jealous.

"Congratulations," Reever said. "Move out of the way."

She hit me in the chest instead. "You stay away from Rico, patcher. He's mine. He wants to put his mouth on a woman, he comes to me. Only me."

As I rubbed the sore spot on my sternum, I stared at her, unable to make sense of what she was doing. She was upset? About *that*? "I'll be sure to send him to you the next time he wants to lick body fluids off someone's face."

Reever got me around her and took me back to Medical. There he helped me wash my face and hair. I pulled off my bloodstained tunic and threw it to the floor. The shock faded, and became something else.

"Where's the suture laser?" I looked around.

"There are at least a hundred people around him. You'd be dead before you could activate it."

I took a couple of deep breaths. "He cut Wendell's throat for nothing. *Nothing*."

He held me by the arms and made me look at him. "Killing Rico won't change that."

"Reever, we've got to—" I saw someone walk past the alcove and blinked. "And now I'm hallucinating."

I pulled out of his grip and hurried out into the tunnel. No sign of anyone, either direction. But I couldn't have been mistaken. Not about him.

"What is it?"

"I just saw a ghost," I said, and leaned back against the wall. I closed my eyes for a moment, hoping it had been some crazy figment of my imagination. "I saw Dhreen."

"Cherijo."

Reever sounded odd. I opened my eyes, and saw him starting to slide to the floor. "Oh God, no."

Judging by the levels of phosphates, urea, and creatinine in Reever's bloodstream, his kidney had begun to fail. I had no choice but to put him on the jury-rigged dialysis array to keep him alive.

I'd already surgically prepped an arteriovenous fistula, the artificial junction between an artery and vein in his right leg, to facilitate removing and returning his blood supply.

I would never admit it to Reever, but I was almost glad this had happened. If it hadn't, I don't know how else I would have dealt with witnessing Wendell's murder.

"Get comfortable, you're going to be doing this three times a week until we find you a new kidney. You're also going on a new diet. No more splurging on the sodium and potassium, got it?"

As I hooked him up to the machine, I explained how the rig's dialyzer filtered the toxic substances out of his blood.

He watched his blood flow through the tubing into the rig. "How long will this work?"

"Forever." I smiled down at him. "Okay, not forever. But long enough. All I have to do is find a donor organ that matches your tissue type."

"That will be difficult, given our present circumstances."

"I'd give you one of mine, if I could." I thought of Kao—I couldn't help it—and blinked hard. "I wouldn't recommend it, though."

"How are you feeling?" he asked me.

Why lie? "Scared."

"Can you tell me what happened with Rico, before he murdered Wendell?"

I told him everything, including my part in seeing that Wendell got killed by telling the chief about the drugs.

He thought it over for a while. I kept busy by making unnecessary adjustments on the rig. "It's not your fault, Cherijo."

"I know." Or I should have known. "But why would Rico pretend these people are cursed?"

"It may not be a pretense. Such superstitions are common among primitive cultures. Many Terran races believed sickness resulted from divine malediction."

"These are modern Terrans who have chosen to live this way. When they belonged to the Four Mountains tribe, they were regularly examined and treated by state-funded physicians. That's the law, even on the reservation. They know better."

"Perhaps they have chosen to forget."

"It doesn't matter. I'll find a way to treat them. I have to go back—they'll be suffering from barbiturate withdrawal."

"You can't go alone."

"I'll take Kegide with me." Before he could argue, I held up one hand. "Don't give me a hard time about it. You need to stay here. Besides, it's not like he's going to say anything to Rico."

By the time I tracked down Kegide and made him understand what I wanted to do, I had to stop back at the alcove and take Reever off the rig. Who immediately insisted on going with us.

"This isn't going to be pleasant," I told him. "You're still weak and tired."

"I feel better." He picked up the Lok-Teel and propped it on his shoulder. "I'm coming with you."

Kegide led us back to the exiles' hogan. I could hear the groans and cries from a hundred yards away, and took out a syrinpress.

"I'm going to infuse them with mild opiate to help with the withdrawal symptoms, then I'll do the penicillin screens. They're going to have a hard time of it for the next couple days." And I still didn't know if the penicillin would do anything to rid them of the infection.

I went inside the hogan, and saw most of my patients were considerably more animated now. Feverish, covered in sweat, and experiencing delirium tremors.

Reever put down the Lok-Teel, who went right to work cleaning up the mess.

I handed Reever and Kegide the gloves and masks I'd brought. "I need you to help me hold them down."

It was an unpleasant business. Some of the hybrids spit and snarled, and tried to attack us. They were too weak to do much more than make noise. Others wept and pleaded for the drug they believed kept them from suffering.

"Your body has become dependent on it. It isn't helping you anymore," I tried to explain to one, fairly lucid young woman. "You'd have to keep taking more and more of it to keep the pain from coming back. In the end, it would kill you."

She clawed at me, suddenly furious. "Then let me die!"

Out of the fourteen patients I examined, only one showed a mild dermal reaction to the penicillin screen. If I could find a way to culture the spirochete and see how it reacted to penicillin, then I could possibly use it to treat them. After I took more blood samples, we gave them bed baths and made them as comfortable as possible.

I checked all three of us to make sure we hadn't been infected with the spirochete before sending Kegide back for food. He returned with a large pot of stew and a jug of water, but no one wanted to eat or drink.

"Try." I spooned some of the stew into one young man's mouth. "You need to eat something."

"We are cursed by the gods," he said, knocking my hand away. "Leave us alone to die."

"The curse thing again." I stood up and addressed all of my new patients. "Listen up. I know you've been told you were cursed. That's superstitious nonsense. You've been infected with a disease that comes from bacteria."

"What kind of disease?" he demanded.

I had no choice but to admit, "I don't know yet."

Someone screamed with weak fury. "You are torturing us!"

"Okay, I'm torturing you. Good reason to rest, and get better, right? Then you can come after me for doing this to you."

I collected my supplies and told them I'd be back to check on them as soon as I could. We left, followed by the sound of more shrieks and curses.

"It's so nice to be appreciated for your work." I ran a tired hand over the back of my neck.

Reever was holding the Lok-Teel, who appeared to be gorged. "How long will it take until they recover?"

"Physically—a couple of days. Psychologically the addiction and the belief in the curse have done a lot of damage. It'll take longer to fix that." I looked at my Man Mountain. "Kegide, I need to come here again. Can you bring me back tomorrow?"

The big man shook his head.

"Rico will be suspicious if you disappear too often."

Reever glanced back at the hogan. "When you come here, I want to be with you."

"You're not a doctor." I wished I could get Hawk to come with me, but I suspected he'd not only refuse, but he'd also tell Rico about it. Then someone else's throat might get slit. Like mine.

We went back through a different tunnel, and I noticed a large recessed area filled with books. It must have been the vault Wendell had told me about, the one filled with books—

I halted. "The books. That's it." Kegide motioned for me to keep walking. "I know, I'm coming."

I quickened my pace and we made it back to Medical in record time. I went immediately to the box of books I'd been reading and started digging through the volumes.

"Bacterial Metabolism Studies. Epidemiology in North America. Synthetic and Natural Antibodies." I took a few more out and set them all to one side. "It had to be in one of these."

I carried the pile of books over to the exam table. They were charming to look at, but heavy. Then I grabbed the first one and skimmed through the pages.

Reever peered down at it. "Wendell's books?"

"Uh-huh." I tucked a piece of loose hair behind my ear and flipped through most of the first chapter. "I knew I'd seen that bug somewhere before. It was in one of these. I'm sure of it."

It took about three hours to find the photographic illustration of the spirochete. Unfortunately the wood-pulp page was crumbling, and it was impossible to make out the name of the bacteria in the caption or the text. Nor did the photograph exactly match the bacteria I was seeing in the outcasts' blood samples.

"Not identical, but close. They have to be related."

I read what was left of the page, which detailed the antiquated methods of dealing with outbreaks of sexually transmitted diseases. Latex prophylactics. Irregular blood screens. Even abstinence was recommended as an effective method of control.

"Abstinence?" I snorted. "No wonder someone invented cascade innoculants."

Despite that rather criminal naivete, the doctors had been intelligent enough to realize that STDs were passed through body fluid exchanges. My patients had been both male and female. It was reasonable to assume my spirochete had been transmitted the same way.

I flipped through another half dozen pages, until I found the description of the tests performed to identify the various kinds of STDs. One of them, the rapid plasma reagin series, remained in use by a few remote clinics who couldn't support a regular laboratory array. I'd seen it done in a village in Asia once.

Working off the hope that the test could prove helpful, I ran the RPR series on the blood sample. Results returned a host of antibodies responding to the bacterial invasion. These particular antibodies were ones I *did* recognize.

"Mother of All Houses." I stepped back from the scope.

"What is it?"

"It can't be." I ran a fluorescent treponemal antibody absorption test anyway. It confirmed the RPR's positive screening.

I went over to the unoccupied treatment table and sat down on the edge, trying to understand what I'd just determined. I knew exactly what the spirochete was now. Any first-year medtech student who'd paid attention during their history classes would have recognized it.

At the tame time, it wasn't possible. It couldn't exist.

"Cherijo?" All this time, Reever had been sitting quietly off in the corner, watching me. "Did you find something?"

"Yeah. I found treponema pallidum." I looked at Reever, then shook my head. "It's right over there, under the scope. I don't believe it, but it's there."

Reever went over to the scope to have a look. "Treponema pallidum is the name of this disease?"

"It's the name of a bacterium that caused a disease. One that was eradicated from Terra during the twenty-second century." When he glanced my way, I gestured at the scope. "What you're looking at, Reever, doesn't exist." And, with the slight change in its appearance, may have mutated.

"It seems very active for a nonexistent micro-organism."

I went to the med supply containers and checked my stores. I had enough penicillin to deal with the outbreak, as long as it was confined to those dozen hybrids. I'd need to get my hands on doxycycline or tetracycline now; it was possible some of the patients would have stronger allergic reactions to the treatment, which would take about two weeks. As long as the mutation didn't mean the bacterium was antibiotic resistant.

"How contagious is it?"

"Remember the Core?"

He lifted his head from the magnifier. "That bad."

"Almost."

I recalled what I knew about the archaic disease. The symptoms differed from one person to the next; the bacteria often created "carriers" who showed little sign of the infection, but were highly contagious. Others would come down with severe symptoms almost at once. If the outcasts had been infected and active with any other member of the tribe before being exiled to that shack, this bug would spread like wildfire.

"I have to find a way to run tests on everyone in the tribe."

Reever sat down beside me. "This infection—is it terminal? Will you need a quarantine?"

"No, it isn't fatal, as long as we catch it in the primary and secondary stages. As for a quarantine"—I laughed once—"the only way I can do that is to keep everyone from having sex, which, given Rico's attitude and the tribe's superstitions, is also highly unlikely."

He picked up the book I'd been reading. "Urethritis. AIDS. Gonorrhoea. Herpes Simplex. What are they?"

"STDs. See there"—I pointed to a section in the text—"they used to call them 'venereal diseases.' "

"Which one of these does treponema pallidum cause?"

"Syphilis."

Chapter Ten

Desperate Bargain

My worries about mutation proved to be unjustified. Most of the hybrids showed an immediate response to penicillin therapy, and after fourteen days, the outcasts' blood tested negative for syphilis on the RPR. That left only the drug addiction to deal with.

Wendell, I learned, had been selling them barbiturates for weeks. The mild opiate I gave them only took the edge off the worst of the withdrawal symptoms. Gradually they stopped having the tremors and night sweats, but the psychological dependency was still presenting a problem.

Reever came in very handy in that department.

He accompanied me on all my surreptitious visits to the sewer shack, and started talking with the patients waiting for me to examine them. He used their native language, and at first I was too busy to adjust my wristcom to pick up whatever it was he said. Most of his conversations remained one-sided; the hybrids were good at ignoring people they didn't like.

Slowly, some of the outcasts started responding to Reever. First they swore at him. Then they pleaded.

Slowly, they talked, and finally, they listened.

By the beginning of the third week, the hybrids began

gathering in a circle with Reever as soon as we arrived. I walked around scanning them from behind while he talked. He used a lot of hand gestures, and sometimes spoke without stopping for a good hour.

One day he made everyone laugh. That was when I adjusted my wristcom and started listening in.

He was telling them all about our adventures. Stories that came from our captivity on Catopsa, the systems we had traveled through on the *Sunlace,* and the devastating plague on K-2.

I liked listening to Reever. I never realized how differently he had experienced everything, until he described the first time we met.

"I had finished my work translating for the morning's new arrivals, and went to the Training Center to see an old friend. Ana Hansen, a woman I respect and worked with, came to see my friend as well. With Ana was this very small Terran. If it had not been for the physician's tunic she wore, I would have thought her a child. I could not stop looking at her."

One of the outcasts eyed me skeptically. "Because of her beauty, *Nilch'i'*?"

"No, only because she was the smallest Terran I had ever seen."

Everyone looked at me then, and a couple of the women giggled.

I sniffed. "I'm not *that* small."

"As she walked by me, I felt an immediate connection to her. As if she were a telepath, like me, reaching out to me. Then a vision came to me. A vision that would come true."

Visions were very important to Native Americans, and the Night Horse outcasts proved no different. They leaned forward and made gestures with their hands for him to continue the story, eager to hear all about Reever's vision.

I remembered that. Reever, standing beneath a gnorra tree, surrounded by white light. Holding a woman's wrists in his hands, in front of his face. Although I hadn't realized it at the time, they were my own wrists. . . .

"Ana introduced her to my old friend. Their meeting was not congenial."

That was an understatement. Lisette Dubois had been six feet tall, blond, beautiful—and completely hostile. "It wasn't my fault she didn't like me."

Reever glanced at me. "Lisette was always self-conscious about her height. Small, feminine women intimidated her."

"Feminine? *Me*?"

"I realized I had better defuse the situation, so I interrupted the meeting."

"You asked Ana if the Council had instituted a Health Board," I said.

"It was a joke."

"You have a terrible sense of humor. No one ever gets it."

He went back to his story. "Ana introduced us, and told me that Cherijo was a newly transferred physician. Lisette wanted me to leave, but I thought I had better find out more about this strange Terran woman."

I snorted. "You asked me when I planned to leave, if I remember correctly. You also asked if I was Asian, and said a couple other rude things."

"No more than you did. You acted very secretive." To the outcasts, he said, "She considers her maternal ancestry to be of little value."

Everyone gave me a condemning look. The Night Horse, like the Navajo, were a matriarchal society.

"Hey, I didn't know, okay?" I gestured toward my husband. "Then he said on some planet in a system two light-years away from that one, I'd be ritually sacrificed for having blue eyes."

"Is this true, Reever?"

"Quite true. I meant it as a warning—to remind her that she was a stranger on an alien world."

"He's so helpful that way," I said.

"Before I left the Trading Center, I looked back at her. That was when I had my second vision."

I perked up at that. "What second vision?"

He reached over and traced the line of silver in my hair. "Of watching you, with this streak in your hair, and our child in your arms."

"Nice." Boy, that one hurt. "I hate to break this up, but story time is over. We'd better get back before we're missed."

The men clamored for more. Then one of the women touched my stomach.

"Changing Woman brought forth the People from her own body. Yours will be a very special child, loved by all, sought by many."

I didn't say a word; I just nodded and walked out.

We weren't as lucky as we had been in the past, for Milass was waiting at the alcove with a couple of the hybrid players I'd worked on.

"Where have you been, woman?" He pushed me into a wall. "These men are hurt and in need."

Reever rolled in front of me before I could stop him, and shoved Milass back. "Keep your hands off her."

Milass jerked a blade from his belt. "You should have killed me when you had the chance, whiteskin."

"No!" I grabbed Reever's arm, but he shook me off. "You can't fight him. Not in your condition."

"I will not *fight* him." Reever made it sound like he intended a lot worse.

"Come then, what do you wait for? Your woman's permission?"

I noticed the players watching both men. "Stop him, Or I won't lift a finger to help any of you again."

"*Secondario.*" One of them was brave enough to step forward. "We are needed in the arena."

The little twerp ignored him. "She will do as she's told."

That's when Hawk limped into the middle of things. "Milass. There is no need for violence. He protects his woman. It is the way. Let her treat the players' wounds now."

For a tense couple of seconds, nobody moved. Then Milass sheathed his knife. Reever didn't back down, but he didn't lunge, either. The chief's *secondario* said something really vile and stalked off.

I heaved a sigh of relief. "I'm starting to like this way thing." When Hawk would have kept going down the tunnel, I blocked his path. "Oh, no you don't. I'll need a hand with this."

Both of the hybrids had just returned from a shock-ball match; both were sporting multiple contusions, minor stress fractures in their forearms and calves, and localized thrombosis. I didn't figure out why until I saw the burns on their hands and feet.

"You guys got a couple of penalties, right?" One of them nodded, and I swore. "Testosterone. It should be outlawed. Hawk, I need two infusers, fifty milligrams sodium bicarb, twenty-five grams mamutanol per liter, line-push."

Reever came over to watch as I finished the scans, supervised the infuser applications and showed Hawk how to start cleaning the worst of the gashes. "What do hormones have to do with these injuries?"

"You men have too many of them. Here, Duncan, you help us with these splints. Hawk, if I don't get some decent bonesetters soon, I'm going to break *your* legs."

A couple of hours later, Hawk asked if he could look over their charts as I was hooking Reever up to the dialysis rig.

"Why? Think I messed up?"

"No. I am only curious."

"Curiosity is good." I handed him the charts. "Would have been nice if you'd helped me when Rico cut Wendell's throat open."

"I cannot go against my chief." He gave me a faintly guilty look. "No matter how much I wish to."

I went over to the container and started my weekly inventory of supplies. I had to keep a close eye on the antibiotics stock. As it was, I'd used nearly a quarter of it treating the hybrids. Another thing to bug Hawk about.

"Patcher, I don't understand." He showed me one of the charts. "You put here the fractures were caused by muscle contractions. Bones cannot be broken by muscles."

"Sure, they can." I counted my syrinpresses and frowned; one was gone. "Alternating current passing through the body cycles, and with each cycle, the muscles contract. If you've got voltage higher than one kilowatt, and sufficient duration, the jolts can fracture every bone in your body. We won't even discuss distal soft-tissue ischemia, entry- and exit-point thermal injuries, spinal cord damage, rhabdomyolysis, myoglobinuria, cardiac and pulmonary arrest. Both your players were hit five or six times, and at least once with maximum jolts."

"I see." Looking even more bewildered, he went back to studying the charts.

Reever looked interested, too. "It sounds as if they were almost electrocuted."

"They almost were." I recalled Reever hadn't spent much time on Terra. "These players were all penalized during the game. The sphere they use to score points is controlled by a computer system, which monitors the plays. Whoever commits an illegal motion while in contact with it triggers the computer to register a penalty. The player then gets a nice, automatic bio-electrical shock."

"It sounds barbaric."

"Yeah, but it packs the arenas, I'm told."

"I was at the game," Hawk said suddenly. "I saw what happened to them. They knew what they were doing."

"Which makes them idiots, as well as injured," I said.

Hawk shrugged. "The Night Horse won."

Damn men and their damn stupid games. "The Night Horse are going to end up crispy little piles of ash if they keep getting that many penalties per man."

"I will so inform the chief," Hawk said, then departed without another word.

Two weeks passed without incident, during which I got a lot of work done. I continued follow-up maintenance on the hybrid players, finished the last of the antibiotic therapy with the outcasts, and even got Juliet fattened up a bit.

I also spent considerable time trying to figure out how to get out of *Leyaneyaniteh*. Kegide willingly escorted me around the outer tunnels, but he refused to disarm any other traps or proximity fields. He didn't understand any of my arguments as to why he should help me and Reever escape, so there was nothing I could do about that.

Joseph had intensified his efforts to find us, and we often heard distant, muffled sounds of glidetrucks taking off and landing on the surface. The village had been searched again, according to Hawk, and this time the inhabitants questioned at length.

I couldn't worry about Joe. My immediate problem was Reever's kidney, which had now completely shut down. The dialysis rig was proving only about eighty-percent effective, so he became more tired and weaker as the days passed. The toxic buildup in his blood was inevitable. So was the end of my patience.

"If I could just take you to an organ transplant center for a couple of hours, I could fix this." I sat down by the table where he lay quietly watching the machine finish its three-hour cycle. It was late, but I preferred to do his dialysis at night, while the tribe slept, so we wouldn't be interrupted. "A donor bank, a surgical suite, and a nurse. That's all I'd need."

"Don't get upset. You've done all you can."

I laughed, once. "Oh, sure. I'm the creation of the man who pioneered organ transplantation research in this century, and I can't . . . even— Wait a minute." I got up and looked at the vault of stone above us. "The lab. All we have to do is get on the subway and go back to the lab."

"You want to go back to The Grey Veils?"

"Yeah." To save his life, I had to do something he'd never agree to. Which meant inventing a cover plan he'd buy. "I must be brain dead, why didn't I think of it before? Joe has an entire wall of cloned organs, growing on artificial scaffolds."

"He may not have one that is a tissue match."

He'd picked up a little *too* much medical knowledge, hanging around me. "No problem. I'll just get the equipment I need and bring it back here so I can clone one for you myself."

"Do you believe the Night Horse chief or your creator will allow you to access the facility and help yourself?"

"I don't tell Rico, and we don't let Joe catch us. I can get us into the mansion undetected, and get what I need." He didn't know I could never transport all the tech necessary to clone his kidney, even with ten subway systems running. "All I have to do is convince Kegide to guide us back there."

"You don't need Kegide." Reever sat up as I disconnected his leg shunt from the machine. "The outcasts will do it."

"How do you know they can? Or will?"

He gave me a mild look. "They told me all the Night Horse know how to operate the subway. They are also very grateful for what you've done for them."

"Then by all means, let's capitalize on their gratitude."

Reever was weaker than I thought, and had to lean on me to make it the last hundred yards into the sewer pipe. Before we reached the shack, one of the men came out.

"We heard your footsteps." He stared at Reever. *"Nilch'i',* you are ill. What is wrong?"

"Nilch'i' needs help," I said, and explained the situation.

The outcast stroked his chin. "If the chief discovers we have done this, he will kill us all."

"Then we'd better be quiet, and hurry, don't you think?"

The man disappeared into the shack without another word. Just as I was getting ready to give up hope, he emerged with three more men and a makeshift litter.

"Put him on here. We will carry him for you."

I helped Reever stretch out, and wrapped a blanket one of the men handed me around him. "I need to get into the underground research facility, where Rico found us. Can you take us on the subway, and guide us there?"

"Yes. But you must return to the tunnels before morning comes."

"I can do that." I was starting to believe my own story.

The outcasts carried Reever through the sewer system up to the subway platform. From there, only two of the men went with us on the old transport. We had to travel nearly an hour before we reached the sewer system beneath my creator's estate.

The men carried Reever to the same access panel Milass had brought us through, and helped me get him in. I refused to let them accompany us inside.

"Is there another place you and the other hybrids can go to, where Rico won't find you?"

The outcasts nodded. "You are not coming back, are you?"

I couldn't keep them in the dark any longer. "No. He'll die without this surgery tonight. I'm sorry."

The hybrid smiled slightly. "You lie for him, not yourself. We will make ourselves safe. Walk the rainbow, patcher."

I figured Joseph hadn't reprogrammed the lab and maintenance drones to deal with me voluntarily returning to the facility, so when the first one approached, I tried using the old medical priority access command imperative.

"Unable to comply. That command series has been deleted."

Well, he'd been smart enough to figure out how I'd overridden the system the last time. I was prepared for that, though, and squeezed Reever's arm.

"Emergency surgical procedure, initiate assistance to surgeon Dr. Cherijo. This file supersedes all contradictory submenu commands," he said, exactly the way we'd rehearsed it.

"Identify for voice analysis."

I'd scored another point; Joseph hadn't bothered to create a voice-print file for Reever in the facility database.

"Identity: Duncan Reever, chief of Surgical Services, New Angeles Medical Center."

What Reever had done was make himself, in essence, my creator's old boss. The old hospital hierarchy files kicked in, and the drone responded exactly as I'd hoped.

"Thank you, Dr. Reever. Emergency surgical procedure file does not exist. Create, or cancel?"

"Create."

The drones were now under Reever's complete voice control.

"Emergency surgical procedure new directive: All

commands issued by Dr. Cherijo equal commands issued by Dr. Reever. Supersede all contradictory submenu command directives and acknowledge."

"New directive acknowledged."

At last I could say something. "Prepare for organ transplantation procedure in Development and Engineering." Reever started to sag, and I tucked his arm over my shoulders. "Move your rollers!"

I managed to support most of his weight and helped him over to the berth nearest the organ specimen wall. He collapsed and slipped into unconsciousness. After I checked his vitals, which were terrible, I ran to the console. Since the new commands enabled me access to Joe's full database, I keyed up the organ stock inventory in a few seconds.

"Okay, colon, heart, intestine large, intestine small—There, kidney stock available." I ran my finger down the screen, following the column of tissue types. Then I input an inquiry, and got the final answer.

No match available.

I ground a few molars together. "Always has to be a challenge, doesn't it?"

I input another inquiry, this time for the cellular sample stock inventory. I got lucky. Joseph had stored a sample of kidney cells that matched Reever's tissue type.

I pulled the sample, examined it, and loaded it onto an organ scaffold. "Begin whole kidney formation process. Extrapolate approximate length of time for cloning full organ for transplantation purposes, and display."

"It takes four weeks," Joseph said behind me.

I went motionless.

"Where have you been, daughter?"

"We took a long walk through the mountains." I took a deep breath. "He doesn't have four weeks. He doesn't have four hours."

"You should have taken that into consideration before attempting this larceny."

He was calling *me* a thief. If that didn't ice the cake. "Transplantation isn't my specialty."

Reever, who'd suddenly woken up, jerked into a sitting position. "Run!"

"I can't." I went over to the table and made him recline, then saw his eyes. Icebergs were warmer. "Don't look at me like that."

"You knew. You knew he wouldn't catch us here."

"I was pretty sure he still kept the floor sensors armed. That's how he caught me sneaking out a few times during secondary school." I turned to my creator, who was recoding the door panel. "Don't bother. We're not going anywhere. We need your help."

Joe smiled slowly. "You must allow me time to properly appreciate this moment."

"Gloat next week. He's in critical condition." I put a hand on Reever's forearm when he tried to sit up again. "Stay put and act like you're in critical condition, please."

My creator made a leisurely survey, then started curling his upper lip again. "Why should I help you? He means nothing to me."

"Because if you do save him, and release him when he's healed, you get me." I wondered if I should have him sign something. "Along with my full and voluntary cooperation, and use of my body for whatever twisted, sick experiments you can think up, for the remainder of my existence."

Reever made a harsh sound. "No. I won't let you."

"Lay back down, or I'll sedate you." I turned to my creator. "Well?"

Joe's smile got wider. "I agree."

Reever argued with me until the very last moment before we started, when I infused him with Valumine. "You could have escaped. You don't have to sacrifice yourself for me."

I snapped on my gloves and peered over the edge of my mask at him. "Too late."

He fought to keep his eyes open. "Cherijo, you despise him. Don't trade your soul for my life."

"What if it were me on the table, dying, and you were the one he wanted? Wouldn't you do the same thing?"

"Yes." He closed his eyes. "But—"

"No buts."

I'd never operated side by side with Joseph. He'd observed many of the procedures I'd performed as a medical student, but only so he could tear apart my technique once I got off shift and came home. Now we stood on opposite sides of our patient. The man I loved. The rival he hated.

Joe leaned over the table. "Are you ready?"

"Wait." I went to the monitors and double-checked the leads. "I want to make this crystal clear before we start. If you try anything, mess up anything while we're working on him, I'll know."

"Obviously, you will."

"I'll also have a laser and several sharp instruments close at hand." I nodded toward the setup trays. "You've seen me perform an emergency colostomy, haven't you? Imagine how it would feel without anesthetic."

"I took the same oath you did. I also gave you my word. I will not harm him."

"Good. I hate eviscerating people. So much noise, so much mess." I checked Reever's brain waves. He was sleeping peacefully. "Since we don't have a donor organ, and we can't clone a new one in time, what are you going to do?"

"You should have kept up with your research journals." Joseph powered up the laser rig. "I've developed new procedures since you left Terra."

"Gee, I thought you were too busy chasing me around the galaxy to get any serious research done." I held out my hand. "I'll open him up."

He held on to the lascalpel. He really was afraid of me. I enjoyed seeing that.

"Don't get your gown in a knot. I gave you my word."

"You've lived with alien barbarians for three years. I'm not convinced I can trust you."

"The aliens use swords, not lasers. Just relax."

"Why do you want to open him up?"

Now he was starting to get on my nerves. "Look, the repair work is yours, the grunt work is mine. Hand it over."

He reluctantly gave the instrument to me. "Very well."

I waved it in front of me. "See? I'm not burning your face off with it. Much as I'm tempted."

I made the initial incision, over the freshly healed scar of his previous operation, and clamped back the tissues to reveal a kidney that was, for all intents and purposes, dead.

"Damn. How bad?"

He scanned the organ. "It's eighty-one-percent non-functional. Necrotic tissue is present, though the amount is negligible. You're fortunate you decided to return when you did. Another couple of hours and the organ would have been unsalvageable." He paused for a moment, lining up the scope. "How did you get out of the lab?"

So he hadn't found the access hatch. "We tiptoed."

"You said you'd been in the mountains. The closest mountain range is over sixty kilometers from the estate."

"No wonder my feet hurt."

He held out a gloved hand. "Lascalpel."

I didn't want to give it back to him, so it hit his palm with a little extra, unnecessary force.

Joe ignored that and looked through the scope. "It appears you repaired the original trauma and restored systemic circulation. However, the cellular damage was too extensive for the organ to continue functioning. The other kidney is missing. Removed?"

"He doesn't know. It could be a birth defect, or it was excised during infancy." Though how that could have happened without leaving a scar, I had no idea.

"Interesting. The remaining kidney should be enlarged." He carefully entered the organ with a scope probe and surveyed the interior. "You must have worked on him at some kind of medical facility. Which one?"

"Oh, I did that in the mountains, too. Amazing what you can accomplish with a sharp stick, a few vines, and some moss."

He held out his hand again. "Hypercellular injector."

I glanced at the tray. "The what?"

"The long instrument to the immediate left of the suture laser."

I picked up what looked like a syrinpress that had been miniaturized, with a few dozen infusion ports added to the tip. "What's it do?"

Dark blue eyes narrowed above the edge of his mask. "Do you want me to teach you this procedure, or perform it?"

"I want you to tell me how many patients survived it."

"All of them."

I slapped it in his hand. "Remember what I said."

Whatever Joe was doing was fine, delicate work. He stayed in the organ and on the scope for the next two hours. Occasionally I had to apply suction and take care of a few bleeders, but otherwise I was made to feel about as useful as a structural post.

"There." Finally Joe pushed the scope away and tossed the bloodied injector onto the discard tray. "I've repaired the vascular occlusions, and seeded the organ with hypercellular implants. The new cells will restructure the kidney, and replace the dysfunctional tissue."

I wasn't going to take his word for it. "I want to see what you did on the scope."

He stepped aside. "As you wish."

I upped the magnification and studied the work he'd done on Reever's kidney. New, pink organ cells were already beginning to flush the gray surface of the organ. "It looks almost like cancer."

"It operates with a similar replication and replacement process, at a far more rapid and efficient growth rate. Like carcinogenic cells, the organic hypercells will replace existing tissue and reinstate organ function without further treatment."

"Will he need anti-rejection therapy?"

"No. The cells rebuild themselves by utilizing existing systemic material. His body will not attack it."

"Congratulations, Doctor." I pushed the scope aside and grabbed the lascalpel. "I'll close, and monitor."

"You may, until this evening. The drones will care for him while you will change for dinner, and our night together."

Oh, yes. Our night together.

I spent the next six hours monitoring Reever, scanning the site and witnessing the gradual reformation of his kidney. The hypercells replicated and replaced the damaged tissue with astonishing speed. It was probably the most miraculous process I'd ever seen, outside of the development of a human fetus. Once again, Joseph had found a way to radically change Terran medicine for all time. He'd also saved Reever.

I had no problem dealing with that. Joseph owed me.

As Reever's condition continued to improve, I turned my attention to what I had to do tonight. Pulling off the rest of my plan presented some problems. It was all going to be very tricky. I'd also have to leave Reever alone for several hours. A couple thousand variables were involved.

Anything might happen.

Reever stirred, then gradually came out of the anesthetic. He immediately tried to reach for me, so I took his hand. "Cherijo."

"Hey, blue eyes." I stroked the blond hair away from his brow. He was still pretty groggy. "How many wives do you see?"

"One." His voice rasped on the word. "Joseph?"

"He's up in the mansion. Don't worry about him."

He tried to lift his head from the berth, then grimaced and closed his eyes. "What happened?"

"I talked old Joe into helping us out. He's invented a new way to handle organ damage. He injects replacement cells into the organ, and they replicate and rebuild it. You'll have a brand-new kidney in a few hours."

"Complications?"

"All kinds of them." I rolled my eyes. "None that will bother your kidney, I hope."

He didn't appreciate my joke. "What does he want?"

"Something he's not going to get. No, don't try to sit up. Look at me." I checked his pupils. At this rate, he was going to be ambulatory in a few hours, so I removed the restraints. "You stay here and rest. I have to go and deal with him now."

He didn't like hearing that, either. "Stay with me."

"I wish I could. Duncan, you know I have to put an end to this. Trust me, I won't resort to violence." Unless I had to. "I'm going to try to reason with him. If he doesn't cooperate, I'll drug him. Then we're getting out of here and leaving Terra. Sound good to you?"

From his expression, I could tell he wanted to argue with me. "Be careful."

"I will." I kissed him. "Rest now."

The lift was open and waiting for me. So was Joseph, just outside the door panel up in the house. He took my arm.

"I meant what I said," I told him. Not yanking out of his grip took some effort. "I'll cooperate."

"Forgive me if I find your sudden acquiescence suspect."

Normally Joe was completely oblivious to anything but his own schemes, but occasionally he anticipated me. Time to do my song and dance.

"Look at it this way. Even if I wanted to walk out of here, Reever is in no shape to be moved. I'm not going to trade his life for my freedom. Besides, is there any possible way for me to get out of this fortress now?"

"I did not think so, until you escaped the last time."

"You taught me a lot of things, Joe. One of them was how to keep my word." I didn't mention the fine art of lying through my teeth I'd picked up since leaving Terra. "I want Reever alive, and out of here."

"We shall see."

He took me to my room, where one of the housekeeping drones stood waiting with more impractical garments.

"I haven't had a decent shower in a few weeks," I said, and pretended to scratch my scalp. "Mind if I clean up before the experiments begin again?"

He gave me a vaguely alarmed look. "Do a dermal parasitic scan before you cleanse. You have thirty minutes."

I waited until he left, then tried to dismiss the housekeeping drone. It ignored me completely, which made it very easy to disable. A server of water dumped over it shorted the control panel long enough for me to yank the power core. "One down, two to go."

I retrieved my treasure box, and as promised, Maggie's cache of discs were hidden inside. I turned on the cleanser unit to full stream and let it cloud up the lavatory before going in there. I had to hide the discs on me, which took a silk scarf and some creative tucking and draping.

The dress Joe wanted me to wear was fully and conservatively cut, thank God, so the scarf didn't look out of place. I unbraided my hair and let it get damp, then stepped out of the fog back into the bathroom.

A study of my reflection made me adjust a few folds. Whatever was on the discs, there was no way I was letting Joseph get his hands on them. "Okay. Best I can do." I went to the console and did what I needed to do there. "Time to ruin Daddy's entire night."

Knowing my creator, he'd be waiting in the formal dining room for me, so that's where I headed. I'd watched him input the access code to the lift, so I knew I could get back down into the facility. All I had to do was disable him long enough to get Reever on a gurney, up and out of the mansion, and into a glidecar.

Piece of cake.

Joseph had changed into his party tuxedo, a sober-looking affair that made him look like a penguin. I refrained from pointing that out as I took my place at the table. Might as well give him a few minutes to savor the triumph I was about to take away from him.

"You remembered how I like your hair," he said, surprising me.

It was down so it hid the bulges in the scarf around my neck. "I'm glad you like it. What's for dinner?"

"Summer quail with raisin-oyster stuffing."

"Oh, boy." I controlled a wince. "My favorite."

The kitchen drone delivered our meal in short order, and I spent a few minutes pushing quail around my plate while Joe lectured me on his new transplantation techniques. If I closed my eyes, I could have gone back in time three years, and found myself doing the same thing, only pushing bits of lobster while he gave me a mini-seminar on bowel resections.

"Tell me something," I said, interrupting his oration. "What would you do if you found out I'm sterile?"

"You're not." He cut up his quail the same way he operated on Reever—with precise, absolute accuracy. As he sampled the meat, I finally recognized the gruesome side to our profession. "You were ovulating the day I brought you here."

Ovulating, yes. Able to reproduce, no. Why had he missed that? "What about my immune system?"

"I've taken that into consideration. After my personal insemination, specific genetic adjustments, and a regime of immuno-suppressants should protect the fetus for the duration of your pregnancy."

"Really." I gave up the pretense of eating and drank some of the red wine he'd poured for me. A California merlot, one of his favorites. It resembled congealed blood in color, and old sterilizer solution in taste. "Far as I know, my immune system will render anything inert and useless. You'd better go with the in vitro method."

He actually reached out and put his hand on mine. "I do not plan to use artificial insemination."

I dragged my hand away. "I doubt you could implant a gestating zygote . . ." I stopped, and reconsidered his statement. "When you said personally impregnate me, you mean *personally*? As in having intercourse?"

"Yes."

I dropped my fork. I tried to say something. Nothing came out. I took a deep drink of the lousy merlot.

"I didn't create you simply to be the perfect physician and human." He placed his utensils down and flattened his hands against the table. Like he was bracing himself.

I needed some bracing, too, and quickly downed the rest of the merlot. "You—"

"I created you to be my wife."

PART THREE

Consanguinity

CHAPTER ELEVEN

Not To Be Trusted

Everything I had never understood about my creator for the last twenty-nine years abruptly snapped into stunning, nauseating clarity. I must have sat there in silence for a full five minutes as I saw my entire existence turn upside down.

He'd made me to be his *wife*.

I'd misjudged the motives behind everything he'd done. He'd programmed me genetically. He'd taught me to obey him. he'd isolated me from other men. He'd convinced me to take up his profession. He'd instilled in me some, if not all, of the values he held sacred.

Not because he'd wanted to be a good *father*.

When I'd left him, he let me go only so far. He had allowed me my alien experience on K-2, to test my immune system and to instill in me the hatred of non-humans he had. Only it had gone all wrong. I'd become fascinated with aliens. I'd even fallen in love with one. I'd refused to come back to him.

Of course he'd come after me with a vengeance. Not because he was being a good father, or he considered me a lab rat.

He'd made himself a *mate,* and he wanted her back.

Panic set in. I shoved my chair back away from the table and got up. "You're sick."

He came after me. Slowly, with great poise and dignity.

"I have been training you to take your place at my side since you were born. You are an accomplished surgeon who can understand and share in my work. You have been brought up to appreciate the finer aspects of Terran existence, unsullied by alien cultural pollutants. You were physically engineered to be an attractive female and a highly responsive partner."

He'd tinkered with *that*? "Stop. Stay away from me."

He did stop. "I designed you to be the perfect woman for me. This is your destiny, Cherijo."

"You made me so you could mate with yourself," I said, and saw him extend a hand. "Don't touch me. Unless you want to pull back a bloody stump."

"Think of what we will do together." He smiled a little as he watched my face. "As husband and wife, we will produce the children who will chart the genetic future of the human race. We will continue my research and resolve the threat to our way of life. It will be an incredible journey for both of us."

He was completely insane. "Incest is still against the law."

"You're not my daughter, or my sister. Only a sentient being qualifies as such, under Terran law."

"So you made sure I wouldn't meet the specifications."

"Naturally, there will be no officially recognized union between us. I have no need for the bonds of marriage. You are my property."

"Your own little brood mare."

"You cannot become pregnant with an alien's child. Only a Terran can breed with you. That is why the World Government consented to my proposal thirty years ago. You and I will have children who cannot be corrupted by alien DNA. Their children, like you, will be unable to crossbreed, thus preserving our heritage forever."

I'd always known my creator was brilliant, and narcissistic, but this went way beyond the worst megalomania. Somehow, he'd convinced himself that he was God, and it was time to rewrite Genesis.

Even scarier, he might just pull it off.

"I see." I centered my weight on my feet. The calm Xonea had taught me to seek inside myself settled over me. You had to be calm to beat the daylights out of someone. "Is that all you have planned for me and the human race?"

"We can discuss it in more detail, as long as you cooperate. If you resist, I will have the drones attend to your linguist friend." He took my cold hand in his. "Shall I signal them now?"

We stood like that for a minute. Joseph had rarely touched me when I was a child. Now I had the final puzzle piece. And I could use it.

"You're in love with me."

He jerked, then tightened his fingers.

"That's why you never bothered getting married." Hard to fake the bewildered wonder in my voice, but I managed. "It was always me, wasn't it?"

"My only personal inconvenience was waiting for you to mature." More sure of me now, he led me back to the table. "I felt the result merited the effort. No other man could match your intellect, potential, or talent. No other woman would suit me, for the same reasons. In time, you will come to understand."

I'd walk into the backwash of a starshuttle discharge vent first. Time. I needed to buy a little more time. I waited as he pulled out my chair, then I sat down.

"Why didn't you raise me to regard you as a lover instead of a father? You could have saved yourself ten, maybe twenty years of frustration. Not to mention all those inconvenient explanations to your colleagues and friends."

"I am not a pedophile." He said that as though it made everything all better, and took his seat. "I required a valid reason to be involved in every facet of your childhood and adolescence, both in public and private situations. I'd hoped you'd naturally gravitate toward me as you went through puberty, but when it became apparent you preferred to pour your passion into your work, I was willing to delay the inevitable." He offered me another glass of merlot.

"No, thank you." After this night, I'd never be able to drink wine again. He wanted to talk clinical, we'd talk clinical. "What about my psychological reaction to the prospect of incest?"

"The potential damage was an acceptable risk. You're a highly intelligent woman. Once I explained my rationale, I felt confident you would accept the change in our relationship. You accepted everything else I required of you."

That I had, idiot that I'd been. Why hadn't I ever picked up on this? "But the blackmail sure comes in handy, doesn't it?"

"It does." He finished his quail. "You have been controlling your temper admirably. What I have to say to you now will be difficult for you to accept, but it is important to start out with complete understanding."

If *he* thought it was going to be tough to listen to, I was positive *I* didn't want to hear it. I needed just a few more minutes. "Knock yourself out."

"You have an emotional attachment to the linguist, which I would not have permitted, had you been living here. I had no control over your choices after you left Kevarzangia Two, much to my regret, but I anticipated this happening. As a result, congress with me initially may be unpleasant for you at first. Until such time as you feel willing to participate, I will provide you with tranquilizers."

He was going to drug me before he raped me. Only Joe could make that sound logical. I refused the dessert offered by the serving drone. "You can't drug me into submission forever."

"You will adjust in time. Loss of control and ability to surrender to a familial authority figure is a common sexual fantasy among otherwise dominant women."

He'd even managed to make rape sound respectable. "You have the research to back that up?"

He nodded, then frowned. "Your hatred of me was a concern, at first. I failed to take into account your penchant for independence and competitiveness. All that will be corrected as our relationship progresses to the next level."

"So you think eventually I'll kick off my footgear, incubate your child, and take up permanent residence in the food prep area?" A faint odor reached my nose, and I sniffed. "Just like that?"

"One area we will need to work on is your irreverent speech patterns. I tolerated them when Margaret was alive, but they are extremely annoying."

"Why not cut out my vocal cords? Then you don't have to listen to anything." My internal time clock and the smell said it was just about time, so I got to my feet. "Can we cut to the chase?"

"I suggest—"

Whatever he was going to suggest fell to the wayside as the household thermal sensors went off. Several staff drones rushed in, displays blinking, alarms chiming.

"Dr. Joseph, a room console in the east wing was cross-wired, and set fire to the bed linens draped over it."

My creator gave me a furious look. "You gave me your word."

"I told you I'd cooperate." I studied the deplorable condition of my fingernails. "I didn't say a thing about avoiding arson."

"Keep her here. Send all maintenance drones to put out the blaze." Joe put down his wineglass and gave me his famous disappointed look. "I'll deal with the linguist myself."

I picked up a knife from the table. "No, you won't."

I could have disabled him. I certainly would have, if twenty screaming, knife-carrying Indians hadn't burst into the dining room at that exact moment.

Two worlds collided right in front of my eyes.

Faces smeared with colored pigments, bare chests gleaming under the chandelier optics, the Indians charged at me, Joseph, and the drones like the front line at a shockball game. Chairs went flying and smashed against the embossed floral wall coverings. The long dining room table was upended, and the remnants of our meal scattered.

They got to me first. I didn't resist when someone's strong arm snatched me off my feet and I was carried to an out-of-the-way corner. By then I'd realized it was the Night Horse players I'd treated, evidently sent to rescue me.

Polished metallic drones tried to fend them off, with static discharges, which didn't even faze the shockball-hardened athletes. The drones ended up hitting the walls and being reduced to jumbles of components.

I peered around Small Fox's arm to see what had happened to Joseph. He was already gagged and tied to a chair. The Indians circled around him, jabbing at him with their knives and screaming insults.

Then the dark man walked in, and everyone fell silent.

"How is it one of the blood lives like a whiteskin, alone in an enormous hogan filled with objects obtained by his greed?"

Rico bent down and picked up a piece of quail from the floor. He sniffed at it, then tossed it back down.

"He eats the whiteskins' food." He came over to

Joseph and inspected him. "He cuts his hair and wears the whiteskins' clothes. This is not the way."

"He is not blood," Small Fox muttered.

"But he says he is." The chief bent over my creator, who was staring at him, wide-eyed. "He takes the blood for his own."

Joseph strained against his bonds, his gaze bouncing from Rico's face to mine. He looked quite uncharacteristically terrified.

Rico, in contrast, seemed almost serene as he pulled a blade from his belt and tested the edge. "His life should belong to those he has wronged."

I didn't know what to do. I didn't want to see the chief slit another throat, but I couldn't think of a single good reason to stop him from killing Joe.

Things got even more complicated when Rico strode over and held it out to me. "Here. His life is yours."

I took the knife. So it would be my decision. Killing him would solve a lot of problems. Nearly all of mine. It would keep him from wreaking havoc on the future of the human race. Then I thought of the hypercellular procedure, and the fact Joseph had never been able to recreate me.

I handed the knife back to the chief. "No."

"He is the one who hunts you." With a single jab, Rico buried the knife in the highly polished surface of the dining room table. "End it now, or you will look over your shoulder forever."

I shook my head. "Thanks, but I have to leave. I'm going to get Reever." I started for the lab.

"You're coming with us." The chief nodded to Milass and Hawk, who grabbed my arms.

My heart started pounding out of control. I couldn't leave Reever here. Joe would dissect him alive, an inch at a time, out of spite. "If you want me as your cutter, my husband goes with us."

Rico mulled this over for a moment. "If he comes back, he comes as one of us."

"Fine." Reever wouldn't care if he had to pretend to join the tribe.

I walked over to my creator. He was still struggling, trying to free himself. I bent over so my words were for him alone.

"Before I go, I want to thank you for saving Reever. I love him. My life would have very little meaning without him. We have the rest of our lives to be together. You made that possible." I moved around so he could look into my eyes, so he could see my hatred and disgust. "That's the only reason I'm not using that blade on you."

On the way to the lab, a few more drones got in the way. The players mowed them down. Once we stepped onto the lift and descended into the research facility, the men began congratulating each other and comparing whatever they'd swiped from the mansion.

"You should have killed him."

I looked at the small man behind me. Milass had painted his entire face black, and was wearing Joseph's dinner jacket. "There are plenty of people in that category."

The little twerp grinned, his small teeth white against the paint. "Any time you wish, woman."

We got off the lift, to be greeted by the thermal sensors triggering an alarm. A virtual barricade of maintenance drones rushed toward the lift. It took the Indians a little longer to plow through this line. At one point, I picked up a dismembered extensor unit and started hammering on a couple myself.

Felt pretty good to be beating the components out of something.

I led the Night Horse through the resulting pile of fizzling bodies to the lab and Reever. The sight of the malformed fetuses in the embryonic chambers seemed to mesmerize the Indians, who shuffled back and muttered some things to each other.

Reever, who was semiconscious, was still too weak to travel under his own power. "We'll need to rig a litter to carry him. I also need to take some equipment and supplies with me." Including all the antibiotics I could get my hands on.

"This place smells of whiteskin trickery," Milass said. "We should take nothing from here."

I ignored him and finished redressing Reever's torso brace. Only when I went into Research and Development to load up a medical case did the little twerp get nasty.

"No." He appropriated the case and flung it across the lab. "You will not bring evil spirits into *Leyane-yaniteh*."

"Get lost." When he didn't, I looked for Rico. He had followed us in and was over by the embryonic chambers, studying one of the specimens. "Chief? I need to take these supplies for Medical. Call off your deranged midget."

The chief regarded me, then his *secondario*. "Why do you object, Milass?"

My nemesis spat on the spotless floor. "She will curse us with the Shaman's trickery."

"Make an effort and don't be stupid for once." I showed Rico the syrinpress units and surgical supplies. "These are things we need down there."

"Take what you can carry, patcher," Rico said at last.

That wasn't going to be much. I cleaned out Joseph's stocks of antibiotics and confiscated some lightweight instruments. One of the hybrids had some mild cardiac damage from the syphilis infection, so I added a couple of biomechanical replacement units to my pack, in the event his condition worsened.

The thermal sensors above us stopped blaring. A different alarm went off in their place.

"That's the security grid. Joseph must have gotten loose. Area authorities will be here any minute now." I saw Rico pick up a suture laser, and hurried over to him. "Put that down, it's dangerous."

He pointed the laser at one of the embryonic chambers, and activated it. The narrow beam cut through the malleable outer housing and duralyde began to pour out through the tear. There was a sickening plop when the occupant of the chamber slid out and hit the floor.

"Stop it." I tried to take the laser from him, but he shoved me away and used the beam on another chamber. I felt his anger again. It slapped at me with an icy hand. "Why are you doing that? You're killing them!"

Rico stared at me for a moment. "They are better off dead."

The other Indians covered their mouths and noses and backed away as the smell of the embryonic fluid hit them. Milass dragged me out of the lab, and kept me from going back in after the chief.

The specimens were too small to survive on their own. Even though I knew Joseph had created them, and meant to experiment on them, I could have never destroyed them like that, in cold blood. "He doesn't have to kill them!"

"He is the chief," Small Fox said, tugging me away from Milass. "Come, help us with the litter."

My eyes burned and my hands shook as I helped the men rig a litter for Reever. The smell of the duralyde followed the chief as he emerged from the lab a few minutes later.

"Did you rupture all of them?" I asked.

He gave me the suture laser. "Yes."

"Why?"

He washed his hands at the cleanser. "They were filled with evil."

Oh, that made perfect sense. "You're a murderer."

"Yes." He dried his hands. "I am."

I didn't talk to him after that. We got Reever back through the wall panel, and into the tunnels. It was a close thing, though. I could hear security forces running through the corridors of the research facility just after Hawk closed the panel.

"They've never found this access pipe?" I asked Hawk as we made our way into the sewer system.

He didn't answer me. Guess he was mad.

Everyone was quiet on the long trip back on the subway transport. I sat by Reever and kept him on continuous scan. Milass played guard and sat watching me.

Rico manned the controls, but the faint smell of duralyde drifted back. It made me want to vomit. Why had he done it?

The subway came to a halt, and we entered the tunnels. I watched carefully as Rico disabled the traps, memorizing their location this time. I had no intention of exchanging one kind of captivity for another. As soon as Reever had healed, we were getting out.

As soon as we emerged from the sewer system, Milass latched on to my arm.

"Chief?"

Rico looked at me.

"I'm not trying to escape. Tell him to get off me."

"You told the old man you'd do what he wanted, didn't you?" Rico asked me. "And then you set his house on fire and stole his medicine. Hold on to her, Milass."

The *secondario* gave me a nasty smile and tightened his grip.

I set up a berth for my husband in the medical alcove and got him hooked up on a monitor. Renal function had been nearly completely restored, but he was still very weak. I was about to perform a second scan series when Milass grabbed me by the back of the tunic and hauled me out into the tunnel.

Rico stood waiting, arms folded. The rest of the raiding party formed a ring around us.

I looked at all of them. "Problem?"

"You were welcomed into our tribe, and yet you deceived us."

"I'm sorry about that." I didn't have time for this shame-on-you stuff. "Excuse me, I have a patient to take care of."

Milass forced me down on my knees instead. "Look at the chief, woman."

"Okay." I looked up at him. "And?"

"You are not to be trusted."

"Obviously." I thought of Wendell, and put a clamp on my temper. "I'm sorry we left without permission, and I'm grateful that you helped us escape again. You have to understand, this isn't our home. We want to be free, the same way your tribe chose to leave the reservations and live here. We don't belong here."

"You belong to me," he said.

Milass hit me, so fast and hard it sent me sprawling at his feet.

Rico moved to stand over me. "If you attempt to escape again, I will have the linguist's life."

I spat out some blood and pushed myself up. "I understand."

The chief cocked his head to one side. "Do you?"

Milass drove his foot into my side, and bone cracked. The explosion of pain made my vision double, made me curl over and groan. He kicked me two more times.

"If you lie to me again," Rico said through the haze of agony surrounding me, "I will cut out your tongue. Do you understand that?"

His little demon hauled me up, and I clutched my abdomen, trying to protect my rib cage. The dark man was waiting for an answer, I saw, and managed a nod.

Milass drew back his fist, and clipped me across the jaw. I didn't go anywhere that time, because the *secondario* had his fist wrapped in my hair. Some of it separated from my scalp. Blood pooled in my mouth and trickled out the sides.

"You will be under guard until I feel better about you, patcher." Rico reached out one finger, and smeared my own blood over my lips. "Remember what I have said."

Milass let go of me, and I went down. Hitting the stone floor of the tunnel was almost as bad as taking the beating. Rico and the men left, but two stayed behind to take up positions on either side of the alcove entrance.

I stayed where I was for a while. Some time later, hands touched me.

"Don't." I would have shivered from the cold, but it hurt too much.

"You can't stay like this." It was Hawk.

"Ribs." Hopefully he wouldn't want a comprehensive explanation of what was wrong with them.

Hawk didn't try to pick me up, which was a small blessing. "How can I help you?"

A brand-new rib cage would have been nice. "Syrinpress."

He hobbled away. I turned on my back and rode new waves of torment. When I felt his touch again, I squinted at him. "Got it?"

"Yes." He showed it to me.

"Morphinol. Ten cc's. Hip."

"I've never given an infusion before."

Even an overdose would be better than this misery. "Try."

He calibrated the syrinpress, then tugged down the waist of my trousers and infused me at the hip. Then he sat beside me, wiped the sweat from my face, and checked my pulse. "Is it working?"

"Yes." I could feel the burning grip on my abdomen easing a few degrees. I knew my body would quickly absorb the effects of the painkiller, but with luck it would buy me enough time to get up and into some sort of brace.

When I could take a breath without screaming, I held out a hand. "Hold on."

Hawk didn't pull, but provided the anchor I needed. Even so, getting to my feet nearly did me in. As soon as I was vertical, I started moving. Scalding arrows sliced through my lungs with every breath.

Hawk held on to my hands and kept me balanced. "How bad are your ribs?"

"Broken." I got to the exam table. Getting up on it was out of the question. Sweat seeped down the sides of my face as I rested, my hands gripping the edge. I had to pant each subsequent word.

"Hawk. Get. The. Scanner."

Everything became dark and fuzzy, and I focused on my breathing. Short, controlled breaths cleared my head, while the morphinol blurred a little more of the pain. I heard Hawk activate the scanner, felt him moving around my back.

"Four of them are broken, patcher."

"Bone chips? Bleeding?"

"The fractures display clean. There are no signs of internal hemorrhaging."

That took care of my two biggest concerns. Now, how to deal with the broken ribs? I didn't have any torso braces, and I couldn't have him knock me out. Reever had to be monitored, and Hawk wasn't up to that. "Get scissors. Bandage. Players' tape."

He brought a pair of surgical shears, a large dressing pad, and a roll of dermal adhesive to the table. "These?"

"Yes." I panted for a minute. "Cut off tunic." I gritted my teeth as he did that, then glanced down. The skin over my ribs was broken in a few places. Angry-looking bruises spread huge dark circles where Milass's boot had landed. "Clean. Bandage. Wrap."

He gently cleansed the lacerations, dried them, and

taped the dressing in place. Then he began wrapping my torso with the tape. By then the morphinol was starting to back off, and it was a little like having my ribs broken all over again.

"Okay." After he had applied four layers, I held out my hand. "That's good. Thanks."

He put away the supplies, then came over and studied me. "Your jaw is bruised."

"Just sore." I carefully walked over to Reever's berth. "Thanks."

"Don't thank me. You disobeyed the chief."

Shame on you, Cherijo. "So?"

"He might kill you if you cross him again."

I stopped, and turned my head. "He'd better, next time."

My ribs healed, but other things didn't.

Disobeying the chief and escaping from the underground instantly made me persona non grata with the tribe. The players I treated remained silent and kept their visits brief. The few times I went out into the central cavern, everyone pretended not to see me, or went into their hogans so they wouldn't have to.

A leper would have been more popular.

I don't know why it bothered me so much—after all, Reever and I'd been kidnapped twice by these people, and Reever nearly killed—but it did. I missed seeing the warm smiles, accepting the offers to share a meal, listening to the laughter of the children. From what I knew about Indian culture, it would be a long time, if ever, before they forgave me.

I missed Hawk more than anyone. After he'd helped me with my broken ribs, he stayed away from Medical, and took care to avoid me everywhere else. Sometimes I heard him singing in one of the hogans, but I was no longer invited to share in their ceremonials.

That, combined with Joseph's disgusting revelations,

sent me spiraling down into a state of constant depression.

Reever handled everything much better than I had, but I attributed that to the fact that he was used to being treated like a leper. His recovery proved rapid and without any complications. He would have made Terran medical history, if I could have told anyone about it.

"I feel fine," he said as I tried to bully him back onto the berth less than a week after Joe had performed the hypercell procedure. "I cannot remain on my back any longer."

"Oh, really?" I'd been sleeping badly, so my temper was in short supply. "You had major surgery, twice, and I nearly lost you. You'll stay on your back as long as I tell you to. Got it?"

"You've been having nightmares again, haven't you?"

I turned away from the berth. "Take off your tunic. I want to inspect the incision site."

"You did that this morning." He didn't touch his tunic. "Why are you avoiding my gaze?"

"I'm busy." I prepared a syrinpress with the vitamin booster I'd been giving him while he was on dialysis, then realized he didn't need it anymore and tossed the instrument aside. "Okay, I haven't been sleeping very well. This place is making me claustrophobic." And the thought of Joseph and what he'd told me had done wonders, too.

"Link with me."

I closed my eyes and pressed my forehead against the wall. "No, I don't feel like it."

Why?

I was so tired I had to struggle to get my mental walls up. *It's not polite to invade someone's mind without their permission. I thought we'd agreed on that.*

He'd seen something; I could feel it as he withdrew.

"What happened between you and Joseph after my surgery?"

"Same old thing. He wants to get me pregnant, to produce more clones, et cetera."

"No. More than that. You smelled of wine. You never drink."

I could still taste that horrible merlot. "He doesn't want to be my daddy anymore, Duncan. He never did. Just let it go."

"I am not letting it go." He turned me around. "What does he want?"

My temper, never a steady thing these days, blew. "A wife! Okay? He wants a wife!"

For the second time in as many weeks, I had actually shocked Duncan Reever. "He admitted this to you?"

"Sure, he told me. Why wouldn't he? I'd just agreed to let him do anything he wanted to me. What better time to break the news that he made me to be *his* perfect woman."

My husband seemed very troubled. "I had no idea."

"Me either, but he figured with time, and some sedation, I'd accept it." Which sometimes happened in my nightmares, which was why I wasn't sleeping. "According to Joe, I'm too smart to let incest get in the way of true love."

His hands cradled my face. "This was not your doing, Cherijo."

"You know what really gets me the most? All those years he watched me, and the whole time he was thinking—" I wrenched away and drove my fist into the nearest solid object. I ended up with bleeding, throbbing knuckles, and a slightly dented exam table. The pain didn't make me feel any better. "I never saw it coming. Why didn't I see it, Duncan?"

"You don't think the way he does." Reever took my hand and wrapped it in a piece of linen. "There is no perversion in you."

"You know what? I never liked him. He was a lousy father. But he was the only father I've ever known. He's the reason I became a surgeon, and not just because of the genetics."

He tied the ends of the linen and tucked them under the outer folds. "You were a child. You wanted him to be proud of you."

"I respected him. I tried to love him. I can't remember a time when I didn't want to please him." Why was this making me teary eyed? I hated the warped bastard. "He knew that. He *planned* it that way. Told me he thought acting like my dad would make everything easier."

Reever didn't try to touch me again, but let me wander away from him. "We cannot choose our parents. What they do to us is totally without our permission—whether we are cherished, or abused. We can only hope to learn from their actions so we may be better parents when the time comes."

That didn't make things better. It made me want to tear out my hair and dissolve into hysterics. "Shut up, Duncan."

"You have never faced the loss of our child. Perhaps it is time you did. It is a tragedy we will carry with us forever, but we will have others."

"No, we won't." He'd given me the perfect opportunity to tell him, and I was disgusted enough with myself to do it this time. "My immune system will destroy any baby I become pregnant with. Squilyp suspected as much, but we couldn't confirm it until after I had the miscarriage."

"Why didn't you tell me?"

"Because after I lost our baby, Duncan, I forced Squilyp into performing a tubal ligation on me. No more miscarriages. I'm sterile now."

"This is what you've been hiding."

As much I was going to torture him with for the moment. "Yes." I saw his eyes change, and clamped down on the overwhelming despair inside me. "Now you know. Don't worry, Duncan. You'll find someone else to have those babies with."

I ran, and the guards at the entrance silently followed me.

Reever didn't.

I had to return to Medical eventually—my two shadows would only let me go so far, and no farther. When they marched me back, Reever was gone. I checked my hand, went over my charts, and brooded. If I'd had a couple of nurses and some jaspkerry tea, I could have closed my eyes and pretended I was back on the *Sunlace*.

Reever didn't show up that night or the next morning, but Hawk did. He came in during one of my procedures, a small vid unit under his arm.

"Why are you here?" I was in the middle of working on Small Fox's back, half of which I had successfully denuded by electrastim. "Strain your throat or something?"

"You will want to watch this." He put the portable unit on the makeshift worktable where I kept my charts.

I told Small Fox I'd kill some more of his follicles later. After he dressed and left, I inspected the unit. "Where did you get this?"

"Veda Wolfkiller sent it down to us. She saw and recorded the original broadcast," he said, and programmed it for replay.

The news recording began with their lead story— Joseph Grey Veil, walking down the steps of a familiar federal building. Drone reporters went berserk as soon as he emerged.

"Dr. Grey Veil, how have the authorities responded to the break-in at your estate?"

"Will you state the events surrounding the abduction of your property?"

"Have there been any leads in identifying the perpetrators?"

Joe paused and stared into the drones' recording devices. He seemed a little upset. "Officials have assured me they are continuing their pursuit of the individuals who burglarized my home. I have no information on the whereabouts of my property or the identity of the criminals. I am making a public appeal for all Terrans to assist in the investigation and help me recover the experimental subject who was taken from my research facility."

"You reported the criminals were renegade Indians. Do you think they have a grudge against you for your role in removing non-Indian residents from the Four Mountains reservation?"

I looked at Hawk. "He did *what*?"

"Watch," was all Hawk said.

"The Cultural Standards I helped develop during my office as Official Shaman to the Native American Nations have nothing to do with this outrage. My property was stolen, and I want it returned."

"League Colonel Patril Shropana claims your clone was directly responsible for the loss of life during the Varallan incident. Would you care to comment?"

Joe started to say something, but a familiar figure pushed in front of him and started spouting League law.

"My appeal to the World Government Committee has been taken under advisement. We will hunt down this criminal female and bring her to justice."

For a moment, Joseph and Patril gave each other ugly looks, then went their separate ways, still pursued by the media. Hawk reached over and switched off the vid.

"They search for you—the Shaman, and now the League forces as well. The entire property surrounding the estate has been combed every day. Joseph Grey Veil has not yet found the tunnels, but we think it will be soon."

"I see." I regarded Hawk. "Why didn't anyone tell me Joseph had you kicked off the Four Mountains reservation? Why the fairy tale about Rico's exodus?"

He just gave me that inscrutable Indian stare.

Oh, I forgot. I was still the resident leper. "Fine. I've seen the vid. Go away."

"Rico has summoned you to the sweat lodge. You will come with me now."

"No, she won't." Reever stood in the doorway. He sounded exhausted and none too happy.

Hawk shuffled around to address him. "She is in no danger."

"He had four of her ribs broken the last time he saw her." He wiped his face on his sleeve. Why was he so dirty and sweaty? "She is not going anywhere near him."

Hawk made an impatient gesture. "If she does not come now, he will come to her and do worse."

I wasn't risking more of my ribs or Reever getting into another knife fight. Besides, the last thing I wanted to do was hang around and hear what he had to say about my big confession.

"I'll be fine." I picked up my medical case and followed Hawk out of the alcove. When I passed Reever, he put out an arm to block my exit.

"I will be waiting for you."

"Sure." Maybe I'd stay in this sweat lodge for a few weeks.

I followed Hawk out to the central cavern. My position allowed me a good view of his distorted spine. I'd never seen a case of scoliosis outside of a dimensional training unit, but Hawk's spine had such a marked curvature that only surgery involving extensive bone grafting would straighten it.

"I wish you'd reconsider letting me take a look at your back." When he didn't respond to that, I sighed.

246 S. L. Viehl

"Okay. Why don't you tell what a sweat lodge is, then?"

"A place we use for sweat baths, to purify the mind and body."

"Bathing in sweat doesn't make you pure." I shuddered at the thought. "It makes you stink."

"It cleanses the mind and the body, and balances the soul." When I would have said more, he shook his head. "You have never experienced it. Wait and see for yourself."

I could reserve my opinion, but no amount of waiting and seeing was going to convince me sweat did anything but smell.

Hawk led me past the central fire and to a small, domed structure set far back into one corner of the cave. Some kind of mud had been used to seal the spaces between the stacks of flat rock and arched boughs forming the outside of the sweat lodge.

"What's in there?"

"Darkness, heated stones, steam, and fire."

Oh, brother. "How about I wait outside?"

"It is nothing to fear." He gave me a twisted smile. "The sweat lodge is like the womb of a mother. Within is darkness, like the time before birth, before learning and knowing. The heated stones are the approach of life, and the hissing steam the power of creation. The fire is the undying light of eternity."

"Very poetic." I folded my arms. "I'd still like to wait outside."

"Go on." He pulled back some kind of a small, tightly woven hatch and gave me a little push. "They're waiting for you."

Inside the extremely hot, smoky, humid interior was a circle of men sitting around a pile of rocks stacked over a low fire in a shallow pit. They were all stripped down to the skin. One of the men was shaking a wet bundle of straw over the hot stones.

The dark man sat at the head of the circle. His

shadowed face lifted, and he stared directly at me. I wrapped my arms around my waist and waited.

"Patcher." Rico pointed to an empty place at the foot of the circle. "Sit. We have things to speak of."

I sat. The man sitting next to me was passed a decorated pipe, and the smell coming from it made me suspicious. Some sort of drug, I thought, judging by the enlarged condition of his pupils. Maybe a hallucinogen. When he passed it to me, I handed it to the next man without sampling it.

Milass addressed me next. "Woman, the chief wishes to know why the Shaman persists."

I drew a blank. "What Shaman?"

He pointed in the general direction of the sewer/subway passages. "The one called Old Joe."

"Dr. Grey Veil believes I'm his property."

"Why?"

The smoke was starting to get to me, and I smothered a cough behind my hand. Explaining that I was a virtually immortal clone wasn't the prudent thing to do. I had no idea how the Night Horse felt about genetic engineering. "He tested some of his medical theories on me."

"Which theories?"

"Improvements on my immune system and brain development."

Rico leaned over and murmured something to Milass, who nodded and muttered something back. They did that for a couple of minutes.

"Excuse me." The lack of oxygen made me lightheaded. "Can I go now?"

"No," Milass said at once. "You will answer other questions."

"Okay. As long as I don't pass out first."

The subsequent questions Milass asked me had nothing to do with genetic engineering. He wanted to know about my childhood, what schools I had attended, and details of my life at The Grey Veils. I answered each briefly.

Then, unexpectedly, Milass said, "The League commander says you are a murderer."

"Maybe I am."

Milass smiled sourly. "Both the Shaman and the League offer a great reward for your recovery. Perhaps we should take advantage of it."

"Perhaps you should." I got to my feet. "May I go now?"

"No," Rico said to Milass.

The psycho dwarf pointed to the ground. "Sit."

I sat.

Milass continued to question me about my youth. It seemed a little ludicrous, to be sitting there talking about entertainment privileges and meal schedules with a bunch of drugged, naked men, but I dutifully reeled off the facts. With each sentence, I became aware of how closely everyone was listening.

Why? What did my childhood have to do with Joe and the League hunting me?

At last Milass stopped and abruptly gestured to the hogan's entrance. "You go now."

"May I ask a question before I do?"

Rico nodded. Milass gave me the go-ahead.

"I saw an alien man in the tunnels. His name is Dhreen; he's from Oenrall. Do you know him?"

Milass consulted with Rico, then said, "Yes. He has sanctuary here."

He was probably spying for Joseph. But if he was, why hadn't Joseph stormed this place? "Why does the Night Horse provide sanctuary to an alien male?"

Rico muttered something to Milass.

"We do not explain ourselves to liars." The little twerp grinned and pointed to the door. "Leave."

CHAPTER TWELVE

Centerfield

I emerged from the sweat lodge more confused than when I had gone in. My tunic was soaked with sweat, and I smelled of whatever they had been smoking in that pipe. I needed a thorough cleansing, a cool drink, and a place to hide and think things over.

Why was Rico so interested in my past? Why not ask me himself? Was having Milass as his mouthpiece supposed to impress me? Intimidate me? I didn't get it.

My guards took up their positions on either side of me, and I gave up the idea of hiding out somewhere. Might as well go back and face the music.

All thoughts of Rico and bathing and confronting Reever disappeared when I heard a woman laughing from the alcove and walked in to find Reever sitting on the exam table, apparently talking with a young Indian woman. She had her hand on his chest, her fingers playing with the lace of his shirt.

I wondered how she'd look after an amputation to the elbow. "Having fun, you two?"

She turned, and I saw it was Rico's girlfriend, Ilona something. The same woman who'd hit me after the chief had murdered Wendell.

Since I wasn't zoned out with hysterical shock this time, I noted all the usual reasons to loathe her—she was absolutely gorgeous. Long, glossy black hair, golden skin, and exotic dark brown eyes. She had wrapped herself in a *biil* woven in a scarlet-and-white pattern that set off her coloring beautifully.

Suddenly I felt grubby.

Ilona sniffed the air. "Do you never wash, patcher?"

Very grubby. "Maybe I'd have more time if I didn't have to deal with people loitering around Medical." I went to the cleanser unit and started unfastening my tunic. When I felt the Indian woman watching me, I pulled a privacy screen between me and them.

I took my time cleaning up, while Ilona continued her conversation with Reever as if I were invisible. She did most of the talking, going on about her last visit topside and how Rico was going to raise a new hogan for them up there as soon as the shockball season concluded. Harmless stuff, but it was the way she said it—in that breathy, female voice, punctuated with coy little giggles—that really got under my skin.

Finally I was clean, and dressed. I shoved aside the screen, startling Ilona, who merely frowned at me and then kept going on about some rug she was weaving. Evidently she planned to stay here all day and chatter, and Reever wasn't doing anything to discourage her.

"I hate to interrupt this fascinating conversation, but could you excuse us?" I said to Ilona. "I need to talk to my husband."

"I came to hear about *Nilch'i*'s recent dance with death." She gave Reever a brilliant smile. "Tales of daring intrigue me."

"Yeah?" Something green and ferocious snarled inside me. "Here's what happened: His kidney failed and I cut him open and fixed it. That's the whole story, so run along now."

She didn't. "You take all his fire from him."

Keeping the peace until I could figure a way to get

me and Reever out of here was important. More important than knocking her on her backside. "I keep him warm enough, Red Face."

Her pretty mouth became a thin, tight line. "Red *Faun*."

"Whatever." I gestured to the entrance. "Good-bye."

She sauntered over, tossing her head so her hair swung like a black silk curtain. "The chief utters your name too often. I grow tired of hearing it."

"Really." I showed her some teeth. "Does the chief also mention he's keeping me and my husband as prisoners here?"

"Now that the whiteskin patcher is dead, Rico says we need you." She spat on the floor. "I say the blood needs no part of a lying snake."

The tribe had once compared me to a goddess. Now I was a snake. Why couldn't I make normal friends, like everyone else? "Instead of flirting with my husband, why don't you have a little chat with your boyfriend, see what you can do to get us out of here."

That made her mad, judging by the way she shoved me back. She called me something, too—something that my wristcom refused to translate.

I returned the favor. "Look, Pocahantas, do whatever you want. Just leave."

A moment later we were down on the stone floor, her on top of me. She got in one good left to my chin before I rolled her off my newly healed ribs and slammed her into a storage container. Before things could get worse, strong hands yanked us apart.

"Let me go," I muttered, twisting to free myself from the restraining grip. "I'm not going to hurt her. A lot."

Reever was pulling Ilona up from the floor, helping her regain her balance, and totally ignoring me. "Are you all right?" he asked her.

"Hey. *Hey*." I pushed at the hands gripping me. "Damn it, let go!"

Odd-shaped fingers clamped down harder on my shoulders. "That's enough, Doc."

I froze, then shook the loose hair out of my face so I could see. This time I definitely wasn't hallucinating. "Hello, Dhreen. Take your damn hands off me."

My Oenrallian ex-friend hauled me over to the cleansing unit instead. Reever, I saw, was leaving with Ilona.

Had I really been afraid to face my husband? Now I was ready to rip his lungs out through his nose. "Reever, don't you go anywhere."

"Settle down, Doc." To my husband, Dhreen said, "You'd better give me a few minutes with her."

As my husband led her out of the alcove, Ilona fired her parting shot. "I am not done with you, snake."

"Come and see me anytime, Red Face. Anytime."

As soon as they disappeared, I twisted out from under Dhreen's spoon-shaped fingers on my arms and whirled on him. "You can get out, too."

He only grinned and thrust his hands in his trouser pockets. "Not content to see me again, Doc?"

"I'd hoped to be spared the pleasure." I pushed my hair back and refastened the clip holding it off my face.

Two years hadn't changed Dhreen, who still looked like an oversized kid. Oenrallians didn't appear to age until mid-life, which for them was around one hundred and fifty revolutions. He still sported his mane of blazing orange hair, out of which sprouted two red nubs that weren't horns, but his version of ears. He wasn't wearing the usual pilot's flight suit, but his gaudy purple tunic and trousers suited him just as well.

"It's been an extended interval, hasn't it?" He was giving me the once-over. "You haven't changed at all."

"Spare me the 'gosh, it's good to see you' speech." I stripped the exam table and remade it. "What are you doing here? Didn't Joseph have another spy mission lined up for you?"

"We need to talk about that."

I dumped the dirty linens in the sterilizer unit. "I heard all I wanted to hear the last time I saw you."

That had been on the *Perpetua,* after I had turned the League fleet over to the Hsktskt. When Joseph had revealed he'd hired Dhreen to take me to K-2, become my friend, and report back to him on my activities.

"You only heard Grey Veil's side of it—not mine."

I cleaned out the lines on the infuser rig, using compressed air. The flatulent noise expressed my opinion better than I ever could.

"There were just intentions for what I did."

I ran out of things to clean, and walked to the entrance of the alcove. Or tried to. He caught my sleeve.

"Stop disregarding me, Cherijo."

"Ignoring." I couldn't help correcting the way he slaughtered the Terran language. "I'm *ignoring* you, you stupid jerk."

"I didn't do it for compensation."

"How noble of you. Excuse me, the waste level is getting intolerable in here."

That didn't shake him off. "I was hopeless. I'd already gone to the League and everyone else I could think of. They all declined to aid me."

"Uh-huh." I studied my nails, which were as usual in deplorable condition. Maybe I should just surgically remove them and save myself the grief. "Are you done now?"

"I didn't want to hurt you. We were friends."

"Yes, we were." That got to me, when nothing else would have. "So you can imagine my shock when I found out you worked for Joseph. It's not the first time you've sold someone out. We both know that."

Dhreen winced at my reference, but then, he should have. He'd transported me from Terra to K-2, and served with me on board the *Sunlace,* acting like nothing more than a good friend. In reality he'd been hired by Joseph to do just that—be my friend, follow me around, and report back on what I did. I'd only found out when the League cornered us in Varallan, and Joseph had openly gloated over it.

I smiled at his discomfort. "You know, you really shouldn't keep doing this. Betraying people, I mean. I'm nice. The next victim may decide to separate you from your genitals."

"I didn't have a choice. He promised to help my people."

"Fascinating as I'm sure that particular story is going to be, I'll pass on hearing it. Now, I want you out of here. Now."

"Doc—" He let go of me. "Fine. Maybe, like you say, I deserve it. But I didn't pretend to be your friend to get close to you. I've never had a friend, before you."

"Treat the next one better," was my suggestion as I watched him go. "If anyone is ever stupid enough to trust you again."

I didn't allow myself to think about Joseph, Dhreen, or how I was going to get out of Rico's underground prison. Over the following weeks, my focus was making sure nothing went wrong with Reever's kidney, scanning my patients for syphilis (so far I'd found no new cases among the Night Horse), and finding a way to elude my guards so I could track down the outcasts. I could escape later.

One of the players I treated told me Joseph had several Elders from the Night Horse village detained and brought to New Angeles for questioning. To add insult to injury, the League had set up a command post just outside the village.

Reever disappeared for long stretches of time, generally at night. Ilona started hanging out at Medical, hoping to catch him on one of his infrequent visits.

She harassed me. I ignored both of them for the most part.

Then there were days I didn't.

"There is no reason for you to be hostile toward Ilona," Reever said, after preventing another tussle and sending his new groupie out of Medical.

"I see." I thought about punching him, but started his weekly exam instead. "Take off your tunic." I looked over his compact musculature, and an awful image of him naked with Ilona on an exam table coalesced in my head. "Why are you defending her?"

"Ilona is young and only wants attention."

She wasn't the only one. "You'd better watch your step, Reever. Her boyfriend likes to play with knives." I finished my scan of his torso and handed him back his tunic. "And please remember, I'm fresh out of ways to repair kidneys." I looked at the entrance, and saw the guards were talking. Without much effort I projected a link. *Have you found out anything on the outcasts?*

He shook his head.

If Rico had found them, I know one of us would have heard about it. They may have already left the tunnels and gone up to the surface. Hopefully, Joseph and the League wouldn't find them.

They still need a hiding place, he reminded me. *Many of them will never pass as full-blooded Terrans. They're still down here. I've seen signs out in the sewers.*

Why are you still going out there? You don't know if Rico's set up new traps. And what if you get caught?

He pulled something from his trouser pocket—a remote device, identical to the one the chief had used to disarm the traps. I darted a glance toward the entrance and made him put it back.

How did you get that?

He picked up the Lok-Teel, and concentrated on it for a minute. It formed a mask in his hand. A mask of Rico's face.

Very clever. I folded my arms. *Doing that on Catopsa nearly got you executed. What if he misses it?*

The outcasts are our only allies here; we will need their assistance if we are to escape. I will return the device tonight. He plumped up the berth linens and arranged them to appear as though someone was sleeping under them. *I need you to make the tribe think I am ill and staying here for the day.*

What if someone decides to peek under the linens?

You will keep them from doing so.

I rolled my eyes. *I always get the easy part. All right, I can probably drop a few comments about you getting a nasty head cold, and how I've isolated you in here so it won't spread around the tribe. I'll go out to the central cavern now, to get the guards away from the entrance. How long do I keep this up?*

I need at least three hours.

I hadn't left the alcove since the day before yesterday, which gave me an excellent excuse to stomp out of there, grumbling about claustrophobia, Reever's fictitious head cold, and having no help. Right on cue, my two shadows followed me out to the central cavern. I surreptitiously checked my wristcom. Three hours. He'd better not lose track of time wandering around out there.

Once I reached the center cooking fire, I made myself a cup of tea from the perennial clay pot warming in the ashes, and sat down beside the speaking rock. One of the older women was sitting with a couple of the teenagers, telling them some kind of story about a coyote.

"—and when the Dove maidens saw Coyote's fine wolf-skin quiver and the circles he had painted on his face, they honored him as someone of consequence and hearkened to his many lies. Coyote told them the Dove people needed no longer hunt, for with a thought he, Coyote, could make any animal lay down and die. When their hunters returned at dusk, the

Dove maidens hurried into the village and told them of this wondrous visitor and what he had promised—"

"You enjoy hearing tales about the Trickster?" Hawk asked behind me, making me jerk in surprise.

"About as much as I like you sneaking up on me like that." I said it without heat, though, because I was glad to see him. Until I saw his skin tone, which was almost pasty. "Are you feeling okay?"

"I am well." Awkwardly, he lowered himself down beside me. "I have been occupied with performing the Blessing Way."

"What's that?"

"A chant way, used to ensure good luck, good health, and blessings for good hope."

"Right." I'd never understand religion. "You're not doing this for sick people I should be seeing in Medical, I hope."

"No." He stretched out his legs, and for the first time I saw the faintly distorted shape of his musculature. "It is customary for us to perform the Blessing Way twice per revolution. The rite ensures good hope at any stage of life for all who wish to be sung over." He massaged one of his calves absently.

"Are your legs bothering you?"

He looked into the fire. "Sometimes."

"If you'd let me have a look at your back, I bet we can fix that, and a whole lot of other problems."

He laughed once. "Thank you, patcher, but no. I am used to this body. Changing it will not make me happy."

"You'd be surprised." I decided not to push, finished my tea, and rose to my feet. "I have to make my rounds. Want to join me?"

Since most of the tribe was still avoiding me, I'd gotten into the habit of visiting the various hogans to check on my current cases, and two pregnant women who were both in their third trimesters. Hawk agreed, and hobbled after me as I got started.

Many Belts, my first mom-to-be, was doing fine.

She'd put on a few pounds, but according to my scanner it was mostly baby. The fetus had dropped, and a quick pelvic scan showed her cervix already three centimeters dilated.

"Another week, I think." I checked her vitals and recorded them on my data pad, while the anxious father hovered at my elbow. "Want to see your son?"

He nodded, then grinned when I showed him the interuterine scan on the display. "He has two arms, and two legs, Many Belts," he said to his wife.

Already an experienced mother of twin girls, Many Belts rolled her eyes at me. "Better than to see four of each, I think."

Kegide was hovering outside the hogan of the younger pregnant woman, and made some urgent gestures I couldn't quite interpret.

"What does he want?" I asked Hawk.

"I do not know, but I will go with him." The hunchback took Kegide's outstretched hand and let the big man lead him away.

My second mom wasn't doing so well. She had a vaginal infection, and was showing signs of first-stage toxemia. I infused her with mild antibiotics and told her mother, who had come down from the surface to care for her, to keep a close eye on her fever.

The older woman wanted to know if evil spirits had possessed her daughter, which led to a long discussion to simplify the prenatal complications and dispel both women's fears. By the time I was done, I had passed the three-hour mark. I couldn't stall the guards much longer. I stepped out of the hogan and bumped directly into Milass.

"Excuse me." I tried to go around him, but he just sidestepped to compensate. "What?"

"Where is your gutless whiteskin mate?"

"Sick with a head cold in Medical. Why?"

"He was seen leaving your hogan last night." He turned around and headed for the tunnels.

I hurried after him. "Someone must be mixed up. Reever didn't go anywhere." I caught up to him. "He's very ill and contagious."

Milass ignored me and kept going.

If Reever wasn't back, this could get ugly. I increased my pace until I passed Milass, and hurried to Medical ahead of him. When I got there, I saw the lump of linens on the berth, and my heart sank.

Milass strode in and headed for the berth. I put myself between him and it. "He's sleeping. Come back another time."

That got me pushed to one side. "Why are you so alarmed, patcher? Are you hiding something here? Or is something missing?" With a big, nasty grin, he ripped the top linen from the berth.

Reever pushed himself up and blinked. "What is it?" he said, in an appropriately hoarse voice.

Milass muttered something and stalked out.

I sagged against the side of the berth. "God, that was close." Then I saw the two round bumps sticking up in Reever's light hair, and groaned.

Dhreen pulled the edge of the Lok-Teel mask down from his right eye, and winked at me, then stretched back out and promptly went to sleep.

I took my guards on another stroll, and came back after another hour of meaningless wandering. Dhreen was gone. Reever and Hawk were standing in the tunnel outside Medical, talking in low voices.

"Problem?" I asked, giving my husband a hard look.

"News has come. Black Otter was hurt in the game today." Hawk nodded toward the tunnel. "Before we could bring him here, the referees had him taken to a whiteskin hospital."

Damn, I hadn't been able to solve his skin problem. "They'll know he's a hybrid as soon as they take his uniform off."

"Yes. It is possible we may recover him before he is deported, but he cannot play on the team again." He turned to Reever. "We will begin training tomorrow."

"Training for what?"

"*Nilchi'i'* has been chosen to replace Black Otter as centerfield runback."

"*What?*" I didn't wait for an answer. "No. I positively forbid it." Hawk didn't say a word. "He's just had major surgery, damn it!"

"It is what the chief orders. Identity chips are being arranged. As soon as we have them, he will join the team."

Hawk left. Reever didn't say anything. Not that I would have noticed—I was too busy throwing a temper tantrum.

"He's nuts! That's what he is. How can he expect you to go out there and play that demented game for him? You'll be electrocuted the minute you step on the field!"

That made him raise an eyebrow. "I think I can avoid incurring any penalties, Cherijo."

I stopped pacing. "Don't you start overproducing testosterone on me now, Reever. That kidney may be healed, but it's still fragile. Those reformation cells are still taking hold." I kicked a stone. "Why doesn't he get one of his own people to replace Black Otter? Why does it have to be you?"

"Perhaps he'd rather sacrifice someone who doesn't belong to the tribe."

I'd had enough of what Rico wanted sacrificed. "We'll just see about that."

I tried to talk to the chief. I sent a dozen requests through my guards and Hawk to be granted an "audience."

Rico ignored me.

When my efforts at being diplomatic failed, I tried the direct approach, and went to confront him. As soon as I got within ten feet of the chief's hogan, my guards politely but firmly steered me away.

"You may not go there. The chief does not wish to speak with you."

"Is that right? Well, the chief can go to hell!" I shouted at the hogan, hoping he'd hear me. All that got me was a fast march back to the medical alcove, and after that I wasn't allowed even within yelling distance of Rico's hogan.

In the meantime, Kegide arrived every morning to collect Reever, and led him off to the surface and the practice field outside the village, to train. According to what Reever told me, there were men in the village who were veterans of the game, and they scrimmaged against the Night Horse players during each practice session.

"Apparently the goal of the runback is to keep the sphere in motion while crossing the length of the playing field, until an attempt can be made to kick the sphere into the touchzone. Each successful touch-in awards the runback's team four points."

"How thrilling. Hold still." I cleaned a laceration on his shoulder and dressed it. "If all you have to do is kick the damn thing, why are you getting so banged up every day?"

"Kegide plays the position of blockback. He attempts to prevent me from crossing the field, kicking the sphere into the touchzone, and also tries to take the sphere away from me."

"This involves knocking you down, right?"

"Yes."

"God." I saw the slight curl on one side of his mouth. "You're enjoying this, aren't you?"

"I have never participated in a cooperative athletic competition before." He shrugged. "It is interesting."

"Uh-huh." I pulled his tunic back down and swatted him on the arm. "Stop being so interested. Your kidney is more important than your success at team sports."

It was frustrating. Since I wasn't allowed to attend the practice sessions, all I could do was scan him and treat whatever wounds he received when he returned from the surface. At first, Reever got battered pretty regularly. Gradually he began showing up with fewer injuries, and then hardly any at all. My insistence on scanning him was virtually unnecessary.

What really bothered me was when he started getting interested in the game.

"I was able to score three times today," he said after a couple of weeks of this nonsense. "Defense prevented the village team from scoring any points at all." He looked down at my scanner's display. "I have found a very effective running pattern. No one was able to successfully tackle me."

"You're becoming such a jock." And I hated it, but I didn't say that. "Stay right where you are. I'm not done checking your spinal cord."

"I am fine." He pulled his tunic over his head. "I am looking forward to playing at the professional arena tomorrow."

Men. Give them a chance to compete as athletes, and even the brightest of them turned into instant Neanderthals.

"Not without this." I went to my worktable and brought back the special torso brace I'd made for him. It wasn't much, but it would provide some protection for his abdomen. "Wear it under your uniform."

He fingered the padded material, which I'd reinforced with sheets of flexible plas. "If the officials permit it."

I could care less about the rules. "Don't let them see it."

He looked at me oddly for a moment. "Cherijo, if something happens to me, I want you to leave this place immediately."

"Oh, sure, no problem, seeing as I can come and go as I please."

"Find the outcasts. They will help you."

"I have two mothers about to give birth, and a syphilis carrier to track down. Plus, the minute I appear on the surface, Joseph's men will grab me," I reminded him. "We're stuck here for the moment. Don't worry, nothing will happen to you."

I hoped.

Things happened to Reever after he started playing professional arena shockball. It wasn't as easy as the scrimmages with the surface villagers, and he always came back from every game with muscle strains, tears, bruises, and cuts. I started laying out therapeutic packs as a matter of course.

In direct relation to his injuries, his enthusiasm for the sport seemed to grow. I found I had to constantly bite my tongue or I ended up showering him with acidic sarcasm about the supposed allure of professional competition.

In the meantime, I kept trying to get to Rico, but he refused to see me.

One day Reever came back with five other players needing treatment. They were all in bad shape. He walked in with three of them, carrying the other two. I performed a quick visual and had the two unconscious men put on berths first.

"Multiple fractures, deep tissue thermal injuries, blood clots all over the place." I scanned the other player, then tossed down the instrument in disgust and started the infuser lines. "How many penalties did they take, Reever?"

"One had six. The other, seven. We're all burned. Take a look at him first." He pushed another player toward me. "He was penalized while at the bottom of a pileup. The sphere malfunctioned in his hands. It took several minutes to reset the computer."

"God. Look at this mess." I relived an old nightmare from my past as I carefully scanned the player's broken, charred fingers. "Sit down over there before you pass out." I turned and yelled at the guards. "Get Hawk in here, now. I need some help."

Several hours later, I finished wrapping the burns on Reever's hands and feet, and looked over the other players, now resting comfortably. "I've never seen injuries this bad before. What went wrong at the game?"

He pulled off his jersey, which had a huge number fourteen on each side, and the name *Nilchi'i* emblazoned across the back of the shoulder yoke. "The Gliders are trying to progress to the semifinals for the playoffs, and the teams challenging them are much harder to beat. Rico does not want the team to lose. He ordered the plays to be run, knowing we would be penalized."

"Why didn't you just refuse to play?"

"I did at first." Reever looked at his bandages. "Milass told me that if I did not run the plays, he would come back here and use his knife to blind you."

I got indignant. "And you believed him?"

"I wasn't going to take a chance."

"That is good, whiteskin. Because I would have carved her eyes from her head."

We both turned around to see Milass standing in the entrance.

"Come to see the damage you've done?" I asked, gesturing to the unconscious men. "They're going to be out of action for a couple of weeks."

"If they are truly men, they will survive."

Suddenly, something clicked. "You were a player. That's how you got those burn scars on your face." Fury surged through me. "Is that why you're forcing these men to nearly kill themselves every time they play this stupid game? So they can be as homely as you are?"

"They will bear their scars, as I do."

I wanted to lunge at him, but Reever had a hold on my arm. "You'll be bearing a few more by the time I get through with you, you little twerp."

"Any time, patcher." He plucked out a blade and waggled it at me, like a taunt. "Come to see me any time."

I made Reever and the other patients comfortable, then pulled Hawk out into the tunnel.

"I'm not going to stand by and keep treating these players for self-inflicted wounds. You get me to Rico so I can tell him that personally."

"No."

I wanted to break some of my knuckles on the nearest stone wall. Instead, I took a couple of slow, deep breaths. Control. That was what I needed. Control and a couple of fully charged pulse rifles.

"Hawk. You've worked Medical long enough to know how serious this situation is. These men are risking their health, and possibly their lives, to win a game that is meaningless."

"It means a great deal more than you understand." Hawk looked at my expression and lifted one warped shoulder. "There is much more at stake in playing for the junta than mere victory. The Night Horse are the only Native Americans competing professionally. We represent a lost ideal, we fight for ethnic recognition."

"So weave more rugs. Stage more ceremonials. Sing more chants. Whatever," I said, throwing out my hands. "Anything would be better than forcing these men to court electrocution just for the sake of putting some numbers on a four-story vid screen."

"They are not forced to play, patcher. They do it willingly, for our chief, for our people."

"Your chief doesn't give a damn about anyone but himself."

"On the contrary." Hawk looked up, and the intensity of his gaze made me take a step back. "Rico has prevented hundreds of our people from being deported. He created *Leyaneyaniteh* for their sake, not his own. He preserves a way of life that has been otherwise reduced to a few paragraphs in the databases of museums."

"That doesn't give him the right to ask these men to deliberately injure themselves in these games."

A strange smile curved his scarred mouth. "They are happy to do it. Suffering for the good of the tribe is a noble thing. It is an expected thing." He looked back into the alcove. "I will help you finish making the chart notations, but I will not speak any further on this."

"Fine."

We went back to the patients, and completed the tedious task of recording the individual case particulars on their charts. Hawk moved over to Reever, who was watching both of us.

"Your woman does not understand the ways of men," Hawk said.

"You would be surprised what she knows," Reever said, then he made a long, trilling sound.

"No whistling." I turned around. "You're going to . . . Hawk?"

Hawk was pressed back against a console, his face completely blanched. He stared at Reever with utter horror.

Reever sat up, and trilled something else. This time it was a bunch of different sounds, all mixed together.

The hunchback nearly fell flat on his face as he stumbled for the entrance.

I watched him go, then turned to my husband. "Now what's this all about? What did you do, mess up one of his chants?"

Reever stared at the entrance with a thoughtful expression. "Something like that."

CHAPTER THIRTEEN

Dolts to Fix

I thought being shunned, kept prisoner, under guard, and having to treat my husband and the other shock-ball players for self-inflicted injuries was bad enough.

Silly me.

The next game was scheduled a week later, and no one was permitted to remain on the injured roster. I was told to put support casts on the players with bone fractures, and protective dressings on everyone's burns. Except their hands—I found out junta rules prohibited players from insulating their hands with anything. The hard way, of course.

"Bandages won't insulate them against the sphere," I argued with Milass, when he came into Medical carrying the bundle of dressings he'd removed from the players. "Those burns are still healing."

"They are Night Horse. They will play without them." He dropped the ripped bandages at my feet. "They need none of your whiteskin coddling."

"How about nerve damage? Do they need that?" I yelled after him as he stalked out.

I lectured Reever on being careful until he left the alcove to join the other players going to the arena.

Then I sat down to wait, until my guards came to get me. By the arms.

"You are to attend the games," one of them said when I asked what the hell they thought they were doing.

I tried to twist free. "No thanks."

"It is not a request, patcher." One of them shoved a medical case into my hands, then pushed me ahead of them.

"Yeah. It never is."

I hadn't been out of the tunnel since escaping from Joseph, so emerging into the sunlight took a few minutes' adjustment. We weren't at the surface village—that route hadn't been used since Joseph and the League had taken up permanent residency there—but in the middle of a park of some kind.

By the time I got my bearings, the Night Horse were hustling me across the manicured grounds toward a glidebus parked on an access road. On the side of the bus was a stylized mural of a shockball player with black-feathered wings sprouting out of the back of his jersey.

"Who's that? Vulture Man?" I asked, pointing to the bus.

"He is the Glider."

So that's where the team got their name from. "What is he? Some kind of Indian hero?"

One of the guards chuckled. "No, patcher. The Glider is very real. He has been seen flying through the mountains for years. Many whiteskin have tried to capture him, but without success."

"He must be an alien, avoiding deportation."

"The Glider is a great figure of legend among the junta."

"I still think he looks like a big vulture."

They made me get on the bus and walk past seats filled with Night Horse players dressed in bulky protective gear.

I was shoved into the seat beside Reever. "What's going on? Why do they want me at the game?"

He put a hand over mine. *I don't know. I heard Milass tell the men to go and get you. He was angry. If you see Rico, don't antagonize him.*

That's going to be hard.

The glidebus pulled out onto the empty road and started heading toward the dense cluster of ground and hover-buildings I recognized as downtown New Angeles.

I'd say this is a great time to try to escape, if we had the cats with us. There was no way I was leaving Jenner and Juliet behind. Not with knowing how casual the Night Horse were about what went into their tribal cooking pot.

We will be even more closely guarded than we are below.

The glidebus pulled into a restricted area behind New Angeles arena and the players silently filed out. Waiting outside the doors to the team locker room were a pair of junta officials. One of them noticed me and put a hand up to stop me from entering.

"No fems in the locker room."

"She's the team patcher," Milass told the official, sticking out his chest and trying to look taller. "She's come to observe the game and make recommendations to our chief on how to reduce penalties."

"Here's one," I said. "Stop letting them play this idiotic game."

Both officials stared at me as if I'd told them to let the players run around the field naked.

"Cherijo," Reever said behind me, in a familiar warning tone.

"A good joke, patcher." Milass wrapped his hand around my upper arm. "She's amusing, isn't she?"

"Not as much as you are, trying to walk around on your toes like that. Have you ever considered putting lifts in your footgear?"

The officials laughed and waved us through. I thought Milass might just fracture my humerus before we got inside. When the door closed, he flung me against a row of storage units.

"Not another word out of you."

I swung out with the medical case, and rammed it into his groin. He folded over with a groan. "Keep your hands to yourself, or I'll do a lot more than talk."

Milass slowly straightened. "You'll die in my hands one day, bitch."

Reever didn't like hearing that. I could tell by the way he moved into that strange, alert sort of stance he did right before he wiped up the floor with someone.

Don't antagonize Rico's little pet rattlesnake, I thought. "Are we done now?" I asked Milass. "Or do you want to dance some more?"

He looked at Reever, then me. "The chief is waiting for you." The *secondario* pointed toward the other end of the locker room. "That way."

I needed to talk to Rico. Badly. "All right. Let's go."

"Cherijo—"

"I'll be fine. See you later."

I kept my case between me and Milass and followed him out to a lift panel. Once inside, I looked out through the viewer panel at the tiers of the arena, which were rapidly filling up with eager fans, and wondered where Rico's seats were. "What does the chief want to see me about?"

"He will tell you."

"Want me to ask him about that footgear for you?"

That got me slammed face first into a wall panel, and made the lift rock slightly. "Insult me again, woman." Milass said against my neck. "I am enjoying it."

"Try this instead." I stomped on his instep, then drove an elbow into his stomach. He staggered back and hit the opposite panel. I turned around and rubbed my bruised cheek. "Have you ever considered therapy? The extensive, mental kind?"

Before he could hit me again, the lift stopped and the door panels slid open.

We weren't in the stands, but at the entrance to a private arena box. I'd only seen one before, when one of Joseph's colleagues had invited us to his to watch a game. My creator had been so disgusted by the so-called sport that we'd left after the first fifteen minutes of play, and never repeated the experience.

That was one of the few times I'd ever agreed with my creator—shockball was stupid, pointless, and barbaric.

The box was three times the size of the one I remembered, with luxurious furnishings set up stadium-style, with rows of chairs equipped with personal vid screens. You could watch the game on the wall-length viewer in front of the chairs, too. It was programmed to display the field at eye level.

Terrans liked to see pointless, barbaric stupidity on a wide screen.

No one would go hungry or thirsty while watching, either—tables crammed with platters of gourmet food lined the walls banquet-style. A waiter, dressed in a modified Glider uniform, stood at a well-stocked bar. A second waiter, this one a drone, made a slow circle around the box, offering a tray of canapes and another of champagne.

But this box didn't belong to a wealthy doctor. There were very familiar woven rugs hanging on every wall. Bundles of multicolored corn in decorated baskets formed a huge centerpiece on a main banquet table. Traditional Navajo music played softly in the background.

How did the Night Horse rate a box like this? Then I spotted the only other two occupants of the room.

The chief and Ilona sat in front of a huge screen, which projected the image of the center of the playing field below us. They weren't wearing the clothes I'd gotten used to seeing them in. In fact, if you ignored the braids and the dark skin, Rico and Ilona could have passed for a pair of wealthy Caucasians, dressed in their best party clothes.

All I could do was stand there and gape.

The dark man turned his head, smiled, and rose to his feet. "Dr. Torin, welcome. Come and join us for a drink." He went to the drone and took a pair of flutes from the champagne tray.

Ilona pouted as I walked over and accepted a flute of champagne from her boyfriend. He wore the very latest trend, a four-piece black suit in an optic illusionary motif of red checks. Joseph had a couple of the same suits, minus the blinding pattern.

"Nice place you have here." I gestured around me with the champagne glass. "It's good to be the chief of the Night Horse, huh?"

He laughed. "This is nothing more than what is allocated for the owner of a participating team."

I spilled some champagne on my footgear. "You *own* the Gliders?"

"Come, sit down with me. Ilona will give us a few minutes to talk, won't you, my beautiful one?"

His beautiful one scowled, got up, and flounced out of the room without another word.

I sat down gingerly on the expensively upholstered chair Rico indicated. Real fabric. "How does an Indian who lives in a cave and runs an alien underground afford to buy a professional shockball franchise?"

"Night Horse players donated their salaries to our tribal fund, until we could purchase the team."

We watched the last minutes of the pregame show through the viewer. Two thousand gyrating women in micro-mini skirts danced and waved various glittery accessories to the music from dueling drone bands on either side of the field. Around the top of the arena, huge vid screens projected holoimages of cartoon animals in shockball uniforms getting electrocuted by fumbling oversized spheres in various comical plays.

Even more ludicrous was the sight of what had to

be two hundred thousand fans filling every available seat, nook, and cranny of the arena. Nearly all of them were wearing modified team jerseys and other ridiculous paraphernalia related to the sport—black plasfoam wings on their heads for the Gliders, and twin foam stardrive housings for the opposing team. Some had even painted their faces with team colors.

And I'd thought the Indians were prehistoric.

"Why didn't anyone ever mention that your people owned this team?"

"We do not discuss our tribal concerns with outsiders."

That put me in my place. So much for being of the blood. "Must have taken the players a long time to accumulate the money."

"Only a few years. After the Native American Remuneration Act, Indians entering into any free enterprise qualify for matching federal funds." He sat down next to me and sipped his champagne. "Not all whiteskin laws work toward our detriment."

So Rico really owned the Gliders. That totally blew away my perception of the poor, ignorant, deprived renegades. And from the smugness he was radiating, he was enjoying my reaction.

I went to check the time on my wristcom, then saw I'd left it in Medical. Rico was, on his own, speaking stanTerran. Very educated, erudite stanTerran.

Suddenly, I wasn't sure anything I'd seen or heard over the past months was the authentic package.

I refrained from commenting on the amazing improvement in his personal situation and speech patterns, and watched as the dancers cleared off the field, making way for the two straight lines of players from each team. I stood up automatically for the World Government Anthem. Rico didn't.

As the last notes of "Our Terra, Unified" faded away, the fans cheered so loudly that the viewer panel vibrated from the decibels. I sat back down and handed my untouched flute to the passing drone.

"Why am I here, Chief?"

"I thought you would enjoy watching your husband play. He has become one of the most popular members of our team."

I could see that for myself. Hundreds of fans in the arena wore the Gliders' number-fourteen jersey, and there was a swelling chant of *"Nilch'i'! Nilch'i'!"* already echoing around the field.

"I'd rather talk to you about these injuries the players have been receiving."

"Later. We have a real chance at making the playoffs for the World Game." He continued, talking about the team's performance since something called the "preseason."

I tuned him out after the first sentence and glanced back at the lift, the only exit from the private box. The demonic dwarf stood in front of it, stuffing his face with the tray of caviar-topped toast triangles he'd taken from the drone. He caught my eye and snarled, his teeth black from the fish eggs. So much for slipping out when I wouldn't be noticed.

"Reever's kidney isn't going to take much punishment," I said to Rico, when he finally ran out of game stats. "Some of the other players should be benched for the rest of the season."

"Nilchi'i'" tells me he is fully recovered."

The Wind was going to get himself smacked, if he didn't stop trying to be Super Terran. "Who's the doctor, me or him?"

"You are a woman." He flicked some fingers at me. "You do not understand what drives a man to win."

I could feel the heat creeping up my face. Stay cool, Cherijo. "I understand what ruptures an internal organ."

"There are other, more important matters for you to attend to." He leaned forward, getting close to my face. "You have been punished long enough, I think.

You belong to us now. Accept it, patcher. I can make your life much more pleasant."

The sudden, inexplicable perception smashed over me, much stronger than before. I wondered for the first time if he was doing something deliberately to drag me in like this—hypnosis, maybe? I bit down on the inside of my cheek until I tasted blood. Slowly the assault on my synaptic functions faded back to a faint, nonthreatening buzz.

"Don't do me any favors, Chief," I said. "I like my life tough."

I saw Reever trot out onto the field, carrying his helmet. Seeing his number-fourteen jersey made the crowd cheer. My throat tightened when he joined the double rows of players and took position directly in the center. Some buzzer went off and the players tightened the straps on their helmets before crouching over in a distance-runner's stance.

"Is it starting now?"

"Yes."

On the field, nine players from each team lined up facing each other. The computerized game sphere popped out of a heavily shielded box at the top of the arena and dropped down to hover between the lines. It shimmered and tiny rainbows flickered around it.

I recalled reading a psych text about some long and painstaking research on what colors and textures most appealed to the senses. The resulting data had ended up determining the design of modern sports equipment, like the shockball game sphere. I could see the attraction. Even I felt like reaching out and grabbing it.

When everyone was in position, a drone official rolled down the length of the gap between the lines, then turned near the sidelines and fired a small, ornate pistol into the air.

Every fan in the arena shrieked as the two sides descended on the sphere, their arms folded in front of their jerseys, legs kicking at each other and the sphere. Someone got it out of the middle and went down on his knees, cradling the sphere between them. It was Reever.

"We have won the starting offense driveline," Rico said.

"Yipee." I watched a couple of the players slap Reever on the back as they helped him to his feet. The chant of *"Nilch'i'! Nilch'i'!"* got a lot louder. I winced as one of the opposition spit on Reever's face mask. "Oh, isn't that against the rules?"

"No. Spitting on another player is a time-honored tradition."

Well, what did I expect? I was on Terra, after all.

From there the game wasn't difficult to follow. The Gliders tried to kick and bounce the sphere down the field toward a small silver box being guarded by two of their opponents, armed with sticks with wide, padded ends. The other team, dubiously named the Nu-York StarDrivers, tried to stop them by throwing their bodies to block the sphere during passes, and colliding with the players kicking the sphere.

One of the Night Horse, not Reever, acquired a penalty on the second play. The sphere rose from the ground, hovered over the teams, then dropped and landed in the hands of one of the players.

"How does this penalty thing work?"

"The sphere is linked to a remote computer. It records any illegal motion and penalizes the players immediately after the play is done."

"How does it know which player made the illegal motion?"

"It reads the sensor grid under the playing field. The grid identifies the offender by the transmitter implanted in his helmet."

I hissed in a breath as the man suffered a hard jolt of bioelectrical energy, which knocked him off his feet. The crowd, naturally, began cheering.

"What did he do to deserve that?"

"Watch the arena vid."

On the small screen by my chair, the view of the field was temporarily blacked out, and the penalty displayed. "Illegal use of hands?"

"Junta rules specify the players are not to touch the sphere with their upper bodies."

"How do they know he used his hands? I didn't see him grab it."

"He probably didn't do anything more than brush it with a few of his fingers. The sphere is highly sensitive. It will register any contact, no matter how insignificant."

As the game went on, the level of excitement in the arena peaked. Grown men and women began leaping up and down in front of their seats, screaming at the players on the field. The viewer panel never stopped vibrating, and I couldn't imagine how noisy it was, outside our insulated box.

There were amusing moments. One young woman rushed onto the field and had to be hauled off by official drones. Despite her expensive business suit and carefully groomed hair, she acted like some kind of crazed psychiatric patient, screaming obscenities at the visiting team as she frantically waved a small flag bearing the home team's emblems.

To watch apparently intelligent beings embarrass themselves with such juvenile enthusiasm for what had to be the *stupidest* game in existence made me wish I'd been born on a Hsktskt planet. At least with the lizards, violence had some meaning.

Another player, this one on the StarDrivers team, was shocked. The decibel level reached a new crescendo.

"Why do they scream when someone gets penalized?"

"They cheer because they like seeing the players get hurt."

"That's disgusting."

He shrugged. "That's shockball."

Milass came to sit on the other side of me and leaned over to address the chief. "Should I begin?"

"Yes."

Rico's *secondario* brought over another tray of food and sat beside me. He held it out.

"No, thank you," I said politely, thinking he was offering it to me.

"Hold this for the chief." Milass scooped up a couple of dessert tarts and started munching on them. "How many times did the Shaman take you to sporting events?"

I took the tray. "Once."

"How old were you?"

More questions about my childhood. I ignored him. "If you want to know something, Rico, why don't you ask me yourself?"

"I must attend to the game. Answer Milass."

It was hard to concentrate; I couldn't take my eyes off Reever. Plus the questions Milass asked were extremely annoying.

"How many hours of leisure were you permitted each day?"

"Were you permitted to go on holiday, and if so, where?"

"How many times a day were you permitted to eat?"

Reever took a bad hit and went down under a pile of three opponents, and I jumped to my feet. "No!" The tray went flying. The drone waiter hurried over and began cleaning up the mess.

Milass yanked me back down. "Answer me."

"I could have as much leisure time as I wanted, I went on holiday with my paid companion twice a year, and I ate three times a day. Satisfied?"

Rico said nothing, but made a languid gesture.

The questions went on. Really idiotic questions this time, about how much credit I was given and what toys were provided for me and things like that. The more I told them, the more I sensed Rico withdrawing. It was as if my answers disgusted him.

Maybe they did. I hadn't ever given much thought about how privileged my childhood had been—who did? Although Joseph had never been an affectionate parent, he had literally showered me with material things. The real motives behind his generosity still made me sick.

To Rico and Milass, however, the facts probably made me sound like a thoroughly spoiled brat. I was relieved when the halftime warning went off, and Milass got up and went to the lift.

"Come. You will see to the players below."

I saw to the players. There were dozens of minor electrical burns from the many penalties incurred by the team in the first half. Reever included.

I got to him as quickly as I could and wiped the sweat from his face as I ran my scanner over him. "Are you okay?"

He nodded and leaned back against the storage unit behind him.

"Rico had me up in his private box. I've been watching the game. Guess what? The Night Horse tribe owns the Gliders." I injected him with a mild analgesic and treated fresh burns on both of his palms. "Do you have to keep playing?"

He took his clear plas mouth protector out before he answered. There were teeth marks in it. "As long as I stand upright, yes."

"Can you run these plays without getting the penalties?"

"I'm trying." He regarded the protector without expression. "The plays are deliberately flawed so we can gain maximum advantage on the field."

"Who's calling the plays?"

"Rico schedules them before the game."

I straightened and glanced at the next player waiting for treatment. "I'll try to talk to him about it."

Reever closed his eyes. "Be careful."

*   *   *

The twenty-minute interval went by too fast, and the players were signaled to return to the field. I went back up to the private box with Milass. This time I didn't try to bait him while we were in the lift. I was too busy formulating an argument to use with the chief.

Rico was busy, too. I walked in to find him with Ilona on his lap. He was lazily fondling her body while she purred and rubbed her cheek against his. Her eyes widened when she saw me step off the lift.

"What is she doing here again?"

"She is my personal patcher." Rico pushed her off and slapped her backside. "Go back to our hogan, sweet one. I will return after the game."

Ilona made sure to bump shoulders with me on her way to the lift. Oddly, Milass went with her, leaving me alone with Rico.

"Your girlfriend doesn't like me," I said as I sat down.

"She is young," he said, as if that explained it all. "What do you think of our game?"

"It's revolting. Brutal, criminal, and meaningless. I think whoever invented it should be shot. They should give each of those spectators a couple of electrical burns, make the players get some psych therapy, and throw the team owners into prison."

"You do not like it."

"It disgusts me."

He stretched and smiled at the viewer. "It is not a woman's game, I think. Though there are several female players on other teams."

The chauvinist didn't sound too pleased about that. "But not on your team."

"Not mine." He waved to the drone, who brought over a plate with fruit-flavored sherbets. "Women have a simpler purpose in the great scheme of things."

"Like sitting on your lap and letting you paw them?"

"Why do you ask?" He licked some ice from the silver spoon in his hand. "Are you intrigued by my attentions to Ilona?"

"Sure. I always wonder why other women have such bad taste in men."

He threw the drone's plate at the viewer panel, splattering it with a rainbow assortment of sherbet, which immediately began to melt and drip down all over the immaculate red-and-black floor covering.

He stood up, towering over me. "You have been overindulged since you took your first breath."

"You should have been around the last three years." I went to help the drone clean up the new mess, but the dark man seized me by the wrists and pushed me down on my knees. "You're ruining my trousers."

"You serve me," Rico said, tightening his grip. "Say it."

He wasn't just angry. He looked ready to kill me. We were alone; there was no one to stop him.

I remembered my four broken ribs, which made it easy to say the words. "I serve you."

For a long moment we stayed in that position, me on my knees, him ready to strike. My heart pounded in my ears, driven by the waves of fury rolling from him. Slowly his fingers uncurled, until he released me.

"Watch the remainder of the game."

Then he simply walked to the lift and left me there.

I waited a few minutes, then tried to get out myself. The lift didn't respond to my summons—he'd apparently locked me in.

I took the opportunity to search for weapons or anything that I could use to defend myself. There was nothing—even the utensils on the banquet table were made of thin plas and therefore totally useless.

At last I dropped in a seat and watched the violent

escalation of the game on the field below. Reever was still playing centerfield, still getting the sphere on every other play. The tally board showed the gap between the teams' scores—the Night Horse were winning.

But not without paying a heavy price. Four of Rico's players were penalized so frequently they dropped out of the game with injuries by the final quarter. The replacement players evidently weren't as skilled and for nearly the entire final twenty minutes of the game, Reever ran the sphere.

I watched, mesmerized by Reever's speed and the thundering approval of the screaming fans as he moved toward the touchzone. I didn't cheer when he scored points. All I could do was let out whatever breath I was holding.

The game ended at last. The arena vids lit up with the final score: Gliders—35, StarDrivers—7.

"Way to go, Duncan," I said to the image of my husband as he was carried off the field on the shoulders of his teammates. "At this rate, your kidney may last a whole month."

Milass emerged from the lift.

"You will attend to the players now."

Back down to the locker room, where I did another full round of treating injuries. This time the burns were much more severe and there were several cases of thrombosis and minor stress fractures to be dealt with. Reever hadn't been hurt as badly this time, but that didn't make me feel any better.

"Did you watch the entire game?" he asked as I scanned him.

"Yeah. Real riveting, seeing you get pounded like a filet of veal. I especially liked it when the other guys spit on you. Sports traditions are so heart-warming, aren't they?"

"There is a reason for what I'm doing, Cherijo."

"You'll have to explain it to me some time." I finished my scans and dressed the new burns on his palms. "Gee, look. The insides of your hands are starting to match the outsides."

He studied the new injuries, and flipped his hands to display the old scars. "I will heal."

"But not before next week." I checked his pupils, and then his ears. "I assume you're playing again."

"I have to."

"Never say I stood in the way of you enjoying yourself, Reever." I clicked off my optic magnifier and thrust it back in my case. "Excuse me, I have other dolts to fix."

My first shockball game was not to be my last. Rico insisted I be brought to every subsequent game leading up to the final playoffs for the World Game. In between treating players, I sat in his private box and submitted to more interrogations by Milass.

Reever kept playing, and wild applause broke out whenever he took the field. Women began rushing at him after the games from the sidelines. He ignored them, but that didn't make me feel any better. Bad enough when it was just Ilona being his groupie. Now he had thousands of women wearing number-fourteen jerseys to every game.

After one match that sent the Night Horse into overtime play, Rico summoned the entire team up to his private box to celebrate their victory. That was when Reever overheard Milass questioning me, and pulled me aside later to ask me about it.

"I don't know," I admitted. "Rico seems to get some kind of charge out of hearing about my childhood." I looked over at the chief, who was drinking with the players. He was telling a story everyone thought was funny, judging by the amount of laughter.

"You don't see how he looks at you when you speak with Milass," he said, looking worried—for

Reever, anyway. "He's angry about something. I can almost sense it."

"You feel it, too?" I asked, then I bit my lip. "Damn."

"What are you talking about?"

I hadn't meant to let him know about the weird connection I shared with Rico, but he was already steering me into a private corner.

Tell me.

He linked to me so fast that I barely registered the mental connection now. *It's nothing, really. Just, I can tell what he's feeling sometimes. Whenever he gets close to me.* I looked at my footgear, which I was shuffling nervously. *Look, I don't have any feelings for him. I mean, other than disgust and revulsion and what I'd normally feel toward a murderer. But no matter how hard I try, I can't turn this thing off.*

We have never tested your telepathic abilities.

We both looked at Rico, both of us thinking the same thing: *What if he can pick up our thoughts?*

I decided to use my voice. It seemed safer. "If I was a telepath, wouldn't I be able to read anyone in the room? The only people I can do it with is you and . . . him."

Reever's hand went under my chin, and he made me look up at him. "I am not jealous of Rico."

"You don't have any reason to be."

"I know that." But his eyes were so cold. "You've been keeping this from me as well, haven't you?"

"Yes." I was tired of the anger and the lies. "There's something else we need to talk about."

"Not here." He leaned forward, and murmured the rest against my ear. "I'm going to try to link with him. We have to know if he's a telepath, or just a transmitter. We also need to find out all of his plans for us. See if you can separate him from the group, just for a moment. I don't want anyone else to see what I do."

"Okay. Wait here." I took two glasses of wine from

the passing drone waiter. "Be prepared to ad-lib your way through this."

I wandered through the crowd over to Rico and the players, and squeezed in beside the chief. To get his attention, I handed him one of the drinks. "Do you have a minute, Chief?" when he frowned, I added, "Reever and I want to have a private toast." I held out my hand and turned up my smile, like we were all good pals.

He folded his hand over mine. "Of course."

I led him over to the corner where Reever was waiting. "Look who I ran into, honey. Chief, my husband wants to make a toast." I lifted my glass, and gave Reever a glare.

Reever lifted the drink he'd snatched from a nearby table. "To the glory of the Gliders, and the coming World Game. May we make you the owner with the most wins in the junta."

We all clinked our glasses together, and drank. Somehow, I had ended up with another merlot. I nearly choked on it.

"Why do you toast to our success, patcher?" Rico asked after a healthy swallow. "You despise this game."

I gave him a goofy smile, as if I was a little drunk. "I guess it sort of grows on you after a while."

"We're both looking forward to the championship games." Reever held out his hand. "Wish us luck, Chief."

"You have what will serve you better—skill and heart." Rico took Reever's hand and shook it.

I watched the chief's eyes glaze over for a few seconds, and the two of them stood there like statues, not moving or even blinking. Finally, Reever released the chief's hand.

"Luck will be welcome, too." Rico had sort of a blank look. Then, without saying another word, he turned and went back to the group of players by the viewer.

I moved in front of Reever, trying to block him from the gazes of Milass and the other Night Horse. He was pale and beads of sweat had broken out over his upper lip and brow. "Are you okay?"

"No." He wiped a hand over his face and stared at the chief. "I linked with him, but I— His mind—"

I saw Milass heading our way. "We'll talk about it later."

Later turned out to be that night, in our hogan.

It is safer to use telepathy, Reever told me. *He cannot read us, and it will be easier to explain this way.*

You looked terrible after you linked with him. What went wrong?

His mind does not operate the way a Terran's usually does. He thinks almost completely in images—memories, I believe.

What are the memories of?

Reever obliged by summoning up the images he'd seen. I watched the mature Rico looking at himself in the mirror, and seeing the image transformed into a young boy with a battered face. Rico picked up something to eat, and melted into an emaciated adolescent.

He'd been beaten, and starved. No wonder Reever had been upset. *I'm sorry. I had no idea he'd been through that kind of thing, or I would have never let you do this.*

It explains much about his need for dominance and control over others. Reever pulled me closer. *That much of his character I understand completely.*

It made me think for a minute. *Is that why you became a linguist? So you could control others? Because of what your parents did to you?*

It was more out of my need to control my environment. Many times in my youth I found I couldn't communicate with the beings around me. It was frustrating, especially when I was left behind while my parents were out gathering data in the field. I was never beaten by my parents, or intentionally starved, but inadvertently through their negligence, I suffered the same deprivations.

I was glad they were dead. *I can't believe they did those things to you. You were just a little kid.*

I survived. You survived. But Rico . . . He shook his head. *He is completely without conscience or remorse for what he does. That much, his parents taught him.*

I tried to make out the image Reever had retained of Rico's parent, but all I saw were huge, black-and-white blurs were shaped like hulking monsters.

Maybe. I was beginning to have my own suspicions about the source of Rico's mental imbalance. *I have to find a way to examine him, somehow.*

That will not be easy.

I live for the day something is.

We both sat up when a loud, automated screech sounded throughout the cavern.

"What's that?"

One of the players stuck his head through the entrance flap to our hogan. "Intruders have penetrated the entrance traps to one of the outer tunnels. Come, we must hide."

We followed the other members of the underground down a tunnel into a section of old subway I hadn't seen before. Behind us, the rumble of collapsing rock and weapons being fired in the distance sent deep vibrations through the stone walls.

At the end of the ancient platform, Hawk was standing at the entrance to some kind of room, ushering people in.

"What's going on?" I asked him, and he waved me and Reever over to one side.

"The Shaman discovered the entrance to the sewer pipes from his underground facility a few days ago." Hawk pointed back in the general direction of the estate. "We didn't expect him and his men to find the traps so quickly, but they may be using wide-range thermal proximity scanners. Our scouts report they're also using some kind of chemical detectors."

That made no sense, until I remembered the solution that had splashed everywhere when Rico had destroyed the embryonic chambers. "We must have tracked the duralyde in here. That's how he found us. What happens when they get to the central cavern? Are we going up to the surface?"

"They won't. Rico is sealing off access to all the tunnels that lead to the cavern. They've all been rigged with frequency displacers in the ceilings."

"Hawk!" someone called from the tunnel.

He pointed into the room. "Go in the bunker now. We reinforced this section to resist collapses. There will be many when the displacers are activated."

Inside the large bunker, which had once been a large, tile-lined lavatory, it was cold, dark, and crowded. Someone put up a couple of temporary emitters, while a few of the women started handing around blankets. Reever and I found a place against one wall and stood with our backs to it, watching and listening to the tunnels collapse.

"What are these displacer things he was talking about?" I asked him, keeping my voice low.

"They're used in mining to create tunnels and break down rock into workable ore. The units tap into the atomic frequencies of the stone, then alter them at the molecular level. The stone molecules subsequently disintegrate, and the solid mass turns to gravel."

"How charming." I looked around at the tired faces of the Night Horse, waiting patiently for the all-clear. "Any chance we can get our hands on one?"

"Possibly."

The vibrations abruptly stopped. An hour passed before Hawk called for everyone to return to the hogans. Reever and I went back, but neither of us were able to sleep very well. My still-ringing ears kept me staring at the roof for the rest of the night.

CHAPTER FOURTEEN

A Promise to Keep

When I heard the women preparing the morning meal outside, I left Reever to go and check on the cats, whom I'd left in Medical. They were both hiding under the equipment, but I coaxed them out with a bowl of leftover stew.

Ever the practical stray female, Juliet didn't waste time, but got right to wolfing down her meal. Jenner paced around her protectively, giving me some surly looks.

"Hey, it wasn't my fault the guy in charge decided to blow half of this place last night."

Jenner sat down beside his hungry companion and regarded me without a shred of sympathy. *You're never around when things start going boom.*

"Yeah, I know. I'm sorry."

"Patcher."

I turned to see a couple of the men standing in the entrance. "Did someone get hurt?"

"The chief wishes to see you. Come with us."

I was escorted to the central cavern, where nearly the entire tribe was assembled around the fire. Milass was standing on the speaking rock, holding something and shaking it.

"We offer nothing but life and meaning and purpose and *this* is how we are repaid for our generosity. It is beyond forgiveness this time. Our way of life is threatened. Our lives are threatened. *We* are threatened."

Rico was standing below, and he didn't look happy, either.

I turned to one of the guards. "So who's in trouble?"

I got my answer when I was led up to the speaking stone.

"Patcher." Milass threw down the object at my feet. It was a tunic, torn and filthy. My physician's tunic, which had disappeared a few days ago. "You led the whiteskins here. You showed them the way into the tunnels."

The demon dwarf had gone way too far this time. "Um, no, I didn't."

"We found this where the whiteskins broke in from the sewers. It is yours."

"Yes, it's mine, but—"

"You treated the unclean cast out from this tribe."

"Yes—"

Rico came up and grabbed me by the hair. "I trusted you and you betrayed all of us. How did you lead them in here? Did you work a spell? Did you mark the way with magic? Is that how their machines led them to us?"

"No!" He was scaring me. "I don't do magic or spells. It was the duralyde from the lab. We must have gotten it on our footgear."

"Let her go."

It was Reever, and he was not happy. Hawk came up behind him and grabbed his arms.

"She is a *chindi,* intent on destroying *Leyaneyaniteh.*" Rico shoved me forward, toward one of the tunnels no one was allowed into. "I will deal with her."

The last I saw of Reever was him struggling with Hawk, then going still as Hawk said something to him. When I stumbled, Rico dragged me back on my feet by my hair. My scalp burned as I kept trying to free myself.

"What are you doing? This is crazy!"

The chief kept dragging me forward, past the stern faces of the tribe and into the forbidden tunnel. Once inside, he hauled me down what seemed like miles of rock to a wide, open area. Where we stood hung over a huge, dark hole like a cliff. He forced me to the very edge.

"I believed you were one with us. I treated you as one of the blood, and you do this to me. You betrayed me."

"I didn't betray you!"

"Lies!" He shoved me over the edge, and held me for a moment, dangling by my hair. I clawed at his hand, trying to hold on. "If only he could see you now."

He let go and I fell into the dark abyss below. I screamed, waiting for the bone-shattering impact, but it never came. I simply kept falling and falling.

Something came out of the dark at me from below, and claws sank into the right side of my abdomen.

Animal? Monster?

The wrenching grab sent me spinning out of control, until my head smashed into hard rock. My last thought was of Reever, and how glad I was that Rico hadn't made him watch me die.

I didn't expect to survive that fall, much less wake up in Reever's arms. It was a lot like how I'd woken up, after coming in direct contact with the Core back on K-2. Especially the being naked and floating in water part.

Maybe I'm just having a flashback.

I opened one eye, not sure if I was going to trust my senses. No, I was definitely naked, and absolutely floating in water. If this was a flashback, it was happening inside a dimensional simulator.

A dimensional simulator that strongly resembled a cave half filled with an underground lake.

Reever was doing something to one side of my face. The same side that was throbbing. I'd hit the side of the pit there, I remembered. There were more aches and pains. I felt the distinct sting of lacerations below my ribs and gingerly touched them. Claw marks. Big claw marks.

There really was something in that hole.

"They are not bad," he said. "I don't think you'll need sutures."

"Thank you, Dr. Reever." I opened the other eye and looked around. "Mind telling me what happened?"

"Rico threw you into an interior shaft."

"I remember that part." I winced. "Ouch, stop. That hurts."

"We almost didn't have time to get you before you fell too far."

"We?"

He looked over at the side of the pool. So did I. Hawk was lying facedown under a blanket, apparently unconscious. I jerked up and found the bottom of the pool with my feet. "What happened to him?"

"You'd better see for yourself."

I got out of the pool and went to Hawk. He wasn't unconscious, only curled over and in considerable pain. As soon as I pulled the blanket aside, I saw why.

"I need my medical case right now. I left it in the bunker," I said to Reever, who disappeared into an opening in the rock wall beyond the pool. I started a therapeutic massage to loosen the cramped muscles along Hawk's abdomen and back, talking to him as I worked on the knotted tissues. "This is why you never wanted me to scan you."

He looked up at me, and managed a nod.

"Now that I know, are you going to let me help you?"

"Can . . . you?"

I sat back on my heels. "Yeah. I think I can." I got the rest of his clothes off and rubbed his limbs briskly to promote circulation. That's when I saw the open sores. "God, you've been infected, too. Who was it? One of the outcast women?"

He shook his head, and refused to answer any more questions. Reever arrived a few minutes later, and handed me dry clothes along with my medical case.

I scanned Hawk, took a blood sample, and confirmed he had first-stage syphilis.

"I'm going to start you on antibiotics to treat the venereal disease, but I have to know who gave it to you so I can stop her from spreading it." He didn't answer. "Once we get the syphilis cured, we'll start you on a regime of physical therapy." I adjusted my scanner and performed a spine series. "Maybe some minor surgery, too. But I need to know whom you've been having sex with. Not because I'm nosy. They're going to need treatment."

The analgesics I infused him with helped dull the pain of his cramped muscles, and he sighed. "I am the tribe's only *hataali*. It is my place to perform the *Tł'ééjí*, the Night Ways."

"Which is?"

"The necessary ceremonial to cure the diseased one."

Not this Indian superstitious nonsense again. "There may not be just one diseased person. Dozens of people could be infected." Be nice if I could confirm and actually do something about that. "A lot of singing and dancing won't cure syphilis."

He closed his eyes. "It is what must be done first."

"No, the entire tribe needs to be inoculated, including the woman who gave you this disease."

"If I fail, I will tell you everything you need to know."

I laughed once. "Look, I'm all for cultural integrity. But praying to your gods to get rid of venereal disease is about as intelligent as throwing the only doctor you have down a bottomless pit."

Hawk gritted his teeth. "Our way is not meaningless."

"It's a primeval attitude." My display indicated his penicillin screen was negative, so I infused him with the antibiotic. "Wake up and join this century."

"The old ways are our balance."

I threw up my hands. "Fine. Go on and do your song-and-dance routine. When some of your children are born blinded by this outbreak of syphilis, I'll remind you of this conversation." By the time I was done ranting, he was asleep.

Reever wrapped a thick piece of linen around me and started rubbing me down with it. "You cannot force them to follow the dictates of modern science."

"I'm not planning to." I sighed as he unraveled my wet braid and began drying my hair. "It's simple geometry, you know. The longer we wait to treat the carriers, the more people they can spread the disease to." I thought of the wedding ceremonial we'd attended. "Maybe even some of the villagers topside. That feels nice."

He draped the damp linen over my shoulders and worked his fingers through the worst of the tangles. Then his hands slowly stilled, his fingers spreading on either side of my throat. "I thought I'd lost you again."

"Me, too." I turned around. "Have I lost you?"

"What makes you think you have?"

"The shockball. Ilona. What I did—" and what I still hadn't told him. "Duncan, I meant it. What I said. If you want to find someone who can give you children, I won't stand in your way. Although you could do better than Ilona—"

Suddenly he was pulling my hair. "Do you love me?"

"It doesn't matter what I feel. You can—"

Really pulling my hair. "Answer me."

"Of course, I love you. But if you don't stop yanking on my scalp, I'm going to—"

He hauled me over to a cavity in the rock, away from Hawk, and threw the linen down on the stone floor. His tunic followed. "Show me."

We hadn't been intimate with each other since before his surgery. I'd been too scared, too upset, too angry, too ashamed. Everything that had happened since we'd been taken from the *Truman* had conspired to tear us apart. Most of it was my doing.

So if I felt like a virgin all over again, I was justified.

My hands trembled, and I couldn't look at him as I stepped closer. I shivered with cold that had nothing to do with being wet in a dark cave. I wanted his warmth, his touch, his love.

What did he want from me?

"Do you know what I thought, when I nearly lost you after that knife fight with Milass?" I slid my arms around his waist, and rested my cheek against his heart. "I thought, how could he do this to me? How could he go and get himself killed, and leave me alone? I don't want to be alone, Duncan. I can't do it anymore. You made me forget how."

I ran my hands up his sides, until I could feel the thickening scar from the two operations. Then I clenched my fist, and hit him on the side of the arm.

"I've never been so angry with you. Don't you ever try and die on me like that again." I was shouting, my voice echoing in the cave, and I couldn't care less who heard me. "And don't you ever even *think* about leaving me!"

I let the rage and pain direct my hands as I pulled his head down and pressed my mouth to his. I let all the sadness and fear I'd been locking away spill out and wash over both of us, with that single kiss. His long hair was wrapped around my fingers. His heart pounded against mine.

This was where I belonged. No other place but right here, with this man. His woman. His wife. And no one was ever going to take that away from me.

We were both on our knees, and I was sobbing. He kissed my wet eyes, my brow, the curve of my cheek. Blindly, I chased his mouth until I caught him. He held the back of my head with one scarred hand, and kissed me.

The pain abruptly exploded into passion.

What followed was a blur of sensation and wanting and movement. I felt his hands rasp over my skin as I dug my fingernails into his shoulders. Sweat made our bodies slick as we landed on the pile of garments and linen, the stone beneath bruising me in a dozen places.

I didn't care. The need inside me had become a snarling, ravenous beast and it was long past feeding time. When his teeth scored over my breasts, I groaned and dragged my nails down his back. He pushed his legs between mine, and I arched up, aching for him, greedy for the hard thrust that would fill me and encompass him.

He held back, clamping one hand in my hair, watching me as he waited. For what I didn't know, didn't care—I had to have this. I had to have him. I jerked my hips up, trying to force him into me.

"Open your eyes, Joey. Look at me."

I looked. "Do you want me to beg now?"

He bent until his mouth was just resting against mine. Golden hair spilled around my face. "Would you beg for me?"

Even now, after all this time, he needed the words. Once I'd actually resented it. Now I'd give him as many as he wanted to hear.

"I'd beg for you. I'd lie. I'd steal. You know, I already have." I lifted my hand and took his, and brought it to my lips. "And, though it might take some time and effort"—I kissed the scarred back of his hand—"I'd find a way to die for you."

He didn't push or shove or thrust his way into my body. He sank into me in slow degrees, a centimeter at a time. We didn't mate, we melded, until he was so deep inside me that all the emptiness I'd ever felt vanished.

"You don't have to beg, beloved. Or lie, or steal." He traced the outline of my lips with his fingertip. "I have been yours since the first moment." Slowly he moved, gliding out and in, pressing deeper. "You don't have to die for me, Cherijo. You'll have to live."

"Show me," I whispered.

I don't know how much time passed after that. Pleasure burst through me so many times as I moved under him, and still he kept rocking our bodies together, taking me with slow, determined restraint. He seemed driven to maintain his control over himself and me. I held on, taking what he gave me, returning it when he allowed it.

It wasn't dominance and submission, it was male and female, so elemental and inexplicable that I barely understood it myself. All I knew was he needed this, needed me in ways I hadn't begun to understand. As I needed him. After tonight, there would be no question about what lay ahead in the future for us.

Whatever happened, we would never be separated again.

In the end, when he finally lost the battle with his own need, he pressed my face against his chest, and pulled us both up from the ground. He moved until he stood with his back against the cave wall, his hands on my hips, working me over him. I braced myself with my hands on his shoulders and stared into his eyes.

"You'll live for me," he said, his voice hoarse, his lungs dragging in air. "Say it."

"I'll live for you. I love you."

"Forever. Promise me forever."

"I promise you, Duncan. Forever."

"Cherijo." He wrapped his arms around me, shuddering as he cried out and poured himself into me.

I held on, I lived for him. I loved him.

We spent the night on that bumpy, uncomfortable cave floor, and I couldn't remember a time I'd ever been happier. Duncan and I were together, body and soul, and that was all I wanted. That was paradise enough for anyone.

Hawk's groans were what brought me back down to earth. Reever watched me as I got up and slowly dressed.

I smiled down at him. "Good morning."

He folded his hands behind his head. "Yes, it is."

If he'd been a cat, he would have been purring. "Don't look so smug. We've got work to do." I found his clothes and tossed them at him. "I need to get to Medical for more supplies for Hawk."

He pulled on his trousers. "We will all go back up to the occupied levels."

"But I'm supposed to be dead."

"We will tell them you survived."

He walked with me over to where Hawk was. I knelt down beside him. "How are you feeling?"

"Not as good as you, I think." Hawk rolled over so I could check his back. "I don't want anyone to know, patcher."

"No one knows?" Hawk shook his head, and Reever and I exchanged a look. "Duncan and I won't say anything." I turned to my husband. "Can you get him up to Medical by yourself? I'll tell you what you need to do for him."

Hawk groaned. "You cannot stay here, patcher."

"Sure I can. Even if you tell them I somehow survived the first fall, they might try to do it again." I made a face as I helped the Indian to his feet. "And, as thrilling as the experience was, I really don't care for a repeat."

"No one will assault you," Hawk said as I slipped his arm over my shoulders. "You are not the first person I have taken from the pit."

"I thought you said no one knew."

"No. The others were unconscious when I took them." Hawk looked sheepish. "The tribe believes I appealed to the gods for their lives, and they were returned from the spirit world."

"I'll try to remember all that. What about Rico?"

"He will not remember what he has done. He never does, when he is in a rage."

Reever took Hawk's other arm. "The chief will not attack someone returned by the gods, will he?"

"It is not the way."

"I hope you're right." I looked at the man we had propped between us. "Are you sure, Hawk? You're not in any shape to defend me or Reever."

He chuckled. "I was rather hoping to see you· defend us."

"Now he gets a sense of humor," I said to Reever.

I left the men outside the medical alcove to pick up my cats and more supplies. And walked right in on Milass, going through every container in the place.

"Find what you're looking for?" I asked, then folded my arms and leaned back against a wall as he jumped to his feet.

Even his scars turned white. "You're dead!"

"Am I? That would make me a ghost, haunting *you*." I raised my arms and made a horrible face. "An angry, vengeful, surgically knowledgeable ghost."

"He killed you. I made sure he killed you this time."

So I was right—he'd planted the tunic. "Why did you go to all the trouble of framing me? Do you really hate me that much?"

He didn't answer that. He yelled, rushed past me,

and kept going on down the tunnel until he was out of sight.

The cats came out to stare at me. "Don't look at me. I didn't make all that racket." I turned to the entrance. "Reever, bring Hawk in here."

I took care of the muscle strains, then Reever helped me get Hawk dressed and back on his feet.

He tried walking and grinned at me. "I have not felt this good in years."

"You're welcome," I said, then couldn't help adding, "even better, I didn't have to sing a note."

Hawk limped out into the tunnel to talk with Reever, so I went over to the containers to put everything back in place. A short time later, the first of my patients walked in.

"Can you look at my leg?" Hawk must have done some fast talking, because the man didn't look even vaguely spooked. "We've only got a week until the World Game."

I examined the infected burn on the lower half of his leg, cleaned and treated it, then went back to straightening up the mess Milass had made. For a few minutes, anyway. More patients came in to congratulate me on my celestial return, and could I check this or that injury for them?

Milass came back, his face absolutely blank. "The chief wishes to see you."

"The last time I saw the chief, he wasn't in a very good mood. Tell him I can't make it."

"He does not hold you responsible for the intrusion anymore." Milass gave me what could be construed as a pleading look.

On another day, I would have needled him a little more, but I was still in my glowing-with-happiness mode. "Look, twerp, I'm busy. Get lost."

"Patcher, it is Ilona he blames now. He is not rational today. You must help her."

I set down the box of skin sealer I was repacking and sighed. "All right. Give me a minute, will you?"

After telling Reever and Hawk an abbreviated version of the truth, I went to the central cavern with Milass. "What did you mean, he's not rational?"

"Some days the chief is as you saw him at the arena. Some days he is as he was at the pit, with you."

"So today is a pit day, not an arena day?"

"Yes."

"Terrific."

"He will not harm you. He has exercised his rage many times. Now he indulges himself with drink and food in celebration. Much of what he says makes no sense."

I got to see that firsthand when Rico hailed me as Milass and I entered his hogan. The chief was dirty, drunk, and acted as if he'd never thrown me down a cave shaft.

I pulled out a scanner. "Looks like he's really been celebrating. I'd better have a look at him."

"Do not approach him yet," Milass said. "Wait until he invites you near."

"Patcher! We have prevailed over the whiteskin. You should have been there."

"Sorry I missed it." No, I wasn't.

The interior of the hogan was so dark I couldn't make out who was with him, until Milass got a fire going. The flames illuminated everything—two guards standing behind Rico, who was sitting on the antique chair I'd seen him use once or twice before. Then I looked down.

His feet were resting on top of a body. A bleeding body, wrapped tightly in rope. Ilona's swollen, battered features were slack, but from the whistling sound coming from her broken nose, she was still breathing. Someone behind me made a similar noise, and I glanced back to see several League troops huddled in chains against the walls of the hogan.

"You've noticed my new footrest."

"Yes. It's . . . very decorative."

"Ilona was the one who led the League into the tunnels to get you. She confessed it to me. She is very sorry she made it seem as if you were to blame." He frowned. "Did I shout at you for that?"

"Yes, but not very much. So you beat her into confessing, is that right?"

"I found her with the League men, and she got on her knees and told me everything." He drank from the bottle he held and wiped his mouth. "Then I beat her."

"I'm glad we've got that straightened out." How long had he beaten her, and how much damage had he done? How was I going to convince him to hand her over to me so I could find out? "Who are these other men, Chief?"

"Scum who thought they could challenge me."

"Oh, they're crazy men." Casually I walked back to have a look at the wounded troops. One of them was in bad shape, and just my luck, the worst enemy I had in the League besides Joseph. "It looks like you caught a pretty important guy here."

"The one gasping over there? Shropana, is it not?"

"One and the same."

"Do not concern yourself, patcher." Rico waved an unsteady arm. "He does not breathe very much. He will be dead soon."

"Maybe not." I knelt down and checked him quickly. What I'd been worried about since I first examined him was about to happen. I rose to my feet. "He's a powerful man, Chief. One who could possibly prove more beneficial alive."

"Possibly." Rico looked at Shropana. "He has not long to live, though."

"I can keep him alive. He needs a heart operation."

"Another patient for you, huh? Eventually every-one comes under your hands," Rico said, then laughed uproariously. "There is nothing you can do for him here. Let him die."

"On the contrary, I can do a great deal, if you'll let me borrow your new footrest."

"Why?"

I gave him a cool smile. "Patril here needs a new heart. Ilona won't be needing hers much longer."

The chief gave me an owlish stare. "You mean to cut out my footrest's heart and give it to the alien?"

"The organs are compatible," I said, hoping my nose wasn't getting longer. "The League will pay you a fine reward for his return. Or, you can keep him here as a hostage against future attacks. The worst that can happen is they both die."

Rico laughed again. "I like how you think, patcher. Very well." He kicked Ilona's body toward me. "Take them."

CHAPTER FIFTEEN

Initiation

Milass helped me get enough men together to carry Ilona and Patril to the alcove, but he made it obvious he didn't like the idea.

"I got her out of there for you, didn't I?" I asked him. "What's your problem now, shortie?"

"You will not harm her to save him," he said as he directed the men carrying Ilona to a berth. Once she was on it, he took out his knife and began slicing through the ropes binding her limbs.

I left explanations for later. What I had to do now was get Patril prepped for surgery. I thanked the other men for helping us as they left, then did my preliminary scans. The Colonel's heart could go at any moment. I was out of time and options—if I didn't do the procedure, he would die.

"Did you hear me?" the demonic dwarf came up and gave me a push. "You will not cut out her heart."

"I have no intention of cutting anything out of her, you moron. It was the only way I could think of getting her out of there before Rico did anything worse."

Milass didn't thank me. I think I would have dropped dead of a heart attack myself if he had. He did agree to go and find Hawk and bring him back to assist me.

Once more I grumbled under my breath about my lack of nurses as I completed the prep work and got Shropana sedated. As soon as he was under, I set up the instrument trays and cordoned off the area. I couldn't make a sterile field, but I got everything as isolated as I could make it. Before I scrubbed, I went to check on Ilona.

Rico had done a good job on her; she had extensive facial fractures and all of her ribs and fingers were broken. Ilona wouldn't be weaving anything for a couple of weeks.

She'd regained consciousness, and stared at me as I infused her with painkillers. "You help me—why?"

"I'm a masochist. Go figure." I watched her drift under, then went to scrub and take care of my other pain in the ass.

Hawk limped in just as I finished gearing up. "Get sterile, we've got cardiac transplantation surgery to perform."

"A transplant?" His mouth sagged open. "You can't do that down here."

"I'd better find a way, or this man will die." I looked into the swollen, canine features of the Colonel who had chased me across the galaxy. "Believe me, his death is one I really don't want on my conscience."

Hawk scrubbed while I went to set up the laser rig and the heart-lung machine which would keep Shropana alive while I installed the replacement heart. A couple of scans made me readjust the calibration of the Jarvik biomechanical replacement unit I'd swiped from Joseph's lab; it wasn't going to be a perfect fit. Still, it would serve as a temporary fix until I could get him out of the tunnels and up to a regular medical facility.

"You know something, Hawk? I think I'd amputate

a limb just to have access to a nice, big, well-stocked medical facility."

"The gods do not give us more than we can handle. I know this man," Hawk said as he took position by the instrument trays. "This is the one who has been asking for your execution."

"Yep." I adjusted the optic emitter to give me maximum light over Shropana's brisket.

"Is there anyone you will not operate on?"

"First rule of being a surgeon: You don't get to pick and choose who ends up on your table." I powered up the rig and leaned over. "Here we go."

My first radical decision was not to remove Shropana's diseased heart, but to perform a heterotopic transplant, which would leave the native heart in place. To do this, I didn't sever the diseased organ from the atria, but refitted them to pair off with the Jarvik replacement's connections.

Hawk spotted what I was doing at once. "Why do you put the machine heart on top of the old one?"

"To give Colonel Shropana a heart with eight chambers, instead of four. The Jarvik will take care of circulatory supply and return, and the other four can do whatever they want."

"Would it not be easier to take the old heart out?"

"Easier, sure, if he was human. He's not, and this unit wasn't designed for his species. I'm hoping a better-equipped surgeon can salvage the native heart, and remove or replace the Jarvik."

If we ever got Patril back to the League.

I started the work on the pulmonary arterial and aortic junctions. From the amount of plaque in his vessels, I'd have to adjust his medication regime and his diet while he was with us. That would make me even more popular with the bad-tempered military mogul when he woke up.

"How will it continue to function?" Hawk asked me. "You said you have no power core."

"Don't need one. We're going to do this the way they did before autonomous power cores were invented. See these air lines?" I indicated the tubes I would be putting in the chest wall. "They're going to do all the hard part. We'll rig him to an external compressor that will feed pressure through the lines."

"I will sing for him later," Hawk said.

It sounded like all we'd need was a song, but as soon as I tested the Jarvik, things got complicated. The biomechanical heart had to be recalibrated twice before it attained the proper pumping sequence and speed. As soon as I performed the preclosure test activation, an internal safety valve shut the unit down.

"It still thinks he's human," I said, scrambling to disable the safeties. I could only pray the components wouldn't seize up while they were running at three times the set rate. "One more test, and then we'll plug him in."

The second test was successful. Now I had to take Shropana off the machine that was keeping him alive, and see if all my hard work would do the same.

Hawk murmured something under his breath as I switched on the external compressor. There was an instant of silence before the Jarvik began to pump. Shropana's vital signs elevated slightly, then leveled out.

"It worked." The skin around his dark eyes crinkled in a surgeon's smile. "You made it work."

"Piece of cake." I watched the Jarvik for a few minutes, just to be sure. Then I showed Hawk how to close, and suture the long incision.

At the cleanser unit, he scrubbed in silence.

I worried for a minute that I'd demanded too much of him. "Not what you expected?"

"No. It is so much more . . . beautiful. Like dancing inside a soul." He glanced over at Shropana, then at me. "How long does it take? To learn to do these surgeries?"

"As long as you want it to take."

He discarded his bloody gloves. "I want to do more of this. I want to learn more. Will you teach me?"

"We won't get in any more alien cardiac replacement cases, I think." I thought of Vlaav, and how I had wrecked that. "Still, if you're willing, I'll start you off."

Hawk didn't have much time for lessons over the next nine days, as he began the Night Way. I joined the tribe every night for the chanting and ritual sings that, according to my new student, would attract holiness and repulse evil.

I didn't know about the curative effects, but the ceremony involved the entire tribe, which made it very loud, anyway.

"Explain this to me," I said to Hawk as I adjusted his back brace on the morning of the ceremonial. "How is it that a tribe who owns a major shockball-team franchise doesn't give in to the temptation of material wealth? I mean, Rico has to be taking in millions of credit a month, just from the arena ticket sales and advertising."

"Most of the profits are reinvested in the team. The non-Indian players must be paid, of course. The Night Horse contribute their portion to the tribal fund."

"I thought Rico used all that to pay for purchasing the Gliders."

"Now we use it for to provide dowries for our men." Hawk nodded toward a group of villagers from the surface. "Ten will return to Four Mountains this month, to offer for their brides."

"I thought you had broken off with the Navajo."

"Not in marriage. It is forbidden for our men to marry within the clan. We have been sending young men back to the reservation to seek brides and settle down for many years. The Four Mountains clans have welcomed them."

That bothered me. Why was he really sending his people back to the surface? He'd led them from Four Mountains, started a new tribe, and moved underground rather than stay on the reservation and live under "whiteskin" laws. Now he was funding the way for the Night Horse to rejoin the mother tribe?

Could he be trying to deliberately infect the Navajo, and through them the general population, with syphilis? It might take months, even years before someone identified the cause and treatment for the disease, and by then it would constitute a worldwide epidemic.

I rejected that idea at once. Sure, Rico might slit someone's throat, or beat up his girlfriend. But he wasn't sophisticated or psychotic enough to attempt that kind of random, global destruction. Someone like my creator might pull it off. But the Night Horse chief was no Joseph Grey Veil. Besides, Rico still thought the disease was a curse from the gods.

Hawk explained that the first day of the *Tł'ééjí* was devoted to the purification and consecration of the special hogan built for the ceremonials. Hawk called it "The Day of the East."

"Today we perform the first rite of exorcism, the breath of life," Hawk said to the crowd gathered around the Night Way hogan. "There will be prayer ritual, the cleansing of the sweat bath, and honor to the sacred mountains."

I refrained from pointing out there weren't any mountains around, and went in for a few minutes to watch the festivities.

It was interesting, in a Navajo kind of way. Hawk used special gourds and lots of corn meal and pollen to purify and consecrate the hogan. Everyone chanted without stopping. I wondered idly how much breath control it took to accomplish that, and how many sore throats I was going to have to treat tomorrow.

"Here." Hawk thrust something covered with beads

and feathers in my hands. "Offer this up to Changing Woman for us."

It was some kind of elongated pot filled with ground, dried corn. "Um, I don't exactly know any prayers," I told him.

"Cast it into the fire, and say what you will."

I went to the fire, and shook out some of the corn-meal over the flames. Prayers. Right. Like I knew.

Might as well keep it simple. "Changing Woman, accept this offering and bestow your blessings here."

Despite my cynical attitude toward religion, performing the offering moved me. The smell of the corn burning was sweet and pervasive. I could almost feel the weight of the eyes watching me. Beyond that, there was a feeling of connection to something I'd never recognized in myself before.

Come on, Cherijo. Next thing you know you'll be abandoning your laser to hold sings for injured patients.

The assembled repeated what I'd said, only in Navajo. I turned to hand the pot-thing back to Hawk. He looked amused.

"Your blood is red after all, patcher."

I stayed until the purification rites were through, then headed back to my alcove to check on my patients and make sure Rico hadn't recovered from his hangover and come looking for a heart-less Ilona. Reever was feeding the cats, but I spotted his shock-ball uniform hung over one of the containers. I kicked it over, and that got his attention.

"You know I must do this, Cherijo."

"We didn't get around to discussing why the other night."

"Not for the reasons you think." He picked up Juliet. Since he was her favorite human, she let him. "We'll talk after the game."

Shropana's mechanical heart was still ticking, but he was very weak and couldn't be brought out of sedation just yet. I made note of his vitals and ran some routine cardiac screens. The native heart was functioning at about twenty percent, which was enough to keep it alive. The Jarvik did the rest of the work. Due to his advanced age, recuperation would probably take a few months.

Ilona was in much better shape, although I'd immobilized her in multiple bonesetters. She wasn't going anywhere for a while, either. She also tested positive for first-stage syphilis, which made me wonder if she was the carrier. I just couldn't picture her with Hawk. Since she was asleep, I didn't wake her, but added her meds to her infuser line.

I moved the privacy screen back in place, and stacked the containers we'd been using to help conceal Ilona's presence. Then I sat down to watch Reever dress.

"I hate to admit it, but you look good in protective padding. How much longer are you going to have to do this?"

"The World Game is next week." He strapped on his shoulder padding and pulled his jersey down over it. "Why were you surprised that I enjoyed the competition? All cultures participate in some form of sport."

"Shockball is not a sport. It's an excuse to electrocute people."

"Avoiding penalties is quite exhilarating."

"So is avoiding my bad side." I went over and kissed him. "Don't get on it anymore."

"Patcher."

I went back behind the partition, and found Ilona awake and agitated. Now that the meds had worn off, I wondered how much of a fuss she was going to kick up about being under my care.

"Hi." I checked her abdomen and saw that the inflammation around her ribs had gone down considerably. Sympathy pains still made me grimace. "How are you feeling?"

"Foolish," she said. Her face, still beautiful despite

the swelling and the bruises, was serious. "You saved my life. Why?"

"I was bored and had nothing better to do." I sat down beside her berth. "Mind telling me how you got mixed up with someone like Shropana?"

"I saw him on the vid broadcast. I thought it was a good idea. I could give you to him and get money for my people. I went up to the surface to seek him out." Ilona closed her eyes. "He said he wouldn't hurt anyone. He only needed to know how to get into the tunnels."

"He lied, but then, he's good at that."

Her bottom lip trembled. "Does Rico think I'm dead?"

I sighed. "Ilona, Rico wanted you dead. Rico tried to kill you. Rico gave you to me so I could kill you."

"He will kill me as soon as he finds out I am alive."

I thought of the outcasts. "Not necessarily. I can help you get out of here, but I need some information first."

"What do you want to know?"

I was almost positive she was the carrier, but I couldn't exactly accuse her of sleeping her way around the tribe. How did I put this diplomatically? "You were infected with a sexually transmitted disease called syphilis. It's very contagious. I need to know how many men you've been with so I can treat them."

"One."

"Ilona, this is really important. Don't kid around, okay? Tell me their names."

"There has only been one. Rico."

"But Hawk was infected, and some of the outcasts, and—" I stopped. "Just Rico?"

She gave me an ironic look. "Do you think Rico would share his own woman with the rest of the tribe?"

"No." That put a lot of things into swift perspective. "So you're telling me you're not his only woman."

Ilona sighed. "It is not the old way, but Rico takes whoever he wants. He told us it was his right. We do not have the kind of sexual taboos the whiteskin have. Though Rico forbids our women to be with more than one man, our men can have as many woman as they wish."

I wonder how the logistics of that actually worked out. "It has to be one of the other women, spreading it to the men."

"No, they were infected by Rico, too."

"He has sex with other men?"

"Of course." Ilona didn't blink. "He enjoys taking whoever he wants—whenever he wants."

"Great." No wonder Hawk refused to tell me where he'd gotten the disease. Since Ilona was tiring, I told her to rest and moved the privacy screen back into place.

I turned around to see Dhreen standing in the entrance to the alcove. He looked like someone had tried to feed him through a disposal unit.

"Where is she?"

"Out making new friends already?" I went over to help him get to a berth.

He wouldn't let me touch him. "I tried to stop him, and then they said he'd given her to you." He grabbed the front of my tunic with his bloody spoon-fingered hands. "Did you cut her up? Did you?"

"I didn't cut anybody up, and when I do, I sew them back together." I glanced down at his hands. "Do you mind?"

He let go. "Where is she?"

"Ilona, right?" He nodded, and I pointed to the privacy screen. "She's back there."

"She's alive?"

I thought about torturing him a little, then decided not even Dhreen deserved that. "Yes."

All the color drained out of his face and he started sliding toward the floor. I grabbed him and hauled him over to my exam table. Slinging him up on it was even more fun.

"Did Rico do this to you?" I said as I scanned him. he was more battered and bruised than Ilona was.

"He doesn't like anyone obstructing his judgments."
He latched on to my wrist. "She's going to be okay?"

Evidently Dhreen had a little love quadrangle going
on between him and Ilona and Milass and Rico.

"With a little time and care, yes, she will. Glad to
see you're concerned with someone other than yourself." I put his hand down at his side and calibrated
a syrinpress. "What's the matter, she owe you money
or something?"

"It isn't like that." He closed his eyes.

"Would you mind telling me exactly why you're
down here?"

He didn't look at me. "It's not because of you, if
that's what you think."

"Pardon me if I find the coincidence a little tough
to swallow."

"Your parent didn't require my services after we
reached Terra. I didn't have enough credits to purchase a new ship, so I hired myself out for surface
transport."

"The kind legitimate transportation companies
wouldn't touch, I imagine."

His mouth curled. "You know me too well. I got
word of this place in the tavern district. The chief
hired me to convey the players to regional games and
do a little resource management on the side."

"Smuggling, you mean." I infused him. "Good story,
Dhreen. I almost believe it."

"Doc." He opened his eyes. "You've got to get her
out of here before Rico finds out she's still alive."

"I plan to. Forgive me if I don't ask you to help."

"I don't care what happens to me. Just get her away
from him." The painkiller I'd administered started
taking effect, and his voice slurred. "Please, Doc.
Keep her away . . . from . . . him. . . ."

I finished my scans and set his collarbones and right
shoulder, then sutured the various cuts and gashes

he'd gotten. He still looked like a kid, just the same way he had when he'd picked me up on Terra.

My mouth thinned. Dhreen was a grownup, just like the rest of us. He'd lied his way into my life one time, and there was no way I was going to extend a second invitation.

I couldn't allow Hawk and the others to keep fooling themselves with Indian rituals and protocol—if Ilona had told me the truth, it was possible Rico had infected nearly every adult in the tribe. Since members of the tribe were not only going topside to play shockball, but were also moving back to the Four Mountains reservation, the disease could easily get out of control.

Way out of control.

Modern doctors would have a problem diagnosing and treating patients with syphilis. Their diagnostic units would identify the treponema pallidum bacteria, but it had been so many centuries since the last reported case of STD that I doubted if any symptomatic or treatment files even existed. They'd probably think it was something new, and waste months going through the World Drug Administration's painstaking procedural process to have a standardized inoculate approved.

If there was one thing a sexually transmitted disease didn't need, it was months to spread.

There was also the very strong possibility that, once prevalent among the general public, the syphilis would mutate into different strains. Strains developed in crossbred carriers would be resistant to Terran antibiotics, creating a whole new set of headaches, and possibly an incurable mutation.

I went to the consecrated hogan to talk to Hawk. From the outside of the door, I could hear he was in the middle of one of his unending prayer sings.

"The ts'aa *has a pathway to the coming dawn.*
The pathway leads out to the edge of the world,

The place that can be felt by the singer in the dark,
The place that opens to the dawn in the east—
Here under the east, it is a holy place,
Here beneath the triangle stone, it is a holy place,
Here at this consecrated hogan, it is a holy place,
Here at this fire, it is a holy place
Holaghei . . ."

My guards took up position on either side of the hogan.

It was purely superstitious nonsense, but the words throbbed in me. My unruly Indian blood again. No matter how the clinical side of my brain attacked the problem, I still felt the draw of my heritage, the beauty and serenity of the Night Horse way.

Compelling, but it wasn't going to kill off a single *treponema pallidum.*

That was the end of the song. The occupants of the hogan filed out, carrying baskets of corn that had been blessed, to use for the evening meal.

After the last person left the hogan, I stepped inside. Hawk was sitting in an awkward position, obviously in deep meditation. I waited another few minutes, then politely cleared my throat.

"Patcher." He opened his eyes. "Changing Woman smiles upon you."

"Changing Woman would be yelling, if she had my problems." I went over and sat down beside him. How would one of the tribe ask him? "I need your help, *hataali.*"

"I am here for you."

"I know who is the syphilis carrier. Ilona told me, and I don't think she would lie about that. Rico is the one responsible for infecting the tribe. For infecting you."

Hawk didn't respond.

"The silent treatment isn't going to work this time. As much as I respect you, and want to honor your traditions, I can't continue to stand back and do nothing."

He got up and hobbled over to the fire. He crouched down and prepared two cups of tea, and handed one to me. When I took it, he said, "It would be like asking a bird not to fly."

"Or a *hataali* not to sing." I sipped the tea, which was hot, dark, and pungent with fresh herbs. Crushed mint leaves swirled around the bottom. "How would you feel, if you were in my place?"

"Torn between two worlds. As I feel now." He stared into his cup.

I still didn't understand what it was about *Leyaneyaniteh* that kept him in the underground. Hawk didn't belong here. He belonged where he could feel the sun on his face—

I looked down at the tea leaves in my cup. The baskets of corn. The pot of stew bubbling over the central cavern cooking fire. Something that had been subconsciously bothering me for weeks suddenly snapped into focus.

"What more must you do?"

I put aside the new mystery to deal with matters at hand. "First, I absolutely must send a signal to the doctors at the Four Mountains reservation. The reservation medical facilities have to know what the disease is, how to test the general population for it, and what to administer as a cure."

"The chief is the only one of us with access to any communications equipment, and it is all located within the arena."

"I need to examine Rico. Can you get me in to see him?"

He hobbled over to the door and looked out into the cavern. "Rico has gone to the surface, to make arrangements for the entire tribe to attend the World Game. He will not be back until the day before the game."

That was a week. "What about testing the other members of the tribe here?"

"They will not voluntarily allow you to examine them, not until you pass the initiation ceremonial. The chief left instructions to accept you back into the tribe only *after* you passed the test."

I clenched my teeth. All that meant was a big fat no to everything I'd asked. "How long until the initiation?"

"It is held in four days from now."

"I guess you can't move it up on the schedule." He nodded. "Terrific."

"Will a week make that much difference?"

"This is a STD. A single night of romance makes a difference." I put the tea down and joined him at the door. "All right, Hawk. Out of respect for tradition, and because I have no other choice, I'm willing to wait one more week. But call off the guards. You can do that much for me."

He smiled. "Very well."

I smiled back. Respect for tradition had gotten me exactly what I needed.

Reever finally contacted and arranged a rendezvous with the outcasts. On the third day of the *Tl'ééjí*, we moved Ilona out of Medical and into the outer tunnels. Dhreen, whom I'd reluctantly allowed to visit Ilona daily, insisted on going with us.

"You do one thing to mess this up," I told him, "and I'll tell the chief all about this little love affair of yours."

"You would not do that to Ilona."

"I'd do it to you. Speaking of Ilona, you'd better watch your step there, too."

Dhreen looked hurt. "I care for her."

"I've seen how you treat people you care for. Just how did you two lovebirds get together, anyway?"

"We're not together. Not literally." He looked

down at the litter he was carrying with Reever. Ilona was asleep. "This isn't the initial time the chief employed his fists on her. I saw him knock her down the first time I came here. Since then, I got her away from him when I could. She told me she had no option but to be with him. I know all about that. We became friends, then . . ." He shrugged, embarrassed.

I looked sharply at him. "Then you'd better remember what I said."

The outcasts were waiting for us as we emerged into the sewers.

"Patcher." A very healthy-looking hybrid led his group out of the shadows. He grinned at me and slapped Reever on the shoulder. "*Nilch'i*'. They say nothing can catch The Wind in the arena."

"I haven't chased him yet," I said, which made everyone laugh. "We hadn't heard anything from you in so long—I was worried. Where have you been hiding?"

"We found a passage above the old subway that leads to the surface, and made a place for ourselves in the forest. The villagers will not go there. They fear the Glider will descend from the trees and take them to his lair. Now it grows too cold for us to stay there, so we are moving into the western conduits." He pointed down toward another section of the sewer. "We will be there until the snows pass."

One of the women stepped forward to have a look at Ilona. "This is the chief's woman. They will search for her when she is found missing."

"No, they won't," I said. "They think she's dead."

Reever briefly explained the situation, which dispelled the last of the hybrids' doubts.

"Good. We will keep her with us until she is able to travel. Then we can see she returns to her clan at Four Mountains."

Ilona suddenly clutched at my hands and wailed, "I don't want to go! I want to stay with Dhreen!"

Dhreen gave me a desperate look. "I'll go with her and make sure she's all right."

Infatuated Oenrallians were more tenacious than Larian flatworms. "We've already been over that. I can make a dead woman disappear, but you'd definitely be missed." To Ilona, I said, "You know you have to go, Red Face. I'll do my best to keep him safe."

She stopped crying and scowled at me. "Faun. Red *Faun*. Why can't I stay in hiding? No one has seen me."

"I can't keep chasing people out of Medical, Ilona. Someone is going to get suspicious. Then Rico will come to finish what he started."

"You're sure she'll be safe with them?" Dhreen jerked his thumb at the hybrids.

"They're our friends. She'll be fine. Talk to her, Dhreen."

The Oenrallan knelt down by Ilona's litter and carefully took one of her broken hands. "Doc's right, my precious. The chief's crazy. I couldn't stand it if he hurt you again. You have to go with them now."

"My precious." Gee, he had it bad.

"I'm afraid." Ilona groaned as she tried to reach for him. "Come with me."

"I'll come as soon I can." He bent over and rubbed his cheek against hers. "I'll figure out something soon. I promise."

We all watched as Ilona's litter was carried off by the outcasts. She sobbed Dhreen's name until they vanished into the sewer pipes.

"I can't leave her out here by herself," Dhreen said, staring after them.

True love. I needed an aspirin. "She's not going to be by herself. They'll take good care of her. I know you're worried, but if you want to keep her alive, she has to stay out of sight."

"Don't simulate the sympathy." He turned on me.

"You want to despise me, okay. But she's just a kid. Don't unleash your disillusionment with me and make her pay for it."

"Pardon me. I'm not very fond of you, but I won't take out my frustrations on your girlfriend. If I'd wanted to do that, why the hell would I go through all this?"

"Grey Veil. Your parent could have tutored you on some of his maneuvers. He has more than a Hsktskt raider fleet."

I walked back into the tunnels. Behind me, Reever started talking to Dhreen in low, rapid Oenrallian. I didn't bother to switch on my wristcom.

"Cherijo." Reever caught up to me.

"I go to all this trouble for her, and he thinks I'm doing it to set him up. The ingrate."

"He doesn't understand friendship."

"I can see why." I scowled over my shoulder at the sullen Oenrallian, who trudged several yards behind us. "Who wants to be friends with him, anyway?"

"You should talk to him about what happened at Joren."

"I was there, I remember what happened." I made an irritable gesture. "Just let it go, Reever. He thinks I'm just like Joseph, and I'll never trust him again. Whatever friendship we had is over."

Hawk continued performing the Night Way ceremonial. The first four days were devoted to exorcism rites, group sweat baths, and unending prayers. After an all-night sing on the fourth night, Hawk went into "the Healing" phase of the ritual and made his first great sand painting.

I'd read about them, naturally, but to see Hawk actually making the dry painting on the cave floor was something else.

He held different colored materials in his fist, and crawled to a specific spot. Slowly and carefully, he trickled the colored stuff in a specific, geometric pattern. Already he'd laid out a complicated design, with hands, spirals, snakes, and stick figures bent over, gathering something in small baskets.

"Sa'ah naaghéi, Bik'eh hózhó," he chanted.

I went to the other side of the dry painting, where he could see me and my voice wouldn't startle him. "Can I talk to you while you do that, or will it mess you up?"

"Talk as much as you like. However, try not to sneeze in this direction."

I already smelled the pollen, and gave him a mock-warning sniff. "What is that stuff you're using to make all the different colors?"

"Crumbled clay, sand, cornmeal, pollen, and crushed larkspur petals."

"If it's supposed to be a painting, why not use paint?"

"The *'iikááh* is not a permanent thing. Only vegetal materials and sand are used, so the painting can be destroyed before *tse'yi,* sundown."

"You take hours to make this thing, and you're going to sweep it up before it gets dark?"

"Yes."

"Hawk, you need to take up another hobby." I looked around at the gathering circle of children watching both of us. "The little ones seem to like it."

"They take part in the ceremonial tonight. It will be their initiation into the spiritual life of the tribe."

"Really." The children weren't just fascinated; some of them looked terrified. "This initiation scary?"

"Children must learn the greatest secret of the way."

I noticed that wasn't a "no." "Which is?"

He glanced up from the dry painting. "You will learn that tonight, when you are initiated."

"Me?" I sat back on my heels.

"Isn't it time you rejoined your people, Cherijo? In

spirit, you're ready to embrace all the mysteries of the way."

I'd been initiated into a lot of things that no one had bothered to properly explain to me. "Tell me something, Hawk. Does any of this involve things like accidental betrothals?"

He laughed.

Reever escorted me to the consecrated hogan that night, but he was not allowed inside. Only me and a group of kids were admitted.

I saw Hawk, painted and wearing some kind of ceremonial jacket, standing beside a pile of bundled sticks. One of the older women directed me to sit with the girls on the south side of the fire. The boys had already stripped down to breechcloths and were shivering on the opposite side. The low chanting swelled, and suddenly a figure wearing a white mask burst into the hogan.

"Who is that?" I asked the trembling girl next to me.

"The *Yei*," she whispered back. "My mother says they put bad children in a sack and take them away and cook them and eat them."

Nice, what they told their kids for bedtime stories. "Why don't we tell them to leave?"

The little girl looked blank. "You cannot tell the gods what to do."

The *Yei* danced around the girls' side of the fire, sprinkling something over our heads. Then another figure, this one in a black mask, ran into the hogan and started touching every girl with an ear of corn.

Once all the girls had been sprinkled and touched, the dancers went to the other side of the fire. The oldest boy got up and stood apart from the others. The *Yei* started dancing around the boy and sprinkled something over his head. More cornmeal, judging by the way it looked.

Then the black-masked dancer ran over and grabbed a bundle of sticks. He also started dancing around the lone boy, then struck him on the back with the bundle. The boy bit his lips and didn't make a sound.

I got to my feet. Cornmeal fell off my head and made a circle around my feet. "Hey!"

Someone grabbed me and held on. "Do not interfere. It is the way."

I was getting extremely tired of "the way." Just the thought of letting this clown in the mask hit all those boys made my blood boil. I thrust away the hands holding me and yelled as the masked figure hit the boy again. "Knock it off!"

It was obvious no one was going to stop them, so I went over and placed myself between the masked dancers and the quivering boy.

"Whatever this means, you can do it without hurting him."

"Life is pain. Truth is pain," Hawk said from behind me. "He is not hurt, Cherijo."

"He has welts on his back. Bleeding welts," I pointed out. "You're going to have to do this another way, because I'm not sitting here and watching you beat these children."

"The blows must be given."

"Fine." I pushed the nearly naked boy toward the fire, stripped off my tunic, and presented my back to the two masked dancers. "I'll take them."

"You would have to take three for each male child."

"I said, I'll take them."

Hawk shook his head. "You would have to take them in silence."

"What happens if I yell?"

"You shame the young men of our tribe."

"Changing Woman offers her compassion for our children," one of the older women called out. "The Goddess cannot be refused."

The dancers looked at Hawk, who made an obscure gesture and hobbled away. The kids were staring at me like I was crazy. I folded my arms and glared at the dancer in the black mask.

"You heard her. I'm a goddess and you can't refuse me. Have fun."

He hit me. The bundle of sticks was actually a pile of reeds tied together, and they hurt. I withstood the blow, and the next ten, in silence. Hawk watched me from a few feet away.

The black-masked dancer kept hitting me, on the back, the arms, and the abdomen. The other dancer pelted me with cornmeal. The kids began chanting my name, low at first, then louder and louder until they were practically shouting it.

I was busy biting my tongue and multiplying. Three blows for each of the eleven boys at the fire. Thirty-three hits. By the time I figured that out I was halfway there, I also started to weave on my feet from the pain.

"Who stands with Changing Woman?" one of the older women yelled.

Two of the Night Horse women came forward and took hold of my arms. That helped—I was about ready to pass out—and supported me. The black-masked dancer was hitting me harder and harder each time. Blood began trickling down my back and arms. My abdominal muscles started to cramp. Not being able to make a sound really made it all the more interesting.

Twenty-nine. Thirty. I was barely aware of the last of the blows. The final one hit me squarely between the shoulder blades, and would have driven me to my knees if the other women weren't holding me. Then all the chanting and yelling stopped, and the dancers stood in front of me and removed their masks.

The one in the white mask was Kegide. The one in the black mask was Milass. As if I hadn't guessed that.

I saw the faces of the kids go rigid with shock as

Kegide and Milass put the masks on the ground. Hawk was handing out little pouches of corn pollen to all the kids.

"So you see now the secret of the *Yei*. Men and women must do much of the work of the gods—remember this."

The kids all came forward to sprinkle the masks with corn pollen. Kegide even picked up the mask so they could look through the eye holes.

"You must never tell what you saw this night to anyone. Especially not your younger brothers and sisters," Hawk said.

The children all promised to keep quiet about the initiation. Then they started surrounding me, and touching the bloody wounds on my arms and back. Some of them smeared my blood in parallel lines on their faces.

"You are truly Changing Woman."

"I was truly in a lot of pain. "Thanks." I let one of the women lead me over to mat, and sank down on it. I couldn't seem to catch my breath. One by one the kids filed out of the hogan, along with the adults, until only Hawk and I were left.

"That was a foolish thing to do, patcher." He brought a bowl of water and started washing the blood from my back. "What is this?"

I tried to look over my shoulder. "What?"

"The cuts are already scabbing over." Hawk squeezed out the rag and the water in the bowl turned pink.

"I heal really fast," I said.

He sat back on his heels. "You have been touched by the gods. Like our chief."

Raising my arms to put on my tunic wasn't an option for a couple of hours. "Yeah, and I didn't enjoy it. Can I borrow a shirt?"

PART FOUR

Equity

CHAPTER SIXTEEN

Twins

The day after my initiation, Reever was summoned with the other players to go to a pregame press conference at the arena. I concealed the palm-sized sensor unit I'd modified to double as a medical scanner in his right forearm pad, and suggested a couple of ways for him to get the scans I needed on the chief.

"If you can't get anything else, do the cerebral scan. Try putting your arm on his shoulder. Position the unit directly behind his head and press the second and third buttons simultaneously. You can pretend to be giving him a hug or something."

"I'll do what I can."

I looked at the vid unit, which was broadcasting news coverage of the pre-World Game festivities. "When you're talking to the media, remember to keep your helmet on." I tucked his queue into the back of his jersey. "The last thing we need is for them to find out 'The Wind' is a wanted fugitive."

He ran a finger down the side of my face. "What are you going to do while I'm gone?"

"Figure out a minor mystery." I caught his hand and squeezed it. "You be careful."

After Reever left for the surface, I casually strolled

out to the central cavern, where the women were preparing food for the midday meal. I hadn't bothered
to help myself to the community stew in weeks, but
now I went over and examined it with interest.

One of the older women beckoned to me. "Are you
hungry? I have bread from the morning meal."

"No, thank you. I was just wondering, are those
potatoes?" I pointed to an open mesh sack next to
the flat boulder used for food prep.

"Yes. New potatoes, very fresh."

Fresh. In an underground cave. With no sunlight.
"May I have one?"

She nodded, a little puzzled. "You would eat it
raw?"

I smiled and shook my head. "No, I don't think so."

I went over and took a potato from the sack. I
brushed a little dirt from it before I dug a hole in the
hot ash with a stick and buried it. Then I started to
walk back to the tunnels.

"Patcher, what about your potato?"

"It has to cook. I'll be back in a little while."

When I got to Medical, I made a slide from the dirt
concealed in my palm. The analyzer balked a little at
my input analysis request, but eventually it identified
three different organic compounds, including horse
manure.

My conclusion: The potatoes hadn't been grown this
far underground.

Working off the theory that using the subway system to transport food to *Leyaneyaniteh* from the surface village would be impractical, I went back to the
central cavern and did some discreet reconnaissance
from behind the cover of an unoccupied hogan.

The women working on the stew occasionally got
up and wandered back toward a certain tunnel. When
I judged the timing was right, I edged along the wall
and went into the tunnel.

It was another section I hadn't been permitted to

explore, part of another subway station. I kept listening for footsteps as I cautiously made my way deeper into the network of platforms and recessed storage areas.

I saw the sunlight before I found the storeroom. It streamed into the tunnel from an open doorway, illuminating everything with a faint, golden glow. Holding my breath, I edged into the room.

Sacks and boxes of vegetables were neatly sorted and stored inside. Above my head, sunlight poured in from a narrow square opening lined with some kind of alloy.

Even better, there was a square wooden platform hooked to a pulley-and-chain fall hanging from the shaft. It was simple to see how it worked. Whenever they needed something, all they had to do was pull the chain, which hauled the platform up through the shaft. Food was loaded onto the platform at the surface, then lowered back down. A primitive, but ingenious, method of assuring the tribe got their veggies.

I got under the shaft and looked up. It was longer than I'd expected, maybe as much as five hundred feet straight up. The shaft itself was too narrow to accommodate more than a few boxes or sacks of vegetables.

But perhaps one small, skinny Terran could fit through.

I heard voices coming near and promptly dived behind a stack of crates. A rat squealed as I dropped and ran past my face to cringe in a nearby corner. I held my breath as the storage room door opened.

"We need three more bushels of corn for the ceremonial. And bring some of those new carrots. Burrow Owl wants to mash them for her little one."

"They were sweet, were they not?"

"Sweet is all that greedy baby wants."

The women laughed and gossiped as they collected the food, then left. I lifted my head cautiously, then rolled my eyes as the rat stared suspiciously at me from its corner.

"I wouldn't hang around here, if I were you. Burrow Owl's kid may decide she wants some stew to go with her mashed carrots."

I got back to the central cavern without raising an alarm, and retrieved my now-baked potato. It proved to be delicious. I made a mental note to prepare some for Reever when he returned from the arena, and returned to Medical to run the daily cardiac series on Shropana.

I'd been backing down on his sedation, gradually weaning him off the heavy dosage. Now he was able to respond physically to reflex and verbal stimulation, although the few times he'd opened his eyes, he hadn't acted very lucid.

Today he was looking better, and his vitals had inched up another few digits out of borderline red range. The Jarvik was thumping along without a hitch. He responded to my voice by opening his eyes and trying to focus on me.

"Hello, Patril." I checked his infuser lines and catheters before giving him his daily sponge bath. The surgical site was also healing nicely. "Miss me while I was gone?"

His eyelids fluttered. A sound came from his lips. Something that distinctly resembled "no."

"Don't spare my feelings now." I finished the bath and carefully changed his berth linens. The liquid nutrient diet I'd put him on had eliminated twenty-five percent of excess body fat, so it was getting easier to handle him. "Your extra heart is working fine, and you're making me very happy by not getting any unnecessary infections. Now if I can get you to a League medical facility, and someone can convince you to stop lining your vessels with enough plaque to choke an elephant, you'll be able to start chasing me again in a few months."

He groaned something in his native language, too low or too obscene for my wristcom to translate.

"Tell you what. When Reever gets here, I'll ask him what that means."

Reever came back that night, a study in surrealistic contrasts. He carried a bouquet of exotic-looking orchids, a plaque with his Indian nickname on it, and a black eye that spilled over into a huge bruise on his left cheek.

I looked up from the chart I was studying and jumped to my feet. "What happened? God, you look like you went ten rounds with the front end of a glidetruck."

"Rico does not like having champagne spilled down the front of his suit." He handed me the flowers and plaque, and sat down on the exam table. "Especially in front of the media."

I set his stuff aside and pushed open his swollen eyelid to check his eye. Other than the surrounding bruising and some broken capillaries beneath the cornea, the eye wasn't injured. The orbital bone and cheekbone had narrowly escaped being fractured, though.

"Bet this hurts like nobody's business. He hit you this hard in front of the reporters?"

"No." He winced as I applied a cold pack and put his hand over it to hold it in place. "He waited until they left." He extended his other arm. "You'll have to check the scanner, but I believe I was successful."

"You must have been, if you got flowers and a plaque. Your face first." I finished examining him and only then did I pull up the sleeve of his jersey and unwrap his forearm. "Did you have enough time to run a full series?"

"Yes. It was a large bottle of champagne."

"Sit back and relax. I'll put your flowers in some

water." I couldn't help chuckling as I took the scanner over to the console to download the data. "While you were out carousing with the boys, I found another way to the surface."

I inserted the leads into the console input panel and transferred the information Reever had gathered. As it downloaded, I told him about the storeroom and the vertical air shaft.

"Even if it is too narrow for me to traverse, you can use it." He changed out of his uniform.

"Keep that pack on your face, and I'm not going anywhere without you." I sat back and ran an analysis on the downloaded scans. The scrolling results made my smile fade. "Oh, boy. This isn't what I thought. At all."

He came over to study the screen while I grabbed the ancient printed book on STDs and started flipping through it.

"Does it indicate that he is the carrier?"

"Looks that way. Hang on, I need to find something."

I waited until the final cerebral series appeared, then cross-referenced the results with information from the old text. Then I put the book aside and rubbed my eyes.

"Okay. Rico is crazy, but not for the reasons I thought. He's in the final stages of paretic neuro-syphilis."

"That is a different disease from what infects the others?"

"No. It just means he's had this disease for so long it's worked its way into his brain tissue. It's started destroying it." That's why he hadn't shown any latent symptoms. He'd probably stopped showing them a long time ago.

Reever perched on a storage container beside me while I ran the secondary scans, and created a patient

data file on the chief. Transferring the data kept my
hands busy, while I tried to figure out the next move.

The problem with tertiary-stage syphilis, especially
when it affected the nervous system, was treatment. I
could destroy the bacteria in his body, but I had no
way to repair the destruction it had already caused.

"Here." I handed him the book. "Read the section
on long-term effects on the neural system." Then
something caught my eye. "What? Can't be."

Reever looked up from the page he was reading.
"Those are DNA patterns."

"They sure are." Maybe I was just seeing things. I
got up, selected a scanner I'd just used and downloaded a file from it. Then I created a split data screen
and ran a side-by-side comparison.

"You already had a sample of Rico's DNA?"
Reever asked.

"No. This sample belongs to someone else." The
two samples were, with the exception of gender and
a few altered physical characteristics, identical.

"What's wrong? You look ill."

I was ill. "The name." I rested my brow against
my hand. "Of course. He's nothing if not consistent
and methodical."

"What are you talking about?"

I tapped the screen. "Rico's not an only child,
Reever. These DNA sequences match. He's a twin."

"Who is his brother?"

You have been touched by the gods. Like our chief.

"Not a brother." I shut the display off. "A sister.
Me."

I got up and checked on Shropana, then wandered
around the alcove for a few minutes. Reever left me
alone. He probably guessed I wasn't capable of coher-
ent speech.

It wasn't every day I found out I had a brother.

I didn't know exactly which one he was, but Joseph

had created nine other clones before me. When we'd confronted each other the first time about my origins, my creator had told me that none of the others had developed properly. I'd assumed that meant they'd died.

Now I had proof at least one of them was alive.

"When I was a kid, I hated being an only child," I said as I sterilized the already-clean spare monitor rig. "You were an only child. Didn't you hate it?"

Reever eased the sterilizer from my white-knuckled hand and tossed it on my worktable. Then he handed me a single orchid. "I had no basis of comparison."

"I did. All my father's colleagues had at least two kids. I'd have given anything to have a brother or sister. I would have loved it." My face felt hot and stiff as I touched the pale lavender, waxy petals of the bloom.

"Now that I know the connection, I see the resemblance." Reever brushed a piece of hair from my face. "He has the same features, the same cast to his hair."

I'd never noticed, but then, I hadn't been looking. "What did Joseph do to him, Reever? What did he do to all the others?"

"We will find out."

"Not like we can go back to the estate and ask him." I shook my head. "I wonder if Rico knows what he is. Of course, he has to know something. How else could he have found this place, unless he'd lived in the underground lab? But how did he get away? Did Joseph put him up for adoption? Did he escape? Does he know where the others are?" I glanced at the blank vid screen, still seeing the ghost images of those matching patterns. "Does he know about me?"

"He must. There are too many concurrences in our present situation for Rico not to have extensive knowledge of you and Joseph." He turned me around to face him. "What did you mean when you said he was consistent and methodical?"

"The name Rico. Joseph would have named him the same way he named me—with the experiment designation." So much for my very original name. "The chief is about thirty-four years old, so it's safe to assume he's Comprehensive Human Enhancement Research I.D. 'C' Organism."

"C.H.E.R.I.C.O."

"He had to know about me. Why else would he kidnap us from the lab? Twice?" So many things made sense—and didn't. My head whirled with the potential avenues of disaster. "Hawk told me Rico won't be back until just before the World Game. We need to get some answers, Duncan."

"Agreed. We should find out what else Hawk knows about your brother."

My brother. I looked down, and saw I had crushed the fragile orchid in the tight knot of one fist. Slowly I uncurled my fingers, and let the remains drop to the floor.

"Hello, Hawk." I stepped inside the consecrated hogan, with Reever right behind me. "Planning out the next dry painting?"

He was scratching the surface of the cave floor with a piece of light-colored clay, which left visible lines in complicated patterns. "Yes. I have three more to make."

"They tell stories, don't they? Why don't you make this one about Rico being Joseph Grey Veil's genetically engineered human construct, and consequently, my brother?"

I expected the *hataali* to show some emotion— shock, dismay, even disbelief—but he didn't. Hawk only played the silent, inscrutable Indian and kept drawing. As far as he was concerned, Reever and I could have been invisible.

I was tired of the lies, the Night Horse, and being invisible. I spotted a wicker jug of water, picked it up, and tossed the contents over Hawk's drawing. The huge splash erased all the spirals and patterns and stick figures, and drenched Hawk. This time he reacted.

"What are you doing?"

"Getting your attention. Now that I have it, tell me about my brother, the chief."

He glanced at the entrance to the hogan, then shook his head. "Do not say that aloud."

"Why the big secret? There some kind of taboo against cloning? I mean, other than our dastardly whiteskin laws prohibiting it. Or doesn't he want anyone to know he's forgotten to send me Christmas signals for the last thirty years?"

"He has only spoken of it to me once, when we first came here." Hawk used a piece of worn cloth to wipe up the floor of the hogan. "He told Kegide and Milass and I about the Shaman and how he had been brought into this world from the great beyond."

Sounded like a legend Rico would invent. "Sorry, there's no great beyond. He came from an embryonic chamber, where he was cloned from Joseph's cells. Just like me." And what else had the chief invented?

"No one may understand how the gods work their magic."

"Joseph Grey Veil is not a god. Neither is *Cherico*."

"Jericho. That is what he called himself when he came to Four Mountains."

"How old was he? How did he get there?"

"I'm not sure. Fourteen, fifteen years old, perhaps. He was found on reservation land, injured and near death. He ran away from the hospital the next morning. Milass found him hiding in the pinyon groves. We concealed him, cared for him."

Hawk went on to describe the younger Jericho, later adopted by Milass's family, gradually gaining influence among the young men of the Navajo. He gathered enough followers to make the tribal council concerned, then opposed them on the issue of deporting illegal Indian hybrids. In a bold move, he led the men and women who would become the Night Horse off the reservation in one night. Hawk and Milass were already his lieutenants by then.

"He kept his promises to us. He created *Leyaneya-niteh* so the hybrids would be safe. He mended the broken ties with the Four Mountain clans. He purchased the Gliders and ensured the entire tribe would never want for anything."

"What about freedom, to come and go as you please? What about proper health care? What about not asking men to risk electrocution in order to donate to the tribal fund?"

"You do not understand what he did for us. The whiteskins were going to send every half-Indian off-planet, and our own families would do nothing to stop them. Rico stood up for us, spoke for us, protected us. We had nowhere to go; he made a place for everyone."

"Giving everything he had," Reever said. "The Navajo have great regard for someone who sacrifices himself for the good of the less fortunate."

Hawk gestured toward the door. "And so it was."

"That's only the beginning of the story. What about when things started to go wrong?" He didn't want to vilify his beloved chief, so I did it for him. "My best guess is the syphilis progressed to his brain after you established your underground here. You'd remember, he would have been a little irritable at first. Quick to anger. Irrational now and then.

"As the brain tissue deteriorated, he would have gone from cranky right into scary. The temper tantrums. The rampages. Memory loss and delusions. How many years has he been abusing the men and women of the tribe? Three? Five?"

"There has been no abuse."

"You mean, everyone just let him have whatever

he wanted? Out of respect? Or terror? I've seen Rico slit a man's throat and walk away whistling. He nearly beat Ilona to death. I think those were mild incidents. Come on, Hawk, tell me, what's he do on his bad days?"

Hawk wouldn't look at me. "There has been no abuse."

"He won't condemn him, Cherijo." Reever took my hand. "Put aside your anger and ask him what we need to know."

Easier said. "Your chief is a very brilliant, sick, dangerous man. I need to know why he kidnapped us, and what that has to do with Joseph Grey Veil. I need to know why Rico is sending so many men back to the Four Mountains reservation. Why this World Game is so important to him."

Hawk's head sagged against the wall. "I don't know. He hates the Shaman, but has never told us why. He needs both of you, but he will not say for what. He sends our men back to the Navajo to spread the Night Horse way. Having the Gliders play in the World Game has always been one of his greatest obsessions."

"Would he confide in anyone? Milass? One of the other men?"

Hawk shook his head. "He keeps his own counsel."

"Do you know if he ever lived at The Grey Veils?"

"He once spoke of it. He called it his prison for thirteen years. I knew then the Shaman was his father."

Knowing Joseph, I'd bet Rico had been subjected to some of the same testing and training that I'd been. "It doesn't make sense. Even if he was a total failure, Joseph would have kept him as a baseline, a yardstick to measure the success of future constructs. And why didn't he do anything about the syphilis he's carrying? Joseph would have made him take some kind of rudimentary medical courses. I had my first anatomy and physiology courses before I began primary school."

"I must complete the ceremonial, but the Night

Way will not help our chief." Hawk looked hopeful. "Can your way save him?"

"I can get rid of the syphilis, but given the advanced stage of his disease, that won't do much. He's teetering on the edge of full-blown psychosis, and the brain damage he has is irreversible."

"He would never take medicines or allow doctors to touch him. That has not changed since he came to the Four Mountains. Even now, he has his food tasted before he eats it."

"I'll find a way."

Before I could do anything about my long-lost brother or the venereal disease that was driving him insane, disaster struck on two fronts.

The sound woke up me and Reever close to dawn after the last day of the Night Way ceremonial. We had stayed up most of the night, and Reever was permitted to observe the Dance of the *Atsálei* and the Dance of the *Naakhaí,* and join in on a beautiful sing called "The Song of the House Made of Dawn." While I already knew I had no singing voice whatsoever, I discovered my husband had a rather startling, mellow tenor.

"You could be an opera singer, with that voice of yours," I said as we made our way to our hogan. "No kidding, this could be a real career option for you."

"I doubt it." He gave me a pointed look. "You, however, should not sing."

"So I've been told, many times." I ducked inside and knelt to bank the fire. I felt exhausted, wrung out from all the revelations of the day and the endless turning wheel of my thoughts. I smothered a yawn. "What other hidden talents have you been keeping from me?"

He pulled off his tunic. "You will have to discover them for yourself."

The last of the firelight danced over his skin, and

suddenly I wasn't so tired anymore. "Sounds like a challenge."

Understandably I was very groggy when, several hours later, things started to rumble and shake. Reever, who was already up and dressed, tossed me my clothes before he disappeared out the door. I had to scramble to catch up.

The entire tribe assembled in the center of the cavern, while the noises got louder and closer.

"What's happening?" I asked Hawk when he limped by us.

"The Shaman has returned with more men, and has blown a passage through to the east subway station. We think he's using more explosives to try to create an entrance to the inner tunnels." A sound from the other side of the cavern made us both turn. "The League forces have also been concentrating their efforts, working their way in from the west."

Attacked from two sides with enemies all around us. Would I ever stop getting in these ridiculous predicaments? Then I remembered Ilona and the outcasts. Their new sanctuary was out where the League was currently blowing things up.

I grabbed Reever's arm. "We've got to get to the hybrids before Shropana's forces do."

Dhreen appeared beside me, his face still bruised and pale from the beating Rico had given him. "Doc, we've got to get Ilona and the others out of those pipelines."

I saw all the entrances were being guarded. "That may be more difficult than you think." I spotted Milass, who was ordering everyone in different directions. Little twerp looked like he was having the time of his life. "Stay here. It's time for me to collect on a favor."

Milass was snapping out orders to his men and barely glanced at me when I came up. "Move the children and the women into the quake bunker. Have the men destroy the perimeter tunnels, all except the ones to the village and the arena drop point."

"Excuse me."

Now he looked at me. "What?"

"There are people out in those sewer passages. We need to get help to them, too."

"The unclean?" I nodded. "The chief already told you, let them die." He turned his back on me.

"No, I won't." I went around and planted myself in front of him. "Who came to me a few days ago, begging for help?"

"That was different." He got a besotted look in his eyes. "Ilona Red Faun is not cursed."

"She couldn't stay here. Guess who I sent her to a few days ago?" At his gape, I nodded. "Uh-huh. She's hiding out with them, and they don't have a chance against armed League troops. They'll all be slaughtered."

He hit me, and I went down. "How could you send her to them?"

"Why?" I pushed my hair out of my face and glared up at him. "What else could I do? I didn't see you volunteering to help me with the problem—and you're the one who dumped her on me."

"They are cursed. Rico forbids us to go near them."

"They're not anymore. I've cured their curse. I can cure everyone, now that I know what it is, and who's spreading it." I resisted the urge to tell him exactly who had been cursing the Night Horse. "You've got to send some men into the sewers and get them out of there."

"Even if I disobeyed the chief, my men couldn't get to them. Your League pursuers have collapsed the western perimeter tunnels. They're cut off, probably buried alive." Hatred replaced the anguish in his expression. "You have her blood on your hands."

He kicked me out of his way and stalked off.

Reever and Dhreen got on either side of me and

grabbed when I would have gone after the demonic dwarf.

"They're trapped," I said to Reever. "We have to get to them. Do you know a way out of here that will take us to them?"

"No. But Hawk might."

We found Hawk outside the Night Way hogan, getting ready to destroy the last of his dry paintings. He listened, then shook his head.

"Is that a no, you don't know the way, or no, you can't help us?" I frowned when he squatted beside the dry painting. "Hawk, this is important."

Dhreen got disgusted fast. "Let's get out of here. Every minute we waste on him, she could be dying."

"Wait." I watched Hawk's patient sprinkling of the dried flower petals and stomped down the impulse to kick the 'iikááh into a big smear. Then something caught my eye. "Reever, you said the tunnels were laid out like a web, right?"

"Yes."

"Look." I nodded toward the spiral pattern Hawk was creating on top of the dry painting mural. "This was finished. He doesn't do that when they're finished."

Reever studied the new design. "He's drawing us a map."

It must have been the only way Hawk could help us without disobeying the chief's orders. On a hunch, I crouched down beside him. "Where are the outcasts? Show me."

He stopped sprinkling the larkspur petals and discarded them on one side in favor of some red sand. Carefully he made a small dot on one of the outer "web" strands.

"And where are we?"

He sprinkled another red dot in the center of the web.

Reever studied the dry painting for a moment. "I know where they are. How do we get to them safely?"

Hawk sprinkled a thin blue line from our position, through the web of tunnels, and over to where the outcasts were located. I looked up at Reever, who nodded.

"Would you take the cats up out of here?" Hawk nodded, and I squeezed his arm. "Thank you."

He started to chant as he added swirls of red along the outer ring of the design.

> *"The enemy is everywhere,*
> *The enemy is inside us,*
> *The enemy is outside us.*
> *We walk the rainbow path*
> *To fight the enemy within us."*

"He is marking the position of the League troops," Reever said.

I judged the distances. "God, they're really close."

Hawk got to his feet, destroyed the entire dry painting with a couple of shuffling steps, and left the hogan.

CHAPTER SEVENTEEN

Change of Course

Since everyone had moved to the emergency bunker, we only had to slip past one of Rico's guards. I suggested the smallest one might be the easiest to jump, but Reever overruled me.

"That man." He pointed to the largest of the guards.

"Reever, he's twice your size. Forget about it."

Before I could stop him, Reever went over to the big guard, and spoke in low tones with him. Then my husband turned and gestured for us to come to him.

"This redeems my debt to you, *Nilch'i',*" the guard said, then he turned and faced the stone wall.

Reever led us past him without incident.

"What debt does he have to you?" I asked.

"You are not the only one who has favors to collect. I took a penalty for him during a game."

"Copycat." I glanced back at the guard. "So why is he facing the wall?"

"Milass ordered him to see that no one went into the tunnels. By doing so, he was not disobeying the *secondario*'s orders." He stopped me when I would have turned toward Medical. "Where are you going?"

"To get Shropana. You're coming with me. This

may be the only chance we have to get him up to the surface."

Shropana was unconscious again, thanks to the continuous sedation I'd been keeping him on. I hooked up the external pump to the side of the gurney and had the men carefully transfer him to it. His artificial heart was still operating smoothly, my subsequent scan revealed.

"Whatever you do, don't drop him." I downloaded his chart onto a datapad and placed it by his side. "And don't knock those pressure lines out of the pump, or his chest."

Dhreen and Reever handled the gurney while I packed a medical case. The outcasts had doubtless suffered some injuries from the explosions, and I hoped they wouldn't be severe. There was only so much I could carry. I spotted the Lok-Teel, looked at Shropana, then slipped the ambulatory mold in my pocket.

When I was finished, the men pushed Shropana's gurney out into the tunnel and we began following Hawk's route to the western sewer system.

The tunnels were in bad shape. Loose rock had fallen everywhere, and the stone walls still shuddered with each new explosion. The closer we got to the sewers, the louder the booms grew. Dust and small rocks began raining down on us, and I held my case over Shropana's chest to protect him. We edged around a couple of half-sprung traps until we got out of the interior tunnels and into the old conduit system.

We emerged into the main sewer line, and discovered all the lights had been knocked out. It was too dark to see what lay ahead. I sniffed the air, and smelled smoke.

Not fire. I'd been badly burned in the past, first during a mercenary attack on the *Sunlace,* then repeatedly branded on Catopsa. As a result, I had an enduring and understandable case of pyrophobia. *Please, God, not another fire.*

"Wait." I pulled an optical emitter from my medical case. "If memory serves me, we need to go left up here, then walk a hundred yards and turn right."

It wasn't easy to do any of that. The damage from the explosives was much worse out here, and the fragile concrete pipes had partially collapsed. Mounds of soil and rock created a labyrinth for us to wade through.

"Where are we?" I asked Reever.

"About forty feet from where the outcasts were hidden."

I looked around. "There?" I pointed to a recessed area above the jumbled rubble that had been a processing station.

Reever nodded.

Small hills of debris blocked every possible approach to the recess. We could climb them, but there was no way Dhreen and Reever were going to be able to get the gurney through. "How can we get to them?"

"We get them to come to us." Dhreen walked over to the pile of loose rock and climbed up until he reached the top. "I can see some light from behind it. Duncan, help me clear this stone away."

An hour of moving rocks made enough of an opening for the outcasts to push through from the other side. To our disappointment, no one emerged.

"Maybe they're farther down the other way?" I tried to see, but the emitter's power cells were starting to fade.

"No, it has to be on this side." Reever went around another hill and vanished. A moment later, he called back, "Over here."

I helped Dhreen maneuver the gurney around the rubble. We had to wrench Shropana through a tight spot, and I held my breath as more rock slid down and pelted us.

The stench of something burning got worse.

I tried not to panic, not to allow my lungs to solidify

from it. Sweat broke out all over me, and I started to shake. My throat was closing up. Soon I wouldn't be able to breathe.

Images of the fire on board the *Sunlace,* when I'd lost Tonetka and very nearly the use of both of my hands, rushed into my mind. I hadn't had a full-blown anxiety attack since leaving Catopsa, but I hadn't been near any uncontrollable fires since then, either.

"Reever, what's burning?" I looked for signs of flame shooting out of some hidden recess. "Is this because of the explosives?"

He helped me and Dhreen wrest Shropana's gurney toward the next opening. "It is from the explosives. The League uses thermal detonator."

That should have reassured me. It didn't. "Maybe I should sit down for a minute."

Reever climbed down and held out his hand. "Squilyp told us this would happen, and when it did, for you to confront it."

"What does that Omorr know anyway?" I grumbled as I threaded my fingers through Reever's. Fear had clamped around my neck like an invisible bonesetter, so I tried to focus on the men and the reason we were trying to kill ourselves. "Do you see them? Are they close?"

"There's another one right up ahead. In there." Dhreen pointed to a shadowy recess in a section of pipe a few feet away.

"Leave Shropana here," Reever said. "We'll come back for him."

We had to climb and crawl over more rubble to get to the outcasts' hiding place. I jerked a few times I felt something a little warmer than it should have been, but saw no fire. Which was a good thing. I think I would have started screaming hysterically if I'd spotted so much as a spark.

The recess had once housed some kind of pumping station, judging from the remnants of the equipment.

A crude door had been rigged and now stood jammed and inoperable.

I felt the metal door, which was cool, then put my mouth by the small open space. "Is anyone in there?"

A chorus of relieved voices answered me.

"Step back, Cherijo." Reever nodded toward Dhreen, and the two of them grabbed the door and wrenched. Metal groaned, some loose rock fell, and then they pulled it out, far enough for the outcasts to fit through.

They started emerging, covered with dust and grinning. A few were injured, and I herded them to one side for a quick triage. Dhreen yelled and swept Ilona up in his arms the moment she appeared.

"It is good that you came to find us," one of the men said.

"I'm sure you would have made your way out eventually. True love conquers all." I watched Ilona cover Dhreen's grinning face with kisses, and shook my head. "I can just imagine what kind of kids they'll have. Short-tempered mercenaries. The universe may never be safe again."

While I dealt with the minor injuries, Reever gathered the outcasts together and decided with them how to proceed.

"We have family on the surface who will help us travel to the Four Mountains reservation," the oldest man said. "We have voted and decided to rejoin our Navajo clans."

That must have been a tough decision to make, seeing as every one of the outcasts still had family members among the Night Horse.

"Weren't these the same clans who were willing to let you crossbreeds be deported?" I mentioned.

"We have made contact with the tribal council. They never wished us to leave, and will not turn us over to the authorities. The chief deceived us."

Another of Rico's many sins. I finished wrapping a support around a sprained wrist and went over to the map Reever was scratching in the dirt.

"You'll need to get past the League troops, and they're probably all over the subway system." I pointed to the place on the crude map where the outcasts had helped me take Reever to Joe's underground facility. "There's a surface access hatch here, right before you enter the lab. It leads to the back maintenance shed on the estate. I doubt the League is watching Joe's grounds. I'd take that."

"What about drones? As soon as they see us, we will be detained."

I thought for a moment. "Is it October twelfth or thirteenth?"

Reever answered that one. "It is the twelfth."

"Tell the drones you're architectural students from the University of California. A group of them comes on the twelfth every year to take a tour of the estate. Thank the drone for its hospitality, and walk away."

The outcast looked down at his dusty garments. "We do not resemble students."

"On the contrary." I smiled. "Native American fashion is the latest trend among young people. The drones won't blip a sensor over your appearance."

"What about him?" Dhreen jerked a thumb in Shropana's direction. "They're not going to think he's a student."

He had a point. "We'll take him out another way."

We led the outcasts back through the opening we'd created and a couple of the uninjured volunteered to carry Shropana. Then we slowly and cautiously made our way toward the subway tunnels.

"Stop," Reever said as we reached the junction tunnel. "Be as silent as possible from here."

We could hear the troops moving on the other side of the walls, and everyone made an effort to be quiet as we filed in. Dhreen, Ilona, and I ended up toward the rear of the group, and we were the first to hear the approaching steps behind us.

"Everyone, down!" I hissed as loudly as I dared, then shrank into the shadows. Beside me, Dhreen wrapped his arms around Ilona.

A detachment of soldiers passed through the tunnels, just where we had been standing only moments ago. I stared at Dhreen, knowing one word from him would bring the League troops running. He had nothing to worry about, he'd only be deported. Terrans didn't even jail aliens—they considered it inhumane treatment of human prisoners.

He'd also get a hefty reward for turning me in—enough to give him and Ilona a start wherever they wanted.

As if he could read my thoughts, I saw Dhreen flash me a smile. And he didn't make a peep.

The troops disappeared down the tunnel, and we all let out a collective sigh of relief.

"You've certainly changed," I said to Dhreen.

"Maybe." He waggled his eyebrows. "Maybe not."

"No more talking until we reach the surface," Reever warned in a barely audible whisper.

We got the Night Horse out first, but Dhreen insisted on staying with us to help carry Shropana. Deliberately, we moved him to another access hatch on the other side of the estate, one I knew was regularly patrolled by security drones.

He was beginning to come out of the anesthetic as we hauled him up the ladder and out of the small portal behind the front gate station. Shropana saw me and struggled for a moment, until Reever clamped an arm around his shoulders and pinned him to the gurney. I knelt beside it, and spoke close to Shropana's ear.

"All the details of your surgery and treatment are on the datapad beside you. Tell them to get you to a medical facility, as soon as possible."

"You . . . did . . . this?"

"No thanks are necessary."

He closed his eyes and didn't make another sound. Apparently he thought so, too.

"I'll stay with him," Dhreen said. "I'll point them in the wrong direction when they want to know where you are."

Now he wanted me to trust him again. Funny, but I was inclined to do just that. To a certain extent. "You just want the reward for recovering him."

He grinned. "I haven't changed that much." He looked at Reever. "Why don't the two of you get out of here now, while you can?"

"I can't go. Not until I treat the infected members of the tribe. Especially the hybrids—they may never see another doctor."

"Still immolating yourself for your patients."

"Sacrificing, and yes, that's part of the job."

He reached out as if to hug me, then thought better of it and offered his hand. "I'll see you again, Doc."

I took it. "You still owe me free passage. When I'm done here, we're going to need to get off this planet in a hurry."

He lifted his eyebrows. "I don't have a ship."

"So? When has that ever stopped you?" I took the Lok-Teel from my pocket and handed it to him. "Put on a happy Terran face, and go up there and steal one."

There were no guards left inside the cave when Reever and I returned. Kegide, however, appeared before us and made some urgent gestures.

"Do you think the League will get this far?"

"Possibly." Reever scanned the area. "The tribe took whatever they could carry, and all the food stores are gone."

Kegide was hopping from foot to foot now and

making the low, toneless sounds that indicated he was
beyond agitated.

"We'd better go with him."

Kegide led us past the emergency bunker, which
was completely empty, and down a long, narrow corridor that ended in a passage up toward diffused light.

I hung back for a minute. The entire area above us
was crawling with Joseph's men. "I can't go on the
surface, Kegide."

"I don't think this goes to the surface, Cherijo. Wait
here while I check." Reever climbed up the ladder
and had a look around, then descended again. "This
leads to old maintenance tunnels under the city
arena."

I looked up. "You mean, the shockball arena is
right over our heads?"

"Yes."

"Wonderful." I shouldered my medical case and
started climbing. "Nothing like hiding in plain view."

"I doubt the officials even know these tunnels
exist." He climbed up before me, and we swung off
the ladder into a pristine passage of whitewashed plas-
crete. "Wait here."

Reever silently strode down the passage and disappeared. I stayed close to the hatch, in case I had to
make a quick exit. A few minutes later he returned.

"They have occupied some of the old storage facilities at the other end of this passage." Reever didn't
look happy. "Milass tells me the chief wishes to see
you at once."

"He isn't happy that we stayed behind, right?"

"He is . . . disturbed."

Great. Rico in a psychotic rage was no one to fool
with. "I don't suppose there's any way I can get out
of this?"

"I will be with you."

We went to the storage areas, where the Night
Horse had set up a temporary camp, and Milass word-

lessly led us to Rico. The chief was working on a computer console in front of an entire wall paved with vid screens. He hailed me as I walked in.

"Patcher! We thought we had lost you."

There was expensive computer equipment crammed in the room, more than I'd seen even in Joe's lab. I struggled to remain calm and keep my tone innocent. "I had to retrieve some medical supplies." I held up my case for emphasis.

"Come here."

I glanced at Reever, who nodded, then slowly approached Rico.

Rico. Jericho. My brother. Even after seeing the DNA strands, it was a little hard to believe. Then I saw what Reever had mentioned—same hair, same eyes, same bone structure. Even our noses made a matched set.

Is that the reason I can sense his feelings? The fabled mental connection between twins?

We'd never shared a womb, the physician in me immediately pointed out. And we weren't really twins—I was at least four or five years younger than Rico. But perhaps it didn't matter. Maybe the connection was formed beyond gestation, in spite of distance and chronological age.

"You are nervous," Rico said.

I was terrified. I didn't know what to do, what to say to him. "Just a little unsettled. What's up?"

"The Shaman has been busy." He tapped the console, and an image of Joseph Grey Veil came up on the dusty screen.

Our creator. "What does he want now?"

"Listen."

Rico enabled the audio, and Joseph's voice came through the panel speaker.

"—have combed the tunnels and neutralized all the traps. They have also placed pulse charges in several

areas. You are boxed in. Release my property, or I
will have the devices detonated—"

"He has been transmitting it continuously since the
assaults on both sides began." Rico switched it off.
"Old Joe thinks he will destroy my *Leyaneyaniteh*."

"He'll do that and worse." I stepped away from the
panel. "Why don't I just surrender to them? As soon
as they have me, the tribe will be out of danger."

"The tribe has never been in any danger, I assure
you." Rico sat back and pressed another keypad.
"Bring in the devices we recovered."

Several of the Night Horse men came in, each one
carrying several small metal boxes.

Reever took one and gingerly examined it. "These
are explosives."

"Defused and quite harmless for the moment." Rico
grabbed one for himself and started tossing it back
and forth between his hands. "We found every one of
them and removed them soon after they were planted
by the Shaman's forces."

I watched him toy with the deadly device. Even if
it was defused, it was still a bomb, and his nonchalant
fiddling was making me feel nauseated. "You may
have missed some."

"No." He gave me a gentle smile, then tossed the
device at me. I gasped as I caught it. "We saw them
plant all of them. When we came here and created
this place, I had recording drones installed in every
tunnel." He turned to the console, and switched on
the bank of vid screens.

Each square coalesced into a different image of the
entire underground world of *Leyaneyaniteh*. The tunnels outside Medical, the cross sections leading into
the sewer conduits and subway systems, all displayed
in perfect detail.

"I like to come here and watch when I cannot be
below," Rico said. "When I cannot be here, I have
the consoles record the images."

What he was telling was he had seen or had accessed recordings of everything Reever and I had done since he'd taken us from The Grey Veils. Everything we'd done, from sneaking around and escaping to . . . I flinched when I saw the hidden lake cavern show up on one screen. Not even on the night had we remained unobserved.

I stopped being afraid. I'd been subject to surveillance before in the past, and I'd never liked it. One bit. I handed him back his bomb. "Didn't anyone ever teach you it's rude to spy on people?"

Some of the men made threatening noises, but all the chief did was dismiss them. "There was much I was never taught, patcher. But I learned what I needed."

"So what are you going to do with the bombs? Throw them back at Joe and his merry men?"

"My men will plant the devices as I have instructed. They will serve my purposes now."

Given the fact we were under an arena that regularly held several thousand people, I could almost bet what his purposes were. "Your men won't blow up the arena for you. They don't hate Caucasians that much."

"The devices will not be used to destroy the arena."

"Where are you putting them?"

"I'm not going to tell you." He sounded like a scheming child. "I want it to be a surprise."

"I don't want to be surprised."

"Very well." He made a show of thinking about it. "I know—if Reever makes the first score in the World Bowl game, I will have all the devices removed and deactivated."

"What if I don't score?" Reever asked.

"Then I will trigger them." The chief said nothing else, and dismissed me and Reever.

"He's lying," I said in a tight voice as we were escorted back to the shelter. "We've got to find a way to warn someone up there."

"I can do it before the game starts. I'll inform one of the drone officials of the threat."

"They'll just arrest you and haul you out of the arena for interrogation. You have to make that first score, Duncan."

"I will."

Reever left me to talk to some of the other players and see if any of them would tell him what Rico was planning. Given the tribe's loyalty to their chief, I didn't hold out much hope of his success. For now, all I could do was set up a triage area and examine the members of the tribe injured from the cave-ins. Someone cleared out a smaller room for me, and after prioritizing the cases, I moved into my temporary treatment room.

Hawk came in later, after the last of my patients, and I took the opportunity to perform his final back treatment.

"You don't have to walk hunched over anymore," I told him as I straightened the curled muscles.

"It is best I maintain the illusion."

Considering his problem, I had to agree with that call. "I think if I lie and say it's vitamin shots or something, I can convince Rico to let me administer antibiotic to the infected tribal members. Once he goes to sleep, I can do the same for him. If I pull that off, will you help me and Reever get out of here?"

Every word dragged as he said, "I will help you."

"Why don't you come with us? Dhreen will probably steal a starshuttle, and there'll be plenty room."

"I cannot go." He looked around, and spread his arms helplessly. "This is my home." His gaze darkened and he stared at his footgear. "I cannot betray my chief."

"Your chief infected you with syphilis. He won't seek medical treatment, so if you stay, he'll do it again. You already know he won't be faithful to you. Come with us."

"I will not leave him." Hawk pulled on his tunic and stalked off.

So much for convincing Hawk to improve his situation.

When some of the men delivered the storage containers with my stock of antibiotic, I decided to go ahead with my vitamin-therapy plan, and took a box of fully charged syrinpresses out to the shelter. Everyone accepted my outright lie without a qualm. I performed quick allergen screens—saying they were to confirm what kind of vitamins they needed—and infused everyone with the proper antibiotic.

I saw Reever a few times, deep in conversation with some of the players. He looked at me from across the shelter once, and shook his head.

He was having no luck.

I didn't see Hawk again until nightfall, when all the lights dimmed and we had to rig some emitters around the different storage rooms. Hawk called me over and pointed to the monitoring room Rico had occupied all day.

"He wants to talk to you."

"Good." Now that I had wiped out treponema pallidum in every member of the tribe, it was time for the final showdown with my brother. "I have some things we need to discuss, too."

I stopped back in the treatment room to retrieve a few things, then went with Hawk. We didn't go to the monitoring room. Instead Hawk escorted me to another chamber. He opened the door panel, but didn't go in. I took a look—it was completely dark inside.

I didn't like dark rooms. "Am I in trouble?" I whispered.

He nodded once.

"Okay." I stepped inside.

As soon as the door panel slid shut behind me, I smelled flowers and food.

"Hello?"

Soft lights flickered on, illuminating the luxurious furnishings of a private boudoir. The tribe had moved all of Rico's possessions up from his hogan, and added a few things—tapestries, upholstered furnishings, and a nice big sleeping platform. Platters of food sat on polished tables. If I hadn't known better, I'd have thought myself back in Joseph's mansion.

"Good evening." My brother sat in a wing-back chair in front of the sleeping platform. He wore a black velvet jacket with gold embellishments. His hair was wet, and he was drinking pale wine from a crystal goblet.

Yep, I was in trouble. "You wanted to talk to me?"

"Come and sit down, Cherijo." He waved toward the matching, empty chair a foot away from his. "I have looked forward to this evening for a very long time."

I went to the chair and sat on the very edge of the seat.

"Have a glass of wine." He held out a second goblet to me.

"No thanks. Alcohol gives me headaches."

"As you wish." He drained half the glass and set it down. "Hungry?"

"No." I felt like a butterfly that was about to lose a wing or two. "Chief, we need to talk about a couple of things."

"Sit back and relax. Tonight I will listen to whatever you have to say."

Which was a rather ominous way to put it. Would my being honest drive him over the edge, or give him a lifeline? I had no love for my brother or what he had done, but I knew what Joseph Grey Veil was capable of doing. If circumstances had been altered only slightly, I could have been sitting in his chair, sipping wine, and dying of a curable disease while plotting to blow up two hundred thousand misguided people.

"At the pre-World Game press conference, I had Reever run a series of medical scans on you. The results are what we need to talk about."

"Of course, the business with the champagne. I gave him a black eye, didn't I?" He seemed pleased that he could remember. "I should have broken his jaw instead." He shrugged. "There's always tomorrow after the game."

"Rico, after running my analysis of the scans, I confirmed you are carrying a sexually transmitted disease. You've infected everyone you've been intimate with since contracting the illness."

"That would be a substantial amount of people."

"Yes, it is. I also discovered that you and I have nearly identical DNA patterns. Do you know what that means?"

"Of course we do. You're my little sister."

CHAPTER EIGHTEEN

The Grandfather of All Monsters

Hearing him say that made my heart sink a little further. I'd been subconsciously hoping to use our connection as an edge. "I never knew I had a brother. Joseph never told me. I wish I'd known."

"He didn't tell you about the others, why bother telling you about me?"

My heart did a flip and I clutched the arms of the chair. "How many others survived?"

"We all survived, Cherijo. Joseph was the proud father of nine baby boys, and one baby girl."

I had eight more brothers. It was too much to grasp. "Where are they?"

"I imagine Joseph has been keeping some of them at the Mendocino facility. I heard rumors of an assistant he sent off Terra, to work with League scientists. Some kind of genius with stardrive design. I imagine he's one of us, too."

"Are you the only one who got away from him?"

"No, dear sister. You escaped, too."

"Rico, I have about a million questions to ask you, but we have to talk about your disease first. What we do to deal with that is the most critical thing right now. Did Joseph ever give you any medical training?"

He ignored my last question as he refilled his wineglass. "My disease. Yes, tell me about my disease."

"You were infected with it some time ago—ten or fifteen years, at least. It's a disease called syphilis. It hasn't existed on Terra for a couple of centuries, so I'm not sure how you contracted it, but—"

"I know exactly how I got it. Would you like to know?"

I leaned forward. "Yes."

"*Yei* gave it to me."

"*Yei?*" That was what the little girl had called the masked dancers during the initiation ceremony. "You mean Milass? Or Kegide?"

"*Yei.*" He got up and started strolling in a circle around my chair. Abruptly he changed the subject. "I've always known about you. I was there when you were born. I watched him drain the chamber and pull you out. I had a good view of the entire procedure from my cell."

His cell. I swallowed hard and shook my head.

"I'd never seen a naked female until that day. When I saw you, all naked and screaming and squirming in his hands, I simply thought he'd neglected to give you a penis. I felt sorry for you, until they took you up to the house." He frowned. "None of us were ever permitted in the house."

He wandered over to a table and took a handful of grapes from one of the platters. He started tossing them, one by one, into his mouth. It was so quiet I could hear them squish between his teeth.

"Did the others know?"

"I'm not sure. He usually kept us isolated from each other. So it wouldn't spoil his tests." He stopped behind me and leaned over so that his warm, fruit-scented breath caressed my cheek. "I would have liked to have known you, little sister. You were the fairest of us all."

"He never told me. If he'd told me, I would have—"

"You would have done exactly what he said. Whatever he said. That is one thing I knew about you, Cherijo. He was so pleased with your compliance that he practically sang your praises every day. Each morning I listened to some new tale about my sister, how intelligent you were, how well you comprehended and achieved the goals he set for you. You were his trophy clone, his superb attainment in human genetic engineering."

It hurt. It hurt to think of all of the years I had spent at the estate and never knew what was happening beneath it. "It may sound hard to believe, Rico, but I was a victim, too."

"Were you?" He came back to his chair and sat down quickly, making a burlesque of his eagerness to listen to me. "Did he beat you? Put you on the treadmill? Did he wrap you in nerve-webbing and set you on the stimulator for a few hours?"

"No, but—"

"Then, he starved you? He liked to see how long we could go without food. Or the temperature chamber, did he ever make you stand naked in blizzard conditions? Did he rupture your eardrums, to see how fast they'd heal? Did he have a drone fracture your arms, and legs, to monitor the density of the breaks knitting back together?"

"No!" I shot up. "Stop it!"

"Did he touch you?"

I meant to shout something else, but those four words knocked all the air out of my lungs. I could barely form one syllable. "What?"

"Did he touch you? Undress you? Fondle you?"

"No." Something was making me feel like vomiting, and it was coming from him. "You knew that, too. You knew what he had planned for me."

"I knew he loved you. I know he still loves you." Rico leaned forward and took my icy hands in his. "I've always known you were the only one worthy of him." He massaged my fingers, warming them. "The perfect woman. Any man would kill to have you."

I had to change the subject. Fast. "Rico, who is *Yei*?"

"One time, just before I escaped, he allowed me to watch you and your companion through an observation viewer. You were almost three, and she had you assembling a model of a human skeleton. You got all the bones right on the first try. All you had to do, he told me, was see a diagram once and you memorized it." His hand squeezed. "It was one of my punishments for neglecting to memorize the entire nervous system."

"I'm sorry, Rico." And I was. "Look, I'll do whatever I can to help you. There's a possibility, with the right medications and therapy, we can repair some of the damage and you can have a more normal life. Just tell me who *Yei* is and I'll—"

"That's all you can think about, isn't it? He's programmed you completely. His perfect physician. His perfect woman. His perfect life partner. Even now all you can think about is fixing me. Do you ever wonder which genes are responsible for kindness and sympathy and caring? Perhaps you could get me a couple of those."

I couldn't take another moment of it, and my voice rose to a shout. "Tell me who *Yei* is!"

"He's the grandfather of all monsters, Cherijo. You know who he is."

I backed away. "No. He wouldn't do that. Not to a child. He told me he wasn't— He wouldn't—"

"But he did." Rico's voice became a gentle caress. "He infected himself from a biosample he'd gotten from one of the research facilities he worked for.

Some archaic, extinct bacteria no one had even heard of. He liked to give us all challenges, didn't he?"

I turned my back on him.

"I didn't know what he intended to do when he put me in the restraints. Until that particular day, the nerve-webbing had been the worst, and I'd gotten used to spending hours wrapped in that. I didn't struggle. I don't think I was even frightened."

"No." I pressed my hands against my ears. "Don't."

"He could have administered it with a syrinpress, but he was a stickler for details. He wanted it introduced to my body the way it would have been when it existed. So he infected me the time-honored way."

I closed my eyes. My hands slipped down to my sides.

"When he was done with me, he infused himself with the correct antibiotic treatment and then he monitored me, to see if my immune system would destroy the bacteria by itself."

"It was just another test to him."

"Yes. Just another test." Rico came up behind me, lifted my hand, and brushed a kiss against the back of it. "Be glad you were perfection, little sister." He got close enough to whisper in my hair. "Brutal things happen to imperfect children."

My face was wet, and I was sobbing. It made it hard to speak evenly. "You never needed me as your team physician. You're using me to get back at him. Have you been signaling him, taunting him about me?"

"I merely made our parent aware that his most cherished creation now belongs to me." He guided me back to my chair and pressed a glass of wine in my hand. "Drink. You've had a shock, and it will help steady you for the rest."

I put the wine aside. "The rest?"

"I have to tell you about my plans. My holy mission, given to me by the gods who watch over little children in the wilderness."

He was descending back into the madness, and this time, I had a front-row seat. *Keep him talking.*

I cleared my throat. "I'd like to hear about it."

"When I escaped from our father, it was revealed to me. In the wilderness, as I lay dying. I am the reincarnation of *Atse Hastiin*—First Man. Born not of woman and man, but of the universal forces that once created the gods.

"Since my enlightenment, I have been waiting for the reincarnation of my *Atse Asdzan*—First Woman. Together we will slaughter the *Yei*, and go on to populate this world and the next with our wisdom, and our children."

"We, as in I'm this First Woman." I made it a statement. Who else could it be?

Rico smiled. "That he loves you makes it all the better."

"You can't infect me with the syphilis, and you can't make me give the disease to Joseph Grey Veil."

Anger slammed over me as my brother reacted to my guess with an outraged scream. "It is not a disease! It is a gift of enlightenment! I have given it to my tribe, to enlighten them as I have been. I have sent it across the mountains so the *Diné* may know the beauty of seeing through my eyes."

I wasn't falling for that. "That's why you've been arranging all those marriages? Sending all those men back to the Four Mountains? You really are trying to create a global epidemic."

For a moment, a flicker of rationality gleamed in his eyes. "The Shaman is consulted on all matters of serious health concerns for the Native American Nations." Joy lit his dark face. "Can you imagine his reaction when he learns his sacred Navajo have shared in the gift he gave to me? Do you think he will observe them to see how their immune systems respond, Cherijo?"

I didn't have to state the obvious. I knew at that

moment that there was no medication, no therapy for him. My brother was totally, conclusively insane.

I tried delicacy first. "I'm sorry for what he did to you. As much as I appreciate the honor you're offering, I have to decline."

That seemed to stun him. "I offer you revenge for everything he has done to you, and to your brothers, and you refuse me?"

Delicacy wasn't going to do a damn thing. "Yeah." I got to my feet. "Let me help you, or let me go."

"You think I need you?" He walked over to me, and with that same, cheerful smile backhanded me with his fist. I went down and out of reflex covered my head with my arms. His foot drove into my bicep. "You're not fit to lick my footgear. But since you refuse me, it makes everything much simpler. I'll let you live long enough to watch your lover die."

Now I dropped my arms. "What are you talking about?"

"My men have replanted all the explosives beneath The Grey Veils. The triggering device is hidden inside the World Game sphere. When *Nilch'i'* crosses the touchzone line, a sensor planted in the field will activate the trigger, and blow Joseph Grey Veil straight to hell, along with his precious research facility."

"Chief."

We both looked over at Hawk, who was standing just inside the door.

"Come and have a drink, old friend. We are celebrating the coming festivities above."

"Grey Veil's facility lies directly within the San Andreas fault zone."

Rico took another sip of his wine. "So?"

"If you detonate those devices, millions will die in the subsequent destabilization."

Rico set down his glass carefully, and started toward Hawk.

"Hawk, get out of here!" I yelled.

"You question me? You, my brother, my lover, my shoulder-talker?"

· Hawk bowed so low his brow nearly touched the ground. "Chief, I respect and honor you in all ways. Let me serve you, let me be your tool. Listen to my words and hear the truth of them."

Oh, God, he was going to end up a smear on the floor covering. "Hawk, run!"

"My warped songbird sings badly tonight," Rico said, caressing Hawk's cheek. Then he began to beat him, using his fists and feet. Hawk never raised a hand or tried to defend himself, so he went down quickly. I tried to pull Rico off and got tossed across the room. My head hit something hard, and everything went black.

When I opened my eyes, Rico was dragging me into a hogan. Ropes bit into my arms and legs. We were back underground, but the cavern was completely deserted. Of course, everyone was still in the underground arena passages.

Had he killed Hawk?

"I will come back for you as soon as Reever and our parent are dead. Enjoy these last hours."

He closed the door covering, then I watched as he nailed it shut.

It took a couple of hours to work my way out of the ropes. Once I'd bound the cut on my arm with a piece of fabric torn from my tunic, I tried to force open the door, but it was sealed tight. There was nothing in the hogan I could use to make a hole through it or one of the rounded walls. They were too thick.

I had to get to Reever before the World Game started, but how? Hawk was either dead or in no shape to help me. No one else knew where I was. It was hopeless.

Then again, when had hopeless situations ever stopped me?

I hammered on the sides and door of the hogan. I screamed for help. Screamed until my throat was raw and my voice nearly gone. I had to keep making noise and someone would hear me.

Hours passed. I alternated yelling with pounding. I kept at it with such concentration that when the door was wrenched open, I nearly decked my rescuer in the face.

"Oh!" I reeled backward and smacked the back of my head. Kegide reached in to help me out, and I threw myself into his arms. "Kegide. Thank God. What are you doing here?"

He smiled, reached down and pretended to stroke a small animal.

"You came to play with the cats. Of course." What should I do first? Disarm the bombs by destroying the trigger. Duncan. I had to get to Duncan. "They're not here, Kegide. Hawk took them up to the arena. Can you take me there so we can both play with them?"

He shook his head, then I remembered. The subway transport couldn't be moved unless it held enough people to pull it up the incline. There had to be another way—

And there was. I took his big hand in mine "Come with me."

In the storage room, I mounted the platform and tugged on the chain. It felt sturdy enough, but getting me up the air shaft would be a tight squeeze. Kegide would have to haul on the chain. Once inside, I wouldn't be able to lift my arms.

With simple words and gestures I showed Kegide what I needed him to do. Then I got on the platform and helped him pull me up to the entrance of the shaft.

It was more than a tight squeeze—I felt like a square peg being forced into a triangular hole. As I ascended, the surfaces of my body, along with my arms and legs, scraped against the shaft's rusty interior. I could hear Kegide grunting in the storage room beneath as he hauled on the chain.

At last I was on the surface, in a clearing behind the villagers' fields. I stepped off the platform and yelled down to Kegide, "I'm out! Thanks!"

Getting to the arena was my next problem. I had no idea how to get out of the mountains and down to the city. The village itself was completely deserted.

They'd gone to the game, too. However, if they'd gone to the city, that had to mean they had more than horses for transportation up here.

I found the old glidecar hidden inside one of the grain storage sheds at the end of the village, and checked the batteries. There was enough charge for a one-hour ride. The trusting owner had also left the ignition sequence uncoded, so I got the engine started with a few jabs on the keypad.

I flew straight up, pushing the vehicle's atmospheric tolerances so I could get a good look at where I was. From this height, it was easy to spot the city, and the small dot that represented the shockball arena.

I might have just enough charge to get there.

It had been years since I'd driven, but I didn't hesitate as I descended and leveled out the glidecar. All I could think of was Duncan, and how little time I had left to get to him. I pointed the vehicle's nose toward the city, and slammed down hard on the accelerator.

I thought nothing else could possibly go wrong after that. I found out differently when I hit the glide lanes leading to the arena, which were choked with fans headed for World Game.

Claxons blared. Voices shouted. Fists waved. And everywhere were the Gliders' team colors, and the number fourteen.

My batteries were going dry. "This isn't going to work."

I ended up abandoning the stolen vehicle in the emergency lane and running the last mile. I shoved my way through the river of spectators flowing into the entrance gate, and came up short when a mechanical arm shot out.

"Present your seating pass."

I didn't have a seating pass. Frantically, I looked around, and spotted a middle-aged man arguing with his wife.

"—shouldn't play? Look at Jory Rask!" the wife was saying. "How many downs did she score last season? Forty?"

"It's a man's game, you don't know what—"

I reached over between them. "Excuse me." I snatched the pass chip from the man's fist. "Thank you."

I shoved the chip in the drone's arm slot and vaulted over it. Behind me, the couple screeched their outrage. I kept going, dodging around concession carts and the long lines of customers winding around them. At last I found a door marked MAINTENANCE, slipped inside, and headed for the lower levels.

A console I passed displayed the minutes left until the game started: twenty-eight. It took me another ten to find my way to the bunkers where the Night Horse had set up camp.

Everyone was gone from there, too. I thought of what I'd told Kegide. Where *were* the cats?

"Cherijo."

Hawk stood at the entrance to the bunker. He looked like he'd been put through a disposal unit backward. Jenner was under one arm, Juliet under the other.

"Thank God." I hurried over to help him. "Why didn't you run when I told you to?" I ran my hand along his spine. "Did he hurt your back?"

"No. Just my front." Hawk's split lips barely formed the words. "I will recover."

"Rico set up my husband to be the trigger for the explosives in the fault. I've got to get to him and warn him about the game sphere."

"I can get you inside the arena as the team patcher, but how are you going to stop Reever from playing? The drone officials don't let anyone near the field."

I took Jenner from him. "Reever and I can communicate in other ways." I knew I could initiate the link, but only if I was physically close to him. "I have to get on the field." I stroked my pet as I recalled the spectator I'd seen hauled away by drone officials. Scratch pretending to be an enthusiastic fan. Team staff members were either seated in the stands or watched from boxes during the actual game. There was no way I was getting anywhere near that field unless—

"Do you know where the players' locker room is?"

"Yes."

"Take me there."

We found a couple of small containers to put the cats in, which did not make us very popular with the felines.

I wrestled with Jenner. "Thanks for bringing the cats, I think."

Hawk tried to stroke Juliet's head and reassure her as he lowered her into her temporary carrier. She clawed both his arms. "After last night, I was afraid Rico might harm them."

Once His and Her Majesty were secure, we carried them with us to the arena's lower corridors level. I filled Hawk in about some of what Rico had revealed to me, including the delusional plot to spread the syphilis bacteria throughout Four Mountains.

"If I am able to get out of here today, I'm finding a way for Reever and I to get off the planet. You need to warn the tribal council at Four Mountains. Tell them everything I've told you about the disease.

Give them the books Wendell found. They will help."
I recalled what Rico had said. "Do you think they'll
try to ignore or conceal it?"

"The old way was to revere those whose minds existed in other worlds," Hawk said. "Rico believes, as
they did, that the mental illness he suffers is enlightenment. But I don't think the Navajo will wait and watch
their people suffer the same fate. They will go to the
reservation doctors."

We were nearly to the underground access panel
when someone stepped out into the hall directly in
front of us. I relaxed when I saw that the figure had
a flight suit on and a smiling, happy Terran face with
two distinct bumps on the top of his head.

"It's Dhreen," I said to Hawk. "He's on our side.
Come on."

Dhreen removed his Lok-Teel mask and checked
his wristcom as we reached him. "About time. I was
going to come down looking for you. Sphere-drop is
in only a few minutes. Reever's playing first string
today."

"No, he isn't." I quickly explained the circumstances behind the pending disaster, then asked, "If I
can get Reever out of the arena, can you take us to
a place where they won't find us for a while?"

"I can get you off planet, if you want."

"You got a starshuttle?"

"I stole it, just like you told me to." Dhreen's smile
wavered a little. "There's only one thing I want in
return."

Probably wanted me to check Ilona and see if she
had a little horn-earned bundle on the way. "Name
it."

"What your father promised to do. Help my people.
Come to Oenrall with me and cure them of the sickness they have."

I'd agree to anything to get to Reever and prevent
California from splitting into a lot of little pieces.

"Sure, I'll go. I don't know about a cure, but I'll give it my best shot." I glanced at Hawk, who was lagging behind. "Give me a minute."

I walked back to where he stood. "You're not coming with me, are you?"

"No. Dhreen can take you the rest of the way."

"I can't repay you for what you've done for me. You've saved my life twice. You opened my eyes to a lot of things I'd never considered, too."

"It is trivial compensation for what you've done for me."

I thought of him living in those underground tunnels, never feeling the sunlight on his face. "Come with us. We'll find a better world."

"No, patcher. As tempting as it sounds, I belong in *Leyaneyaniteh*, with my chief. He will need me even more after today."

"If that's your final word." I put my arms around his contorted body, and hugged him. "I'm going to miss you. Thank you for helping me understand my blood. I'll always think of you whenever I hear anyone sing."

He held me tight for a moment, then let go and hobbled off.

Dhreen led me to the locker room, and the Oenrallian filled me in on the starshuttle he'd "borrowed" from a Terran trade jaunter who was at that moment sleeping off the flask of spicewine he'd consumed, courtesy of Dhreen.

"After I used his access chips, I wondered if anyone would try and halt me, even with the mask. It was more rudimentary than I contemplated. I strolled in purloined it from the nucleus of New Angeles Transport, can you put faith in that?"

If I could understand half of what he was spouting. "Do you know something, Dhreen? The more nervous you get the worse you massacre my native language."

"Literally?"

"Really."

The interior of the locker room was littered with discarded clothes and damp towels. Someone had prematurely opened a bottle or two, and the smell of synalcohol was strong. A maintenance drone trundled around, collecting the used linens for sterilization. It halted as soon as it picked us up on its sensors.

"May I be of assistance?"

Dhreen peeled off his Lok-Teel mask and handed it to me before he went over to the drone. With a single jerk, he tore the entire operational system—core, panels, and circuitry—off the back of the drone. Towels thudded to the floor, then the unit collapsed on top of them.

I just stood there and stared. "That was . . . efficient."

"You still haven't said how you plan to get out on the field."

I located Black Otter's locker, which contained a clean uniform and helmet. He'd been unable to play since escaping the hospital. I slipped the Lok-Teel under my tunic. "You're going to put me in the game."

Once we had stowed the cats in a safe place, Dhreen helped me with the disguise. The outer uniform jersey and leggings were made of a elastic material, suitable for fitting over the various body protectors I had to strap on. The thick protective pads and thermal leggings to prevent discharge burn weighed about as much as I did. By the time he handed me the helmet to wear over my face, I was ready to topple over.

"How do they run wearing all this stuff?" I took an experimental step and nearly went sprawling on the floor. "Never mind run—how do they walk?"

I took a few minutes to practice balancing on the special footgear designed for the synthetic grass of the arena field, then sighed. "This is as steady as I'm going to get."

"Right on time, Doc." Dhreen nodded toward the field. "The amusement's about to commence."

Emerging from the locker room into the players' walkway was an experience. Extra seating had been installed overhead to accommodate the additional spectators for the World Game, and some three hundred thousand fans stood shrieking for their teams.

"Ear plugs," I muttered as we cringed under the solid wall of sound. "I should have remembered ear plugs."

The Gliders' familiar red-and-black team colors dominated the arena, as they were not only the home team, but favored to win this final match. Everywhere I looked, fans sported the mini black-winged hats and divided red-and-black face paint.

Vendors circled on modified hover boards, advertising their wares by using holo-imaged signs slung around their necks. They sold everything, from the traditional popcorn and synbeef dogs to more exotic treats like Fhirrede iced curds and Kirlian colas. The official team bands were trying so hard to outplay each other, their songs tangled into a noisy jumble of notes.

Dancers were still writhing in their glittering costumes all over the playing field, tumbling into acrobatic formations, shooting off small versions of the fireworks that would fill the skies above the arena once the contest was over.

But there wouldn't be any fireworks today, I reminded myself, if I didn't get moving and find Reever.

I stepped out of the passage and onto the boundary between the arena seating and the Gliders' sideline area. I was sweating and terrified I'd be stopped for some ridiculous reason.

"Swagger," I heard Dhreen say.

I turned around. "What?"

"Swagger. Sashay. Strut." He threw up his hands,

in disgust with stanTerran, me, or both. "Walk like you're a shockball player."

I tried to swagger. It was a fairly insurmountable task, with all the equipment weighing me down. Maybe I should take off my helmet, give everyone one of my patented haughty looks. That might chase people away. Just as I loosened the straps, I remembered.

There were no female players on the Gliders' team.
Scratch looking haughty and unapproachable.

As I walked down the sidelines, a couple of drone officials buzzed around me, then scanned the code on my player's badge and whizzed off. The fans hit new heights in sound pollution as they screeched for the game to begin. Glancing up at those thousands of rabid, thrilled faces made my stomach roll.

They can't wait to see someone go down and fry.

The two bands called a temporary truce as the pre-game performers left the field, and began striking up the opening notes of the World Anthem. I had no choice but to follow the Gliders as they trotted out onto the field.

Finally I saw Reever's number fourteen on the other end of the line, but the song was already playing and I couldn't move out of place. I'd have to catch him before he took up his position.

The anthem ended, and the fans cheered. I tried to dart down to the other end of the line, but a drone buzzed in my face before I had gone more than a dozen steps toward Reever.

"Defense will remain on the sidelines. Offense will compete for possession of the sphere."

Just my luck, Reever was on offense. I wasn't.

The Gliders won the drive, and the first play was in motion by the time I spotted Reever again. He ran the sphere, passing it back and forth in a triangular motion between him and two other offensive runbacks. The opposing team smashed into all three of them, and Reever went down on top of the sphere.

I stood frozen, waiting for something to blow.

"First sphere down!" A drone official called. "Second in four point three!"

The stomping and yelling became synchronized, and directed at Reever. *"Nilch'i'! Nilch'i'! Nilch'i'!"*

I measured the distance the Gliders would have to run to get to the touchzone. About sixty yards. Reever and the other players were huddled together at the lineup. Maybe I could catch his attention from the sidelines, call him over before the next drive started.

I tried to link, but I was still too far away. So I waved my arms and yelled, "Duncan!"

A couple of the players on the field glanced at me, but no one moved out of the huddle. Someone cuffed me on the back of the head. "Shut up, Otter! He can hardly hear to call his plays!"

I looked up at Handsome Runner, who was glowering down at me. "Sorry."

"You are not Black Otter." His eyes narrowed suspiciously. "Who are you?"

"Second string," I mumbled, and quickly dodged around him to walk out of questioning range. Along the way, a couple of the players pummeled me with their fists.

"Otter, good to see you!"

"I thought you had taken up weaving!"

"Does the chief know you're back?"

The next drive began, which drew everyone's attention back to the game. I hid behind a couple of line drones, trying to see another way to get on the field, and praying Reever would lose possession of the sphere.

He didn't. The Gliders got to the forty.

I tried to sneak onto the field a couple of times, until the drones got tired of me and warned me one more attempt would result in an auto-penalty. My attempts to link also failed. Reever, on the other hand, was doing a brilliant job of moving the sphere down the field, getting closer and closer to the touchzone.

The thirty. The twenty. The closer he got, the more I shook.

At the twenty, the team lined up in touchzone formation. I knew that from the excited cheers of the players.

"Bring it down, bring it down!"

"Shove that sphere pole down his throat!"

"Go for it, you can do it, you can do it!"

I had to do it now, before the next drive started. I stepped over the boundary line and an official immediately buzzed over to block my path.

"Defense will remain on the sidelines until possession of the sphere changes teams."

I doused the drone with the cup of JocAid I'd gotten for that specific purpose, and ran onto the field. "Duncan!"

He was still in the huddle, still unable to hear me. The sound of the boos and hisses from the fans was merciless. A cluster of drone officials was heading to intercept me. I'd never make it. But I was close enough now to link.

Duncan, damn it, look at me!

Reever straightened and stared out of the huddle, looking around. As I ran toward him, I lifted my hands to take my helmet off so he could see my face.

Duncan, you're in danger, can you hear me? Whatever you do, don't make the sphere-down.

The next thing I knew I was being dragged off the field. I fought, desperate to get loose and get to Reever. Whoever had me held on tight. Through my helmet, I heard the low, familiar sneer.

"Nice try, woman."

CHAPTER NINETEEN

Game Sphere

Milass had stolen my idea and was wearing a helmet and one of the Gliders' uniforms. As he hauled me past the other players and the angry drone officials, I tried yelling for help.

"Stop him! He's crazy!"

Someone snorted. "He's not the one who nearly cost us a penalty by tromping out on the field."

I turned to the stands. "Help! He's going to kill me!"

A couple of men laughed. One woman yelled back, "If he doesn't, I will!"

Everyone on the sidelines ignored us, which made it easy for Milass to drag me away and into the equipment pit. When we were out of sight, he shoved me against the wall.

"Well, little sister." Rico stepped out of the shadows. "You've shown your superior ability once more. How did you get to the surface?"

"Teleportation." I tried to duck around him, but that only got me thrown back against the wall by Milass for my efforts. "Get out of my way, Rico. I'm not going to let you kill him."

"There's nothing you can do to stop it. They won't

let you back on the field now. Listen. The sphere is in play. The Wind is about to blow itself out."

"No!" I went crazy, throwing myself at him, clawing at his face, beating him with my fists. "He heard me, he heard me tell him! He won't do it!"

"Even if he doesn't make the score, he still dies." He got my hands pinned to the wall and his face in mine in short order. "I've programmed the computer to administer five penalties to him. If they don't make sphere-down by the end of the first interval, he gets automatically charged with delay of game and unsporting conduct and a few other things. Shock, shock, shock, shock, shock. Each one more severe. The last one is special. It's three times the usual voltage."

Milass laughed. "That should cook him like a Founder's Day turkey."

There was a strange moaning sound to one side of us, and I looked over. Kegide stepped into the light, and made the odd, keening sound again. In his arms were both of my cats. Juliet stayed curled up against his broad chest, but Jenner lifted his head, sniffed, then jumped down to come after me.

"Everyone leaps to defend you. Even your precious little pet." To Kegide, Rico said, "Put the animal down and come here."

Kegide shook his head.

"He doesn't understand, Chief," Milass said. "Let me do her. I've been wanting to for months."

Rico took a pistol out of his tunic, raised it, and shot Milass in the face. The blast decapitated him. I screamed.

"Never tell me what to do," Rico said to the headless corpse, still twitching on the floor. "I am your chief." He turned to Kegide. "I gave you an order, follow it."

"Jenner!" I shrieked.

Rico glanced down at the floor. My beloved pet was

crouched right in front of him, ready to spring. "Keg-ide! Come and get this mangy animal away from me."

Kegide didn't move.

"Very well, I'll do it myself." My brother aimed his weapon at Jenner. I shoved just as he fired, and the shot went wide. Jenner stopped playing the hero, screeched, and dove under the benches.

"Kegide," I shouted. "Help them! Get them out of here!"

Kegide carefully set down Juliet instead and came toward Rico, shaking his head, making the raspy, moaning sound.

"She'll have them send you back to where we came from, remember?" Rico snarled at his enforcer. "Remember the little room they made you stay in? I took you from there, I gave you a life. You owe me that life, Kegide." He shoved me into Kegide's arms. "Show me your gratitude and kill her!"

Instead of snapping my neck, Kegide set me aside as gently as he had Juliet. Then he kept advancing on Rico, his hands outstretched.

Rico looked stunned at the big man's betrayal. He lifted the pistol. "I should have left you there to rot, you imbecile."

"Kegide!" I screamed.

Kegide lunged, and Rico fired the pistol. The enormous body stiffened, then dropped short to land at the chief's feet.

I tried to get to him, but Rico grabbed me and put the hot end of the barrel under my chin. "Your turn."

Duncan. I closed my eyes. *I can't keep my promise.*

Someone stepped into the equipment pit. "It's time to stop this," he said. "Let her go, son."

I opened my eyes. Joseph Grey Veil closed the door panel and leaned back against it.

He wasn't carrying a weapon, or had anyone with him. His immaculate business suit and calm, unruffled appearance made him look as though he'd just left a medical conference. He looked utterly confident of his control over the situation.

Probably thought he was. Obviously, he'd forgotten what I'd said to him, the last time we were together.

"Lend me your pistol for a minute," I said to my brother. "Then you can shoot me."

"He's not going to shoot anyone else, are you, Jericho?"

"Why are you here, old man?" Rico's voice changed, went flat. "You're supposed to be at your lab."

"Yes, I know. Unfortunately, I would have been, if I hadn't gotten a signal from Ilona Red Faun. She told me Cherijo would be here."

Rico's grip on me tightened. "Ilona lives?"

"Sorry, I forgot to mention it," I said.

"It doesn't matter. I'll find her later." He sighed. "Well, Father, I'm surprised you were able to get tickets. Have you seen my team play?"

"Yes. They're quite competent."

"We've been trying to get to the World Game for five years. I think changing the starting offense line was the key to winning the semifinals." He sounded like a little boy now, trying to impress his daddy. "I made some other changes, got them to stop whining about penalties. Thanks to you, I learned a little pain goes a long way."

Joseph got tired of listening, and held out his hand. "Jericho, give me the weapon."

"Don't you want your daughter?" Rico's free hand turned my face toward his, and he gave me a leisurely kiss. I didn't move. "She's everything you said she would be. Beautiful. Intelligent. Resourceful. Sensual." He stroked his free hand down the front of my body, and patted my right thigh. "I've thoroughly enjoyed having her all these months."

I thought about telling Joseph that he'd never

touched me, but I wasn't sure what might set either of them off.

"She doesn't belong to you."

"She's been very happy in her loving brother's arms, Father."

"Loving?" Joe let his upper lip curl. "You tried to kill her four times when she was an infant."

"She was so small and helpless, it was practically irresistible. Can you really blame me for what I did when I was a boy?"

"No. I failed in that, Jericho. I failed to recognize the genius behind the psychosis. Even after all the studies."

The studies. When he'd raped his own son.

"Shoot him," I said to Rico. "Or shoot me, because I don't want to listen to another word of this."

"But you don't get a choice, little sister. See, I've had fantasies about this sort of meeting. I never dreamed I'd have the two of you together. Have the chance to exterminate both of you at the same time. My esteemed parent, and my brilliant sister. Scientist and experiment, all rolled into one. Do you want to know why I really bought a shockball franchise?"

"Why?"

Rico giggled. "He hates the game, don't you, Father?"

"She's nothing. A failure. The experiment never worked," Joseph said. "Let her go. Come back to the estate with me. We can talk about the future."

"That's a very good bluff, Father. Unfortunately, I was around long enough to see just how successful number ten here was. She's the one you were waiting for. I think it must have taken superhuman effort for you to keep your hands off her."

"We can talk about everything back at the estate." Joseph looked at me. "Bring her with us, if you like. She has no clinical value to me, but we can use her in other ways."

"You want to share her between us?" Rico sputtered an incredulous laugh. "What a provocative thought. There is more of you inside me than I imagined."

I told Joe what I thought of him. In no uncertain terms.

Rico's grip on the pistol shifted. "Her speech patterns leave a great deal to be desired. No, if she is a failure, Father, let me put her out of her misery."

Our creator looked bored now. "Very well."

Rico's hand tightened on my thigh, then he moved it around toward the small of my back, and gave me a shove. "Give Daddy a kiss good-bye, Cherijo."

I stumbled forward, and Joseph caught me in his arms. He lowered his head as if to kiss me, while I shrieked and twisted against his hold.

But he didn't kiss me. He whispered against my ear, "I love you. Run."

The interior lights went out. Joe pushed me behind him and lunged toward Jericho. My brother shouted something obscene, then I heard the pistol fire as I turned around. I saw the pulse hit Joseph's chest, watched as the front of his torso exploded.

"No!" In spite of everything, I reached out.

The emergency lighting flickered on.

"Go . . ." Joseph wheezed, and staggered the last couple of steps so he could fling his ruined body on top of my insane brother.

I covered my mouth in horror, backing away. Then I remembered Duncan and the explosives, and frantically groped for the door.

Someone's gentle hands eased mine away from the panel. "Wait, patcher."

It was Ilona Red Faun, and with her were about a dozen of the outcasts. They filed in, surrounding me in a protective circle. None of them looked angry, but they were all staring at Jericho, who was still trying to get out from under Joseph's body. His pistol waved wildly in the air.

"Ilona, you traitorous bitch. I'll kill you. I'll kill all of you!"

The outcasts descended on Rico and Joseph. I watched how carefully they disarmed him, the way they lifted him out from under Joseph's body. For a moment, I thought the worst, until I saw the look on Ilona's face.

"No." Even knowing the depths of his depravity and insanity, I couldn't condemn my brother. He'd been a victim of the grandfather of all monsters. "Ilona, he needs to be hospitalized."

"He has done enough, patcher. Even you said you could not cure him. That he will never get better." Ilona knelt beside Milass's headless corpse. She placed her hand on his chest. "He killed my brother, didn't he? Yet Milass was always loyal to him. He would never disobey Rico. He loved him."

I hadn't known Milass was Ilona's brother. That explained a lot.

She sighed, then got to her feet. "This is our chief, our problem. Let us deal with it in our way."

Rico was screaming and demanding the outcasts obey and release him. The pistol disappeared into someone's pocket. Then he was silenced by a dozen hands, clamping over his nose, mouth, and throat. The last thing I saw was him swallowed into the center of the tight circle of bodies, his eyes wide and unblinking.

I couldn't stop them, couldn't process what was happening. All I could do was think of Duncan. "Ilona, I have to get out of here."

"We will take care of them, patcher. Go."

I put on my helmet and went out to the sidelines, in time to see the Gliders' defense leave the field and the offensive team trot out to take their positions. The scoreboard remained at zero on both sides.

Reever had heard me.

I walked up to one of the players I knew. "How much time remaining?"

"Two minutes before interval end." Small Fox glanced at me and his eyes widened. "Patcher? Is that you? What are you doing here?"

Beyond us, Ilona and the outcasts silently vacated the equipment pit and returned to the spectators' stands.

I hoped that now, at last, our brothers were at peace. "I had to talk to Rico."

Ilona went over to a security drone and said something. The drone immediately buzzed past me and entered the pit. A minute later more drones descended on the sidelines. They'd be notifying arena security about the dead bodies any moment.

I adjusted my helmet. I had to do it now.

A drone intercepted me as I started toward the field. "You were seen going into the equipment pit with the dead man. Security wishes to interview you about the nature of his demise."

"I don't know what you're talking about," I said, keeping my voice low and rough. "Can't this wait until after the game?"

"Do not leave the arena," the official warned me.

I saw the drones carrying the bodies out of the pit. My brother was dead. My creator was dead.

My husband was going to live.

I hid behind an equipment rack to do what I needed, then emerged with my new face. When the interval clock sounded the one-minute warning, the Gliders lined up for the last play.

This was it. My last chance.

There was only one person who could walk onto the field and not be automatically stopped by the officials. Knowing that, I headed for my husband.

A drone buzzed in front to me. "The team owner must not disrupt the game—"

"I'm just going to have a word with my players," I said, in a low growly tone. "One minute."

Confused, the official rolled back out of the way. My Rico-mask worked, but only for a moment. Someone must have identified Rico's body, because a horde of drones left the sidelines and headed for me. At the same time, the play was called, and the sphere put into motion.

I had fifty meters to cover before I could get to Reever, who was heading directly for the touchzone, so I ran.

I ran the way Xonea had taught me, with fast, long strides that pulled at the muscles in my legs. If we survived this, I was going to be sore as hell.

Duncan!

Reever looked over, saw me. His face turned to stone and he kicked the sphere into play.

He thought I was Rico. I peeled off my Lok-Teel mask. *Duncan! Stop!*

Reever worked the sphere toward the wide white line. But why? Then I remembered the drones carrying the bodies out. He must have thought Milass's headless corpse was mine.

My husband was trying to commit suicide.

"Duncan!" I screamed. Then, with every bit of mental ferocity I could put behind it, I repeated the call in my head. *Duncan! Stop!*

A few inches from his goal, Reever suddenly came to a halt and looked over his shoulder at me. I glimpsed the interval clock. Twenty seconds left. I held out my arms.

Pass it to me now.

Cherijo?

Just give it to me! I screamed in my mind.

He almost fell, then bent and scooped up the sphere. The crowd shrieked with rage and got to their feet. My ears rang as the noise increased with every step I took.

Reever threw the sphere to me just as the interval clock ran out. I caught it and went down, holding it against the ground with my body.

Gliders helped me to my feet. The game computer registered five penalties on the player's board, all charged to Reever. A drone announced them as they were listed.

"Illegal pass. Illegal reception. Illegal number of players on the field. Illegal assumption of position."

Another drone buzzed near me. "Release the sphere. Penalties must be discharged."

There was no way in hell I was letting go. If I did, the sphere would act like a homing device, go directly to Reever, and kill him. I turned, and ran for the sidelines. I'd drop the sphere into the nearest bucket of water I could find. Hopefully that would short out the triggering device.

I hadn't counted on the efficiency of the game computer, or the rule that stated if a non-penalized player refused to release the sphere, they had to take the jolts instead.

The first jolt hit me like a sledgehammer. I staggered and nearly fell, then righted myself. Five penalties, like that? That wasn't too bad. I could handle that.

The second jolt was harder, and longer. This time I did go down, on both knees. The bioelectrical charge stabbed up through my hands and sent arrows of bright pain through my arms. Only when the jolt ended was I able to get up and keep going.

I could hear the other players running after me. A drone got in my path and I jumped over it. Thirty meters and three more penalties to go. I ran over to the sidelines, hoping that would stop the charges. Players lunged to get out of my way. Couldn't blame them—if I touched any of them, they'd get a taste of the penalty jolts, too.

"Cherijo!"

I don't know if it was Reever's voice or the third jolt that knocked me off my feet. I went flying, body writhing uncontrollably, and landed on the spectators' side of the retaining wall. When I stopped twitching, a couple of furious fans heaved me back over and onto the field.

I sat up in time to get penalty number four, which sent me into convulsions. Vague images of players surrounded my burning field of vision. Someone was yelling my name. Two men held a third back.

My immune system was good, but would it hold up under the increasing strength of the shocks?

Well, you're going to find out, aren't you, smartass?

Maggie stood over me, and held out her hand.

"Come on, get up. The next one won't be for another ten seconds."

I cringed and rolled away. "Don't touch me. Someone will take it away."

"Baby, ten seconds in your world is about ten hours here." She took the sphere away from me and tucked it under her arm. "Damn stupid game. We thought these people were civilized, until we saw one of these sporting exhibitions." She made a clucking sound as she dusted off my uniform. "Really ruined the theory you evolved from primates for me."

"Primates? Evolved?"

"Yeah, well, Terran primates are a lot more sensible than homo sapiens. Don't go calling them family." She surveyed me. "So you saved Reever and everyone who had the lousy idea of building houses on top of a shifting tectonic plate. Proud of yourself?"

"What do you want?"

"What I always wanted. You get the discs?" I nodded. "Good girl. Now you take them, and Reever, and get off this planet. There are star charts contained in one of the discs, you'll be able to use them to get to Jxinok. It's easy to find even if you can't decipher the star charts. Go to Oenrall—"

"Dhreen's world?"

"Yeah, Dhreen's world. Once you get there, take a left at the second moon."

"Juh-zin-ock?" I tried out the word. "That the name of your homeworld?"

"Bingo."

I was beyond exhausted, and hurting, and she was worried about giving me directions. "And what am I supposed to do when I get there?"

"You'll find out all the answers on Jxinok." She looked around at the arena. Everyone around us was frozen, as if time stood still. I finally understood that here, with Maggie, it did.

"Will I see you there?"

She looked down at herself and laughed. "No, little girl. I'm dead. All you see are some memories I gave you."

"Interactive memories."

"I was an interactive kind of gal."

"Did you know about Jericho?"

She stopped smiling. "Yeah, I did. I was the one who got him out of there."

"What about the others? Jericho said they all survived."

"They did. If you could call it that." Maggie turned, and suddenly we were back at Joseph's underground facility, in the Research and Development room. A group of dark-haired boys sat playing a game. They ranged in age from three to twelve. One of them had a particularly chilling smile.

Rico and his eight brothers. My eight brothers.

"Jericho was almost a success," Maggie said. "The only problem was his immune system didn't work right. And the fact Joe had turned him into a full-blown sociopath by the time he was four."

I began noticing something was physically wrong with each of the other boys. One had a deformed head, another possessed withered legs. "What about the others?"

"Some he put out for adoption. Two had to be institutionalized. By the time you came along, they were almost all gone. All except Rid and Rig. They stayed and eventually became his research assistants. Rid's in Mendocino. Rig's out cruising with the League boys."

Joseph was dead. Who remained behind? "Are any of them still at the estate?"

"No. They were moved as soon as you got old enough to wander around the mansion. It doesn't matter."

"It doesn't matter?" I whirled around. "They're my brothers. My *family*."

"They were raised like laboratory rats, Cherijo. Most of them don't have the personality of a drone on auto-replay."

"You two made sure I wouldn't ever find out."

"You met Jericho, wasn't he enough?"

Jericho, who like me had only wanted our father to love him. A few genes' difference, and I might have ended up chief of the Night Horse. "Go away, Maggie."

"I will. When you tell me you're going to Jxinok."

"I'll go to your damn homeworld. Satisfied?"

"Oh, no, baby. The dead are never satisfied." She straightened my jersey and dusted off my helmet. Then she pinched my cheek. "But getting you there, yeah, that will do, for now."

Someone helped me to my feet, and led me out onto the field. It was a drone official, moving me away from the crowd. Everyone had fallen silent.

"We cannot disable the game computer," the official was saying. "If you do not release the sphere, you will die."

Even now, if I released the sphere, it would automatically seek out Duncan. I wasn't going to let that happen. Going out on the field was to protect everyone else, I realized. I stumbled along, ears ringing, vision blurring.

Jericho was dead. Joseph was dead. I clutched the hot sphere tighter between my palms. They were dead, but Reever would live.

The official checked the player's board. "The last penalty shall be administered in five, four, three . . ."

The hysterical crowd chanted down the clock, then suddenly hushed. Behind me, a woman screamed. Everyone was on their feet, looking up at a lone figure, standing on the edge of the highest tier of seats.

Another crazy fan, determined to have the best view. What a game.

The final, lethal jolt hit me. It knocked me flat on my back. The alloy between my hands began to glow a dull red. I clenched my chattering teeth and endured the charge, holding the sphere up, high above my head, so everyone could see.

Look at me. Watch me burn.

I forgot about the pain when I saw the lone figure leap out into space, and fall. Thousands of voices shrieked their shock and horror as the figure hurtled down toward me and certain death.

As I twisted and writhed, so did the figure. Was it some kind of poltergeist, suffering with me, burning with me? No, it was tearing off its outer clothes. Another dark-haired twin who arched up and at the last moment spread out his two enormous, gleaming black wings.

Hawk.

I watched my friend as he broke his own fall and turned it into a slow, graceful glide. No one moved or made a sound, so I could hear his wings beating against the air currents. It sounded like a heartbeat.

Then someone started to chant, "Gliders, Gliders, Gliders!"

More voices chimed in, and soon everyone was

chanting the word. For a hunchback who had turned into an avatar. The black-winged Glider of New Angeles myth. Now Hawk had revealed his secret, not only to his tribe, but to everyone on Terra. I was proud of him.

I let my head fall back once I saw he could sustain his flight, and let the pain roll through me. My teeth screeched against each other. The flesh on the insides of my hands began to smoke.

"Cherijo!"

Hawk swooped down and grabbed me, plucking the sphere from my hands at the same time. He was wearing some kind of insulation gear, so the jolt didn't affect him. His talons crushed the sphere before dropping it, then he folded me against his chest.

"Reever," I managed to say.

"Look." Hawk hovered, and pointed. On the other side of the field, Dhreen was helping Reever, Ilona, and the cats into a glidecar he'd landed on the sidelines. "Are you ready to go now?"

Oh yeah, I was ready. I nodded and held on.

Hawk flew up and out of the arena, and glided above the regular traffic lanes. I looked down and saw Dhreen following us below. They weren't the only ones.

"League troop units," I said. "They're coming after us."

"They'll have to get through the Night Horse first."

I watched as several glidecars deliberately smashed into the troop vehicles, disabling them. The faint sound of Indian voices hooting with triumph made me smile. "You guys are handy to have around when someone wants to escape." I looked up into his dark face. "But I thought you were staying."

"I can't now." Hawk smiled. "You forced my hand, you know."

"I did nothing of the sort. This was all your idea."

I grinned, painfully. "But you made one hell of a sphere-down, pal."

Hawk flew until we were over some deserted agricultural fields, then finally glided down to the ground. He grimaced as he set me on my feet and folded his wings.

"I know those exercises you showed me how to do strengthen them, but they still hurt every time I fly."

"Keep at it." I inspected the spinal junctions, where his wings were connected to his back. I would have felt them, but my hands were too burned to use. "You're using muscles that you've been binding down for years. The atrophy was the biggest problem, and that's gone. In time, they'll stop aching and you'll be able to fly longer."

"Not on Terra." He reached back and touched the top of one wing, stroking the short black feathers covering it. "At least now I won't have to pluck these out of my chest anymore."

Or face having his wings amputated to better pass as Terran, I guessed. That must have been why he'd never told Rico or any of the other Night Horse.

"See? And you thought Small Fox had problems." I looked around. "Any particular reason you decided to stop here, other than getting tired of hauling me around?"

"We're expected." He nodded toward a nearby line of trees.

I walked with him to the edge of the field, and saw Dhreen and Reever waiting for us. Both of them were holding a very disgruntled cat in their arms. Beyond them was another, smaller clearing, and a large object covered with brush.

Reever handed Jenner to Hawk, then pulled me into his arms. "You shouldn't have done it." He kissed me, hard and angry.

As soon as he let me up for air, I smiled. "What,

and let you get fried? Who has the superior immune system around here?" I snuggled against him, exhausted but happy. "I was so scared."

"I was frightened, too." He kissed the top of my head. "Now we must leave, or the League will catch up to us."

"Is that big heap under those branches over there what I think it is?"

"Dhreen's starshuttle."

I looked at the Oenrallian pilot. "You mean Dhreen's *stolen* starshuttle."

Dhreen shrugged and wrapped his arm around Ilona. "As long as it maintains a stable flightshield, what does it matter?"

We all went to the shuttle and boarded. It was a Terran flagship, a luxurious craft that planetary officials used to transport League dignitaries. It definitely would be missed.

We all elected to stay at the helm, and strapped in. I jumped when a dark-haired woman walked into the cabin.

"Ilona? You're coming with us?"

"Yes." She smiled and sat down beside me. "Dhreen is very clever, isn't he?"

"Yeah." I eyed our pilot. "He's just full of surprises."

Hawk was having trouble with his harness, so I leaned over and clipped him in. He was sweating and staring at the viewport.

"Don't be nervous. Dhreen has survived out in space for years. He probably doesn't even know how many crashes he's walked away from."

Hawk's wings folded around him like a cloak. "That does not give me a great deal of confidence."

After putting the cats in their carriers, Reever sat down across from me. He never once looked away from my face.

"I had to do it. More than your life was at stake."

"I know."

"You're still mad."

"You broke your promise to me." He didn't crack a smile. "I will be mad for some time."

"I guess you're entitled. Do you think you'll forgive me by the time we get to Joren?"

"Perhaps."

I hid a smile and gripped the armrests as Dhreen initiated the flightshield. "Dhreen, how are you going to get us through the security grid?"

"No worrying, Doc. This baby is equipped with a full camouflage array." Dhreen's spoon-shaped fingers danced over the pilot's console. "Once we're in the upper atmosphere, I'm going to enable it."

"What does a camouflage array do?" I asked Reever. "Make us disappear?"

"Not exactly."

We lifted off and headed straight up. G-force kept me plastered to the seat, until the shuttle's flightshield altered the molecular composition of the ship, and we started slipping through gravity. That was when Dhreen yelled, "Watch this!"

I looked out the viewport, and suddenly we were surrounded by hundreds of shuttles. All identical to ours.

"I get it. Camouflage as in try to guess which one is real," I said.

"They're all real," Reever assured me. "As real as we are."

Which, given the peculiar mechanics involved with flightshielding, meant we were all visible—and invisible.

I sat back in my seat and closed my eyes. "Wake me when we get the signal."

"What signal?" Reever asked.

"Didn't I mention it?" I yawned. "The cavalry is coming."

CHAPTER TWENTY

A Gift for Duncan

The League had mustered all the ships within the Sol Quadrant, and sent them after us. Dhreen didn't seem worried about that, even when I pointed at the converging blips on the sensor screen about an hour later.

"No worrying, Doc. I already signaled our friends the Jorenians, and the *Sunlace* is waiting for us, just beyond Jupiter. Right where you said they'd be."

Reever glanced at me. "You sent for the Jorenians?"

"It was my last request—you know, my Speaking. I asked them to come to Sol as soon as they'd finished repopulating the slaves. I told Xonea we'd find a way to rendezvous with them." Seeing the familiar nautilus shape of the *Sunlace* made my eyes sting for a moment. Then I saw two more Jorenian ships hovering just beyond HouseClan Torin's star vessel.

"Three Jorenian ships?"

"Xonea probably figured we could use the extra firepower." Dhreen flew directly at the *Sunlace,* and signaled for permission to dock.

"If you have my ClanSister on board, you may," Xonea's deep voice said over the audio. "If you don't, go back and get her off that miserable world she was mistakenly born on."

I went to the helm. "Hi, Xonea. You don't like my homeworld?"

"Of course I do—but your homeworld is Joren." He made a gesture that blended affection and relief. "Welcome back to your family, Cherijo."

"Xonea, we've got about twenty League ships on an intercept course with us. You'd better prepare to transition—quick."

"As soon as you land in launch bay, we will transition. *Sunlace* out."

The *Sunlace* and the two flanking ships transitioned a few minutes after we landed in launch bay. I got to go through the dimensional shift while clutching my seat harness and swearing to join the Hsktskt just so I didn't have to watch reality melt around me.

Once we were cleared to disembark, I walked out and saw Salo and several large Jorenians waiting for us. They were armed and not smiling.

"Isn't anyone happy to see me?" I demanded.

Salo nodded, but his eyes were fixed on a spot beyond my right shoulder. "We have some HouseClan business to attend to here, healer. You and Duncan should go to your quarters."

I turned around and saw he was staring at Dhreen, who was having a hard time blinking. Then I recalled how my adopted family felt about people they thought had harmed me.

"Oh, no." I backed up until I bumped into Dhreen. "I shield the Oenrallian Dhreen, Salo."

Slowly the killing rage left the grim expressions of the Jorenians. Salo lowered the huge, curved sword he'd been ready to use and gave me a frown.

"You never allow us to carry out ClanKill against anyone, Healer Cherijo."

"I can't stand the sight of all those ripped-out intestines." I let out a sigh, walked over and nearly dislocated my spine giving the *Sunlace*'s second in command a hug. "Good to see you, big guy. How are Darea and Fasala?"

"The light of my life, as always." He touched his brow to mine. "Eager to see you as well. But I think perhaps you should go to Medical first."

Medical. Yes, I definitely was ready to go to Medical.

"Make sure no one chops up Dhreen while I'm gone." I grabbed the cats and Reever and headed directly for a gyrlift.

"I want Squilyp to look at those electrical burns on your hands," Reever said as I pushed him into the gyrlift. "Why are you in such a hurry?"

"You'll see." I tapped my foot on the floor of the lift. "Can't this thing go any faster?"

Squilyp was waiting for us at the entrance to Medical Bay. So was Alunthri.

After I gave the Chakacat a hug and exchanged relieved greetings, I turned to my former resident. "Well?"

He looked at my hands. "You've been burned again."

"Minor." I flicked my fingers to show him. "What about the experiment?"

"What experiment?" Reever asked.

Squilyp hopped over and put two of his three hands on my shoulders. "Cherijo, it was a complete success. It *worked*."

At least, I think that's what he said. A moment later, I was flat on my back, with someone waving an ampule of ammonia under my nose.

"Okay, okay!" I slapped the hand away. "I'm up."

Alunthri paced nervously around me. Reever didn't let me stand, but picked me up instead. "She's endured more than burns. You'll need to do a complete workup on her, Senior Healer."

"I should live long enough to see the day she allows

me to do one," Squilyp said. "Put her on the trauma
table and I'll start my scans." He saw my expression
and shook his head. "We can discuss the experiment
after I bring you the results. Let me make sure you're
all right, for Duncan's sake."

"Hurry up," I said. "I've been waiting almost a year
and I'm not going to wait another second more than
I have to."

Reever jumped right on that. "A year? For an experiment? What sort of test was this?"

Alunthri muttered something about its thesis and
beat a hasty retreat.

I didn't want to tell him until Squilyp brought us
the results. I bit my lip and stretched out on the table.
"Let Squilyp scan me first."

That took only a few minutes, and then Squilyp left
us to go to get the test results. I couldn't sit still, so I
got up and did his rounds for him. Reever trailed after
me, still looking puzzled.

"Cherijo, this experiment, what is it?"

"You can't stand being in the dark, can you?" I
grinned. "Well, you'll just have to wait this time. Because I don't think you'll believe me until you see it
with your own eyes."

Xonea came in a few minutes later, and nearly
crushed me with one of his brotherly hugs.

"I never want to go through this again," he said
against my hair. "First we thought we'd lost you to the
Hsktskt, and now to the Terrans. You cannot leave us
again. I will not let you." He held me at arm's length.
"You are thinner. You are *burned*."

I saw the familiar, kin-have-been-harmed, get-the-
swords expression and patted him on one muscular
blue arm.

"I'm fine. I burned myself. Come and sit down and
tell us what's happening with the war. Reever and I
have been out of touch for months."

Anything to keep me from thinking about what Squilyp was getting.

Xonea shook Reever's hand and led us into Squilyp's office, where he updated us on the League's escalating war with the Hsktskt. Started by my own creator in order to retrieve me from the Hsktskt, the war had exploded across a dozen quadrants throughout the galaxy. It was moving forward, like a deadly tide, and getting close to Terran space.

"We should return to Joren at once," he said. "We can better safeguard you on our own territory."

Reever and I exchanged a glance. "I don't think that's such a good idea, Xonea. Remember what happened the last time?"

He looked a little annoyed. "We have improved our planetary defenses."

"Great. I hope you never have to use them. Joren is still remaining neutral in the war, isn't it?"

"Yes, for now. However, news of atrocities on both sides may compel Joren and some of our allies to form a third defensive force to protect our homeworld quadrants."

That wasn't such good news. "Neutral usually means staying out of the fighting, Xonea."

"We will do what we must. If League or Hsktskt forces enter the Varallan system, we may have no choice but to fight."

"Well, Reever and I are going to stay away from Joren, just as a precaution." I recalled my promise to Maggie, and to Dhreen. "There are some other places we need to go."

We debated just where to go for a few minutes. The boys wanted to fly to the other side of the galaxy, and find a nice, unoccupied fertile world for me and Reever to settle down on.

Gee, just what I'd always wanted: to build a house I'd have to clean myself. My patience, which had been thinning ever since Squilyp left, reached a breaking point. "According to what you've told us, the war isn't likely to reach Oenrallian space. Why don't we head that way?"

"I'd heard you shielded Dhreen." Xonea glared at me. "Why?"

"My creator basically blackmailed him into doing what he did. It really wasn't his fault. Besides, even if everyone stays mad at Dhreen, you can't blame his people for his actions."

"True. We have yet to explore that particular quadrant." Xonea tapped his finger against his lips. "I think it may be a viable alternative."

I wasn't going to mention that Maggie's homeworld was in the same quadrant—there would be time enough to analyze the discs and tell everyone about that later. "Where are our other passengers?"

"Waiting for us at the reception."

I groaned. The Jorenians loved to throw parties. "Not another one."

"You are a popular member of our HouseClan, Healer. Get used to it." Xonea looked up as a nurse called him over to the main console. "Excuse me."

I started pacing again. My ClanBrother came back a minute later.

"It seems Squilyp needs my assistance."

"With what?" I demanded.

"A minor problem, easily dealt with." Before I could say anything, he shook his head. "Patience, ClanSister, you will soon have all you desire. I will meet you both at the reception in a few minutes."

The reception was held on level seven, in the new environome someone had put in around the galley. Now everyone could dine in the simulated surroundings of whatever world they chose. It disoriented me for a moment, to step off the gyrlift and into Marine Province on Joren.

"Wow, someone has been busy." I took Reever's

hand in mine. "Listen, no matter what happens when Xonea comes back, I want you to remember something."

"What is that?"

"I love you." I smiled at him, then stepped forward to greet what looked like the entire crew.

Everyone had missed me, judging by the number of times my ribs were compressed. Wonlee made me put on a plas-lined frontal engineering shroud so he could give me a squeeze without impaling me on his spines. I spotted Dhreen and Ilona over in one corner, talking to a couple of the nurses, and left Reever to see how my Oenrallian friend had fared with my adopted family.

He had his arm around Ilona and was making jokes about water on Terra. "It looks clear enough, until twelve hours later, and then the microbes hit you—"

"Hey, you two." I stepped into the circle. "Anyone seen Hawk?"

"Not since we left the shuttle." Ilona snuggled up to Dhreen. "We have been busy."

"So I see." I gave her a stern look. "You are not allowed to breed for at least two months. We'll discuss why when I give you your followup exam."

"Yes, patcher." She gazed at the big warrior men and women surrounding us. "Your tribe is most impressive. I have never seen such people."

I thought of my own reaction when I'd landed on the mostly nonhuman colony of K-2. "Another reason it's good to leave Terra. Are you okay with that?"

"I am bonded to Dhreen. Where he goes, I follow."

Dhreen gave her waist a squeeze. "And where you go, I follow."

"Keep that up and you two will go in circles." I spotted Hawk on the other side of the galley and smiled. "I'm going to go check on our other guest. Behave yourselves."

It took me a few minutes to work my way through

the crowd over to Hawk, who had his wings to a hull panel and was gingerly sampling some Jorenian tea.

"Awful stuff, isn't it?" I whisked the server from his hand. "It took me a couple of months before I could manage to drink more than a few sips." The professional side of my brain kicked in and I glanced at his back. "How do they feel?"

"Sore. But good, too. I don't think I could go back to binding them down again." Hawk stretched them out slightly. Many of the Jorenians were eyeing him with open curiosity, and it was making him nervous. "Your tribe, they will allow me to accompany you and *Nilch'i'* to your destination?"

"Of course. They're always happy to welcome friends of the family along for the ride." I went to a prep unit and dialed up more familiar Terran tea, and handed it to him. "Try this, it's chamomile and mint."

The taste of the unsweetened tea seemed to relax him. "No one seems to mind that I have wings."

"Or fur." Alunthri joined us. "The Jorenians aren't like Terrans. They enjoy the diversity of life in the universe."

I looked at the door panel for the hundredth time. If my ClanBrother and that damn Omorr didn't show up soon, I was going to go hunt them down myself.

"One of the pilots told me we're going to the Liacos Quadrant."

Hawk was talking to me again. "That's right."

"My father's homeworld lies along our route there. Would it be possible, I mean—"

"Can we make a stop? Of course." Reever came over, and I automatically blocked my thoughts. I patted Hawk's arm. "You're among my friends now. I hope you'll give them a chance to be your friends, too." I smiled at Alunthri. "They've enriched my life quite a bit."

"Cherijo, may I have a moment?"

I excused myself, then went with Reever to another

unoccupied corner. As I looked back, Hawk began having a conversation with Alunthri, and two fascinated Jorenians who had approached them in my wake.

"I think we have another potential member for House-Clan Torin." I looked back at Reever. "What's up?"

"Why are you acting so agitated?"

"I'm just, uh, excited to be back where I belong."

"If that's so, why are you blocking your thoughts from me?"

"Because I'm thinking about killing two crew members with my bare hands."

Duncan turned to the viewport and made a frustrated sound. "I could understand why you were blocking your thoughts on Terra. But we are among friends now, Cherijo. It isn't necessary."

Maybe it was time I went to find Xonea and Squilyp. "Stay here and I'll—"

The crowd between us and the corridor door panel suddenly parted, forming a wide gap between them. I saw why, and froze.

Xonea was standing at the other end of the gap. In his huge arms he was holding a yawning, blond-haired toddler.

There she was.

"I know you think my telepathic abilities are an intrusion, but if you would only consider how they deepen our intimacy—"

She was a tiny thing. Of course the Jorenians made everyone look dinky. Her hair was so blond it was almost white, dead straight, and nearly touched her shoulders. Her features were rosy and yet not baby-pretty. No, she looked like a miniature adult.

"Uh, Duncan?" I blindly swatted at him, unable to take my own eyes away. "Turn around."

Xonea started walking toward us. The sleepy child rested her cheek against the wide vault of his chest, making her look even smaller. Given her rapid gestation, the six months I'd spent in sleep suspension on the League ship, plus the time on Terra, she would be about a year old now.

Reever took me by the arm. "I love you, Cherijo. I don't want there to be any more walls between us. Let me in."

"I will, in a minute. Would you please turn around?"

"Even now you are distracted. Has someone—"

I grabbed his arms and shoved him around. He went very still. "Xonea."

Xonea stopped a few feet away, and the entire room fell silent. "I regret I was not able to join you sooner. My ClanNiece Marel often becomes grumpy when woken from a sound sleep."

I could sympathize with that.

"One of the disadvantages of being gestated in an embryonic chamber," I said, my voice cracking a little. "You get spoiled."

At the sound of my voice, the child lifted her head and looked at me.

Xonea gave me an indignant look. "She is not spoiled."

Squilyp hopped down the gap after Xonea. "Yes, she is. In fact, she's terrorized the entire ship since emerging from the chamber I raised her in."

Marel reached out to the Omorr and smacked him lightly on the arm.

"She likes to hit people, too," Squilyp said in a dry tone. "Just like her mother."

Xonea set Marel down on her feet, and the little girl stared up at me. Hawk appeared on the edge of the crowd, distracting the toddler for a moment. He smiled as she headed straight for him, then patted the lower part of one of his wings.

"She has the same eyes as you, Cherijo."

"Yes, she does." I knelt down and held out my hand. "Marel?"

Marel took a couple of steps forward on unsteady legs, then looked back at Xonea. "Mine?"

"Yes, Marel." To me, my ClanBrother said, I showed her photoscans every day so she would know."

The little girl pointed to me. "Mine."

"Yes, Marel." I'd waited over a year to hear that. "I'm all yours."

The baby toddled over and reached up for me with her tiny hands. I carefully lifted her and closed my eyes at the feel of her slight weight in my arms. Her hair was so soft beneath my palm.

Oh God. She *was* real. "Hello, sweetie."

"Mine mama." She patted my cheek and gave me a delighted, four-toothed grin. Her eyes changed from green to blue. "Where been, Mama?"

My throat hurt. "I've been trying to get back to you, sweetie."

Marel thought about that. "Stay now?"

"Yes, I'll stay now. I won't leave you again." I turned slightly. "There's someone else here who wants to meet you."

She looked at Reever with a great deal of interest. "Him?"

"That's him."

"Mine?" She cocked her little head, then reached out her other hand.

Something incredible happened when that small hand touched Duncan's face. The blank mask that I'd never seen him without vanished. Then he smiled.

Duncan Reever *smiled.*

Our daughter patted his cheek. "Mine daddy."

Look what's coming in December...

❏ **BIKINI PLANET**
by David Garnett
Rookie cop Wayne Norton went to sleep in the swinging sixties—and woke up 300 years later. Now he's out of time, out of touch—and caught up in a battle for dominion over the galaxy's most prized vacation hotspot...
458605/$5.99

❏ **THE SILVER CALL**
by Dennis L. McKiernan
Bestselling author Dennis L. McKiernan's mythical novels of Mithgar are among the most cherished stories in the pantheon of fantasy fiction. *The Silver Call* collects two of the earlier novels—*Trek to Kraggen-Cor* and *The Brega Path*—in one volume for the very first time.
458613/$6.99

❏ **MECHWARRIOR #4: INITIATION TO WAR**
by Robert N. Charrette
A newly-recruited battalion of MechWarriors prepares to go head-to-head against a vicious army of Mech raiders...
458516/$5.99

Prices slightly higher in Canada

Payable by Visa, MC or AMEX only ($10.00 min.), No cash, checks or COD.
Shipping & handling: US/Can. $2.75 for one book, $1.00 for each add'l book;
Int'l $5.00 for one book, $1.00 for each add'l. Call (800) 788-6262 or
(201) 933-9292, fax (201) 896-8569 or mail your orders to:

Penguin Putnam Inc. P.O. Box 12289, Dept. B Newark, NJ 07101-5289 Please allow 4-6 weeks for delivery. Foreign and Canadian delivery 6-8 weeks.	Bill my: ❏ Visa ❏ MasterCard ❏ Amex_____(expires) Card# _____ Signature _____

Bill to:
Name _____

Address_____	City _____
State/ZIP _____	Daytime Phone # _____

Ship to:

Name_____	Book Total $ _____
Address _____	Applicable Sales Tax $_____
City _____	Postage & Handling $_____
State/ZIP _____	Total Amount Due $ _____

This offer subject to change without notice.   Ad # ROC (7/01)